"The twisty plo   s kept me turning the pages as I fell in love with Becca and Alex all over again."

Trisha Wolfe, author of Fireblood

"It had a gripping plot, plenty of exciting twists and turns and some pretty fantastic characters which all combined to keep me glued to the pages."

A Dream of Books

"If this is any notion of what Julianna Scott can do, I cannot wait to see what is next. *The Holders* was refreshing and just one heck of a good read."

The Book Cellar

"I am so thankful this is only the beginning of a series because I couldn't imagine not being able to read a continuation of Becca's story. *The Holders* is a novel too entertaining and emotionally charged to pass up!"

Lovey Dovey Books

"There are a lot of other things to love about *The Holders* – a detailed history and Celtic element come to mind – but it was really the characters that sold this novel for me."

More Than Just Magic

"It was just perfect easy, indulgent reading, and I absolutely loved it."

Liberty Falls Down

JULIANNA SCOTT

The Seers

STRANGE CHEMISTRY

An Angry Robot imprint
and a member of the Osprey Group

Lace Market House,   Angry Robot/Osprey Publishing,
54-56 High Pavement,   PO Box 3985,
Nottingham   New York,
NG1 1HW   NY 10185-3985,
UK   USA

www.strangechemistrybooks.com
Strange Chemistry #24

A Strange Chemistry paperback original 2014

Cover art by Lee Gibbons
Set in Sabon by Argh! Oxford

Distributed in the United States by Random House, Inc., New York.

ISBN: 978 1 90884 446 0
Ebook ISBN: 978 1 90884 447 7

Printed in the United States of America
9 8 7 6 5 4 3 2 1

For Grace Pleskovich, mo dheirfiúr.
My biggest little fan.

CHAPTER I

"Do you think if I passed out, she'd let me sit for a few minutes?" I mumbled, as my legs started to twitch.

"Probably not," Chloe smiled, amused by my growing irritation and no longer bothering to hide it.

"*Ne pas se voûter!*" came a shrill bark from behind me, followed by a hard slap on my back, "*Se dresser!*"

"Don't slouch," Chloe translated quietly.

"Yeah," I ground out from between clenched teeth, "got it." My French may have been nonexistent, but the Seamstress from Hell, also known as Madame Loute, had knuckles that spoke for themselves.

"Don't worry," Chloe said from her comfy seat in the corner, "you're almost done. Besides, if you were to faint and land on a pin, you'd bleed, and that would stain. Then you'd have to start all over again."

I huffed a sigh and looked back up at the one window on the opposite side of the room, and began to count the ripples in the ancient glass – again. The right pane had eight, one of which looked like the top of an apple, while the left pane had ten ripples and looked like an old man with crooked eyes.

That had been the previous two and a half hours of my life; standing in a dusty classroom in the basement of Lorcan Hall, starring at rippled glass and imagining patterns into it to pass the

7

time. All so I could get fitted for a gown, so I could attend a gala that I didn't want to go to, and meet a bunch of people I already knew I wasn't going to like. I had been standing perfectly still for so long my legs were starting to shake, and if I was poked with one more straight pin, I was going to pop the shriveled uppity seamstress right in the nose.

"You know," Chloe added, "there are people out there who would kill for the chance to have a custom gown made for them." Her inflection made it clear she was counting herself in that number.

"Yes, and there are *other* people out there who prefer to shop the old fashioned way; in a store with dresses lined up on racks, and all you have to do is try them... *AHH!*" I yelped with a flinch as yet another pin stabbed me in the shoulder.

OK, that one was on purpose...

Luckily for her, before I had time to seriously consider any form of retaliation, Attila the Seamstress pulled out the last pin and a few strips of sewing tape, and stepped back as the waves of green silk rippled down into place. "*Voilà*," she said with a proud raise of her chin. "*Fini.*"

"Oh... Becca..." Chloe whispered, starry-eyed, "It's beautiful! *Très magnifique, Madame!*" she added, touching Madame Loute's arm.

"*Merci, ma chérie*," Madame Loute replied, patting Chloe's hand with what actually might have been a smile. Honestly, I shouldn't have been surprised. The two had been buddies from day one, while I, the woman's actual client, had remained little more than a pincushion.

Though not a *French*-speaking pincushion, which I was pretty sure was a big part of the problem...

"Are we finished?" I asked, finally relaxing my shoulders.

"*Non! Rester!*" she snipped, holding her hand out like she was trying to stop a bus. "*Bouger les bras*," she ordered, with an upwards flip of her wrist.

Clueless as to what was being demanded of me, I looked to Chloe for a translation, but before she could say anything, Madame Loute came at me and grabbed both my elbows.

"*Bras! Bras!*" she snapped, as she began to manually flap my arms up and down.

"She wants to know if you can move your arms all right," Chloe said, unable to stop herself from giggling at my involuntary chicken dance.

"It's good," I said, darting my tongue out at the still-laughing Chloe.

After a few more flaps, Madame Loute seemed satisfied and let my arms fall to my sides. "*Quelque chose ne va pas avec tes seins...*" she mumbled with a shake of her head as she stared at my chest. "*Comment se sentent-ils?*"

Again, I turned to Chloe who now had a hand over her mouth to hide the fact that she was straining not to laugh. "She says there is something wrong with your boobs."

"...What?"

Chloe nodded. "She wants to know how they feel."

"How do my boobs *feel...*? Um, fine?" I said with a shrug. "I've got to be honest, no one's ever asked me that before."

"*Elle est à l'aise,*" Chloe told her.

I'm not sure what Chloe said, but whatever it was, a moment later – and without warning or apology I might add – Madame Loute reached up and grabbed my chest with her cold, bony hands, and squeezed like she was honking two horns. I couldn't stop my eyes from nearly popping out of my head, while Chloe snorted a laugh and had to turn away.

"*Trop petit,*" Madame Loute sighed, releasing her hold on me and walking toward the door. "*Je reviendrai dans un instant,*" she said, then disappeared into the hallway.

"*Petit?*" I said, glaring at Chloe as soon as the door closed. "Did she just call me small chested?"

Chloe laughed. "Caught that one, did you?"

"Cranky old bitty…" I mumbled, glancing down at my chest. "It's her fault anyway. With all the holes she's been poking in me, I'm surprised I haven't flown around the room like a popped balloon."

"She's only trying to help," Chloe smiled. "And just look at you," she added, her eyes glued to my new gown. "You look amazing!"

"After all this, I should hope so." I turned around to face the full-length mirror propped up against a bookcase. It really was a magnificent dress, there was no denying that. Deep emerald green silk with an embroidered front, ornate scooped neck and flowing draped sleeves that fluttered elegantly when I walked. It was by far the nicest item of clothing I had ever put on.

"What's wrong?" Chloe asked, obviously having noticed the face I was making, "Don't you like it?"

"No, no, I do. It's incredible… really."

"Then what's the matter?"

"Nothing I guess, it's just… I don't know, you don't think it's a little… 'Maid Marian crashing Cinderella's ball'?"

Her eyes went dreamy. "Yes, that's exactly what it is," she mooned, "and it's perfect."

"Right," I chuckled, realizing I should have expected no less from Lorcan Hall's resident Happily-Ever-After expert, "but let's remember that this is a formal Gala, not a costume party. Are you sure I won't look silly?"

"Oh no! Not at all! Everyone dresses traditionally for these things, it's expected. You would look strange in anything else. Trust me, this will be perfect," she assured me, letting the silk of my skirt slide over the back of her hand. "I wish I could go…" she sighed, her bottom lip slowly making a more pronounced appearance.

"I'm sorry Chloe, I wish you could come too, but there is nothing we can do. Only Jocelyn, Cormac, Alex and I were invited. And technically Alex wasn't invited, but Jocelyn wants him with us, so they are *allowing* him to come. The Bhunaidh are pretentious jerks Chloe, you know that."

"Yeah…"

"And jerks aren't worth your time. You're better off here."

"Sure," she groaned. "Better off here by myself, while you all get to go to a castle, and attend a gala, and wear gowns and tuxedos, and dance under the stars…" she gushed in a voice becoming more melodramatic by the second.

"OK, first of all," I cut in, "it is forty degrees out there, so no one will be doing anything under the stars besides shivering. Secondly, these people are pretentious jerks. Just look at *Madame Loute*," I scoffed in an exaggerated French accent.

"She's not really one of them," Chloe pouted.

"Exactly! She's not one of them, she only *works* for them and yet still she acts like the Queen of Sheba! Besides, what kind of people hire personal designers, anyway? And not only hire them, mind you, but sends those designers to make clothes for other people? Who does that?" OK, I was venting now, but I couldn't help it. I've never had patience for stuck-up people.

"It was a gift, they were just trying to be nice," she tried again, but even I could tell she didn't believe her own words.

"Maybe. But more likely, they were worried that whatever I was going to wear wouldn't have been good enough for their oh-so-important affair."

She sighed again, but nodded this time. "You're probably right," she allowed, "But really, wcan you blame them? Who knows what you would have shown up in, you are an *American*," she added with a laugh.

"Worse," I laughed, "I'm an American *teenager*! I could have shown up in yoga pants and a sweatshirt."

"Don't forget your flip-flops."

"Nah, it's too cold for flops, I would probably have gone with sneakers," I winked.

"Right," she giggled, though the sadness lingered slightly.

"We'll be back before you know it," I said, taking her hand and giving it a playful shake.

"But what if you *need* me?" she whined, in a last ditch effort just as Madame Loute came back in.

"We'll be gone for less than a week," I grinned, "I think we'll be OK. But I promise, if for some reason I need to time walk…" I paused as Madame Loute pulled out two large foam bra cups, "…*or hide a body*…" I added quietly with an evil smirk, "you'll be the first one I call."

To the great relief of all involved, after cutting a few stray threads and the placement and adjusting of the bra cups – which was borderline creepy – my new gown was finally done. Once sprung from the fashion dungeon, I walked up to the main entrance of Lorcan with Chloe. She needed to leave for class, I needed to breathe air that wasn't laced with mildew, dust, and fabric lint.

"What time do you all leave tomorrow?" Chloe asked as she pulled on her coat, almost managing to not pout.

"Early. We are supposed to be on the road by 8."

"OK," she sighed, definitely pouting now, "I'll come by and see you tonight before you go."

"Sounds good," I smiled, as she looped her bag around her arm and headed off to class.

I stepped outside and leaned against the pillar at the top of the entrance steps, watching Chloe as she made her way up the path toward campus. I really did feel bad for her. I knew how much she wanted to help and be involved in the Order, and honestly I didn't really understand why she couldn't. Jocelyn had told her it wasn't safe for her as her ability was too weak. While true, I never saw why that would be dangerous for anyone, however in this instance I was happy the situation was as it was. Chloe was the best friend I had, and much as I would have loved to have her with us at Adare Manor, that was the last place in the world she needed to be.

From what I'd heard, these Originals – or Bhunaidh, as apparently they liked to be called – were a group of Holders who thought way too highly of themselves. They measured a person's worth only by the bloodline they were born into and the strength of the ability they possessed. To even be worthy of associating with them you had to meet their standards, the biggest of which was that you had to be a pure-blooded Holder; as in, no non-Holders in your bloodline. At all. Any Holder, even a full Holder, who was born outside of their circle and thus not pure-blooded, was deemed tainted and unworthy in their eyes.

And as for non-Holders, they might as well not even exist.

Chloe was not only born of two non-Holders, but the strength of her ability was unimpressive at best. There is no way these self-righteous snobs would have ever considered her worthy enough to associate with them, and were she to come with us, I knew exactly what would happen; she would show up wide-eyed and innocent, someone would insult her and hurt her feelings, and then I would have to kick their ass. Which, while completely justified as far as I was concerned, likely wouldn't go over very well. So whether she realized it or not, Chloe really was better off staying home.

Still standing at the top of the steps, I looked out into the afternoon fog, and let the cold wet air fill my chest. The sky was steel gray, the mist of the fog hung just over the ground, and the evening shadows had started to stretch their legs. It really was beautiful. So beautiful, in fact, that I decided to stay out and enjoy the view a bit longer. Why not? I mean, how often did people take time to truly admire the beauty around them every day when it is so easy to take it all for granted? I had always been told that it was important to remember to slow down every now and again and appreciate life's little pleasures, so that's what I would do; I would sit on one of the benches surrounding Lorcan and take in the sights and sounds of this magnificent campus. I would relax and spend some time enjoying the day.

It would be revitalizing and inspirational. It would be profound and meaningful...

...and was in no way stalling.

After all, stalling involved doing something that was pointless or unnecessary; this was neither. I was trying to improve myself. I was communing with nature...

I was...

...*damn it.*

OK, maybe I was stalling... a little. I knew what needed to be done – what I had promised myself I would do – but now that it was time to make good on said promise, I wasn't nearly as confident as I had been the day before when I'd made it. However, I was quickly realizing that were I to continue with the avoidance game, "admiring the beautiful outdoors" was not the way to do it – at least not in November.

With a frustrated shiver I stepped back into Lorcan, trying to warm my icy fingers against my arms, staring down the long hallway that, were I not a sniveling coward, I should be walking along right now. The hall leading to Jocelyn's office.

The Order had a meeting scheduled that evening to go over everything before the four of us left the next day. The meeting was in Jocelyn's office at 4.00. It was currently 3.38. Cormac, Min, and Mr Reid all had classes until 3.55, and Alex was assisting Mr Anderson with a tour set to end at the same time, thus none of them would get to the meeting until just before it started. I had known all this the evening before, and told myself that I would use this opportunity to arrive early to Jocelyn's office so that the two of us could actually talk for a minute or two alone and break this weird sort of stalemate we had going on.

Refusing to be the one who chickened out, I took a deep breath and started to slowly make my way down the side hallway, studiously keeping my fingers from fiddling nervously with the hem of my shirt. Jocelyn, my father, and I hadn't been alone together since our "talk" a few weeks ago, and, while I'm pretty sure that neither of us would actually admit that we were avoiding the other, I knew we kind of were. It wasn't that we hadn't seen each other at all, because we had. We'd even spoken a few times briefly, but it had always been in a group. This would be our first one-on-one, and the fact that I had no idea what to say to the man was more than a little unsettling.

But weird or no, I'd recently decided that I would at least try. And really try, not pretend to try while actually remaining skeptical and bitter like I'd done before. Well, OK, there may have still been some skepticism, but now it wasn't so much about him as about whether or not an actual relationship between us could ever truly work. Strange as it was to admit, it seemed possible, but we'd really never know if I didn't at least give it a shot. And yeah, it would have been nice not to have to be the one to initiate things, since the last effort had been made by him when he finally told me the truth about why he'd left us all those years ago, I knew it was my turn.

About halfway down the stone stretch, I reached out with my ability, focusing on the office ahead to see who I felt inside. I told myself I was just making sure Jocelyn was in fact there, ignoring the tiny hope that he wasn't. There was indeed an ability in the office that I immediately recognized to be Jocelyn, but no others within the vicinity of the office, which meant he was alone.

Damn. So much for that...

Or, umm... good.

I paused in front of the office door, took a deep breath, and scanned the room one last time – you know, in case someone had materialized out of a wall or something in the last thirty seconds. OK, that was a lame hope, but hey, around Lorcan, that may not have been as crazy as it sounded.

But no, still only Jocelyn.

OK; this was it. No way around it now, and I would not be a wimp. I took one last breath, I set my jaw, pushed the queasy feeling in my stomach to the side, and knocked on the door.

Chapter 2

"Come in," Jocelyn called.

I'd known he was there, but still for some reason I still jumped a little. I pushed the large wooden door open slightly and leaned in to find Jocelyn standing behind his desk, stacking textbooks into piles. When he looked up and saw me, it was clear he was shocked.

"Becca?"

"Yeah, sorry," I said, praying my voice sounded normal, "I know I'm early..."

"No, it's fine," he said with what I assume was supposed to be a smile, though he was still too surprised for it to look natural. "Come in."

He pretended not to watch me walk over to one of the armchairs by the desk and take a seat, while I pretended not to notice him pretending not to watch.

Yeah... this wasn't awkward or anything.

I pulled my feet up under me in the oversized chair, making much more out of straightening my pants than was really necessary as it gave me an excuse to stare at my legs as the seconds ticked by while I tried to come up with something to say. I didn't just want to stare at him while he stacked books, but what was I supposed to say? Was he going to say anything? Should I just look out the window and pretend I'm daydreaming?

Had we been in a cartoon, I was pretty sure we'd be due for a cricket chirp right about now...

"How have you been feeling?" he asked, the sudden sound startling me.

"Fine," I said, knowing he was talking about my Iris-induced near-death experience a few weeks ago. "Back to normal."

"Good," he nodded, followed by another bout of heavy silence.

OK, this was getting us nowhere. I'd forced myself to make good on my resolution to "try," and I wasn't about to let the effort it took to get this far all be for not. He'd asked me how I was, so it was my turn to say something, and sticking with questions seemed the best way to go.

"So um... Do you know these people?" I asked, proud of myself for speaking, even if my tone hadn't actually sounded as casual as it had in my mind. "The ones we're going to see I mean, the Bhunaidh?"

"No," he said, seeming to relax slightly, "not personally, or at least not well. I've met the head family, Brassal Bloch and his wife Alva. They have two children, both attending University now, I believe."

"What do you mean 'head family'? Are they in charge?"

"Something like that," he nodded, as he started moving the stacks of textbooks to the bookcase on the wall, lining them on the empty shelves toward the bottom. "The Bhunaidh have their own, very unique way of life, and to them, the Blochs are essentially their... well, royal family, I suppose, for lack of a better description."

Royal family? These people were just getting better and better by the minute.

Realizing it was totally lame of me to just sit and watch a man walk back and forth with stacks of books when I had functioning limbs, I got up and stepped over to the desk. "OK," I said, picking up the next stack of books and handing it to him, "royal families, galas, private personal tailors; these people really are as bad as everyone says, aren't they?"

"I don't know if 'bad' is the best word, but I'm sure you would think as much," he said with an emphasis on "you," as he took the books from me and turned back to the bookcase.

"*You'd think as much*?" I said, mimicking his tone. "Should I be offended? Kinda feels like I should." I'd known what he meant, but me being me, I couldn't help but fall back into one of my most tried and true comfort zones: sarcasm.

Unfortunately, he didn't recognize the joke in my undertone. "No," he said, looking up quickly, clearly thinking I was mad – though given our more recent history, I couldn't really blame him. "I only meant..." but he stopped when he saw that I was smiling. Relaxing, he took the next stack of books from my outstretched hand. "What I meant was that growing up as you have in this era, you are used to the idea that people are equal no matter their circumstance. The Bhunaidh don't operate that way."

"Yeah, I've heard all the holier-than-thou crap."

"It is not crap to them. They call themselves Bhunaidh, or Originals, because their bloodlines are directly descended from the Holders of ancient times."

"Good for them," I mumbled, passing over the last of the books. "Surprised they are letting us come to this gala at all."

Jocelyn chuckled slightly. "Actually, when I asked if we could attend their get-together this year, they were thrilled. They have been trying to bring me into their fold for decades. Of course I didn't mention that we were, in fact, coming to find one of their own who is possibly a spy for Darragh. I can't imagine that conversation would have gone well."

"Wait, they want you in their little Holder club? Why? I thought it was only pureblooded Holders allowed. Weren't your parents normal? I mean wasn't that the whole prophecy deal?" I asked, trying to remember what Min and Alex had told me about all the old stories. From what I could remember, it was said that a full Holder would be born whose ability didn't come from anyone else in his line, and that his son – or as it turned out, daughter; me – would be the Holder destined to awaken the Iris.

"That was the deal," he grinned, "yes. But in my instance, bloodline is of little matter. I am *Bronntanas*," he said, rolling his eyes slightly. "Not only am I worthy," I smiled at that distaste in his voice at the word "worthy," happy to know that he seemed to find this as ridiculous as I did, "but I would most certainly be quite a large feather in their collective cap. The Bhunaidh know more about Holder lore and our legends than anyone. It is an immensely serious matter to them, almost like a religion."

"Religion?" I was trying not to giggle, as I probably shouldn't have been, but I couldn't help it. "So, does that make you the God?"

Luckily, he smiled too. "No, not God," he chuckled. Then, with a grin added, "Moses, at best."

I was about to continue my line of questioning, but stopped when a subtle pulling sensation began to bloom in my chest. Immediately my heart picked up as the fuzzy warmth grew, spreading down my arms and up my back, making my neck tingle and my stomach flutter. It was a feeling I'd experienced for the first time only a few weeks ago, however since then I'd grown so used to it that part of me felt strangely empty when it was gone. It was exciting, like sitting down to watch a movie you'd been waiting months to see, while at the same time soothing as a hot drink after being out in the snow. It was comforting, it was fulfilling, it was thrilling, and it was nerve-racking.

It was the feeling of the Anam bond... which meant Alex was nearby.

A moment later a knock at the office door had both Jocelyn and I turning – him in curiosity; me in anticipation.

"Come in," Jocelyn called, standing and walking around to the front of the desk.

"Afternoon," Min's voice said, as she entered the room followed by Cormac, Mr Anderson, and Alex.

He met my eyes the moment he came through the door, then,

quickly surveying the room and seeing that I had in fact been the first to arrive, looked back at me and raised his eyebrows slightly, impressed. I lifted my chin just a touch in a subtle, "That's right, I'm awesome," kind of way, to which the corner of his mouth twitched and his eyes sparkled, their stormy blue irises laughing at me.

As they filed in to the large office and began taking seats around the large coffee table in the center of the room, Alex walked by my chair and ran the backs of his fingers discreetly down my arm as he passed, sending hot chills racing along my skin, heating my neck, and prickling my ears. He didn't say anything, but he didn't have to. Everything about him told me how happy he was to see me. The last time we'd been together was the morning before last, just before Alex left with Mr Reid on a short scouting trip down to Cork, in the south of Ireland. I knew he'd gotten back that morning, but between my endless dress fitting and Alex helping Mr Anderson with a campus tour, this had been the first chance we'd had to see each other. It was wonderful to have him close again, and I really was trying to convince myself that the combination of seeing him and the amazing – though short-lived – feel of his touch was enough. It should have been enough, at least to get me though this meeting... but it wasn't. When it came to Alex, nothing would ever be enough for me, and though I usually did a good job of keeping my sappy, sentimental, lovely-dovey thoughts under control, that afternoon, it wasn't happening. Embarrassed as I was to admit it, at that moment... I would have done *anything* for a kiss.

But of course I knew that wasn't going to happen, not with so many people around. Alex and I never kissed in public. In fact, we never did anything more than hold hands unless we were alone. Every so often he would give me a peck on the cheek, but that was it. Alex preferred our more... um... *personal* exchanges to remain a private matter. He was definitely a gentleman, and held nothing higher than our relationship and the bond we shared, and while I knew that there were girls my age that would have frustrated by such old-fashioned discretion, I found it charming.

At least normally. However, on days like this, it was the best and worst kind of torture. The need for his lips on mine was like the tickle of a feather I couldn't scratch, and as Alex sat at the end of the couch nearest my chair, I kicked myself for not thinking to move over there myself before they'd arrived.

OK… time to focus on something else…

Luckily, Mr Reid chose that moment to come rushing in, completing our group.

"You're late," Mr Anderson grumbled, as Mr Reid took the seat next to him on the second couch.

"I'm not late," Mr Reid said under his breath, pulling his sleeve back and displaying his wristwatch to Mr Anderson. "We were to begin at 4 o'clock, and it is 4 o'clock."

"Aye," Anderson said, pushing Reid's wrist back, "we were to *begin* at 4, not *arrive* at 4."

"We have several things to go over today," Jocelyn began, putting an end to the mumbling and starting the meeting. "First off, we need to determine which classes will need to be covered in Cormac's and my absence…"

It quickly became clear that the first portion of the meeting would have nothing to do with me, so I tuned out a bit, breaking my "focus elsewhere" vow as my eyes slid over to Alex. He was sitting casually, elbow leaning on the couch's armrest, chin resting on his knuckles, evidently listening intently to the conversation across the room about schedules and curriculums. Or at least that was how he appeared. However on closer inspection, I realized that his eyes, which should have been focused on the speakers, were glancing sideways at me as though he were waiting for me to look at him. When our eyes met, he smiled ever so slightly then looked down pointedly at the coffee table in the center of the room before looking back up to the conversation, again seeming perfectly attentive.

More than familiar with this game, I looked down at the table where his eyes had been moments ago, and sure enough, a few moments later the pattern of the wood grain on its surface began to move, twisting and curving until the dark veins formed words floating in the pale chestnut background.

"*Hi.*" The lines swirled again. "*I've missed you.*"

Following his example, I focused my gaze on the scheduling conversation while simultaneously reaching across to Mr Anderson, connecting with him and assuming his ability. Over the past few weeks I'd made several strides in honing my ability, but the one I was most happy about was my newly-developed power of stealth. It had taken some time, but I had finally reached a point where, if I was careful, I could connect with other Holders and use their abilities without them realizing I was doing so. I knew it didn't really get me much, but it still made me feel slick.

Not to mention how handy it was when partaking in candid conversations during boring portions of meetings...

"*I missed you too,*" I imparted carefully, making sure that Alex was the only one to get the message.

"*I was hoping you would be over here,*" the table read, while at the same time Alex moved his hand from his chin to the couch, drumming his fingers lightly on the edge of the upholstered arm.

"*I know, sorry.*"

"*No problem. I'll just have to wait a little longer.*"

I couldn't help but laugh inwardly at that last message, particularly at the level of detail he was using in his casts. He had even gone as far as to use the knots in the wood grain for his letter "o"s.

"*You know that no one else can see this,*" I glanced over to him quickly, "*you don't have to work so hard.*"

"*You don't like the table...?*" the grain spelled out, then slowly dissolved back into its rightful pattern except for one wispy spot that slid over to the edge of the table, down the leg and on to the floor. It melted into the carpet causing the fibers of the Oriental rug to ripple and then move, rearranging the images of gold leaves and ornate flowers into words. *"How about the rug"* I was about to answer when a growing pattern of frost on the window opposite me caught my eye. *"Or the window?"*

"OK, now you're just screwing with me."

I saw his lips twitch as the writing on both the carpet and window disappeared, only to be replaced by black letters hanging in the air a few feet in front of me. They were a squared font and appeared one at a time as though an invisible typewriter was floating in the air.

"All right then, boring it is."

I smashed my lips together to keep from smiling and made sure to keep my eyes on the discussion. *"Stop making me laugh, we're going to get caught."*

"Looks like you need to learn to control yourself." I glanced over again to see his eyes sparkle as the corner of his mouth raised a bit.

So he thought he was funny, did he? Well I could be funny too…

"I thought I was doing a good job controlling myself," I imparted innocently, *"because all I want to do is jump into your lap and kiss you until we can't breathe."*

I had to give him credit, he didn't move, but I did note – with satisfaction, I might add – that his stare became much more direct, and his hand, which had been resting casually on the armrest, started to slowly grip the fabric as a warm pink hue began to flood his ears.

"Or," I continued, starting to feel a bit warm myself, *"if you'd rather, I could kiss my way down your neck until–"*

"Not fair," came the floating words again, though this time he didn't bother with the pretext of writing it out one letter at a time.

"Oh, don't worry," I told him, unable to hide my grin at his ears which had gone full-on red, *"I'd play fair… you'd get to kiss me too."*

He took a deeper than average breath, squirming a bit in his seat.

"Becca?"

Damn it! "Yes?" I said, looking up at Jocelyn who was clearly expecting an answer to a question I'd not heard.

"I said I am trying to arrange our meeting with Brassal and Alva for before the gala tomorrow night. I know they would like to meet you, and it's best to get it out of the way if we can."

"Oh, yeah," I nodded, hoping he was just assuming that I'd been daydreaming – which, had Alex not been in the room, would likely have been the case – and smiled. "Sure, no problem. Will you ask about Ciaran then?" I asked quickly, both curious and hoping to play off my distraction.

"Nice save," the floating letters said. Even in their hovering silence I could tell they were sarcastic.

With everyone else looking at Jocelyn as he retook his seat, I glanced over at Alex and quickly poked my tongue out at him. He smiled and turned the *"Nice save"* still hanging in front of me into a heart before letting it waft away like a puff of smoke.

"Maybe," Jocelyn finally said. "We will have to see how the day plays out. It is a delicate matter, so if there are others around, I may wait for a better time."

"Aye," Mr Anderson said. "Can't imagine they will be thrilled that we plan to accuse one of their own of being a traitor. Could tarnish their reputation, you know," he added with a scoff.

"What do you plan to tell them?" Mr Reid asked.

"Only that I wish to speak with Ciaran and ask them to set up a meeting."

"Why do you need to ask permission?" I asked.

"I'm not asking permission, but I do want to keep them apprised of the meeting. Anderson is right, they will likely not be happy that Ciaran is suspected of association with Darragh and I do not plan to tell them until I must, but I also do not want it to appear that we are attempting to operate against their own people behind their backs."

"But what if they say no?" I continued, already suspicious of all of them. "I mean, what if they know he's working with Darragh? What if they all are?"

"That would be highly unlikely, my dear," Cormac smiled.

"Until now, none of the Bhunaidh have ever been known to be involved with Darragh or any of his associates. In fact such a thing is looked down upon and would likely result in a permanent dismissal from their society."

"But this Ciaran guy is obviously up to something, why not others?" I asked.

"Well first of all," Jocelyn said, "we don't know that Ciaran is guilty of anything yet. All we know is that Taron was in contact with him, and that surrounding those dealings are holes in his memory."

"Holes? What do you mean 'holes'?" several of us asked overtop of one another.

I'd known that Ciaran Shea was the only unaccounted for person that Taron – the dirty backstabbing traitor who was still currently under house arrest in his room at Lorcan – had been in contact with. Jocelyn had discovered that during one of the first readings of his mind just after the "incident" a few weeks ago. However, he had never mentioned anything about memory holes, though it appeared that I wasn't the only one out of the loop.

"When did you realize that, Jocelyn?" Min asked.

"Only a few days ago," Jocelyn sighed. "When my subsequent readings on Taron didn't produce anything useful, I took a closer look at the memories involving Ciaran. That is when I noticed the inconsistencies: missing periods, partial conversations, and so on. They were well disguised, but once I realized what I was looking for, the holes became obvious."

"What exactly is a memory hole?" Alex asked, making me happy to know that I wasn't the only one who was lost.

"An absence of information, or a break in the stream of consciousness," Jocelyn answered. "From the time we are born to the moment we die, our brains are always active, constantly collecting information. Even when asleep, our sensory organs continue to function, adding to the string of memories, thus this string would be continuous from birth to death."

"So then, what would cause a hole?" Mr Anderson asked.

"Nothing natural," Jocelyn replied. "The only way that a string of consciousness can have holes is if a memory or group of memories is removed."

"Could it have been an accident?" Mr Reid asked.

"No," Jocelyn shook his head, "absolutely not. It was deliberate, and I am more than sure it was done with Taron's consent in an attempt to hide information. Had Taron been unwilling, there would have been tension, strain, or fear within the memories surrounding the gaps, but there is none."

"He allowed someone to erase his memories?" I asked no one specific.

"Why have we not yet fed him to the hounds?" Mr Anderson growled, clenching and unclenching his fists.

"Taron's fate will be determined by what Mr Shea has to tell us. Until then, he stays where he is," Jocelyn said.

"Aye, but we could at least knock him around a bit in the meantime," Mr Anderson grumbled quietly, earning him an elbow in the ribs from Mr Reid.

I would have been more than happy to voice my agreement, but as I knew the subject of Taron was a touchy one, I kept my opinions to myself – though not without making a mental note to secure a front row seat should Mr Anderson ever get the chance to make good on his threats.

"We will be largely playing the situation by ear," Jocelyn said, deliberately moving the conversation on. "I am not sure how Brassal will react to the news about Ciaran, or even how much I will disclose to him, but regardless, I feel confident that if we can assure him of our discretion in handling the matter, that he will be more than willing to help us however we may need."

"And you'll be sure to let us know if you need anything?"

"Of course," Jocelyn nodded. "Let's just hope it's smooth sailing."

CHAPTER 3

Twenty long minutes later, after covering everything from packing to the weather, the meeting finally began to wrap up. I sat quietly the whole time, silently praying that every new topic would be the last, doing my best not to tap my foot, drum my fingers, or do anything else that would let on how antsy I was. All I wanted was for this now seemingly endless meeting to end, get away from the crowd, and have Alex to myself for a few minutes. The five short feet that separated the two of us were little over an arm's length at best, but in the current scenario it may as well have been a mile, and after more than an hour, it was starting to irk me. We hadn't attempted to communicate again since nearly being caught, yet somehow the silence and feigned ignorance of each other had only made my need to be closer to him build, bubbling under my skin like fizz in a soda. My only consolation was the fact that he didn't seem to be faring much better. His once relaxed posture had become strained and his leg couldn't seem to keep still, bouncing the hand that rested on his knee. The hand that I'd soon be able to slide my own into and feel his fingers close around mine, his thumb tracing invisible patterns on the back of my hand like it always did. I sighed quietly as I thought about...

Wait... I sighed?

Seriously? *I sighed*?

Dear Lord! What the hell was happening to me? When did I become such a sap...?

"All right then," Jocelyn suddenly said, "does anyone have anything else?"

Ignoring my internal embarrassment at my apparent swooning, I held my breath, willing everyone in the room to stay quiet.

"Very well then," Jocelyn nodded after an excruciating moment of silence. "If that is all, we'll adjourn. Have a good evening everyone, and I'll be sure to keep you all informed."

As everyone began to stand I glanced over at Alex who was already looking my way with a smile that made it all I could do to not jump out of my chair.

"Shall we?" he asked me quietly as he stood.

"Let's," I grinned back, already feeling the tingle of heat in my hand as I reached for his. However, my legs had barely had a chance to completely straighten before our bubble was burst.

"Not you two," Jocelyn said from behind us, stopping both of us in our tracks. "We need to have a discussion before you leave."

Of course we did...

I let my lonely hand fall back to my side with an tiny sigh, turning to face Jocelyn, and only then seeing that Min had also hung back and was coming over to join the three of us.

"Are the rings ready?" Jocelyn asked her as she approached.

She nodded, reaching into a small pouch she pulled from the pocket of her dress. "Yes," she said, turning the pouch over and letting two small silver circles roll into the palm of her hand. "Now let us hope they work."

I squinted down at the ringlets, having no idea what to make of them. They were perfectly round and slightly cylindrical – very much like a wedding band, though they were far too small to be intended for anyone's finger. Honestly, they looked like bangle bracelets for a Barbie doll.

"What are those?" I asked as Min reached around the side of my neck and found the clasp of my Scaith's chain.

"They are charmed Saol rings," Jocelyn said while Min attached the ring to the closure of my necklace. "I asked Min to make them for the two of you. They will disguise your Saols from anyone at the manor able to read them."

"OK, why?" I said, pulling the clasp of my chain around to the front so I could see it.

"Anyone who can read your Saol will instantly know everything about you that we don't want them knowing," he explained. "When it comes to your ability, the less people who know, the safer you are. As far as the Bhunaidh are concerned, or anyone else for that matter, you are simply a Holder – not even a full Holder at that – and in no way exceptional."

"Sounds like fun."

"There," Min said, after taking a step back and studying me for a moment. "Good."

"It works?" Jocelyn asked.

Min nodded. "I see nothing but the mildest compulsion ability. Nothing that will attract any undue attention."

"Why do I need one?" Alex asked as Min turned her attention to him.

"Becca's ability is not all we need to disguise. Her ring also hides her bond to you, and this one," she handed him the second ring, "will hide yours to her."

"Again," I said, not loving this idea, "why?"

"Because your bond is also exceptional," Min answered, "and would certainly raise a few eyebrows, particularly amongst the Bhunaidh, who frown on the Anam bond in general."

"We don't want anything to draw more attention to you than is absolutely necessary, and allowing everyone to know that you share a reciprocal Anam bond with another Holder would do exactly that. Anything that places you under extra scrutiny also places your actual ability in danger of being discovered. Which is why, while we are at Adare Manor, it is imperative that the two of you keep the same distance from one another as you would a casual acquaintance."

"Wait, what?"

"At least when you are anywhere within the public eye," he nodded.

"The rings only do part of the job," Min chimed in, "but they cannot cover the bond entirely, at least not one as strong as yours. All the typical Saol markers of a bond are masked by the charm on the rings, but if someone had a mind to look hard enough, they would be able to see it. That is why you must make sure that no one has any reason to get nosey."

"It won't be a problem," Alex said, prompting a cocked eyebrow from me. "They're right," he said, seeing my unamused frown in his direction.

"Just being Jocelyn's daughter will have every eye in the place on you as it is," Min said patting my arm. "No need to add to it and invite trouble."

"Yeah, OK," I relented, as it was clear there was no argument I could make. "I get it."

Satisfied, Min turned to help Alex attach his ring to his Sciath, careful to save him the embarrassment of having to completely remove it. Jocelyn turned to me, slightly angling his shoulders away from Min and Alex and tipping his head down as if to signal the start of a semi-private conversation.

"Speaking of being related," Jocelyn said, his lowered voice sounding a bit nervous. "I should let you know before we leave that while we are with the Bhunaidh, you will need to use the name Clavish." He looked up at me in a guarded fashion, as if he thought I might violently reject the whole idea. I did feel my brow furrow, but it was more out of confusion than anything else. Clearly it didn't read that way to Jocelyn because his tone was borderline apologetic as he quickly continued. "That is how they have always known you. I never allowed anyone outside of a few members of the Order know the name Ingle, it simply seemed safer that way–"

"No, no," I cut in, hoping to ease his nerves. "It's fine. I was just confused, that's all. No big deal."

"You're sure?" he asked, though the lines on his face did seem to relax.

"Absolutely."

"Good," he said, then after a moment added, "thank you," which I wish he hadn't.

"No problem," I nodded, willing the awkwardness I felt creeping back in to go away.

"I know it will be odd for you, but I do believe it is best for everyone this way." He'd said "everyone," but his eyes told me what he'd really meant.

Mom.

The question that had been bothering me for a while reared up in my mind, and as much as I didn't want to get back to this particular subject with him just yet, I couldn't let it go anymore. "No one's..." I paused, glancing down at the rug. "No one's going to hurt her or anything, are they?"

The notion had been haunting me since I'd learned that Taron had been working for Darragh all those years, and the idea that she was back in Pennsylvania all on her own just waiting to somehow be used against us was one that kept me up more nights than I'd like to recall.

He didn't answer immediately, which, even while unsettling, I appreciated. It meant he was trying to be honest and not just give me the quick answer he knew I wanted to hear. "I have done everything I can to make sure that doesn't happen," he said, as I looked back at him. "The Order is not without resources. Protection charms have been placed on your house as well as the hospital and places she frequents, and I have sent men to watch over her."

"You have?"

"Three," he nodded. "All former students who are more than

capable of keeping an eye on her and even offering protection and assistance should the need arise."

I hated to do it, but I had to ask. "And we're sure..." I left the question hanging, but he knew what I meant.

"Yes, they can be trusted. I read them all thoroughly before I gave them any information."

Wow. I knew how much Jocelyn disliked using his ability, so for him to have put his ideals aside and read the minds of three different people voluntarily was no small thing. I knew that Taron's betrayal had been a blow, but it was clear he would not be making the same mistake twice.

"OK," I said simply, letting him know that I trusted his judgment. It wasn't a perfect scenario, but just knowing that she was in fact being looked after and that we would know if she was to get into trouble was enough to ease my mind, at least for the moment.

With a nod, Jocelyn walked over to his desk while I turned back to Alex and Min, crossing my fingers that they were done and Alex and I could finally get away. When I saw him waiting for me patiently, the excitement in my stomach bubbled back to life. I took his hand as we walked toward the office door, no longer concerned with who might see. All I cared about was the fact that I was a mere twenty steps away from the kiss I'd been waiting all afternoon for. My pulse quickened and my lips hummed, all in anticipation of the moment Alex and I made it through the door and around the corner. We were nearly there, close enough now to reach for the handle, pull open the door, and...

"Alex?" Jocelyn called from behind us. "One last thing, do you have a minute to go with me to vehicle services and pick up the car for the trip? I need to register you as an alternate driver."

A half hour later – and still kiss-less – I was taking my frustrations out on the unassuming piles of clothes stacked on my bed when I heard a knock on the door to my room.

"Becca?" Before I could answer, I heard the handle click and looked up to see my brother Ryland's curly red head pop through the door.

"Hey," I said, flipping the lid to my suitcase open, "What are you doing here? Don't you have soccer practice?" Ryland had only joined the team a few weeks ago, and the idea that he was actually a part of any sports team still blew my mind.

"Nope, not today," he shrugged, shuffling over to the bed without bothering to close the door. "Coach is sick. No," he continued, as I moved to shut the door behind him, "leave it open, it's hot in here."

"OK," I said, not at all hot, but not caring enough to argue. "So, no practice…" I prompted him to continue.

"Yeah," he nodded, plopping down on the foot of my bed. "So I came to say hi."

"Really…?"

"Yep. So, what's up?"

I cocked an eyebrow, but I wasn't about to question him further. Honestly, I was kind of thrilled he came to see me on his own without me having to initiate a visit like I normally did. It wasn't that I never got to see him, but lately the kid had more social appointments then there were hours in the day, which didn't tend to leave a lot of room for entertaining older sisters. Life at St Brigid's had turned him into a new person, and I was thrilled that he was finally able to have the normal happy life that a kid deserves.

I really was.

But, great as it was for him, for me – selfish as I felt admitting it – it was still kind of hard. The whole concept of not needing to constantly be there to defend or protect him was still new, but I was doing my best to get used to his newfound independence. Even if it meant I didn't get to see him as much as I would like to.

Sudden as it was, if he wanted to hang out, I wasn't about to look a gift horse in the mouth. It was clear I had been his plan B for the afternoon; that was fine by me, I'd take what I could get.

"OK, then," I said casually, turning back to my packing efforts. "Nothing's up, what's up with you?"

"Nothing," he sighed. "You guys still going to the castle tomorrow?" he asked as he nudged my suitcase to the side with his foot so he could sprawl out across the bed.

"Make yourself comfortable, why don't you?" I chided, picking up the stack of shirts he'd knocked over. "Yep, tomorrow morning."

"Is it really a castle? Do you get to stay there?"

"Yes, it's a real castle," I said, smiling at his enthusiasm as I stuffed a handful of underwear into my suitcase, "but I doubt it's the kind of castle you're thinking of. The inside has been renovated dozens of times, so now it's basically a really nice hotel. People have weddings and parties there all the time."

"Oh," he frowned, let down. "But it still looks like a castle on the outside, right?"

"Pretty much."

"Is there a moat?"

"No moat," I chuckled, "sorry."

"Dungeon?"

"I doubt it." And even if there was, odds are it would have long since been turned into a wine cellar.

Ryland said something else, but I didn't catch it. I was distracted by the unmistakable feel of Alex approaching my room. I looked up, expecting to see him smiling in the doorway – but it was empty. That was odd…

"What's wrong?" Ryland asked, as I looked out into the empty hallway through the still-open door.

"Nothing," I said, glancing around the room once more before eyeing the ceiling. Alex's room was directly above mine, he must have gone there first.

"Is that your dress?" Ry asked, pointing to the garment bag hanging over the back of my desk chair.

"One of them is, yes," I said, grabbing my toiletry bag from the bathroom, suddenly eager to be done packing.

"Can I see it?"

"My dress? Why?"

"I don't know, I want to see it."

"I tried to show you the sketch the seamstress did and I believe your exact words were, 'What's it matter, aren't all dresses the same?'"

"I changed my mind," he said, hopping off the bed. "Which one is it?"

"The top bag," I said, giving up the fight with him in favor of starting one with the zipper on my suitcase. "Just be caref–" I stopped short as suddenly it all came together; Ry leaving the door open, feeling Alex nearby but not seeing him, Ry wanting to see my dress... And it almost worked.

Almost.

Just as Ryland's hand went for the garment bag, I reached over and snatched it away. "Nice try," I said, triumphant grin on my face.

"What?" Ry asked, eyes a bit too innocent.

"I wasn't talking to you," I said, laying the garment bags down and turning to the "empty" space in the middle of my room, shaking my head with a scowl. "You are in so much trouble..."

My threat hung in the air only a second before there was a visible ripple in the air and Alex appeared, standing in the corner of my room, a guilty grin on his face.

"That's so cool," Ryland whispered in awe as I glared, crossing my arms.

"You were *hiding* from *me*?"

"Wish I could do that..." Ry continued to moon.

"And you," I snipped turning to him, "this is why you came to see me? So you could help pull one over on me?"

"No," Ry said, defensively, "I came on my own, thank you very much. Then Alex saw me coming in and asked me to help him," he finished, looking over to Alex to back his story.

Alex shook his head. "Nope, didn't happen."

"Did too!" Ry yelled, shocked and appalled at the betrayal.

"Sorry buddy," Alex shrugged, "every man for himself."

Not about to be turned on, Ry grabbed the pillow from my bed and took a swat at him. "Traitor!" Alex easily avoided the assault, stepping back with a laugh, grabbing the pillow and pulling Ry toward him, flipping him around. A moment later, Alex had the pillow in one arm while holding Ry in a playful headlock in the other.

"What he actually came to ask," Alex told me with a chuckle, "was if we wanted to go to dinner tonight."

"Not sure I want to eat with either of you," I said, raising my eyebrows.

"Me either!" Ry mumbled as he struggled against Alex's arm.

"What if," Alex said letting him go, "I make it so no one can see you when we walk back to your dorm after dinner?"

"Really?" Ry asked, perking up immediately. "The whole way?"

"From the dining hall all the way to your room."

"Awesome!"

"I still have to pack, so how about we meet you over there in an hour?" Alex asked him.

"Cool!" he said skipping to the door, completely distracted by the idea of spending a good five minutes of the day invisible. "See you there! Bye Becca!"

As Ryland took off down the hall, I continued to glare at Alex as he went over to the door, shutting it slowly. Once he clicked the lock into place, he slid his hands into his pockets and turned back to face me, his eyes smiling as they looked out from under his eyebrows like a guilty puppy.

"Hi... Sorry... Hi..."

My eyes narrowed as my lips pressed together. "You do not hide from me, sir."

"Sorry," he smiled.

"Mmmhmm." I pursed my lips.

"Maybe I can make it up to you," he suggested, stepping toward me with a sly edge to his grin.

"You better have something better in mind than making me invisible," I said, already fighting to stay stern and keep my longing in check.

"Hmm," he hummed, taking my face in his hands and closing the space between us. "I might have a few ideas."

A breath later and his lips were finally on mine, and all the tension and frustration of the last few hours burned away like fog in the sun. My hands slid up around his neck as his moved down my back, gripping me around the waist as our mouths began to move more fervently against one another. I sighed as the familiar scent of him filled my head, tightening my stomach with every breath, tingling every hair on my body. With a moan he began to come toward me, forcing me back, back, back, until I was pinned between him and the wall. He braced his right arm against the cool stone while his left wound around my middle, arching my back and pulling me against him.

"I missed you," he breathed as his lips left mine to work down my neck, causing my head to loll and legs to shiver.

"You know," I smiled, slowly dragging my leg up his and savoring the groan it triggered, "if you really want to make it up to me..." I left my sentence hanging, though I pulled him harder against me to drive home my point.

I felt his lips smile against my throat, but instead of taking my somewhat blatant offer, he raised his head and kissed me once more on the lips before standing and pulling me into his arms for a far less scandalous hug.

"I don't think today is the day for that," he said, resting his forehead against mine. "Ryland is expecting us for dinner, after all."

"Wait," I said, leaning back and looking up at him, still catching my breath, "we're stopping, just like that? Seriously?"

I don't know why I was surprised; Alex was the king of getting me all hot and bothered then finding any excuse on the planet to stop before things could reach the next level. I'd even gone as far as to start taking a... *ahem* ...certain daily prescription, just to make sure I was ready when the time finally did come, but thanks to Alex's never ending quest to find the perfect situation for us, thus far my efforts had been for nothing.

"You have to finish packing," he sighed, threading his hands together behind the small of my back, "and I have to start."

"Yeah, I know, but it doesn't have to be this second. Maybe tonight we could–" but he silenced me with a light kiss.

"We are leaving first thing in the morning. You need to sleep."

With a frustrated huff, I stepped around him and walked back over to my bed. "Now we need to get sleep?" I grumbled, stuffing the rest of my clothes into my suitcase. "Your excuses are getting lamer, you know."

"Becca," he said, gently grabbing my arm and turning me around, "I'm not making excuses."

"I know," I sighed. "You just want everything to be perfect." I took his face between my hands, "And I appreciate it – really I do. But if you are waiting for perfection we are never going to get there, because there is no such thing."

"Really?" he asked, a mischievous light sparking in his eye. "Because I thought that a luxury room in a five-star castle sounded pretty close."

My eyes popped open. "No way... you mean..."

"But," he shrugged, "if you don't think that – " but it was my turn to kiss him silent.

"You're serious about this?" I asked, my excitement bubbling dangerously high.

"I am."

"Because I'm going to hold you to it."

"Be my guest."

"No excuses?"

"No excuses, no rain checks, no stalling," he laughed. "Though," he added, "I do have to insist on one stipulation."

"Which is?" I refolded my arms, already skeptical.

"That one of us has a room nowhere near Jocelyn's."

"Oh. OK, yeah, that's a good one," I admitted. Nothing puts the damper on romance quicker than having your father in the next room.

"So we're agreed?" he asked, offering me his hand to shake.

"Agreed."

CHAPTER 4

When they told me that we were going to a "castle," I hadn't really known what to think. The only images I could come up with in my mind were based on the only two examples of castles I'd ever really known, neither of which were doing me any good. The first was of the only two castles in the US – or the only two that I was aware of, anyway – one in Florida and one in California, both of which had been built by Disney, and as such, obviously didn't count. The other was pictures and drawings in all the fairytales and textbooks I'd read growing up. The history books had shown ancient fortresses which were cool, but clearly not anything that would still be habitable today, while the fairytales depicted grand Camelot-style citadels with stone arches, flag-topped steeples, and drawbridges over sparkling moats, which, though awesome as it would have been, didn't seem any more likely. However, anthropomorphized rodents and lack of round table aside, Adare Manor turned out to be pretty incredible.

I did my best to play it cool as we pulled up the long drive to the entry, but on the inside I was gaping like a kid from the sticks on their first trip to the city. The long white graveled drive up to the entry was lined with perfectly groomed topiaries and flowerbeds that looked like they'd popped straight off the page of a gardening magazine. The walls of the manor were high and white, with windows of all shapes and sizes decorating their faces, each pane shimmering under the afternoon sun like gems.

And if for some reason the building and grounds alone weren't enough to impress, the hustle-and-bustle surrounding them would certainly have done the trick. The moment we stepped out of our car we were swallowed up in as high class a flurry as I'd ever seen. There were dozens of luxury vehicles being unloaded and whisked away by white gloved valets, scores of servers – in tuxes, no less – passing trays of refreshments to the arriving guests, and more varieties of designer luggage than I'd even realized existed.

And I felt like a chicken at a swan show.

I'd worn the nicest travel-appropriate outfit I owned, and had even taken the time that morning to do my hair and make-up, and until that moment I'd felt pretty good. But now, standing in the midst of a five-star flutter of manicured nails, air kisses, and French-cuffed shirts, it didn't feel like enough. Luckily, my general distaste for these people eased the self-conscious itch I felt crawling up my back.

Almost, anyway...

However, there was something else that was off, and it had nothing to do with rosebushes, fancy cars, or self-esteem. It was a feeling in my head; a strange haze round my mind as though my brain needed to blink. It started just before we pulled up to the Manor and seemed to be growing by the minute, becoming almost overwhelming. As one of the valet/bellman teams came over to our car and began unloading, I stepped over to the edge of the drive and out of the way, trying not to stumble.

Holders. They were all Holders. Of course I'd known that would be the case, but I hadn't given any thought to how it would feel – and I clearly should have.

"Are you all right?" Alex asked quietly, coming over to stand beside me.

"Yeah... I'm, um... fine." Or at least I was trying to appear fine, but I knew I was blinking way too much to completely pull it off.

Being able to sense other Holders around me was not new; in fact, it had become so second nature that I barely noticed the brushes of ability on my mind unless I deliberately looked for them. This, however, was like nothing I'd ever experienced. There were Holders everywhere; dozens and dozens of them, all with a corresponding ability radiating from them like a florescent bulb. I could feel them everywhere; nearby, far away, outside, inside, alone, in groups, standing still, moving around – everywhere. There were so many brushes against my mind that I couldn't tell where one ended and a new one began. It was like trying to pick out a single voice in a choir.

"Becca," I hear Alex say again, this time worried. "What's the matter?"

"I…" I paused, blinking again and shaking my head. "Nothing, I just…"

"Jocelyn," Alex called quietly, not waiting for me to finish.

I didn't hear him answer, but a moment later Jocelyn was standing in front of me. "Becca, what's wrong?" he asked, putting a hand on my arm and discreetly leading me further away from the drive.

"Nothing," I said, finally starting to get my bearings. "No really, I'm OK. It's just… there are so many…"

I looked up and saw the sudden realization on both Alex and Jocelyn's faces as they exchanged a glance. "We should have had Min block you entirely," Jocelyn said, concerned. "I hadn't considered that you are not often around so many full Holders. If it is too difficult, you I can call for Anderson to come and get you."

"No," I shook my head, not about to let this get the better of me. "I'll be OK. It's getting better already, I just need to get used to it, that's all."

Nobody seemed convinced.

"Are you sure?" Alex asked. His hand instinctively started to reach for mine, but at the last moment flinched and fell back to his side.

"I'm sure," I smiled up at him. "It's just weird. Like... I don't know, getting used to new glasses."

"Is something wrong?" Cormac asked, joining our impromptu powwow.

"Becca is just noticing how many Holders they have attending this year," Jocelyn told him conversationally, with a look in his eyes that didn't match his tone.

"Ah," Cormac nodded, catching the drift. "I see. I had not considered that."

"Neither had I, but I should have," Jocelyn agreed. "Do you know of an Alchemist here we can trust?"

"No," I said quickly, "there's no need for that." I appreciated that they were all concerned, but I was not about to have them treating me like a baby bird. I knew I could handle this. More importantly, *they* needed to know I could handle it. "Really," I said again, "I will be all right. It's strange, but I'll be fine."

"All right," Jocelyn said with a hesitant nod, "if you're sure."

He waited only a second or two longer before he and Cormac turned and walked back over to the driveway, leaving Alex and I to follow behind. I could tell Alex was still concerned, so I caught his eye before we made it within earshot of the other arriving guests.

"I'm good," I said softly, "really."

He looked down at me with that flicker of fear and worry in his eyes that always caused the overprotective dragon that slept in my chest to rear up.

"Will you tell me?"

He didn't offer an explanation, but he didn't need to. He was asking if I'd tell him if it got too hard for me and I needed help. It was a fair question. If anyone knew how much I hated looking weak or incapable it was Alex, so naturally he would expect me to suffer in silence rather than ask for help. And he was right, normally I would have. Especially when it was a problem that I felt I should have been able to handle, like this one. But Alex was worried, and luckily, my protective instincts always overrode my pride.

"Yes," I said, lifting my hand and wrapping my index finger around his pinky, giving it a quick squeeze. "I promise."

I saw his shoulders relax slightly as the corner of his lips twitched up in a small grin. He turned his head away casually, but quickly shifted his finger within mine, enclosing his entire hand around my own, holding it tightly for a heartbeat before releasing me and stepping away.

By the time we got back to the drive, the car had been unloaded and taken away by the valet, so we turned toward the entrance of the manor and made our way into the enormous foyer. Now *this* was something straight out of Camelot. Stone pillars, molded wood paneling, carved marble mantles, and deep red carpets with gold trim. It would have been ridiculously over the top if it wasn't so incredibly cool. We headed toward the far side of the room where a woman sat at an ornate wooden desk handing out room assignments and other check-in information. The desk was only a short distance away from the main door, and in theory should have been no problem to get to. However, it turned out that crossing a room isn't as simple of a task as it sounds when you are with two of the most popular people in that particular room.

Cormac seemed to know everyone, and they were all very excited to say hello. They would hurry over with big smiles and air-kiss or shake hands, then talk about how long it had been, then inquire about one another's health, then the health of the family if applicable, so on and so forth. Typical fluffy, not-too-deep, reunion conversation that you pull out when you see someone you've not seen in a while but aren't close enough with to bother seeing outside of formal occasions. After the pleasantries were done, Cormac would introduce Jocelyn, Alex, and I to whomever it was he was speaking, while they in turn would greet us politely, pretending just a little too hard not to look impressed by the name Clavish. Finally, whomever it was would promise Cormac that they would meet again later so they could catch up properly before walking off, allowing the next person to come forward, and the process would start all over again.

The other popularity peg in our little group was of course Jocelyn, and while he may have only personally known two or three out of the dozens milling around us, it was clear that they all knew him. I don't think there was a single person in the entire foyer that I didn't catch stealing glances, or gesturing toward him then whispering behind their champagne glasses. Jocelyn had told me that he was kind of a God to these people, but I guess I hadn't realized just how serious he'd been. I glanced up at him expecting him to seem edgy or uncomfortable as he had never enjoyed attention – at least as far as I'd ever known – but he was totally at ease. Did he seriously not realize that practically every eye in the place was on him? He had to.

And to make matters worse, when each pair of eyes were finished gawking at Jocelyn, without fail, they would move to me. They'd look me over, glance back to Jocelyn, then back to me, whispering, staring, pointing, more whispering, more staring...

I felt like an animal on display at the zoo.

Though, I guess I should have expected as much. After all, it was no secret that I was the spitting image of Jocelyn, so it wouldn't have been hard to deduce that I was his daughter. And if he was a rock star, I guess that had to make me at least a backup dancer.

Yeah, it was weird – *really* weird – but if Jocelyn wasn't going to let it bother him, I certainly wasn't going to be the one to fold. Following his example, I stood quietly with my head up, feigning an easy smile I didn't feel, ignoring the nagging urge to shrink back behind one of the stone pillars and disappear.

"Jocelyn!" a dainty yet confident voice suddenly called through the cloud of conversation surrounding us. I turned to see a thin woman with a radiant smile headed our way, gliding through the clusters of chatting guests like a yacht cutting through sea foam.

"*Tá mé chomh sásta d'fhéadfaí tú a bheith linn,*" she twittered, stepping up to Jocelyn and taking his hands into hers, "*tá sé iontach a fheiceáil duit!*"

I was about to eye Alex for a translation, but as it turned out, Jocelyn took care of it. "Alva," he said, leaning down and air kissing each of her cheeks – at which, I am proud to say, I did not so much as smirk. "We are more than happy to be here, thank you for the invitation." Then he took a small step back and turned her to face me. "Allow me to introduce my daughter, Rebecca. Becca," he said, placing a hand on my shoulder, "this is Mrs Alva Bloch. She and her husband Brassal are our hosts this week."

"It's a pleasure to meet you," I said with my best smile.

"*Mo daor, conas álainn go bhfuil tú!*" she mooned, gently placing the tips of her fingers under my chin.

"Thank you," I said, torn between being embarrassed at the compliment and happy that I was able fudge a basic understanding of what she'd said. My Gaelic was still on the piddling side of poor, but luckily I was dating a fluent speaker with a larger than average romantic side, making me more than capable of recognizing the Gaelic word for "beautiful" when I heard it.

"And, my word," Alva gasped, dramatically placing her hand to her chest, "so like your father!"

"Yes," I said, glancing down and tucking my hair back behind my ear, never sure what to say to that. "That's what I hear."

"I am so happy you decided to join us this year, we are overjoyed to have so many young people joining us this year. It can be difficult at this time of year, what with most of them in school or attending university…"

She continued to talk, but I lost all focus the moment one of the servers came over with a tray of champagne. Before he even had a chance to pick up one of the fizzing goblets from the silver tray he held, Alva waved him off with a single flip of her wrist, not even glancing in his direction as she did so – like she was swatting at a bug that was flitting around her ear. The server immediately looked down, his expression hovering somewhere between ashamed and scared as he slunk away like a dog with his tail between his legs.

I swallowed down the thorns of contempt rising in my throat as I continued to listen to her prattle on, no longer remotely interested in what she was saying.

Thankfully, before it would have been my turn to say anything back to her, Cormac came to my rescue. "Alva dear," he chimed in suddenly, "you grow more lovely each time I see you."

"Cormac, you old charmer," she said, stepping over and giving him a cordial but somewhat stiff hug. "I was thrilled to see that you were joining us as well, it's been far too long! How have you been…?"

Ugh. More of this?

I was ready to ask where the ladies' room was just so I could escape for a few minutes, when someone nearby caught my eye. It was a girl who looked to be about eighteen or so years old. She was the first person other than Alex who I'd seen that was even remotely close to my age since we'd arrived, though Alva had said something before I tuned her out about most of the younger Bhunaidh being in school. Maybe this girl was already out or had taken time off.

She appeared to have just entered the room and had pulled another woman – judging by their identical shades of auburn hair, her mother – from her conversation to speak to her, but it wasn't until I saw the mother gesture our way that things got interesting. The mother pointed us out to the girl and whispered something to her, then placed a hand on her shoulder and took a step toward us, but the girl didn't move. The mother tried again, glaring at the girl in a "don't you embarrass me" kind of way, but still the girl wouldn't move. Instead she mumbled something with a small shake of her head then looked away. The corners of my mouth twitched as I watched the quiet argument and snickered quietly; the girl didn't want to meet us. Her mother was clearly trying to get her to accompany her over so that they could introduce themselves just as everyone else had done, but the girl wasn't having it.

Suddenly my hopes began to creep up. Was there actually a person here who was humble and unpretentious enough to realize that mooning over Jocelyn – and by extension, me – was ridiculous? A person with whom I could actually converse without having to fight the urge to punch them? Could I really make a friend here? I had to admit, it would be nice. Particularly considering that Alex and I had to keep our distance from one another and I wouldn't have him to keep me company this week. I looked over more directly, hoping to maybe catch her eye and give her extra encouragement to come over, realizing that for the first time since we'd arrived, there was someone I was actually excited to meet.

That is until our eyes finally met, at which point any hope I may have had for a friend fizzled like a wet match. The ease and grace of her manner may have given off the appearance of a delicate and refined lady, but it took one look in her eyes for me to realize the kind of person I was really dealing with. The kind of person I'd always hated throughout school and done my best to avoid. The kind with eyes that were in a constant state of judgment. Someone who could look at an amazing, enormously over the top gift and say, "I thought it'd be bigger." Someone who had the nerve to look at me, a person she had never met, with a bored derision not even worthy of a bad television commercial, and once again I had the nearly overwhelming desire to shrink away and disappear. Before I could stop myself I looked away, immediately hating that I'd let her intimidate me, and promising myself that it would never happen again. No way was I going to let someone like that beat me – at anything.

Not willing to let her have a total victory, I continued to watch them discreetly from the corner of my eye as the mother tried one more time, prompting the girl to snipe something at her and walk off.

Well, wasn't she a gem...

"Oh, there's Della and Shannon," Alva said suddenly, nodding to the girl and her mother as they both disappeared though an open doorway. "Shannon would be about your age, Becca. Have you had a chance to meet her?"

"No," I shook my head trying to smile, "not yet." *And I don't think I care to...*

"I'll be sure to introduce you at the gala tonight," she promised me with a smile as though she was doing me some favor. "I'm sure you two will be fast friends. And of course we have other young people with us as well, though not so many as we would like, it being in the middle of the school term and all. However, there are some who were on break or took leave to join us. They are all having their own reception in one of the lounges upstairs. Would you care to join them, Becca? I would be happy to escort you."

Oh God, there were more?

I smiled graciously, but on the inside I panicked. No way was I ready to be thrown in a room with the entirety of the junior snobs society, but I was also at a loss for an excuse. Luckily Jocelyn had my back.

"That is thoughtful of you to offer Alva, but we have had quite a long drive and Becca was just mentioning that she could do with a rest before tonight's festivities."

"Oh, of course," she fawned, "What was I thinking, you must be exhausted. We'll get you up to your rooms right away. And not to worry," she added turning to me, "we have plenty of activities for the young people yet to come, so you will have more than enough time to socialize."

Damn it. "Great."

"Now," she said, turning back to the group, "have you all checked in?"

CHAPTER 5

Turns out, no matter where you are in the world, a hotel is a hotel. That's not to say that Adare Manor wasn't by far the most incredible place I had ever stayed, because it absolutely was. However, despite the fact that at one time it had been a true castle and housed only one distinguished family and their staff at a time, that was no longer the case. It was still grand, still majestic, still opulent, but at its core, very much a hotel. And even the nicest hotels have the occasional problem. Luggage gets misplaced, the water heaters break, or in my case, your room key doesn't work.

I don't know what Alva had told the man she assigned to escort me up to my room when she pulled him to the side before we left the lobby, but whatever it was, the poor guy looked like he was about to have a stroke when he slid the key into the lock and it didn't turn. "I am so terribly sorry, Miss Clavish," he croaked, giving the knob one more panicked shake, "I must have been given the wrong key, I don't know how this could have happened..."

"It's not a problem..." I tried to assure him, but his hands still trembled.

"I will go back down and get this sorted, I am so sorry. There is a lounge area I could escort you to while you wait, or perhaps the library? Or I could show you to the conservatory where there are refreshments being served if you would care for…" He finally tapered off as I raised my hand to stop him.

"It's really not a problem," I smiled, hoping if I convinced him I didn't mind that he would calm down. The poor guy looked like he was going to lose his job over a bad key – but then again, with Alva in charge, the idea may not have been that farfetched. "I will just wait for you here, or maybe I'll walk down the hall a bit. It will be nice to have a chance to look around." He nodded, but the tension was still tight in his shoulders. "No need to worry," I added, "take your time. I will be here when you get back."

"If… that is what you would prefer," he said hesitantly.

"It is, thank you."

He lingered a moment longer, probably thinking I would change my mind. I gave him one last smile and a nod, which seemed to finally be enough to get him to turn and hustle back down the hall. As soon as he was out of sight, I leaned against the door of my yet to be seen room with a sigh.

Now what? My first instincts were to slide down the door and veg until the bellman came back, but even though I was alone in the hall for the moment, there was still always the possibility of someone walking by, and Adare Manor didn't feel like the sort of place where one got caught sitting on the floor. I glanced around looking for a chair or bench, but there was nothing in that particular section of the hall, so I decided to go and look for one. After all, it wasn't like there was anything else to do.

I walked down the hall a ways until I reached a secluded back corridor that didn't look to have any guestrooms attached to it, or – as luck would have it – anything in the way of seating. There was however, a bay window on the far wall midway down the hall, that appeared to have a built-in bench beneath it. Not only that, but as I got closer I could see that it was shaded, and piled with at least half a dozen fluffy oversized pillows that were calling me like sirens. Best of all, it had floor length drapes that were only partially drawn, which meant I could easily tuck myself behind them and no one who happened by would be able to see me. Perfect.

With my feet already rejoicing, I made my way across the hall to the window and pulled back the curtain so that I could climb in, only to stop short with a jolt that nearly had me out of my skin.

"Oh!" I cried so loudly it echoed down the – thankfully – empty hall. Hidden in the covered portion of the seat that I had intended to take was a young man who was clearly as shocked to see me as I was him. "Oh, I'm sorry," I continued, bringing my voice down and stumbling back slightly. "I didn't know anyone was here."

"N-no," he stammered as he grabbed for the book that had fallen out of his lap, "I'm s-sorry, I'll g-g-go."

He began to quickly gather up the few other books that had been in the window seat with him, his hands visibly shaking as he stacked them up against his arm. Clearly I had scared the hell out of the poor kid, but he didn't have to leave on my account.

I reached out trying to stop him, but he wasn't listening. "No, please, you don't have to go, really, it was totally my fault. I was just looking for a place to sit, I've been standing for a while, and my shoes suck." I grabbed the last of the books on the bench and handed it to him, keeping my hand outstretched after he took the book from it. "I'm Becca."

He paused, looking at my hand for a second or two as though it might bite him before taking it with his own still-trembling fingers and bowing over it slightly with a nod. "St-teven."

"Nice to meet you," I said, hoping to reassure him a little as clearly his nerves were still getting the better of him – though I couldn't imagine why. Did he honestly think I would be mad over something so silly? Was he just shy?

"P-pl-leasure," he replied.

Ah... so the stutter wasn't nerves after all...

After releasing my hand, he slid back slightly, but didn't run, which I figured was at least a step in the right direction.

He seemed nice enough from what I could tell, and with dark, almost back hair and light green eyes – at least I was pretty sure they were light green, though with them being cast downward most of the time it was hard to tell – he was a pretty good-looking guy. But why was he so skittish? So far, everyone I'd met there had more self-confidence and ego than they had room to store it, yet this guy looked more like a baby bunny ready to take off and hide at the first loud noise.

That was when I noticed something else unique about him: no ability. I could still sense the dozens of abilities all around the manor, but every one of them was coming from a distance and easily ignored. From the man standing right in front of me I felt nothing. He wasn't a Holder at all, just a regular guy. He must have been one of the staff – which would explain the fear at the possibility of having "upset" one of the guests.

Once again I got excited. Now this was someone I could be friends with. Not a Bhunaidh, just an average guy who liked to read. Maybe my hopes for a friend for the trip weren't dashed after all. If nothing else it was a relief to meet someone here who I didn't have to act for or try to impress, and if I did nothing else, I would make sure that he knew I was not one of "them" and he didn't have to be afraid of me.

I turned toward the pile of books he'd brought to the widow seat with him and smiled. "I don't think you're going to get through all of those in one sitting."

Something like a grin tugged at his mouth. "No. I've alr-ready r-read them. I j-just l-like to r-reread my fa-favorite parts."

"I do that," I said, sitting on the edge of the widow seat and picking up the book on the top of the pile. "I read books to death. I may not have read as many as some people but if I've read it, I probably have it memorized. Wow, *Anna Karenina... in Russian*? You read Russian?"

He nodded with a shy smile.

"Jeez... I bitch about having to learn Gaelic, and you can read this while I can't even recognize half of the letters! And let me guess," I laughed, nodding toward the stack of books, "the *Les Miserables* in there is in French?"

He shook his head "no" with a chuckle. "Th-this one is E-English. Th-they d-don't have th-the F-French ver-rsion here... but I h-have it at h-home."

"Well, don't I feel inadequate?"

He smiled again, and I wasn't sure if it was the surprise in his eyes, or the hesitation of his mouth, but I got the sad suspicion that it wasn't something he did often.

"I should probably get back to my room," I sighed as I stood. "The guy should be back with my key by now, and I need to start getting ready for the gala."

"Y-you will b-be at th-the gala?" he asked suddenly, the fear creeping back in to his eyes.

"Yes, I'll be there with my..." I hesitated for a breath, "with the people I came with." I was really going to have to get used to the word "father." "We're here from St Brigid's Academy."

His hand started to shake again "St Br-rigid's?" he repeated. "Y-you're here w-with "J-Jocelyn Cl-lavish...?" His words trailed off as something that sounded akin to terror stretched his voice thin.

Great. Even the staff had been told about us... "Yeah," I shrugged, trying to be blasé, "he's my father, but it's no big–"

"Y-you're R-Rebecca Cl-lavish?" he breathed.

"Well, yeah..." I said, at a loss, "but there's no need–"

"I-I'm s-sorry," he cut me off again, not meeting my eyes as he grabbed for his books and began backing away. "W-we sh-shouldn't... I... I'm s-sorry..." With that he turned and took off down the hall as fast as he could without breaking into a run.

A few hours, a shower, and over a dozen bobby pins later, I gave myself one last look over in the enormous mirror in my equally enormous room, and decided I was satisfied. I had to admit – and believe me, it was painful – that despite all the scowling and poking, Madame Loute really had known what she was doing. Everything about my new gown was perfect; the fit was flawless, the deep emerald color looked great on me, and the style, which I did still find to be a bit Guinevere-esque, was flattering. Hell, even the breast cups had turned out to be a good idea, as they made my usually humble chest look rather glorious – if I did say so myself.

But boobs aside, my biggest accomplishment of the evening was definitely my hair. It had easily been the most tedious portion of my primp-a-thon, but after a plethora of curse words and probably twice the number of hair pins I actually needed, I finally managed to get it looking the way I'd wanted. Chloe would have been proud.

But what would all the Bhunaidh at the gala think?

With a huff, I walked over to the bed and found my shoes, irritated that I would even let myself worry about what they thought. I'd always been my toughest critic, so if I was happy, then that ought to be enough to anyone else. And if it wasn't, that was their problem. I had never let other people intimidate me before and I certainly wasn't about to start now, particularly with a bunch of overstuffed snobs. Or at least that is what I would keep telling myself.

I slid my shoes on, took one last glance at the essentials – hair, makeup, panty lines, etc – to make sure everything was in place before grabbing the key to my room and stepping out into the hall.

I started toward the meeting area that Jocelyn, Alex, Cormac and I had decided on earlier, feeling – yes, I admit – a little like a diva. I was loving the sheen of the silk in the light, and the way the sleeves and train of my gown caught the breeze as I walked, rippling behind me like waves of mist over a stream. It was by far the nicest outfit I'd ever owned and I couldn't help but walk with my head up just a bit higher than usual.

Though as I got closer to the meeting spot, the more I realized that it wasn't only my new clothing-induced confidence that was sparking the excited flutter in my stomach, but the fact that I was only minutes away from seeing Alex, and him seeing me – the first exciting, the second, nerve-racking. Every step I took made my heart pound just a bit faster as more and more questions swirled around my mind. Would he be there yet? What would he look like? Would we get to spend any time together tonight? Would he like my dress? He'd been dying to see it, I'd hate for him to be let down...

God, it was like going to prom!

Amazing dress, hair done, date in a tux, and dancing; that's basically what prom was, right? Take out the "my dad will be there with us all night" part, and it sounded just like the shindig I'd had to miss out on back in high school. One that, until that night, I hadn't even realized I'd wanted. But much as I hadn't expected to be, there was no denying it... I was excited.

I arrived at the large alcove section of the hallway where the four of us had agreed to meet, and before even stepping into the space realized with something between relief and disappointment that I couldn't feel Alex anywhere nearby, which meant I had beaten him. I did however recognize the ability I sensed just a few feet away, so I took a breath and stepped into the alcove to find Jocelyn, standing alone, casually studying a portrait on the far wall.

He must have heard me enter, as he turned, his eyes widening when he saw me. "You... You look lovely," he said after a short pause.

"Thanks," I said, immediately glancing down. "I guess it turned out OK." I twisted my hips a bit so the skirt of the gown swayed, trying to find something to say that would shove off the uncomfortable haze I felt about to settle in, then added with a smirk, "But I still never want to see that woman again."

Knowing my "difficulties" with Madame Loute, he chuckled, and to my relief – and probably his as well – our usual awkwardness didn't seem so bad.

Glancing back up, I took a moment to actually look at him, and when I saw that he was not only dressed in a tux, but also had several other fancy and formal-looking adornments, I was surprised to find myself impressed. Even kind of... *proud?*

"Wow," I said, walking toward him slowly, looking at the large medal and sash he had across his chest. "You look very... decorated."

"Yes," he huffed a laugh, glancing down at himself. "It's a bit much, but for something like this, it's expected."

"Everything's 'a bit much' around here," I said, rolling my eyes.

"It is," he agreed, "though, on that note, I wanted to tell you that you did very well this afternoon."

"Thanks," I said, though I was actually distracted by all his finery and only half paying attention.

I stepped forward so that I could get a better look at his "accessories," such that they were. The one that stood out the most was the medal in the shape of a cross that hung from a deep purple satin ribbon. The medal itself was very large, probably about five inches both from left to right and top to bottom, and was gold in color with silver accents dotted throughout the filigree details. Underneath the ornate medal and ribbon was a sash that stretched diagonally across his chest, which was exactly the same shade of emerald green as my gown. There were also four or five smaller hanging medals attached to his tux jacket, and a half dozen or so lapel pins, each one with a different inlaid symbol or script.

"What is all this?" I asked, and subconsciously reached out to straighten the medal so that it hung flat. By the time I realized what I was doing, it was too late to stop. My heart may have skipped a beat or so, but I acted as though it was nothing and was happy to find that this semi-intimate exchange wasn't nearly as awkward as it would have been only a few days ago.

But I still avoided eye contact, just in case...

"The sash denotes a clan, or a family," he said after a short pause.

"That's why we're the same color?"

"Yes. Alex and Cormac each have one as well."

"So we're a clan?" I asked with a laugh.

"Not in the strictest definition," he smiled, "but to all intents and purposes, yes."

"What about this one?" I nodded toward the medal.

"The medal denotes military service, and the color of the band denotes the war."

I looked up, surprised. "You were in the military?" Sometimes I forgot how little I really knew about him.

"British military, yes." His eyebrows pulled together slightly as though he knew my next question was coming.

"Which war is the purple for?"

He hesitated slightly with something between a wince and a smile. "World War One. Of course then it was called the Great War."

I know my eyes popped open a little bit, but I couldn't help it. "Oh... right..." I forgot, you are so old it's almost creepy. Though I kept that last bit to myself.

"Yes," he nodded, glancing away, "I served in the Second World War as well, but only briefly."

I wanted to let it go, but I couldn't help myself – I had to know. "So..." I paused with a cautious grin, "if you don't mind me asking, how old are you, exactly?"

He laughed quietly, though still looked slightly wary, as if he were worried the answer was going to freak me out. After a moment, he took a breath and replied, "I'll be two hundred and eleven this year."

Wow. "I'm not gonna lie," I said, not quite biting back a laugh, "that's still a little weird."

Luckily he seemed relieved rather than offended at my admission, and smiled. "You think I'm old, keep an eye out for the gentlemen tonight with this same medal on a pink strap."

"Why, what's pink?"

"French Revolution."

He chuckled when my eyes popped open, but I didn't have a chance to comment before I realized – or rather felt – that someone else was approaching our little meeting alcove. Alex.

"I'd better go and make sure Cormac hasn't gotten lost," Jocelyn said suddenly.

"Oh, yeah sure," I nodded casually, playing it off. I was almost certain he didn't need to check on Cormac, but rather he knew Alex was coming and was giving us a moment to ourselves. I wasn't sure whether to be grateful or embarrassed, considering that the only way Jocelyn could have known that Alex was nearby was because I'd done something to give it away... and I really didn't want to consider what that might have been.

Embarrassing reveal or not, Jocelyn didn't hang around to belabor the point. With a nod, he stepped off down the hall, and a moment later I turned to see Alex come around the corner.

I didn't mean to gawk, or blush, or get a goofy grin on my face, but as he stood there just inside the archway of the alcove I'm pretty sure I did all three. Though in my defense, I couldn't help it – he looked amazing. I'd never thought of Alex as "hot," or "gorgeous," or any of the other terms that a lot of girls my age used to describe a good looking guy. That isn't to say that Alex *wasn't* any of those things, or that I didn't find him attractive, as I did. Very much so, in fact. His dark blonde hair was always styled, he dressed very well, and his eyes – which had always been my favorite feature – were the most amazingly clear shade of storm cloud blue you could imagine. The thing was that the specifics of his appearance weren't usually what came to mind when I thought about him. He was Alex. It had never mattered what he looked like.

And while it still didn't *matter*, I was not about to pretend like I didn't *notice*. He was wearing a black tux like Jocelyn, but instead of the white shirt and black tie, Alex's tie and shirt were black, and he also had a charcoal gray vest on under his jacket. His cuffs were French, his shoes shone as though they were new, and across his chest lay the same green sash Jocelyn was wearing.

Not going to lie, there was definitely a flush rising up my neck....

Though red as I was, oddly enough, Alex's didn't blush at all. I'd have thought with me ogling him the way I was, that his ears would be ablaze, but then again, he seemed far too preoccupied to notice the way I was looking at him. Preoccupied... looking at me. His eyes clung to me like condensation on a glass, with an expression that seemed to hover between anger and fear – though deep down I knew it was neither. Still, I couldn't help but feel self-conscious.

Why didn't he say anything? Was he upset? Did he not like the dress? Was something wrong?

I took a breath to speak, but before I could find my voice he was coming straight toward me. He didn't look around, didn't check the hall, or so much as shift his eyes away from mine as he crossed the small alcove in three strides, took my face in his hands, and kissed me.

And dear God... what a kiss...

His mouth moved against mine with more passion than I'd ever felt from him before. His right hand slid up into my hair and gently but firmly held my mouth to his, while his left dropped to my waist and pulled me tightly against him. His fervor poured over me like boiling water over ice, melting me down to my core. I had no idea what had come over him, but whatever it was, it was hot, it was intense, and if he wasn't careful, it was going to bring me to my knees.

But what hit me the hardest wasn't his sudden hunger or intensity, but the hint of something deeper, driving like an undercurrent beneath his passion. It was something I'd never seen from him before, but unmistakable all the same.

Possession.

Alex had never been a dominant or outspoken person in general, but conscious or not, something in him was definitely sending a message: "*She is mine.*" It may have only been implied, but it was definitely there, and the very idea sent a tingling shiver across my skin as I gripped the lapels of his jacket with a throaty sigh. The message was raw, it was primal, and above all else, it was true: I *was* his. And he was mine. The fact that we had to hide it around these people didn't make it any less valid. We belonged to one another.

Forever.

A few short seconds later he pulled back with a husky breath, resting his forehead against mine for a moment before releasing me and stepping back slowly, his eyes glowing. He hadn't said a word – he hadn't needed to. I smiled, hoping he saw the "*I love you*" in my eyes. His answering smile told me he did.

When we heard Cormac's voice come echoing up the hall, we both looked away, doing our best to resume our façade of casual acquaintance. It took some effort, but by the time Cormac and Jocelyn came around the corner a moment later, I was perfectly cool and collected.

On the outside anyway.

"My goodness, Becca," Cormac said, coming up and taking my hand in his. "Aren't you the sight of an angel!"

"Thank you," I smiled, seeing that he too had an array of pins and small medals decorating his tuxedo jacket.

"Yes," he winked. "It's a miracle I can still walk under all these silly baubles, is it not?"

"You look very handsome," I grinned.

"Are we ready then?" Jocelyn asked.

With a collective nod, we all turned toward the hall as excitement once again tickled my neck. I stepped up next to Jocelyn who tentatively offered me his arm, which I took, and together we walked out into the hall and began heading toward the distant echo of festivities, with Cormac and Alex following just behind.

CHAPTER 6

When we arrived at the upstairs gallery where the gala was being held, we stood in the receiving line outside the door, and waited to... be received, I guess. I could see Alva up at the front of the line, smiling and greeting each person or small group as they approached, every bit the charming, elegant hostess.

I stood in line quietly, feigning a fascination with the artwork and the architecture while once again trying to pretend that everyone wasn't staring at us or gesturing our way. At least this time I felt up to par in the wardrobe department, but unfortunately my attire didn't do much to help the uncomfortable itch their eyes sent crawling up and down my back.

"I am never going to get used to this," I whispered as the line took a few small steps forward.

"To what?" Jocelyn asked under his breath.

"The staring, the whispering, and pointing... take your pick." We took another step forward. "How does this not drive you crazy?"

He glanced down, his eyebrow raised. "Who said it doesn't?"

I paused a moment, surprised. "It does?"

"Of course."

"Then how are you always able to look so comfortable?"

"Practice."

I sighed. "So there's no trick?"

"Afraid not." We took another step forward. "But don't worry, they will lose interest after a while."

"We can hope," I added.

"Yes," he grinned, "in the meantime, try to ignore it. And if it helps, you can always think about how bad it could be." When I looked up confused, his grin grew wry. "If they knew," he mouthed silently.

Dear God, he was right...

If they somehow found out the truth about me and my abilities, I'd have had to lock myself in the bathroom for the rest of the trip.

Jocelyn must have seen the color drain from my face, because he chuckled quietly. "Don't worry, we'll on our way back home soon. With any luck, we will get the whereabouts of our friend Mr Shea tonight, so until then," he whispered, as we took the last step to the front of the line, "smile."

"Jocelyn," Alva beamed as she stepped forward extending her hand, "welcome!"

"Alva, you look radiant as ever," he replied, taking her hand and demurely kissing her knuckles.

Wow, he really was good at this...

"Heavens above," she exclaimed, turning to me and fanning herself dramatically. "What a vision you are, my dear! Why, your card will be filled the moment you set foot through the door!"

"Thank you," I said, my polite smile back in place. Though I wasn't quite sure what she meant by that last bit.

"And of course, Cormac... and Mr Bray, lovely to see you as well. Please, allow me to show you all in."

"There is no need for that, Alva," Jocelyn said, glancing at the line. "We could not take our hostess from her other guests. We can see ourselves in."

"Well, if you insist," she said, obviously a bit deflated. "But I will make sure to send Brassal over to greet you this evening, he has been so looking forward to seeing you again. And I shall have to introduce Bastian to your lovely daughter this evening, as well."

"Yes, of course," Jocelyn nodded in agreement, though he didn't share her enthusiasm.

We followed the people before us down the hallway toward the gallery, and as soon as I heard Alva begin to greet the next group and was sure we wouldn't be overheard, I turned to Jocelyn, "Who is Bastian?"

"Her son."

Her son? Wait... was she trying to...

But before I could form the question, Jocelyn answered my expression. "Yes, she is trying to set you two up."

"You knew that and you still said yes?" I asked, appalled.

"Well I could hardly say no."

"I guess," I grumbled.

"Besides, I had expected this would happen," he admitted as we made our way into the gallery. "The Bhunaidh family structure is much like that of the earlier days, when marriage was a contract between families, and little more. Their first concern is making the best match and strengthening their lines. I am *bregbunhass* and you are my daughter, which in the eyes of the Bhunaidh makes you," he paused, trying to hide the smile in his voice, "quite a catch."

"So, what then? Every mother with an eligible son is going to be sizing me up like a horse at the track?" I asked, trying to remember to keep my voice down.

"It is a possibility, yes," he admitted, actually having the nerve to smirk.

"This is not funny!"

"No, it's not," he agreed, though the corners of his mouth were still a little higher than they should have been.

"What's a card?" I asked, hoping to change the subject and take my mind of my new broodmare status.

"What?"

"A card. She said 'my card would be full.'"

"Oh, dance card. It means everyone will want to dance with you."

"Right, right," I nodded, realizing I should have known that.

"Which reminds me," he said, his tone more serious, "should you be asked to dance, you can politely decline, or if you'd rather, I can do it for you."

"Why would I decline? I like to dance." *And I was damn good at it, if I did say so myself...*

"This isn't going to be the kind of dancing you are used to," he said simply.

I could have protested, but I decided to let it go, content to prove his assumptions wrong later. Little did he know that I happened to be quite a proficient dancer, and was familiar with most of the traditional ballroom dance styles thanks to my Uncle Joe. He'd taken me with him to his dance studio for lessons all throughout middle and early high school, and I'd actually become pretty good. Besides, even if I had wanted to say something, the moment we came to the end of the hallway and stepped into the gallery, I was struck completely speechless.

It was a sight I wouldn't have thought was possible outside of a fairytale. The room was almost three times as long as it was wide, with a cathedral ceiling made of deep brown molded wood, a stained glass window that covered the entire far wall, and three enormous crystal chandeliers hanging down from the rafters. Beneath them was a glittering bustle of chiffon, gemstones, and silk, as breathtaking as the room itself. The women were floating across the room in exquisite gowns and dazzling jewelry that probably cost more than the average car, while the men were displaying all manner of medals, decorations, and sashes on what no doubt were the finest tailor made tuxedos. All we needed was a pumpkin carriage with a midnight curfew, and it would have been a storybook come to life.

The four of us walked round the perimeter of the room until we found a grouping of armchairs and settees that were unoccupied and claimed them. Cormac, Alex and I sat, while Jocelyn remained standing, surveying the various clusters of people all chatting and laughing amongst themselves.

"I see Oden Shawn across the way," he said, nodding toward a group of men talking next to one of the huge fireplaces on the opposite wall. "I should go and say hello."

"You go ahead," Cormac said, "I saw Oden this afternoon when we arrived."

As Jocelyn walked over to the group of men, I leaned my elbow on the armrest of the chair with a sigh. I wanted to look over at Alex and see what he thought of all this, but with our encounter in the alcove still fresh in my mind, I quickly decided that was a bad idea. If I looked over I would blush, and if I blushed he would blush, and if we both started blushing… Yeah, bad idea. So instead, I turned my attention to the center of the room and casually watched the ocean of glittering haute-couture and humming conversation ebb and flow around us.

The spectacle of elegant mingling was much like it had been earlier that day in the lobby, with one notable difference: the addition of young people. Alva had mentioned there being other Holders that were closer to my age, but thus far all I had seen was the evil-eyed girl from the lobby that afternoon, the one Alva had called Shannon. But it looked like all the teenagers had come to the gala, each one looking like a perfectly primed and proper miniature of the adult they silently shadowed. At an event like this back at home, I would have expected to find all the younger people together, sitting in their own area, or maybe off talking in a corner, but not here. Here, they blended in seamlessly with the adults, conversing, circulating, and air-kissing like seasoned pros.

I scanned the crowd to see if I saw Shannon anywhere nearby, hoping she wasn't while simultaneously trying to act like I didn't care. It took a moment for me to find her, but when I did somehow I wasn't surprised that she was one of the most stunning women in the room. She was wearing a cobalt blue gown, and her auburn hair was done up like a modern Marie Antoinette. She was standing with her mother, also in cobalt, and an older man and younger boy – father and brother? – both of whom were wearing cobalt sashes.

I looked their way just long enough to get a good look, then moved my gaze on to other groups as I was not about to let Shannon catch me staring... again. No way was I going to let her think that I was in any way impressed by her or her frou-frou hair.

Seriously though, how the hell did she get it to stay up that high...?

Reminding myself that I didn't care, I turned my attention to the other side of the room, which is when I noticed the young man standing by himself against the wall in the very back of the hall. At first he looked strange compared to all the other men in their sashes, medals and other finery. Even the other young men in the room had at least a pin or two and of course a sash displaying their family color. The young man, however, didn't have any medals, ribbons, or sash anywhere. Just a plain black tux and black shirt that perfectly matched the shadows he seemed to be clinging to. It wasn't until I saw his face that I understood the lack of decoration; it was Steven.

"Oh," I said, perking up immediately. Maybe I'd have someone to talk to after all. Of course I knew he was working, but maybe we could hang out for short bits here and there between whatever responsibilities he had.

"Something wrong?" Cormac asked as I stood up.

"No, I'm fine," I assured him, "I just saw someone and I'm going to go say hello."

"I must say, I wasn't expecting you to make friends so quickly," he chuckled, pleased.

I smiled as I passed by him and made my way around the room to where Steven was standing, quietly watching the activity of the room with his hands folded behind his back. Hopefully he wouldn't mind my coming over, but at the very least I wanted to say hi and make sure he knew that everything was OK. He'd kind of freaked out earlier when I'd told him I was Jocelyn's daughter, and I felt bad for springing it on him like that without explaining. With the way the staff was treated by the rest of the Bhunaidh, I could understand his reaction, but I wouldn't have him thinking that he'd done anything wrong.

I was also vaguely aware of the fact that openly socializing with a member of the staff wouldn't be well received by the other guests, but my only reaction there was to say "the hell with it." Steven seemed like a nice guy and that was all I cared about. If they had a problem with me talking to him, they stuff it.

"Hello, again," I said, as I arrived at his post. I didn't know what manner of response I had expected, but it definitely wasn't what I got.

"Wh-what are you d-doing?" he asked, stark fear in his eyes.

"I saw you over here and just wanted to say hi…" I trailed off, unsure what to say.

"Y-you sh-shouldn't be ta-alking to me."

"Look," I said, raising my hand slightly, "it's OK. I'm…" I trailed off again, trying to choose my words carefully. What I would have liked to say was, "*I'm not a pompous jerk like the rest of these people,*" but given that many of the "pompous jerks" were within earshot, that didn't seem the best way to go. Treading lightly, I tried again. "I just wanted to come say hi, I didn't mean to bother you."

He looked at me for a long moment before his eyes softened slightly over the fear. "L-listen, I d-don't think y-you r-realize th–"

"Becca," a female voice cut in, "what are you doing all the way over here?"

I turned to see Alva coming up from behind me, her chipper smile just a little too big. From the corner of my eye I saw Steven immediately bow his head.

"I just came over to say hello," I explained, already seeing where this was heading, and wanting to pop her right in the nose for it.

"Isn't that sweet of you?" she said, though admiration was the last thing I heard in her voice. Without another look at Steven, she wrapped her arm around me and began leading me away. "Why don't we get you a drink? The dances will start soon, and after that, I would be happy to introduce you to all the other Holders your age. I know they all can't wait to meet you."

She continued to talk as she led me across the room back to where Cormac and Alex were seated, while I did my best to keep my cool. I couldn't decide whether I was more furious or disgusted, but one thing I did know was that my temper and I weren't going to be able to take much more of this.

She dropped me off with my party with a twittering farewell like nothing at all important had happened, and the moment she was gone, Cormac and Alex both turned to me with questions written all over their faces.

"Everything all right, dear?" Cormac asked quietly, leaning in.

"These people are horrible," I bit out under my breath.

"What happened?" Alex probed gently.

"I went over to say hi to one of the staff I met earlier, but apparently, he's not good enough for me to talk to."

"She didn't want you talking to the staff?" Alex asked. "That seems strange."

But Cormac's expression didn't look as though he thought it was strange at all. "Hmm," he mused, squinting thoughtfully, "not exactly surprising. Though I do find it odd that she would make such a fuss…"

"It's not even like we were making a scene or anything!" I continued to rage quietly. "We were standing in the corner talking. Or at least trying to talk, which wasn't easy given how terrified these people have made the poor kid!"

"What do you mean?" Cormac asked.

"He is in a constant state of fear, as though he is just waiting for someone to pounce on him and rip his head off! Most of the time he looks like he is too scared to even breathe, much less speak – which he has enough difficulty with on his own without a bunch of pompous, well-to-dos intimidating the life out of him."

Something flashed in Cormac's eyes. "What do you mean by that?"

As that wasn't the question I was expecting, it threw me a bit. "He has a speech impediment of some sort. He stutters a little."

"Is he still here?" Cormac asked, seeming oddly interested. "Can you point him out?"

I looked back over to the corner, but Steven was gone. "No," I said, glancing around the room to see if he'd moved, "he's gone."

"What did he look like?"

"Dark hair, green eyes, about my age. His name is–"

"Steven," Cormac finished for me.

"Wait," I said, my confusion growing, "you know him?"

Cormac nodded. "Who told you he was a staff member?"

"Well, no one. I could tell he wasn't a Holder, so I just assumed, I guess. Isn't he?"

"No," Cormac shook his head a sad sigh, "Steven doesn't work here. He is Brassal and Alva's son."

CHAPTER 7

"Wait... what?" I stammered, barely comprehending what I'd heard. "He's her *son*?"

"Yes," Cormac nodded.

"That doesn't make any sense," I said, picturing the fear in his eyes and the way he'd been treated. "And what happened to this Bastian she wanted to introduce me to, I thought that was her son?"

"He is; Bastian and Steven are brothers, twins actually. But..." he paused, looking wary, "Steven is... not well accepted amongst the Bhunaidh. You see, he was born with certain defects that they consider unacceptable for a family line as ancient and distinguished as the Blochs."

"What, his *stutter*?" I asked, appalled. "That's stupid, he can't..." But something in Cormac's eyes caused my thought to trail off. It was more than the stutter, I could see that. I could also see that he believed it was something that I was already aware of, but I was at a loss. Then I thought back to our first meeting that afternoon in the hall, and why I'd assumed he was a member of the staff in the first place. "He doesn't have an ability."

Cormac gave a small nod.

"How can that be?" Alex asked. "I thought both of his parents are pureblooded. Doesn't that guarantee that any children they have would be Holders?"

"It should mean that, yes," Cormac agreed, "but for whatever reason, for Steven it did not. Bastian was born a Porter like his father, while Steven was born an average mortal, completely without ability." I had no idea what ability a Porter had, but at the moment I could not have cared less.

"Was it because they were twins?" Alex asked interested, while I on the other hand had fists resting in my lap that were hard as rocks.

"Could be," Cormac mused. "There are not many instance of twins in Holder history, much less pureblooded, so that may have something to do with it, though it is far more likely that it is simply a birth defect like any other."

"You're telling me," I ground out under my breath, unable to keep my cool any longer, "that they shun him like some illegitimate bastard child, all because he was born without an ability?"

"Now, my dear," Cormac said, quickly taking my hand and trying to calm me. "It's horrid, I know–"

"Is everything all right?" Jocelyn's concerned voice suddenly came from over my shoulder. "Becca?"

"We were just having a conversation... about Steven," Cormac said casually, though his eyes were still worried.

"I see," Jocelyn said, his tone making it clear that he did in fact know exactly what was going on. "Becca," he said calmly, "the refreshment room is just down the way, why don't we get a drink?"

"I'm fine," I mumbled, not in the mood for the lecture on my temper I knew was coming.

"Becca," he said, his voice deliberate now as he offered me his arm. "You need a drink."

I stood with a silent huff and took his arm, letting him lead me out to the opposite side of the room and through an open door into a large parlor connected to the main gallery. The room was more brightly lit than the gallery and was lined with long tables piled high with what I could only assume were some of the finest hors d'oeuvres, cheeses, and fruits the manor had to offer.

Jocelyn turned us toward the bar area that had been set up in one corner, but halfway there and with no one else nearby, I decided that I'd been silent long enough.

"Do not tell me you are going to defend them!" I whispered as loudly as I could without being overheard.

"I have no intention of defending them, but it is also not your place to condemn them."

"What? How can you say that? This is just wrong! That woman should be–"

"Alva and Brassal provide both their sons with the highest quality of life and the best education available."

"Right," I whispered with a sneer, "never mind affection or love they don't have to earn…"

"I realize that something like this is not what you are used to, but–"

"Oh my God…" I cut in, not believing what I was hearing. "You're actually OK with this!"

Jocelyn paused, scowling at the air in front of him for a moment before discreetly pulling me over to a vacant corner of the room. "No," he whispered forcefully once he was certain there was no one paying us any mind. "I am not OK with any of it. I think it is the most horrid thing in the world for a child to have grown up being treated like an outsider even within his own family. I cannot fathom parents having it within themselves to treat their own child so poorly and the very idea that Alva and Brassal believe that they are justified in their actions sickens me." He paused with a breath, releasing the tension in his shoulders. "But there is nothing I can do. I have tried several times to bring Steven to St Brigid's and give him the chance to escape his life here, but each time it was no use. Brassal and Alva will not allow it, and though Steven is of an age now to make his own decisions, he is not willing to leave against his parents' wishes."

"Why?" I asked, shaking my head.

"I am not sure, though I believe it is simply because that is what his parents want. Difficult as they have made things for him, I believe there is still a part of him that wishes to please them in any way he can."

When he stopped I opened my mouth to speak, but I didn't know what to say. "I'm sorry," is what I finally decided on. I wasn't sure if I was apologizing for sort of losing it, or for actually thinking he would be OK with such a horrible situation, but either way, his eyes softened and he nodded.

"Becca, please believe that I am not asking you to accept or take part in the prejudice toward Steven," he said after a moment, "but I do need you to realize that your actions, while they will never get you into any trouble, could make things harder on him."

I wasn't sure what he meant at first, but then I thought about how Steven kept telling me that I wasn't supposed to be talking to him. I'd taken it to mean that he thought I wouldn't *want* to talk to him, but what if he'd meant that he wasn't *allowed* to talk to me?

"Oh no..." I mouthed as I realized what I might have done. "He isn't going to get in trouble because of me, is he? I didn't know..." Suddenly I felt horrible, and the more horrible I felt for getting Steven in trouble, the angrier I felt toward not just his parents, but to their entire way of life. The fact that it was even possible to get someone in trouble for having a conversation with them was miles past ridiculous.

"I'm sure it will be all right," Jocelyn said. "Just keep it in mind, and perhaps keep your distance in the future if at all possible."

I glanced down and nodded, though it went against every single instinct I had. All I could think about was how much Steven was like Ryland. Ry had spent his life getting made fun of, picked on, or just plain avoided by everyone around him for being different. But through it all, at least Ry had had me to take care of him and protect him wherever I could. Steven didn't seem to have anyone, and I knew it would take everything I had to fight the urge to step in and be that person for him.

I was a protector; had been all my life. If someone was hurt or needed help, then I had to step in and do whatever I could. It was just my nature. Yet now, someone within my reach was suffering and I was expected to stand by and do nothing – or worse, try to help him and inadvertently make it worse. Helplessness was not a feeling I was accustomed to, but for the moment I was prepared to embrace it. Some may have considered that defeat, but only those who are shortsighted. I, on the other hand, knew that helplessness was only a state of mind, and that there was always a way if you were patient and willing to take the time to look for it.

And I was.

"Come," Jocelyn said with a smile, offering me his arm again. "We should return to the gallery. The welcome addresses will begin shortly."

"Sounds like a hoot," I said, earning me a low chuckle.

"Yes, well," he huffed a laugh as I took his arm, "do try to keep your excitement in check."

"I'll do my best," I grinned, as he led me through the refreshment room and back into the diamond-studded snake pit.

"Dear Lord, *another one?*" I grumbled quietly as the seventh speaker took the microphone and began to address the room.

The "welcome" that Jocelyn had mentioned, and that I had thought would be a quick "thanks for coming and enjoy the night" sort of thing, was turning into the wedding toast from hell. The kind of toast where the best man makes his speech then for some reason every distant relation imaginable comes out of the woodwork and wants to "say a few words," and before you know it your dinner is cold and your champagne is flat. Though in this case, instead of quirky uncles and well-meaning second cousins talking our ears off, it was a family matriarch going on about her distinguished line, or an old man covered in medals recounting the thirty-two different wars he'd served in. And of course each person was sure to go on and on about how much being a Bhunaidh had meant to them, and how important it was that the Bhunaidh way of life be treasured, and preserved, and blah, blah, blah… And if all that weren't bad enough, more than half the speeches were given in Gaelic. Though, if nothing else, that did at least give me a legitimate reason to stand next to Alex who would cast the translations for me to read.

Or pretend to read…

"How many more do you think?" I whispered to Alex, who was way better at faking an interest in the proceedings than I was.

He didn't even glance my way, but a moment later smoky script appeared directly in my line of vision, "*Patience is a virtue.*"

I turned my head slowly, giving him my best "not amused" scowl, while of course his jaw was locked to keep from smiling. I turned back to the speaker as he began his monologue – in Gaelic. Great.

"*Should I even bother?*" appeared in front of me, and I smiled. So he did know I'd given up on reading his translations.

"If he's done something interesting," I whisper.

"*What qualifies as interesting?*"

"You know, climbing Mount Everest, wrestling alligators, that sort of thing." No sooner did I finish my sentence, than I watched an anthropomorphized alligator appear at the speaker's side. It was standing up on its hind legs smiling, and had an arm wrapped around his shoulder as though they were the best of friends. "Don't do that!" I snipped quietly, biting back a laugh.

I was seriously considering poking him in the ribs, when something across the room caught my eye. It was a young man, standing just behind that now empty patch of air where the alligator had been. I'd not noticed him before, which was odd as he was wearing a cape – an actual, honest to God *cape* – with a blood red lining and a gold chain closure that draped from his right shoulder to under his left arm, making him somewhat hard to miss. His hair was dark, and he seemed to be on the tall side, while his chest was covered with more medals and pins than I could even make out from across the room – far more than any of the other young men his age. But there was something else about him. Something I couldn't put a name to, but that itched at my subconscious like a buried memory trying to dig its way free.

Then it occurred to me – he looked... familiar? That didn't make any sense. Maybe he just had one of those faces. The sort of person you see and say, "I know it isn't, but doesn't he look like...?" But then who did he remind me of? I squinted, hoping to get a better look, but given the distance between us and the dimmed "mood lighting" of the room, I wasn't having much luck.

I kept my eyes on cape-guy as the addresses wore on, trying to figure out what it was about him that kept nudging at my subconscious, until finally the last of the speakers wrapped up their soliloquy and Alva once again stepped up to the microphone.

"I want to thank you all again for joining us tonight at our commencement gala..."

As Alva continued to conclude the welcome, I took the opportunity to slide over next to Cormac who stood only a few feet off. "Who is that?" I asked him quietly, just behind his shoulder.

"Who, dear?" he whispered back, trying to follow my line of vision.

"The boy there," I nodded, "in the cape."

"Bastian Bloch, Brassal and Alva's other son."

"I feel like I've seen him somewhere before..."

"Well he does look a great deal like his brother Steven, who you've met," Cormac suggested.

"No..." I shook my head, "it's not that..." *But damned if I could figure out what it was...*

After what felt like half a century after they began, the welcoming addresses ended with the call for the first dance to begin from Alva followed by a round of demurely enthusiastic applause. As the crowd began to dissemble, some reassuming their seats around the room while others took to the dance floor,

I watched as Bastian came forward to meet with his mother, finally getting close enough for me to have a good look at him – and my breath stopped in my throat.

It was Brian Connor.

Not "it looked like," or "it slightly resembled." It was. His hair was styled differently, he carried himself in a more regal manner, and obviously he was more dressed up than I'd ever seen him before, there wasn't a doubt in my mind that it was him. For exactly one semester my senior year, Brian had been in all my classes, which had been odd, as I had a completely customized schedule due to my advanced placement. At the time, I hadn't thought much of it, but now it was clear – he'd been planted there.

Suddenly my entire perception of the people surrounding me snapped from haughty and aloof to calculating and sinister. I'd fallen in their trap just like everyone else, believing they were a bunch of self-absorbed elitists, but that ended now. These people knew far more than they let on and weren't nearly as uninvolved and innocent as they made everyone believe. They'd known where Ryland and I were all those years.

And I was starting to get the feeling that they'd been spying on us.

My eyes darted around quickly, looking for Jocelyn who I found walking back the cluster of chairs the four of us had occupied earlier. I hurried up alongside him and took his arm, only at the last moment remembering to keep my voice down. "I need to talk to you."

Immediately he looked concerned. "What's wrong?"

"It's Bastian, I know him."

"Wait," he said, placing a hand on my back and leading me away from the center of the room. "What do you mean, you know him?"

"He went to my high school, his name is Brian, or it was Brian anyway, and he was in every class I took for an entire semester."

I'm not sure what I was expecting him to say, but the sudden calm that washed over his features would not have been at the top of my list. "Becca," he said shaking his head, "I am certain you are mistaken."

We reached our group of chairs a moment later and Jocelyn retook his seat in one of the large armchairs. Not willing to give up so easily, I followed him down, taking a seat on the ottoman at his knee and leaned toward him. "No," I maintained, "it's him, I know it is. Don't you see what this means, they've been spying on us!"

"Becca, I understand that whatever trust you may have had in the Bhunaidh is gone after..." he paused, lowering his voice further, "our discussion about Steven, but that doesn't mean there is a conspiracy or plot hiding in every corner. I appreciate your enthusiasm, but–"

"You honestly think I would make this up?" I interrupted, quickly convincing myself that the strain I felt in my chest was anger, not hurt.

"No, of course not, but I do believe you could be misremembering. You have been out of school for more than two years now. That is a long time and appearances do change – especially in young people. Besides that," he continued discreetly, "Bastian and Steven both attend a private school in France, and I happen to know for a fact that they have not missed a single semester since they began there at age six. Trust me, whomever it is that you are thinking of, it is not Bastian."

He seemed sure, but my gut wouldn't let it go. "I know it doesn't seem–"

But he stood suddenly, cutting me off this time. "We can discuss this later," he breathed sharply, before taking my hand and bringing me up beside him. I was momentarily miffed that he would blow me off, until I turned around to see that Alva had returned to our little circle – and this time, she was not alone.

CHAPTER 8

"Alva," Jocelyn greeted her, as she and Bastian walked up and joined our little group. "The welcome addresses were lovely." *And what perfect timing you have, I added silently.*

"Oh, you are too kind," she smiled, ever the radiant hostess. "I'm so glad you enjoyed them." She took a small step back. "Jocelyn, you remember my son Bastian." She beamed as she gently ushered the young man forward. Ignoring me entirely, Bastian reached out and shook Jocelyn's hand with the practiced grace and poise of a man twice his age.

"Mr Clavish," Bastian nodded smoothly, "it's an honor see you again."

"Bastian, my boy," came Cormac's voice as he and Alex joined us. "What a sight you are! Tall as your father now, I'd say."

"And this," Alva said turning to me, with an embarrassing "last but not least" inflection in her voice, "is Jocelyn's daughter, Rebecca. Becca, this is my son Bastian Connor Bloch."

Connor. Gee... what a coincidence.

"It's nice to meet you," I said, smiling inwardly at my coming victory as reached out to shake his hand. However, instead of the shake I'd expected, he took my hand in his, turning it slightly so that my palm faced downward before he raised it up to his lips.

"The honor is entirely mine," he said against my knuckles before kissing them lightly.

Damn, this guy was smooth. Good thing I knew he was also full of crap...

"Jocelyn," Alva said, after tearing her eyes away from Bastian and myself, "I spoke with Brassal, and he would love to meet with you after the next dance set if that is agreeable."

"Yes, thank you so much Alva. I hope it won't be too much of an inconvenience."

"No, not at all..."

The conversation continued, and I probably should have been paying attention, but all I could focus on was the man still standing only an arm's reach away. His green eyes, his square jaw, even his slightly off center widow's peak, were all exactly that of the boy I'd known from school. And that wasn't even mentioning the blatant proof that was his middle name. It was all there, plain as day, and no way was I going to let it go until everyone saw the truth. And the best way to ensure that was to trap him.

I kept my eyes glued to his face as the conversation carried on around us, just waiting for his eyes to come up and meet mine. Waiting for that deliciously inevitable moment when our gazes would lock and I could witness the spark of panic in his eyes as he realized that I wasn't in the least bit fooled, and that whatever their game was, it was over.

Of course all that would require him to actually look at me, which thus far hadn't shown any sign of happening. Moment after moment passed and he never so much as glanced passingly in my direction. Normally I would have considered his lack of eye contact to be reassuring proof that he knew he was in trouble, but oddly – not to mention annoyingly – that wasn't the read I was getting. In fact, it didn't even look like he was avoiding me so much as completely disinterested in my presence. The way someone would treat a person they'd never seen before and would never see again. But of course it was all a show.

Wasn't it...?

A twinge of doubt started to creep into my mind, but I kicked it back. It *was*.

"Good," I heard Alva say as she began to step away. "We will see you all in a bit then."

No. No way it was going down like this. If he thought he could get away with this by avoiding me... he was wrong.

Doing my best to look charmingly unassuming, I stepped forward slightly, calling out, "Excuse me." They both stopped and turned back, and yet again I got nothing from Bastian. Again a shadow of doubt slipped in to shake my resolve, but again I beat it back. *It's him damn it, you know it is! Don't let them got to you! Maintain!*

"Yes dear?" Alva asked, smiling patiently while I hesitated, collecting myself.

"*Becca...*" Jocelyn whispered pointedly from just behind me.

"I'm sorry," I continued, ignoring Jocelyn's subtle but obvious warning, "I don't want to keep you, and I hope it's not too bold, but I wanted to ask if Mr Bloch," I turned my gaze to Bastian, "would do me the honor of a dance this evening."

For a split second the knot in my stomach felt like it had turned to ice as everyone in our little circle held their breath. Had I gone too far? Was I as off base as Jocelyn thought? What if I was, did I just ruin our chances of finding Ciaran? The doubts buzzed in my head, but before they could break my resolve... I saw it.

His eye twitched. The easy smile never left his face, but for an instant the tension got the better of him. It was the smallest flicker of his eyelid and vanished almost before I realized it'd happened, and though I was probably the only one who'd seen it – I *had* seen it. He was in trouble and he knew it.

I glanced over to Alva to see her reaction, as of course I assumed she would also be feeling the heat, but oddly, she could not have seemed more at ease. More than at ease... she was beaming. Did she seriously think I wasn't going to figure it out?

I mean, she had been the one to bring him over, was she that confident in his acting abilities, or did she just think I was that dumb?

Or... did she not know?

Before I could surmise further, Bastian took a step forward, bowing gracefully. "The honor," he said, finally gathering the nerve to meet my eyes, "would be entirely mine."

I heard Jocelyn quietly clear his throat, but again I ignored him.

"The second set is beginning," Bastian continued, coolly offering me his hand. "May I have the pleasure?"

I paused only slightly and took a moment to listen carefully to the song wafting through the air, praying it was a meter I recognized and would be able to dance to. Silently I began to count. There were three beats per bar which meant three/four time. It was a waltz. A quick glance at the couples who were already dancing confirmed my assessment and the slight tension in my shoulders broke. I had this.

Jocelyn, however, was clearly not as confident in my dancing abilities as I was. "I'm sure Becca would be delighted," he said suddenly, obviously feeling this situation demanded he step in, "but I'm not sure she realizes–"

"I would love to," I interrupted, taking Bastian's hand with a smile.

As he led me away from the group and onto the dance floor, I knew Jocelyn wasn't happy with me, but I wasn't worried. If he was afraid that I was about to embarrass myself by stumbling all over the dance floor, then he was going to be pleasantly surprised. If his fear was that I would probe Bastian about spying on me back in Pennsylvania, well... he was right. But just because I planned to dig, didn't mean I couldn't handle the situation tactfully.

Though, given my history, I couldn't pretend that his fears were entirely unfounded...

Trying to ignore the fact that every single eye in the room was fixed on us as we crossed the it and took to the floor, I kept my head high, my smile easy, and my mind on the mission. I wasn't going to let their whispers and pointed stares get to me this time, not now that I fully understood the sort of shady frauds I was dealing with. These people were as underhanded as they came and had been playing us for fools. And by the end of this dance I planned to be able to prove it.

When we reached an open space in the center of the dance floor, we stopped and turned to face one another. My heart began to kick my ribs a bit as we assumed the dance position and I saw all the other couples twirling around us like extras from a Rodgers and Hammerstein show. Reminding myself that it was just a waltz and that I was more than capable, I held my breath and waited for his lead, trying my best to look as calm and collected as he did. He glanced down at me to confirm I was ready, and a moment later we were gliding around the room like pros.

Or he was anyway.

I was doing my best to keep up, while also making sure not to let anyone realize I was having trouble. I had been prepared to waltz, and we were waltzing all right, but it wasn't the traditional box step that I was used to. Apparently Bastian preferred open footwork, which involved larger steps and a lot more spinning, consequently making it much grander than its box cousin – and more difficult. Maybe this was how he always waltzed, or maybe he assumed that I wouldn't be able to handle the more difficult style and would have to bow out, but either way I was determined to hold my own. The dance may have looked and felt different, but it was still a waltz, and that meant that the footwork was generally the same. My other saving grace was the fact that, while still a lying cad, Bastian was a very strong lead and wittingly or no he was making me look far better than I was. Uncle Joe would have been proud.

As we twirled around the perimeter of the dance floor I waited for him to say something. After all, he had to know that I'd recognized him, so it was only a matter of time before he came at me with something: an excuse, a test question, or maybe even a threat. But the longer I waited the more clear it became that he didn't plan on saying anything... at all. It looked like he didn't have anything to say. But that was fine... because I had plenty.

"Nothing to say this evening?" I asked, keeping my sarcasm – just barely – in check.

"Forgive me," he replied after a moment, though there was a new aloof, almost bored air to his tone, "I am not myself tonight. You look lovely this evening, and are quite a... proficient dancer... for an American."

"The dance?" I asked, gritting my teeth as I let his blatant insult go. "Is that really what you want to discuss?"

"We are *dancing*," he said with a haughty inflection that made me want to stomp on his foot, "so it seemed an appropriate subject. Would you prefer the weather, or perhaps a commentary on the entertainment this evening?"

God, what an ass!

I hadn't known him all that well in school, so I wasn't sure if he was acting this way to try and repel me and my questions, or if "self-righteous dick" was just his natural state, but I was not about to be deterred. "I was thinking something more like Mr Sacklehide's honors English class, or maybe Mrs Tatala's Algebra 3," I said innocently, listing a few of the classes we'd shared.

Certain I had him in a corner, I looked up at his face as I waited for him to respond, looking for the spark of panic in his eyes. Unfortunately, he must have been prepared for my veiled accusations, because all I got from his expression was confusion and a mild hint of annoyance. "Am I supposed to know what you are referring to?" he asked after he realized I was not going to expand.

"Oh, I'm pretty sure you do."

"Then it would appear you are mistaken," he replied casually, actually having the gall to roll his eyes.

So this is how it was going to go? Denials and lies? Playing dumb? Treating me like a pest wasting his precious time? Not a chance. If this asshole actually thought he was going to get away with this, he had no idea who he was dealing with – but he was about to find out.

Game on.

I stared out over his shoulder as I tried to decide my next move, afraid that if I looked at his expression again I might smack him. However, as we rounded the next corner of the dance floor and I saw a pair of blue eyes watching me like fiery ice chips, I realized I wasn't the only one currently teetering on the edge of violence. I couldn't remember a time when anyone had looked at me with as much fury and hatred as those eyes shot at me now. However, it wasn't until I moved from the eyes to the entire face that my shock turned to irritation, as I realized that the glare burning through my head belonged to none other than – surprise, surprise – Shannon.

What the hell was with this chick?

Though no sooner had that thought crossed my mind than I noticed that she wasn't just looking at me but at Bastian too. Her eyes bobbed back and forth between the two of us, and suddenly it became totally obvious what her issue was... and it took everything in me not to grin.

She was jealous.

Were they a couple? Had I cut in on her man? Wrong as it was, I had to admit that my eviler side liked the idea of stepping on her toes way more than it should have. I glanced up at Bastian to see if he had noticed her too, which he clearly had, though he was doing his best to pretend he hadn't.

"She doesn't seem happy," I remarked, perfectly content to stir the pot if it would throw him off his game.

"She wouldn't be," was all he said.

Damn. So much for that.

We danced what was left of the waltz in silence, stopping elegantly on the last beat before joining the others on the floor in a round of light applause for the orchestra. As the next number began, Bastian took my hand and raised it to his lips once again, bowing slightly.

"It has been a pleasure," he said, kissing my knuckles.

"It has," I agreed, with a radiant smile and a small curtsy. We were about to part ways, but just before he was able to release my hand, I squeezed my fingers shut tightly round his own, subtly holding him in place. When he looked up, I kept my smile firmly in place. "Make no mistake," I continued just loudly enough for him to hear, "I am not blind and I am not stupid. I know something is going on here, and I *will* find out what it is."

"I'm sure you will," he said with a patronizing cock of his eyebrows.

Resisting the urge to introduce my knee to his groin, I took my hand back and turned away with my head held high. I made my way back to where Jocelyn, Alex, and Cormac were seated, hoping I would get my internal temperature down to a controlled boil by the time I reached them. That smug bastard made me want to scream, but I'd get him. Even if it was the only thing I managed to do the entire trip, so help me, I would get him.

However, in the meantime, I needed to rein it in, and get myself back under control. Flying off the handle in the middle of the gala wasn't going to do me or my cause any good, which meant I needed something else to focus my energy on. Unfortunately, I didn't happen to pass by Shannon on my way back, as I would have loved to get a good look at the expression on her face, but the good news was that there were three men looking at me with what could only be described as shock on their faces, on whom I could easily focus my attention.

"Becca," Cormac gushed, with a bewildered shake of his head as I arrived back at our little basecamp. "My dear, you were a vision! Where on earth did you learn to dance like that? I had no idea you were so talented!"

"Oh, you know," I said, glancing down a little, embarrassed, "I'm full of surprises."

"No, really," Jocelyn said, appearing to be even more surprised than I thought he'd be. "Where did you learn that?"

I flashed him my best "how do you like me now" grin as I retook my seat on the couch. "Uncle Joe."

"Joe... *dances*?" he asked, sitting in the adjacent chair.

"Yep. He started taking lessons a few years ago, and asked if I wanted to go with him. He's bought me lessons for my birthday and Christmas every year from then on until I graduated."

"Well," he murmured, still looking a bit disillusioned. "I suppose I owe you an apology..."

"Yeah," I flashed a wry grin, "but it's OK. I knew you would."

He huffed a laugh and shook his head slightly before turning his attention back to the dance floor, giving me a chance to look over to Alex who had been sitting quietly since my return. Our eyes met and I raised my eyebrows with a smile.

"*I'm impressed*," he cast in the air in front of me with a grin.

I gave him a quick "yeah, I'm awesome" smirk, but when it only got me a half smile I realized something was off. I pulled my eyebrows together in a silent question, which a moment later he answered, "*I'm fine*." I knew he was lying, but as it was obviously not the time or place to discuss it further, I let it go for the time being.

Besides, I had a slightly more pressing matter to deal with at the moment as a visit to the ladies room was far overdue. I excused myself and headed out to the nearest restroom, and was not surprised to find that even it was beyond fantastic, with a mini chandelier, its own parlor, and a row of vanity tables complete with settees, mirrors, and little baskets filled with emergency grooming supplies like makeup wipes, perfume, needle and thread, hairspray and just about everything else you could possibly have needed. Luckily it was also empty of people which meant there was no one to see me gawk.

I slipped in to one of the stalls and used the facilities – which, I might add is no easy feat when you are wearing full, floor-length gown that you can't get wet, or wrinkled, or dirty in any way shape or form.

I was just about to flush when I heard the door to the restroom open and a conversation caught my ear… or more specifically, a name.

"… is Jocelyn Clavish's daughter, Non, of course it's causing a stir. But that doesn't mean we have anything to worry about."

Me? They were talking about me?

I held my breath as I turned slightly in the stall, angling my head to try and get a look at the speaker through the sliver of space between the door and the doorframe. I could only make out their shadows, but thanks to the inordinately high hair of the shadow to the left, that was all I needed. "Non," she'd called her. Shan*non*. It was her.

"And if it is," Shannon snipped, "what then?"

"Then we change our strategy," the first voice answered, whom, given her tone, I had to assume was her mother. "We knew that minor problems may arise, this is nothing more than that, and we will deal with it. We have worked too hard to allow some no account, American born, partial Holder ruin things, no matter who her father is."

"Holder," Shannon scoffed, "from what Fenton told me, her Mentalist abilities are so weak she barely even warrants the title."

Mentalist? So they'd had someone read me. Looked like the saol ring was working. Well done Min.

"Exactly," the mother said. "And as far as Bastian is concerned, there is no reason to trouble yourself. He has far better taste than to consider someone like her. However," she paused, and I heard the muffled tapping of items being shuffled in a purse, "that doesn't mean his behavior doesn't warrant punishment."

"Gladly," Shannon murmured, her voice distorted as though she was speaking while applying lipstick.

I heard something that sounded like a compact click shut, then the mother continued. "Come, we are going to return to the gallery, and you are going to dance with anyone other than Bastian. In fact you should pay him no attention at all until he approaches you. Ignore him for the remainder of the evening if you must."

"Don't you think that is a bit too much?" Shannon chuckled maliciously. "After having to lug Rebecca around the floor with him for an entire set, he is probably anxious for a decent partner. Did you *see* her footwork?"

"Utter dead weight–" but she was cut off by the door opening, ushering in several new voices.

My nostrils flared as a hundred and one things I wanted to do in that moment screamed in my head. I wanted to step out and let them know I'd heard every word. I wanted to tell them off. Tell them who I really was and that my ability could run circles around everyone else here combined. I wanted to merge with every ability I could sense right there and give them both a show they would never forget. I wanted to scream and yell. Shame them. Call them the most horrible names I knew and mean every word of it.

That's what I *wanted* to do. That's what they deserved.

We all want to stand up for ourselves when the hateful people of the world put us down, unfortunately most of us rarely do. We'll defend others to the grave, but when we are the ones attacked, most of our snarky comebacks and witty retorts go unsaid to everyone but our own bedroom mirrors. But that wasn't me. I didn't hide from tyrants and let worthless arrogant bitches intimidate me. I was tough. I didn't take crap. I stood up for the oppressed and fought off their bullies. But this was different. This wasn't what I was used to. I couldn't fall back on all my old "defend and protect" philosophies that I'd perfected over the years looking out for Ryland, because for the first time in my life the one being bullied... was me.

No matter how much I wanted to put them in their place in that moment, for some reason I couldn't. Shamed as I was to admit it, all I could do was the same thing that almost anyone else would have done in my place: I fumed in silence, hid in the stall until I was positive they were gone...

...and tried not to cry.

CHAPTER 9

A short time later I was finally able to return to the gallery, having both successfully evaded the harpy and her mother, and removed any and all signs of distress from my expression and overall demeanor. I may have let the overheard conversation in the restroom get to me, but there was no reason that anyone else had to know it. I was mad enough that I'd been so sensitive, no way was I about to broadcast it and sulk like a baby.

I hurried back to where Alex, Cormac, and Jocelyn were seated, hoping that I hadn't missed Brassal. I was very interested to meet him; firstly, because I strongly suspected that he was the one who had sent Bastian over to spy on me as it was clear that Alva was clueless, and secondly, I wanted to hear what he had to say about the object of our whole trip here, Mr Shea.

Once I confirmed that Brassal hadn't been by yet, I sat down next to Cormac to wait, not willing to risk missing him. However, as the minutes began to add up, I started to wonder if we were going to get blown off. Alva had said he would meet with us after the second dance set of the night – which was about ten sets ago. What was he up to? Was he talking with Bastian and getting a rundown of the conversation we'd had while dancing? Were they planning damage control? Trying to cover their tracks?

At the hour and a half mark, I ran a few of my theories by Jocelyn, who of course still thought I was crazy. "Don't be absurd," he'd said, when I'd again suggested the possibility of shenanigans. "Brassal is a busy man with dozens of guest to see. He will send for us when he is ready." I didn't press the matter, but for my part, I was a little disappointed in Jocelyn's lack of overall skepticism. For as low as I knew his opinion of these people to be, it was still clearly higher than mine.

At the two hour mark I was about to make another comment when I saw our "hostess extraordinaire" came floating in out of the corner of my eye. Once again she was not alone, but this time, instead of Bastian, she was on the arm of a grown man wearing a perfectly tailored tux, a red satin sash, and a confident smile.

Finally.

"Jocelyn! Too long, my friend, far, far too long!" the man greeted Jocelyn with an enthusiastic handshake.

"Indeed, Brassal," Jocelyn replied, "It is good to see you."

"Do forgive my tardiness, I had some matters to attend to."

Yeah, I'll bet you did…

"No need to apologize, we've been having a wonderful time," Jocelyn assured him. "Alva has truly outdone herself," he added with a nod toward her. Much as I hated Jocelyn playing to these people, I had to hand it to him – the guy knew how to turn on the charm, no doubt about it.

"And this," Brassal said, stepping toward me, "must be the lovely Rebecca I have been hearing so much about."

"Yes," Jocelyn said, placing a hand on my arm and bringing me forward. "Becca, allow me to introduce Brassal Bloch."

"It is truly an honor," Brassal said, taking my hand, though thankfully he didn't kiss it as Bastian had done. I'd had my fill of strangers' lips for one evening.

"Thank you," I nodded, while silently wondering just what he had heard about me… and who had done the telling.

"And this is Mr Alex Bray," Jocelyn introduced Alex who always seemed to be just a foot or two behind the rest of us.

"A pleasure, Mr Bray," Brassal said, shaking his hand, impressing me with his perceived level of sincerity. "And where is Cormac this evening?" Brassal asked, glancing around.

"He stepped away, but should be back shortly," Jocelyn said.

"Well, then I will have to be sure to find him later. Now," Brassal said, stepping back and retaking Ava's arm, "Alva tells me there is something you wish to discuss?"

"Yes," Jocelyn nodded, "that is, if you have a moment."

"Of course," he said, "though I do hope nothing is wrong..."

"No," Jocelyn assured him, though his voice stayed slightly hushed. "I simply wish to make the acquaintance of one of your number and would appreciate an introduction and perhaps a private meeting."

"Is that all?" Brassal asked, looking slightly relived "Of course, of course, no problem at all! Who is it you are looking for? Perhaps he is even here tonight."

"Ciaran Shea."

"Ciaran?" Brassal repeated, confusion furrowing his brow.

"Yes," Jocelyn nodded, "is something wrong?"

Here we go, I thought, scowling inwardly, *let the cover-ups begin...*

"Unfortunately," Alva said, "that won't be possible."

"That is... unfortunate," Jocelyn said, treading lightly. "There is an important matter I need to discuss with him."

"Perhaps it is something that we could help you with?" Alva suggested.

"Thank you, but with all due respect, the matter is somewhat private." He was obviously trying to be as polite and tactful as possible, but at least now he had to see that I'd been right and these people where definitely hiding something. I mean come on; the one guy we'd come here to see, who was probably doing God knows what with God knows who, and now we find out that they have him tucked away somewhere and won't even let us see him?

Conspiracy much?

"It truly is imperative that I speak with him, even if only for a moment. If there is any way I could change your mind..." Jocelyn asked, having no choice but to show his hand a little bit.

"Oh no, you misunderstand," Brassal said, holding up a hand to Jocelyn as though he was worried he'd offended him. "We would be more than happy to introduce you to Ciaran, but..." he paused a moment, "unfortunately, Ciaran Shea is dead."

"Dead?" Cormac asked, stunned as the rest of us. "How? When?"

After we'd found out that the man we'd come all this way to see was undeniably and irreversibly un-seeable, Jocelyn had gone to speak with Brassal privately while Alex and I went off to Cormac.

"We don't know," I said as the three of us gathered in the corner of the gallery. "Jocelyn is finding out now."

"It can't be a coincidence," Alex said.

"Not a chance," I agreed.

"In fact," Jocelyn said as he joined us, his ease of his posture not matching the tension in his brow, "it may just be."

"What did you find out, Jocelyn?" asked Cormac, who, like Jocelyn, kept his stance casual but his voice lowered.

"As I said," Jocelyn continued, glancing quickly around, "Ciaran's death does not appear to be anything suspicious. He passed away of a heart attack."

"A heart attack?" Alex repeated.

"When?" I asked.

"More than three years ago."

Cormac scratched his chin, perplexed. "And there was no sign of foul play?"

"None, nor was there any reason to suspect that there would be. At least, not at the time."

"What the hell could Taron have wanted from a man who's been dead for three years?" I asked, growing more and more frustrated with the entire situation.

"I don't know," Jocelyn answered, glancing around cautiously again, "but I suggest we keep any further speculation to ourselves until we are in private. Cormac, talk to your friends, anyone you are certain you can trust, and find out what you can. The rest of us," he continued turning to Alex and me, "will finish the evening as though nothing has happened. I believe the last dance is about to begin. Afterward, we will all meet in my room and decide what's to be done."

We all nodded then parted ways, Cormac toward his many acquaintances to gather info, while Jocelyn, Alex, and I headed back to our seats near the dance floor. As we made our way through the room, the final dance was announced, and when I realized that it was another waltz, I was hit by a random and very unexpected thought. A thought that impressed me as much as it scared me.

It was the realization that there was... something I could do.

The problem was I wasn't entirely sure it was something I actually wanted to do. Clearly there was a small part of me that did, or the thought would never have occurred to me in the first place. But could I actually go through with it? I guess it would be... I don't know... nice? Weird? Yeah, that too. Plus, everyone would see! Or at least Alex and Cormac would see, the rest of them I didn't give a damn about. But if it went well it would be worth it, right?

Right?

As we approached the small group of chairs we had spent almost the entire night either on or around, I knew I had to make a decision. If I was going to do it, it had to be now or the moment would pass. But did I have the balls?

Yes.

No...

Bah! Yes, damn it! I was not going to wuss out twice in one evening! I was doing this.

Just before we all went to take our seats, I mustered up every ounce of will I had and turned to Jocelyn. It was now or never. I took a breath, and made the leap.

"Would you... like to dance?"

His shock was obvious, even though I could tell he was trying to hide it. We stood silently for an anxious breath until the surprise on his face melted into something that I didn't want to examine hard enough to put a name to. Instead I glanced over to Alex who – bless him – was pretending not to pay attention as Jocelyn and I stood there, hovering in a moment balanced on a razor between impressively improved and incredibly uncomfortable. An eternal second later, Jocelyn finally answered. He didn't say anything, which was probably for the better, but instead turned slightly and offered me his arm. With a wave of relief – and a small pat on the back – I rested my hand in the crook of his arm, caught a small smile as it flashed across Alex's face, then followed Jocelyn's lead out onto the dance floor.

"So, correct me if I'm wrong, but we're basically screwed." I hated to have to say it out loud, but given the events of the evening, that was the only conclusion I could draw.

It was immediately after the gala, and Jocelyn, Alex, and I were waiting for Cormac in Jocelyn's titanic-size suite. My room may have been ridiculously large, but his you could have easily parked a houseboat in.

"That will depend on what Cormac is able to find out," Jocelyn answered, removing his medal sash and jacket and tossing them on the bed. "But our goal is still the same at its root."

"I thought our goal was to talk to Shea."

"Our goal was and is to find out how Shea is connected to Taron and learn what manner of dealings they had. Confronting him would have been the easiest method, but that is not the only way of finding the information we need."

"But only provided that someone else happens to know something," Alex said, sounding about as optimistic as I felt.

"Yes," Jocelyn admitted, "but I'm sure that someone will at least be able to set us on the right trail." He tapered off, looking down at his sash as he slowly coiled it around his hand like you would a silk tie before putting it in a box. "And if all else fails," he continued after a moment, talking almost to himself, "there may be other ways."

I wanted to ask what he meant, but he didn't look like he was prepared to expand, so I decided not to. Though it wouldn't have mattered anyway, because before I could think of something to say, there was a knock on the door.

"It's me," Cormac called as Alex reached for the door.

"Cormac," Jocelyn sighed as the door clicked shut, "tell me you have news."

"I do indeed." He stepped over toward the fireplace wringing his hands with a combination of excitement and nervous tension in his eyes. As Alex, Jocelyn, and I moved closer to him he started his report. "The first few people I spoke with knew little to nothing about Mr Shea, but my friend Aideen McRoy..." He turned to Jocelyn, "You remember Aideen and Devon, don't you?" Jocelyn nodded. "Aideen was an acquaintance of Ciaran's and was able to tell me quite a bit about him. First, Ciaran did pass of a heart attack three years ago, which was apparently quite a long time coming. He had no family and very few friends and lived alone right up until the end."

"That all may be interesting," I observed "but it's not incredibly helpful."

"No," Cormac grinned at me, "It's isn't... but this bit is. He was a Seer."

"A Seer?" Alex whispered, while Jocelyn took a seat in the nearest chair with a long breath, rubbing his face with his hand. Clearly I had missed something...

"Sorry," I spoke up, as everyone reeled from this apparently major development, "he was a what, now?"

"A Seer, dear," Cormac explained. "That was his ability. Seers are prophets, and incredibly rare at that. They can predict coming events, some with pinpoint accuracy. It was a Seer who predicted Jocelyn's birth and abilities, as well as your own."

"So they can see the future?" I asked.

"No, not quite. They do not see the future as, say, a Time Walker can, they can only prophesize. They see how certain events will unfold, but with no specific detail. Take Jocelyn for instance: it was prophesized that a Holder would be born with immense power to parents who had no Holder blood in either of their lines. Specific in what would occur, but the Seer who made these predictions had no way of knowing when it would happen, or where, or to what family, or even what ability this Holder would have." He turned to Jocelyn and continued. "I can't say what Shea's tie to Taron was, but Darragh would be more than interested in a Seer, and anything that Seers might have had to say."

"So it's the prophecies that Darragh is after?" Alex asked.

"We cannot be sure that Darragh is after anything," Jocelyn said, resting his chin on his fingers. "All we know for certain is that Taron was interested in Shea. At this point anything beyond that is speculation."

"There is one more thing," Cormac added, looking hesitantly at Jocelyn. "Aideen wasn't sure where to find him, but she was confident she could find out. In case we wanted to," he paused, and apologetically arched his brow, "pay our respects."

After a long pause, Jocelyn sighed heavily and rubbed his face with both hands. "After three years, I don't know that it will be any use."

"Maybe not," Cormac nodded, "but if we don't get any other leads, it might at least be worth a try. But only if you are up for it, of course."

What the hell were they talking about? I wanted to ask, but somehow it didn't feel like I should. I looked over at Alex to see if he was as lost as I was, but he was listening intently.

"I know," Jocelyn sighed again after another long pause. "And you can find out where he is?"

Cormac nodded.

"All right then," Jocelyn said, looking far more tired than he had a few minutes ago. Then, looking at the time, frowned slightly. "Much as I hate to risk waking Min at this hour, I need to get in touch with her and see if she can get Anderson and Reid together for a call tomorrow. We are going to need their help if we are to continue, and they should all be made aware of tonight's developments. If I speak with her tonight, she might be able to set something up before any of them leave for their classes tomorrow. I will let you know what I hear. Until then, there is nothing more we can do tonight but get some rest."

Everyone agreed and stood to leave, though for my part, I was way too wired to even think about sleeping. Jocelyn showed us to the door, where we went our separate ways, each headed in the direction of our respective rooms. I was immediately irked that I hadn't been able to say a proper goodnight to Alex, though as it turned out, I didn't need to be. As soon as I rounded the corner into the main hallway, I felt a warm pull in my chest followed by the brush of a finger against my arm.

"*Mind if I join you?*" appeared in the air in front of me. I turned to see Alex step up alongside me wearing a sneaky grin like a little boy who'd just stolen a cookie.

"Of course not," I laughed, surprised. "How the hell did Jocelyn let you follow me?"

"*He didn't see me,*" appeared quickly, as Alex suddenly glanced around nervously at the other people in the hall with us, "*and stop talking to me.*" When I shot him a "you did not just tell me to shut up" glare, he quickly added, "*Just until we get to your room.*"

"Why?"

He leaned in toward my ear, just barely whispering, "Because you're the only one who can see me."

Ah.

I don't know if it was the thrill of the secrecy, or just the fact that something was finally going right after a night of letdowns and irritants, but I was suddenly as giddy as a kid in a toy store. The idea that Alex was actually coming up to my room at this hour sent a wave of prickles down my back and a rush of anxious heat to my chest. Did this mean what I thought it meant? Was this it? Were we…

…going to…

"*Why my dear, I do believe you are blushing.*"

Damn it. "No I'm not," I lied. And did he have to grin like that?

"*Shhh…*"

"What?" I breathed through my teeth. "You're allowed to talk to me but I can't talk back?"

"*That's generally the way this works, yes.*"

"Fine," I sighed, really resenting how cute he always managed to be when he was teasing me. "Then at least tell me something I want to know: what were Cormac and Jocelyn talking about?"

"*You mean right before we left?*"

I nodded.

"*They were talking about going to where Ciaran is buried.*"

"Yeah, I got that part, but why?"

"*Probably so that Jocelyn can read him.*"

Chapter 10

"Read him?" The dead man? Ew. Ew, ew, ew.

"*Yes. Or at least try.*" He must have seen my eyes threaten to pop out of my head. "*Sorry, should have warned you.*"

Luckily, a moment later we arrived at my room and were able to slip inside before I blew Alex's cover with my barrage of questions. "H-how," I stammered as I closed and locked the door behind us, "how is that even possible?"

"I don't know much about it, but from what I understand it has to do with how…" he paused, making a face, "*much* of the person is left."

"Oh God… we don't have to dig him up, do we?"

"No, no, nothing like that," Alex assured me, walking to the armchair and leaning against the back of it with his forearms. "He just needs to be nearby. The closer the better, but not *that* close."

I shuffled over to the ottoman next to the chair Alex was on and slumped down in a somewhat disturbed haze. Sure, now that Alex brought it up, I vaguely remembered someone mentioning something once about how Jocelyn could read dead people, but at the time, it had only been an idea. A disturbing one to be sure, but also kind of abstract and far away – like someone telling you they'd been at a party where they'd had to eat monkey's brains; it freaks you out, but from a safe distance. This on the other hand was a different story. Now reading the mind of a dead guy was not only an idea, but it was one that was quite possibly going to be demonstrated for me in the next few days, and honestly, it was creeping me out. Like the difference between the guy telling you he'd eaten monkey's brains, and having him serve them to you. Same idea, but very different when it's up close and personal...

"Now it's my turn," Alex said, coming around the chair and sitting next to me on the arm. "What were you and Jocelyn arguing about tonight?"

I wasn't sure he could tell I needed to change the subject, or if he was truly curious, but if he had been trying to distract me, he couldn't have chosen a better way. "You mean before my dance with Brian?"

"I think you mean Bastian."

"No," I huffed, "I don't. That's what Jocelyn and I were talking about, I know him. Bastian, I mean. I know him. He went to my high school for a year and his name was Brian." I stood and started pacing, all my frustration resurfacing. "He was in every class that I had – which was weird in and of itself, mind you, as I was on a completely customized schedule because of my advanced placement – and yet Jocelyn is convinced I'm crazy."

"He doesn't believe you?"

"Oh he 'believes me,'" – I wagged my fingers in sarcastic air quotes – "he just thinks I'm 'remembering wrong'. He barely even heard me out." I fumed, pacing faster. "How can he not see how serious this is? Not only are these people lying frauds, but they were spying on us! I mean, how did they even find out where we were? And why were they looking to begin with? They are up to something, I know they are."

"And you're sure it was him?"

"Positive."

"So that's why you asked him to dance? What did he say?"

I stopped pacing with a sigh, plopping back onto the chair. "Nothing. I kept trying to catch him in a lie, but he gave me nothing to work with. I even confronted him about it, and still nothing." *The rat bastard...*

"And..." he paused, looking up at me cautiously. "What if it's not him?"

"It *is* him, I know it is! And just because he didn't give me anything solid enough for me to call him out on doesn't mean he's innocent," I insisted, then began counting off on my fingers as I continued. "He looks exactly like the boy I knew, his middle name is Connor which was Brian's last name, and his eye twitched when I asked him to dance."

"His eye twitched?"

"Yeah, like... you know, he was... nervous... or something..." I tapered off with a huff. Why, when I was so sure I was right, did all my undeniable proof suddenly sound so weak even to my own ears?

Alex hesitated a second or two before he took a breath to answer, and I knew him well enough to know it meant he was about to tell me something I wasn't going to like. "Are you sure it's not just a coincidence?"

I was on the defense before my mind even had a chance to admit to itself that it was a reasonable question. "You don't believe me either!" I accused, standing and rounding on him. "You think I'm crazy too!" I knew I was being overly sensitive, but at that moment I couldn't help it.

He stood and stepped toward me, placing his hands gently on my shoulders. "I do believe you," he said earnestly, "or at least I believe that you believe it. But that doesn't mean you might not be misremembering. Hey," he guided my chin back toward him with his finger when I tried to turn away, "you look at me when I'm talking to you, young lady."

I rolled my eyes at his mock-parental tone but smiled in spite of myself, just like he knew I would. The people who love us the most can always find a way to make us smile, even if we are dead set against it – a fact that was often as annoying as it was comforting.

"That's better," he smiled as I looked up and met his eyes. "I do believe you, but I think we both know you need a little more proof before you even consider taking this public." I pursed my lips, but didn't argue. "Right. So, maybe we can do a little digging – quiet digging – and see what we come up with."

"You'll help me?"

"I will do whatever I can to help you prove that Bastian is Brian, or…" He paused dramatically making sure I was looking at him before he continued, "disprove it. All I ask is that you keep your mind open to the possibility of the latter, OK?"

"OK," I sighed, happy that at least he wasn't shutting me down. "At least I'll have some help."

"Always," he smiled. "Actually, I'm kind of glad to hear this guy might not be as perfect as he looks."

"Please," I said with a sneer, "*perfect*? Even without all the spying and lying, the guy is an arrogant, self-assured, ass. Clearly he thinks he's God's gift to the Earth, yet there doesn't seem to be one thing about him that doesn't scream either stuck-up brat, or… Why are you smiling?"

Immediately the small smile I'd caught on his lips and accompanying light in his eyes changed to a show of charming faux-confusion. "What?" he asked, raising his eyebrows innocently.

"You heard me," I probed with a wry squint.

"It's nothing," he finally admitted as his ears visibly warmed. "You two just seemed to be having a good time dancing. And you were doing an awful lot of starring."

"Wait, you were watching me stare at him?"

"No," he huffed, crossing his arms defensively. "I wasn't watching… but that doesn't mean I didn't notice…" He left his thought hanging as he glanced away, looking a bit sheepish.

I paused for a minute, trying to fill in the blanks when suddenly I saw the answer written in the chagrin on his face. "Oh my God…" I breathed, completely shocked. "Are you… are you *jealous?*"

"OK, first of all," he said, with something between a smile and a grimace, running a hand through his hair. "Do you think you could say that like it's *not* the stupidest thing you've ever heard?"

"I could if it wasn't!" I said, pressing my lips together to keep from laughing. "Alex, how could you possibly be jealous of such a–"

"I'm not jealous," he insisted, cutting me off, "at least, not of him, exactly..." He sighed and took a few steps toward the center of the room, scratching the back of his head the way he always did when he was nervous or embarrassed. "It's just, I don't know," he shrugged, "the... situation, I guess. I mean, I'm barely allowed to act like I know you, while this Bastian gets to compliment you, and kiss your hand, and spin you all over the dance floor like some couple from *Gone with the Wind*. And then there was how good the two of you looked out there..." He trailed off, stuffing his hands in his pockets.

I could tell he was frustrated and probably a little ashamed, but what I couldn't figure out was why. I mean sure, it made sense, and it explained why he looked a little strange when I'd come back after dancing, but it still seemed impossible that someone who I considered to be basically perfect and loved more than anything else in the world, could get jealous over, well... anything. Alex was a lot of things, but until that night, I'd never seen him insecure.

I smiled softly, taking the few steps over to him and took face between my hands. "Why, my dear," I said, using his words from earlier, "I do believe you're being silly. You have less than nothing to worry about, my love."

He grinned, sliding his arms around my waist. "I know," he nodded. "It's just hard, that's all. But you wouldn't understand; you don't know what it's like to be madly in love with the most breathtaking woman in the room."

"Yeah," I laughed, rolling my eyes as I slid my hands down to idly straighten the green sash laying across his chest. "I hate to break it to you, but neither do you."

"I just wish it could have been me out there with you," he continued, ignoring my comment. "That is," he added with a chuckle, "if I could actually dance."

"Here," I said, getting an idea.

When I stepped back slightly and took his hand, his eyes popped open. "What are you doing?"

"I think you know what I'm doing. I'm going to give you a dance lesson."

"Becca, we've been over this. I can't dance, and much as I appreciate it, I don't think lessons can correct my second left foot."

"For the record," I said, ignoring his protests and physically squaring his shoulders and positioning his arms, "you are not the only one who wished it was you with me out on the floor tonight. You said you wanted to dance with me, so let's dance. There is no one else here, and luckily for you I already know you're a klutz, so no need to be shy."

He looked like he might refuse again, but then suddenly a strange light sparked in his smoky blue eyes, and he smiled. "All right then, let's dance."

The sudden change in his tone sent a shiver down my back as I began to lead him in a simple box step. Despite his initial hesitation and my jab about him being a klutz, he did very well, and it was only a minute or two before we were waltzing in a slow circle in the middle of my room.

"See, I told you, nothing to worry..." but my thought died on my tongue as I looked up into the smoldering glow of his eyes. A glow that made my eyelids heavy and my neck hot.

As our gazes locked, he slowly slid his arm further around my waist, pulling me in closer and closer with each step we took. My veins began to flood with heat as every detail of the moment intensified; the smell of his cologne in my nose, the silk of his tux under my fingers, the warmth of his touch on my skin, every heartbeat, every move, every breath. Each one echoed within me like whispers through a microphone, haunting and enticing.

As our feet began to slow, Alex leaned down and gently rested his forehead against mine, allowing the tip of his nose to just barely brush against mine, teasing me with the nearness of our mouths. My lips began to ache with the need to feel his pressing into mine, hard and hungry. However this time, to my delicious agony, Alex was in no hurry.

He lingered against my forehead a moment before slowly bringing his lips up and placing a languid and far too light kiss on the space between my brows. Grazing my skin with a trail of languid kisses, he gradually made his way from my forehead, to my temple, then down to my cheek. As he reached my jaw, I felt his right hand move up from my waist and into my hair, his fingers threading themselves in deeply. With a gentle turn of his wrist, he tilted my head to the side, allowing him complete access to his favorite spot of all, the hollow under my ear. My desire spread like fire as his mouth caressed the sensitive patch, sending tingling waves of pleasure rolling over my skin like champagne bubbles rolling up the side of a glass.

"You know," I said, trying to catch my breath, "you're kind of derailing your dance lesson..."

I felt his lips grin against my skin as they slowly started kissing their way across my jaw, growing softer and softer as they neared my chin. "I'm sorry," he murmured in a husky rasp, "would you... *(kiss)* ...like me... *(kiss)* ...to stop?" *(kiss... kiss... kiss...)*

"No," I whispered over a breathy moan.

My eyes rolled back as he placed one last kiss on my chin before bringing his mouth up to hover less than a finger's width away from my own. My breath froze in my chest as his bottom lip ghosted over mine, causing my eyelids to flutter and my jaw to go slack. A tingle began to tickle the backs of my knees as his mouth opened and captured my bottom lip, and when I felt his teeth gently bite down and pull me toward him, I lost all control.

The shudder that ripped through me was so forceful it shook us both, and we fell headlong into the passionate desire of the moment. Our lips molded into one another, moving together in a dance of their own, unhurried but hungry and intense.

Finally able to take part, I ran my hands up his chest and took hold of his tie, pulling him even harder against me, deepening our kiss. Working my hands upwards, I quickly loosened the knot at his throat, freeing the silk tie of his collar and tossing it aside, followed soon after by his jacket. With those gone, my fingers had no trouble popping open the top few buttons of his shirt and slipping my hand inside his now open collar. I slowly slid my palm up to the side of his neck, relishing the low groan that rumbled from his chest and the feel of his pulse racing under my fingers. His hands began to explore me and mine did his, moving continuously at first, rubbing enticing circles up and down my back and across my ribs, but he soon grew bolder, holding me tightly against him as he grabbed and massaged any part of me he could reach.

Our chests rose and fell against one another as our breathing became more and more labored. The feel of his breath on my face, the taste of his mouth on mine, the sound of our mingled sighs and breathless groans...

It was intoxicating.

It was exhilarating.

It was perfect.

...for a moment anyway.

Unfortunately, all it took was the slightest familiar brush against my mind for the brilliant flower of our furor to begin to wilt. Like waking up right before the best part of a dream – immediately you are disappointed and you do everything you can to ignore that it happened and force yourself back to sleep, trying desperately to reclaim the adventure you were on or the discovery were just about to make, but all the while you know deep down that it's no use.

The instant I felt the brush, I kicked it off, tangling my hand further into Alex's hair. It was nothing – just an ability brush from a random Holder who was happening by. They weren't coming here. It wasn't anyone I knew. It wasn't. It... wasn't...

Damn it!

"No," I whispered, squeezing my eyes shut, "no, no, no..."

Alex opened his eyes suddenly, looking down at me as though worried he'd done something wrong. But before he could ask what was wrong, the hanging question was answered by a knock at my door. An entirely different kind of fear ran across his face as both our heads snapped toward the lingering echo of knuckles against mahogany.

"Jocelyn?" Alex mouthed silently, apparently having as hard a time as I was getting his breathing back under control.

I nodded with a wince.

"Go," he mouthed again, motioning toward the door then snatching his discarded tie and jacket from the floor and ducking into the bathroom.

"Coming!" I called out as I scrambled over to the mirror for a quick once-over. My hair and dress had survived our little *encounter* relatively well, though unfortunately the same could not be said of my makeup. I grabbed a tissue from the box on the dressing table and wiped frantically at my face, removing all the tell-tale smudges and smears. Once my face was lipstick free, I darted for the door, taking a deep breath before pulling it open, making sure I was the picture of cool, calm, and collected.

"What's going on?" I asked, trying to settle my tone into that thin line of casual located between too innocent and too guilty.

"You haven't changed yet?" he asked simply, though there was something not so simple behind the glint in his eye.

"Yeah, I was just about to. Did you need something?"

"I wanted to let you know that I spoke with Min and we will be conferencing via phone with her, Anderson, and Reid in my room tomorrow morning at 7 o'clock."

"Oh. Well great," I said, wishing my enthusiasm didn't sound so forced. "I'll be there."

"Good."

"Was there anything else?"

"No, not about tomorrow," he said, his voice eerily stoic, "but there is a mystery you may be able to help me solve. Before coming down to let you know I'd spoken to Min, I stopped by Cormac and Alex's rooms to tell them. But oddly enough," he paused, raising his eyebrows in that "you're so busted" kind of way, "Alex wasn't there. Any thought as to where he might be?"

"Huh..." I said, slowly pursing my lips. Clearly he already knew the answer, so what was he expecting me to say? *"Oh sure, he's here, and actually we were about to get naked when you knocked, so would you mind making this quick?"* Yeah, not the best idea. Despite the hype, honesty isn't always the best policy.

However, as I watched his eyes move from my face to over my shoulder, I realized I wouldn't have to say anything. Glancing back, I saw that Alex had emerged from the bathroom, his tie and jacket – thankfully – back in place. If only his ears weren't red enough to heat the entire room, we might have been able to play it all off.

"You heard?" Jocelyn asked, looking at Alex.

"Seven o'clock tomorrow," Alex nodded, clearly struggling to meet Jocelyn's eye.

He nodded.

The three of us stood silently for the longest moment of my life, no one seeming sure what to say next. All I could come up with was, *"Wow, this is awkward, huh?"* but that of all things really didn't need saying, so I kept it to myself.

"It has been a long day," Jocelyn finally said, somewhat pointedly, "and we have an early start tomorrow. I think it's time we all got some sleep. Good night." With that he turned and walked off down the hall, making it more than clear he expected Alex to follow him.

Taking the obvious cue, Alex came forward, gently squeezing my hand as walked by me. "Goodnight, Leannán," he whispered, leaning down and kissing me sweetly – albeit chastely – on the cheek.

"Stay..." I breathed, gripping the hand that held mine.

There was longing in his eyes, but he shook his head. "Don't know if that's the best idea."

I huffed, but bowed my head. I didn't like it, but I also knew he was right. "Damn it," I mumbled.

"Yeah," he agreed. "But don't worry," he added, stroking my cheek with his thumb, "I don't plan on giving up." With that, he gave me a last quick kiss, then turned and followed Jocelyn down the hall.

I closed the door with a growl and stomped over to the dresser, yanking the bobby pins out of my hair as I went.

Did that seriously just happen? We were so close! Everything was perfect! We were finally... *GAH!*

When I'd thrown down the last of the hair pins and wiped the remaining makeup off my face, I set my alarm for 6.30, slipped out of my dress, and flopped onto my bed, not even bothering to locate my pajamas. As I stared up at the satin canopy, frustrated in more ways than I could even count, I began to make a mental tally of all the epic ways the evening had sucked. First off I'd made a friend, only to discover that he was shunned and mentally abused by his family and there was practically nothing I could do to help him. Next I'd found out that not only was I spied on in high school, but that the spy and his accomplices were more than likely going to get away with it because I had no way to prove it, then was mocked, patronized, and generally treated like crap by said spy. Then I'd been talked about and made fun of behind my back by a catty bitch and her mother, causing me to cower in a bathroom stall like a wimp. After that, we'd found out that the man we'd hoped would have all the answers we came to this nightmare of an event looking for has been dead for years and may end up being no help at all. Finally, I was now going to spend the rest of the night alone in an enormous bed that I should have been sharing with Alex, all because my father caught us about to have sex. Did that about cover everything?

Oh yeah. Great night.

I rolled over with a thrash, punching my pillow into shape as I went. With a string of silent expletives, I hugged my still misshapen pillow to my chest and closed my eyes.

Damn this trip. Damn this perfect mansion. Damn my stupid expectations. Damn it, damn it, damn it...

CHAPTER 11

"You said Brian Connor?" Mom asked, as I heard the flapping of book pages carry through the phone.

"Yeah, that's it. I'm not sure what class he was in, so you might have to check each grade."

"Well, he's not in with the freshmen..." more page flapping, "not a sophomore..."

It was 7 the next morning, and after a night of not nearly enough sleep, I was fumbling around my room trying to get ready, while my mom sat on the other end of the phone line, thumbing through one of my high school yearbooks, trying to find me the proof I needed to nail Bastian to the wall.

"I don't see him in here, honey."

"No," I plopped down on the edge of the bed. "That's not possible; he has to be in there." Even if it turned out not to be Bastian, a Brian Connor would still be there somewhere.

"Oh wait, here he is," she said suddenly, "There is a Brian Connor listed as a senior on the last page in the 'not pictured' list."

Son of a bitch...

"All right, Mom," I sighed pinching the bridge of my nose, "thanks anyway."

"Sorry, hon."

"It's fine. To be honest I should have figured."

"What did you need his picture for?"

"It was nothing. I could have sworn I saw him the other day, and I just wanted to," – *get proof so I could rub his nose in it* – "see if I was right, that's all."

"So," she moved on with an excited note in her voice, "how's the castle? Are you having a good time?"

"The castle's amazing, probably the most incredible place I've ever seen. Just my room alone is almost as big as the whole first floor of our house, and my bed could fit me and about six other people."

"Wow! That sounds lovely! And how is the conference? Is there much for you to do?"

As of course I couldn't tell mom why we'd really come out here, I'd gone with an academic conference that Jocelyn had invited a few of us to join him on. "Yeah, it's fine."

"Doesn't sound fine…"

"The company kind of leaves something to be desired."

"What do you mean?"

"I don't know, they just… aren't my type of people. This whole event that we're at, it's… a school thing," I said, trying to find the best way to explain and school being the best analogy I could come up with, "so most of the other people here are professors and stuff, and I just can't handle how uppity and self-righteous they all are."

"Oh… that's a bummer. But what about the younger people, the ones more your age? Can you just hang out with them?"

"Believe it or not, most of them are even worse than the adults."

"Hmm. Well, you only have a few more days, guess you'll just have to suffer through the rest of your vacation alone in your enormous room and big fluffy bed, you poor thing," she teased.

"Yeah, yeah," I laughed, wishing this trip was as enjoyable as she made it sound. "OK, I have to get going."

"OK sweetie," she said. "Try to enjoy the rest of your trip, and give me a call when you get back to school."

"Will do, Mom. Love you."

"Love you too."

With about the hundredth yawn of the morning I slid on my shoes and made my way down to Jocelyn's room for our call with the rest of the guys back at Lorcan. When I arrived, everyone was already there and gathered around the phone while Jocelyn fought his way through the "dialing out" process. I slid down into a chair hoping I wouldn't fall asleep on the call, though I was at least happy to see that Alex and Jocelyn didn't look much better than I felt. The overall low-energy feel in the room helped to make the awkward, nearly-got-caught-in-the-act elephant in the room a little easier to ignore.

"Hello?" Min's voice echoed through the speaker on the console of the phone.

"Good morning Min," Jocelyn answered, "can you hear us all right?"

"Yes, fine."

"Are Anderson and Reid there with you?"

"Aye, we're here," we heard Anderson say over a yawn.

"Good morning everyone," Reid added.

"I'm sorry to wake you all," Jocelyn began, "but matters have changed."

"Changed?" Anderson laughed without humor, "sounds like matters are bloody well ruined. How are we to find out what Shea and Taron were up to when neither of them are able to tell us?"

"Shea wasn't up to anything, at least not with Taron," Jocelyn answered. "All the occurrences of Shea in Taron's mind were within the last six months, while Ciaran has been dead three years now. That can only mean that Taron was never dealing with Shea himself, but with something or someone involving him. All we need to find out is who or what that was, and we will do that by finding out as much about Shea as we can."

"You think really think it will be that easy?" Reid asked.

"No, I do not believe it will be easy at all, but for now it is our only option. Min, Duncan, I will need you two to gather together all the information you can about Seers. Check the books in the inner chamber, my office, your own libraries, or anywhere else you think there might be anything related to the seeing ability. We will also need a list of the names of any and all Seers we have records of as well as any information you can find about their lineages. If we can determine Shea's family line, it may lead us to family friends who could tell us more."

"Of course," Reid replied. "I can begin right away."

"And I will join him after my morning class," Min added.

"Thank you both," Jocelyn said. "Next, there are a few items I will be needing now that things have changed. Chris, what is your class load today?"

"I've a 10 to 11, and a 1 to 2," Mr Anderson answered, still sounding groggy.

"Would you be able to make a drive out here this afternoon? I can call you later with the specifics on what to bring once I finalize the list."

"Aye, not a problem."

"As for us," Jocelyn continued, turning to look at Alex Cormac and I, "our job will be garnering information here. Cormac will continue speaking to his friends to find out what he can from anyone who might have known Shea." He looked up at Cormac. "There might not be much knowledge to be had, but anything is better than nothing. You never know what might be of use."

"Good thing gossip is an art form around here," Cormac said with a nod. "I'll get what I can."

"Alex will be our fly on the wall," Jocelyn said, turning to Alex. "You can watch and listen to things the rest of us cannot, simply by going unseen. Once Cormac has had a chance to speak to some of his contacts and get leads, you will have more direction and a clearer idea of who to focus your attention on. However, until then, learn what you can, and most importantly, make sure you are not caught."

Alex nodded, while I wondered if either of them saw the irony in Jocelyn telling Alex not to get caught doing something.

Finally Jocelyn turned to me. "Becca and I will go through the books that were brought here for the week from the Bhunaidh archives. They have the most thorough log of Holder lineage and history in existence, and they may contain something we can use. Provided Brassal and Alva agree to grant us access to the books, of course."

"Wait, wait," I said, not liking the sound of that at all. "Grant us access? They could actually tell us no?"

"I don't believe they will, but technically they could, yes. The books belong to them, and the Bhunaidh archives have always been very closely guarded. However, as Alva and Brassal both know you are new to the Holder world, if I tell them that you wish to learn more about our histories, I'm sure they would not have a problem letting us browse whatever volumes they have with them."

They sure as hell better, or I might go ape. These people had long worn through my patience.

"One last thing," Jocelyn added, his tone serious. "I want to make sure that everyone understands how imperative it is that no one finds out that we are interested in Shea. There is no way to know who might be involved in all of this, and there is still the issue of the holes in Taron's memory. Someone had to put them there, and if that someone is here, I don't want to give them the chance to hide. Cormac, make sure that the people you speak to about Shea are trustworthy, and even then, keep your inquiries strictly conversational. Tell them that you and Ciaran were old friends, or that you were once a student of his, or any other story you think will work. The less you divulge the better. Alex, we will be counting on you to listen to any talk you hear about any of us. If you overhear that someone is making too much out of our interest in Shea, or growing suspicious of our intentions, let me know immediately. I will be keeping Brassal appraised as always, but just as before, only as much as I must."

"Will the four of you be staying longer?" Reid asked, causing my stomach to clench. "You are due back the day after tomorrow, but it seems you may need more time."

I looked over at Jocelyn, silently begging him to say no. "I am not sure yet. We will see what we are able to come up with in the next day or so and decide then."

"Jocelyn," Min spoke up after another pause, "forgive me, but I must ask... Do you plan on visiting the site?"

Jocelyn crossed his arms with a sigh, starring at the floor as he spoke. "If I must, yes. However, I wish to give traditional investigation methods a chance first. If we're lucky, a reading may not be necessary. Though," he shook his head with a frown, "even if it does become necessary, after three years, I'm not certain I could get anything that would be of any use."

As I watched Jocelyn struggle with the idea of doing a reading on Shea, I felt bad for him and was impressed by him all at the same time. I was pretty sure there weren't many people out there – Holder or otherwise – who would have had the conviction to stick so solidly to an ideal. But Jocelyn wasn't most people. He didn't believe in reading people, and that was that. Not living, not dead, not ever.

"I think that does it for tonight, and Chris, I'll call you later."

Silence.

"Anderson?" he called, leaning toward the phone.

After another moment of silence we heard something that sounded like a slap. "Wake up you lazy lummox!" Reid whispered sharply.

"What?" Anderson yelped suddenly.

"I'll call you later," Jocelyn repeated.

"Oh... um, yes. Yes, fine."

"Have a good day everyone."

As Jocelyn reached to hang up the phone, I could hear movement on the other end of the line with Reid and Anderson mumbling in the background.

"Bloody idiot..."

"I wasn't sleeping, you half-wit!"

"You were drooling on yourself!"

"That's no reason to hit m–" But Jocelyn disconnected the call.

"Well," Cormac said, standing with a stretch, "I don't know about you all, but I am starving. Shall we get some breakfast?"

"Sounds good," I said, actually excited to see what would be on the breakfast spread.

"I'll have to meet up with you all later. I'm due to have breakfast with Brassal and some of the other men he golfs with. He invited me out with them tomorrow and wanted me to meet the other players. If the opportunity arises, I'll ask him about looking through the archives and see what he says."

"Wait, you golf?" I asked, skeptically.

"I can when I have to. Let us just hope they don't expect me to be any good."

The four of us stepped out into the hall when were said our goodbyes and parted ways. Jocelyn headed off to the left while Cormac, Alex and I took the stairs to the right, following the alluring aromas of baking bread and cooked sausage.

"So," I said quietly to Alex, slowing my pace so that he and I fell slightly behind Cormac, "since you are our resident spy, what do you say you and I do a little snooping after breakfast?"

"Sure," he grinned. "Though it might be hard since we don't have a specific target yet."

"Yeah we do," I murmured, throwing him a sly glance.

It was time to spy on the spy.

"Do you feel anything?" Alex asked, as we stood outside one of the guest suites later that morning. Bastian hadn't been at breakfast that morning, which honestly didn't surprise me, though it had made following him harder considering that in order to follow someone, you first have to find them. Luckily when Alex and Cormac were walking to their rooms just after check in the day before, Cormac had pointed out a smaller hallway and told Alex that those rooms were where the head family always stayed. Figuring it was as good a place as any to start, Alex and I had headed there after breakfast and were now using our respective abilities to begin tracking down our target – me by sensing the abilities nearby to determine if Bastian was actually in any of the rooms, and Alex by making sure that no one who happened by would be able to see us.

"There are two people in that room," I pointed to one of the doors, "and one in there. The two there I don't recognize, but that one," I paused, concentrating on the single ability in the adjacent room, double checking before I went on, "that one is him."

"You're sure?"

"Yeah," I nodded, "I got pretty familiar with the feel of his ability during our dance last night. It's him."

"OK, so we found him… now what?"

"We wait, I guess."

"And if he doesn't do anything out of the ordinary? Or for that matter, doesn't even leave his room?" he asked as we wandered back up the hall toward a set of armchairs by a window.

"OK, Negative Nancy," I glared, "I know it's not a perfect plan, but it's not like we have anything better to do at the moment. Unless that is, you want to go up to the art auction and mingle…"

"Negative Nancy?" he repeated, cocking an eye brow.

"Buzz-kill Betty? Pessimist Polly? Downer Deloris? Gloomy Gertrude? Feel free to pick your favorite, I've got a million of them. Worrywart Wilma is always a classic…"

"OK," he laughed, "now you're just making stuff up. And do they all have to be women?"

"No, but it's funnier that way," I giggled as he shoulder checked me playfully into the side of the first armchair. "Look, I know this is dumb, OK, I get it. But I have to do something – or at least feel like I am doing something. I can't just sit in my room all day and ignore the fact that he's playing us all for saps. Lousy as this plan might be, until I can come up with a better one, this is all I've got. And, if I just so happen to know a talented guy who I can rope in to hide me while I sneak around, so much the better."

"Sounds like a pretty great guy," Alex smiled, resting his elbow on the arm of the chair and leaning back casually.

"He has his moments," I shrugged, pressing my lips together.

"'His moments'?" he asked. "I don't know... Might be hard to rope this guy in to your schemes if that's all the praise he's going to get."

"Don't worry, he's very modest. And if all else fails, I can always charm him with my wiles."

"Then I guess you're all set," he laughed quietly.

We sat silently for a moment or two until I suddenly remembered something Cormac had said the night before. "Hey," I said, shifting in my seat to face him, "I've been meaning to ask you – last night when we were talking about Steven, Cormac called Bastian a Porter. What's a Porter?"

Alex pursed his lips slightly as he thought, like he was trying to find the right words. "Porting is the ability to travel instantaneously. Like teleporting in a sci-fi movie."

"Seriously? Damn it... that's pretty cool. To be honest, I was kind of hoping it was something lame." I knew it was petty, but I was a firm believer that jerks shouldn't get cool stuff.

"Sorry. Though it may not be quite as cool as you think. I don't know a lot about it, but from what I understand, Porters can't simply go wherever they want anytime they want; it's more complicated than that. Their Sciaths also work differently; they aren't tied to them like the rest of us. They still work even when they are removed."

"That'd be nice..."

"Tell me about it," he agreed. "Jocelyn would know more about it, you should ask him."

Suddenly, the loud creak of a door hinge echoed up the corridor, and I turned to see a man dressed entirely in white walking out of Bastian's room. It was him – but what the hell was he wearing? It wasn't until he turned to shut his door behind him that I saw the silver-mesh helmet hanging from the gym bag over his shoulder. It was a fencing helmet.

Ugh... Of course he was a fencer, what was I thinking? Fencing, polo, maybe some croquet. Why on earth would I have expected him to be a break dancer, or a juggler, or anything else even remotely out of the box?

A moment later, the door across the hall opened and this time Alva stepped out dressed in an ensemble looking as though it came straight out of a catalog. It was the kind of outfit that she probably considered casual, but had it been in the closet of a normal person it would have been one of the nicest things they owned.

"Oh, Bastian," she said upon seeing him, "off to practice, dear? I'd have thought you would be there by now."

"Had a late start this morning," he told her as they walked together down the hall. I held my breath as they passed by us, but thanks to Alex they had no idea we were only a few feet away.

"Just make sure you're back in time for the luncheon in the library this afternoon."

"I won't be more than an hour," he assured her.

"All right," she smiled, leaning over and pecking his cheek as they reached the main hall.

They were about to part ways when Bastian looked down into his bag. "Damn..." he mumbled rummaging through his things, "I've got to run back to my room, I've forgotten my gloves. I'll see you at lunch."

"Of course dear, enjoy your practice," Alva called to him before turning the corner and disappearing down the hall.

As Bastian jogged back toward his room, a cast message coalesced in the air in front of me. "*A lunch date and missing gloves. I'm not sure we really have the hang of this "gathering intel" thing.*"

I frowned in agreement, but before I could let discouragement get the best of me, I noticed something odd. Bastian had reached his room... and stopped. He didn't go in or even pull out his key, but instead made a show of adjusting the strap of his bag, trying to hide the fact that he was checking the hallway to make sure no one else was around. After a second quick survey of the hall – and of course oblivious to Alex and I – he lowered his head and walked quickly past his door and up the hall, all the way to the small flight of stairs at the far end. Alex and I both jumped up and followed after him, while I concentrated on the distinct feel of his ability in my mind, singling it out from the dozens of others in the manor and locking onto it, determined not to lose him.

We slipped up to the second floor and continued to follow Bastian through a maze of hallways, moving both as quickly and silently as we could. Finally, Bastian stopped in front of an average looking door in the middle of a long stretch of hall, glancing around once more before opening it and ducking inside.

I was about to make a dive for the door when Alex stopped me. "*No!*" he cast, grabbing my arm and pulling me back just in time for the door to shut in my face.

"I could have made it!"

"But I wouldn't have, and without me, you have no cover, remember? I can't hide you if I can't see you."

"Right," I sighed, carefully stepping back over to the door. Praying that the ancient wood wouldn't creak or groan, I leaned in to listen, propping myself up against the door frame.

The room was silent for a second, then I heard his gym bag unzip and something pulled from it and set down with a soft thud. Then there was more silence... a click... silence...a beep... more silence... then finally a steady stream of tick-tick-ticking that became the distinct sound of fingers on a keyboard.

"What do you hear?" Alex breathed, clearly anxious.

"I'm not sure," I whispered, "but whatever it is... it's definitely not fencing."

CHAPTER 12

"How can you not be convinced?" I said, as loud as a whisper would allow, as Alex and I navigated our way around the second level of the far wing, trying to find a staircase it was safe to be seen coming down. "We caught him in the act!"

"We caught him in the act of lying to his mother. That might not do much for his character, but it doesn't prove he's doing anything wrong."

"What about that one?" I nodded toward the staircase we approached, momentarily ignoring his hole-poking with an irritated sigh.

"I'll check."

He jogged down the stairs while I crossed my arms and leaned against the rail, waiting for the all clear. Alex and I had to part ways as soon as we got back downstairs so he could go and check in with Cormack for an update. That meant that when we got back down to the guestroom level, he wouldn't be able to keep me hidden, and since we were fairly certain that we weren't allowed to be on this floor, he'd been invisibly checking each stairwell we came across, looking for one I could use without being caught.

"I think we're good," Alex said, walking back up. "No one down there, plus I think we are near your room. You should be fine."

I walked down to the first landing to meet him, my arms still crossed, pouting. "This sucks."

"Come on, Leannán, don't be mad," he hooked an arm around my waist and pulled me into his side. "It was a good start. I mean, did you really expect to get all the proof you needed in one shot?"

I scowled at the floor as we stepped off the last stair and into an empty hallway. "I don't know, maybe…"

"What did you want him to do? Sneak off to some secret lair with a sign on the door: 'Bad Guys Only, Mwa-ha-ha'?"

He looked down at me with a smile. "I really hate it when you do that," I said, grinning against my will.

"I know," he said, leaning forward and kissing my cheek, "it's great."

He jumped back with a laugh as I took a swing at his arm. "Get out of here," I said with a playful growl, "you're late."

"I know," he agreed, checking his watch. "Promise you won't do any more spying without me?"

"Yeah, yeah."

"I'm serious, Becca. I can tell you're thinking about it, and it's too dangerous."

"I know that. I won't try anything, I promise," I said, though I was mildly annoyed he could read me so well. "Now go."

A kiss and a wink later, Alex left to meet with Cormac while I headed off in the opposite direction toward my room, trying to piece together a new plan. However, apparently I was thinking a little too hard, as I rounded the upcoming bend without looking and ran right into a startled young man carrying a stack of books.

"Steven!" I said, reaching out to catch him as he stumbled backward. "Sorry about that, I wasn't watching where I was going," – *because I was too busy plotting against your brother* – "but I'm so glad to see you."

"M-miss Cl-lavish," he nodded, looking down.

"It's Becca," I corrected, smiling when he brought his eyes back up. "Look, I just wanted to say I'm sorry for last night. I hope I didn't get you into any trouble," – *ridiculous as that still was* – "I didn't mean to. I didn't realize that it was... even a possibility."

He didn't respond at first, though I was shocked and relieved to see that for the first time since we'd met, he didn't look as though he was about to bolt away from me like a jumpy rabbit. "Do-on't worry," he said with a timid smile, "it w-was nothing."

"Honestly, I just wanted to hang out with you. This," I gestured around us, "isn't exactly the sort of thing I'm used to. Everyone here is so," I paused, deciding I should be nice as several of them were still his family, "different. You were the first normal person I'd met, and I guess I just got a little excited."

He laughed, though his face was sad. "P-people don't us-sually describe me as n-normal."

"Yeah, well they're idiots." *Damn!* That one slipped out before I could catch it, but luckily, he smiled.

Turning to face the way I was originally headed, he motioned for me to continue and the two of us began to walk slowly down the hall. "And don't w-worry about all th-this," he glanced around. "It takes s-some getting u-used to."

"Not sure I have the patience for that. Things are a little more... low key where I'm from. I didn't fully realize it before this, but turns out I like it better that way."

"How l-long are y-you staying?"

"We were supposed to be here through tomorrow, but now it looks like it may be a bit longer. Actually," I said, deciding to take a leap, "there might be something you can help me with. Is there any chance you knew a man named Ciaran Shea?" As soon as I'd finished the question a small knot formed in my stomach. Jocelyn had made it clear that he wanted to keep our digging into Ciaran under wraps, but if no one asked any questions, how were we going to learn anything? Asking a guy who'd lived around these people his whole like seemed like a much better way to get information than leafing through a bunch of old books any day, and besides, who was he going to tell? Everyone around here avoided him like a spilled drink on the floor, no way were they going to listen to him attempt to spread rumors.

"The S-Seer?" he asked. "Yes I kn-new him, but not w-well. Why?"

See, maybe there was something he could tell us. At least it was worth a try. "OK," I said, lowering my voice, "I'm going to level with you. The main reason we came out here was so that we could talk to him. It's kind of a long story, but basically, we found out that someone we trusted was betraying us, and that he was in some way connected to Ciaran, but we don't know how. We were going to confront Ciaran about it, but then last night we find out that he's dead, so at the moment we're kind of at a loss. Is there anything you could tell me about him that might be of interest to someone? Something that maybe could have gotten him into trouble, or would have given someone cause to seek him out?"

He thought for a moment then shook his head. "No, no-othing that c-comes to mind. But I o-only met him o-once a l-long time ago. S-sorry."

"It's OK," I said, a little deflated, "it was a long shot anyway."

Then something lit in his eyes. "It wouldn't b-be his j-journal, would it? Ha-ave you lo-oked into that?"

"What journal?"

"He k-kept a journal with a-all his pr-rophecies in it. M-most Seers do. I r-remember because he di-idn't have any f-family when he died, so my p-parents had t-to oversee his will. In it he a-asked for the jou-urnal to be destroyed, but n-no one could ever f-find it. They as-ssumed he'd des-stroyed himself when he g-got sick."

"A book with all his predictions in it?" Any number of people could have wanted that, including Taron or Darragh. "And no one knows what happened to it?"

"N-not that I know of."

"Steven," I beamed, overjoyed to have actually found out something useful. "You are amazing, thank you so much!"

"H-happy to help," he smiled shyly.

"You've done more than help, you may have just saved our trip! Though," I paused as a twinge of guilt hit me, "there is one more thing, if you don't mind… could you not let anyone know that I asked you about Ciaran?" I hated to ask him as he didn't seem like someone who would be OK with lying – or any good at it for that matter – but I knew I had to at least ask.

I was relieved to see he appeared to only be confused and not upset. "Why?"

"We think there might be people who don't want anyone looking into him, so we are trying to keep it all on the down low for now."

He nodded without hesitation. "I w-won't tell. Just pr-romise to tell me if you f-find anything," he said, with a spark of excitement in his eyes, obviously enjoying the intrigue.

"Absolutely."

As we continued down the hall, I wondered if I could ask him about Bastian and the whole Brian Connor thing, but decided that was going too far. Jerk or no, Bastian was still his brother after all, and I didn't want to do anything that would upset him when we'd finally become friends. "Hey," I said, as we neared the end of the hall, "my room is just down the way, do you want to come back with me? We could hang out for a while and then order lunch to the room."

"I d-don't know," he said, tension beginning to tighten his frame, "I should g-go back and g-get my b-books."

I nodded with a smile, noting how much more pronounced his stutter was when he was nervous. "Yeah, that's fine," said casually, hoping to help him relax, "I just–"

"Steven!" came a sudden bellow down the hall. "What are you doing out here?"

Both our heads snapped to the right where Bastian was storming our way like a charging bull, hands fisted and eyes blazing. He was still wearing his white fencing outfit, though had lost his gym bag and helmet, and was clearly not at all pleased with finding Steven and I together.

"You were told not to leave your room," he scolded, his voice growing softer as he approached while his tone remained just as fierce. "Get back to your suite," he ordered, completely ignoring me, "and stay there until Mother comes for you this afternoon."

"Hey!" I snapped, stepping in between them. "Don't you talk to him like that! He is walking with me because I asked him to, and what we do is none of your damn business!"

Bastian glared down at me like a bear would an unarmed hunter, but I met him toe to toe, unwilling to so much as flinch under his eyes. After a long moment he looked over my shoulder to Steven, jerking his head to the right in a silent command. Obeying, Steven took off quickly back up the hall before I even had a chance to say goodbye.

"What the hell is your problem?" I growled at him the moment Steven was out of sight.

"Trust me," he huffed haughtily, though the fire didn't quite leave his eyes. "I've done you a favor. He's not the sort of person you want to be seen with."

I lost it. "Don't tell me who I want to be seen with, I'll talk to whomever I want! And don't you ever treat him like that in front of me again, or you'll spend the next few days as the one who doesn't want to be seen as you nurse a black eye!"

"Clearly you don't understand the way things work around here."

"I understand perfectly well, thank you, I just don't care! I don't care what you all think about him, and I don't care what you think about me. The only thing I care about is the fact that he is the only person I've met at this pretentious festival of bullshit that can put two words together without spewing either a load of pompous drivel or," I gave him an exaggerated onceover, "blatant lies!"

"Yes, well I suppose lies would abound when you spend your days inventing plots and making wild accusations."

"I'm sorry, what accusations were those? The ones where you're a liar, or the ones where you spent six months spying on my family?"

"I," he looked down his nose at me, "am not now nor have I ever been a liar. And as to the rest, I won't even justify the notion with a response." With a lift of his chin, he turned to go, but unfortunately, I wasn't about to let him have the last word. I had ammo and it was time to use it.

I crossed my arms, cocked, and fired. "Did you have a nice workout?"

"Excuse me?" His tone was almost bored, but something flashed in his eyes.

"Your workout," I gestured to his outfit. "Fencing, yes?"

"Very good."

"Looks like you worked up quite a sweat," I said, eyeing his dry and perfectly coifed hair. "But then I guess sitting at a computer can do that to a guy."

Any traces of aloof detachment remaining in his expression were gone in a blink, and before I'd even realized he'd moved, he was an inch from my face with a flare of malice in his eyes like I'd never seen before. Not going to lie, for a minute… I was scared.

"You followed me?" he breathed, his locked jaw quivering under the strain of his clenched teeth.

"I happened to see you," I shrugged, managing to call back some of my bravado.

"You *happened* to be on a restricted floor?"

"I got lost."

He ground his teeth and took a step back. "You had no right…"

"No," I countered, "I think I had every right to follow you and snoop into your life. I think they call that comeuppance."

"What in God's name do you want from me?"

"I want you to admit you were in Pennsylvania two years ago. I want you to tell me who sent you and what you told them about us. I want you to stop treating me like an idiot and admit I am right! I know you think you are so sly and that no one is ever going to figure it out, but I saw you panic last night when I asked you to dance. You were able to catch it before anyone else saw, but we both know what it was. Why can't you just admit it?"

For the first time he hesitated before answering, as something strange bubbled under the anger in his eyes. Indecision? Fear? Guilt? I wasn't sure what to call it, but what I did know was that it was vulnerable, which was an emotion that, until that moment, I wouldn't have believed him capable of. That is, if I'd really seen it, because a moment later it was gone, the icy glare back in its place.

"I can't admit to being in the States, because it didn't happen," he said flatly, his snooty cocked brow back in place. "I didn't tell anyone anything about you because I don't know anything about you worth telling, nor do I find myself inclined to learn more. And the so-called 'panic' you saw in me last night, was not panic but irritation, and was due entirely to the fact that I have no desire to marry you."

"What? *Marry me?*" Did he seriously just say that?

"I assure you, the idea was in no way my own."

"Are you serious with this," I asked, ignoring the blatant insult, "or are you just trying to distract me?"

"I am quite serious. I find it hard to believe that you haven't seen her intent, but perhaps you don't know what to look for. However, if my mother hasn't yet mentioned it to you, I can guarantee you she has mentioned it to your father."

Was he for real? I mean, sure, Jocelyn had said that as his daughter, I'd generally be considered a good catch, and that Alva would likely try to set up Bastian and I, but he hadn't said anything about her specifically talking to him about it. Looked like he and I would need to have a chat later...

"As you may or may not know," Bastian continued, "marriage for members of our company is quite different from what I would suppose you are accustomed to."

"Yeah, so I've heard."

"My mother has made no secret of the fact that she wishes to see our lines joined, and thanks to your attending this week, she believes this to be the perfect opportunity to make that happen. As I have no desire for such a union with you, I decided the best way to avoid the matter was by avoiding you – an effort ruined by your request for a dance. The last thing I needed was you showing an interest in me and adding fuel to an already well-stoked fire, hence my 'panic.'"

"Please," I scoffed. "*Interest* in you? Don't flatter yourself. I wanted information, not a date." Though I had to admit, I really hated how much sense his story was making.

"Well, I can assure you that was not how the rest of the room saw it. From what I have heard, most expect that our engagement will be announced before the end of your stay here."

"Over my dead body."

"Indeed," he agreed, with a grimace I didn't appreciate.

Much as I was annoyed at the turn the conversation had taken, I knew I had to circle back to the topic. Marriage plot aside, it didn't change his face in my memory or what I knew in my gut to be true, which was that he was playing me.

"And how do I know you aren't just making all this up to throw me off?" I asked, wishing I could have said it with a bit more conviction.

A slimy grin tugged his mouth. "Well, I suppose that could be true. I am a liar, after all, isn't that right?"

"Not exactly a denial," I said, ready to go for broke, "but that's fine. If you don't want to tell me what you are up to, I'm sure your mother will."

I held my breath as his eyes narrowed to slits. "Are you *threatening* me?"

"Sounds that way."

We stood in a frozen standoff as the tension hung over us like icicles in a cave, ready to fall on us at the slightest vibration. Finally, Bastian lifted his head looking much calmer than I would have liked.

"Fine," he said, relaxing his shoulders. "If that is the way you want to proceed, be my guest. Tell my mother; tell anyone you would like. But just know that I will be there right behind you, and after they are finished hearing what you have to say… they will hear what *I* have to say." Pausing, he reached out toward the side of my neck and gently took the chain of my Sciath between his fingers, shifting it slightly so that the clasp was once again in the back, hidden under my hair. "And I think we both know that you are a *far* more interesting subject."

Before I could catch my breath to reply, he turned and walked up the hall, leaving me standing in a stupor.

So much for not knowing anything worth telling…

Chapter 13

ASS! Lying, shady, pompous, two-faced, stuck up, self-righteous ass!
With more vehemently evil thoughts than I had ever harbored against a single person, I stormed through the halls of the manor toward Jocelyn's room. Between spying, talking to Steven, then arguing with Bastian, the last half hour of my life had been the definition of an emotional rollercoaster, but luckily I'd come out of it with information that may actually help us, so I figured the best thing to do was focus my raging energy on sharing what I'd learned.

When I didn't find Jocelyn in his room, I checked in Cormac's and Alex's, but they were both empty as well. I started making my way around the manor, moving from activity to activity, trying to find someone I could unload my information – and pent up frustration – on, but I wasn't having much luck. They weren't having drinks in the main receiving room; they weren't at the lawn bowling tournament; nor were they in the library, the game room, or any of the half a dozen parlors and mingling rooms scattered around the premises. I was about to give up and go back to my room to fume in private, when I passed by the door to an outside patio where there were a few dozen people gathered having drinks and hors d'oeuvres.

I quickly scanned the crowd and found Jocelyn standing with a small group of men not far from the door. Taking a deep breath and collecting myself, I stepped out onto the patio and over to where Jocelyn stood, quietly taking a place just behind his elbow and waiting to be noticed.

"Becca," he said surprised, turning when he saw the other men in his group look my way. "I didn't expect to see you here. Gentlemen," he ushered me forward, "allow me to introduce my daughter, Rebecca. Becca, this is Mr Callaghan, Mr Ryan, and Mr Doyle."

"Pleasure to meet you, Miss Clavish," Mr Callaghan said, as I shook their hands one at a time. "I have been hearing quite a bit about you. It is wonderful you could join us this year."

"Thank you," I smiled, actually caught off guard by his sincerity and overall lack of pride. "I'm happy to be here."

"Keeping your old man in line, I hope," Mr Ryan – apparently a kinetic and the only one with an ability I was able to recognize – said to me with a chuckle.

"I do my best," I smiled, playing along. Why did older people always have to ask things like that?

"I have a daughter, Shannon, who is about your age, Becca," Mr Callaghan said. "I'll have to be sure to introduce you while you're here."

Shannon's dad. Immediately my stomach flipped and I fought the sudden urge to shrink back behind Jocelyn. He certainly looked the part – tall, with dark eyes and brown shoulder-length hair that had more body and style than most women I knew, yet somehow he still managed masculine. What had Shannon and her harpy mother told him about me? He had said that he'd been hearing quite a bit about me. Did he mock me behind my back too, like the rest of his obnoxious family? Would he tell them he'd met me? What would they say?

Dear God, when did I become so insecure?

Damn it, I refused to be this person. I was not going to let some chick I'd never even met intimidate me like a dog barking at a squirrel. Enough was enough.

With as friendly a smile as I had, I nodded. "That would be nice, thank you."

"Weren't the younger folk headed to the stables for an outing today?" Mr Doyle asked, glancing to Mr Callaghan.

"Yes, they are there now, I believe. You didn't want to go riding, Becca?"

"I didn't realize they were going," I said truthfully, "though it's probably for the best. I don't think anyone is in the mood for a trip to the hospital."

As the men chuckled at my lame joke, Jocelyn turned to face me. "I'm glad you happened by, I was about to come and find you. We need to get going."

"We do?"

"Gentlemen," he said looking back to the men, "it's been wonderful catching up, but we have an appointment to keep. I will see you all on the course tomorrow?"

"Indeed, and prepare to be shamed," Mr Callaghan laughed, ribbing the man next to him. "It was a pleasure, Miss Clavish," he added, bowing slightly.

"Miss Clavish," the other two nodded in turn.

"Nice to meet you," I said, then followed Jocelyn back into the manor. I waited until we reached a patch of empty hall before leaning in and telling him my news. "I found something."

He stopped suddenly and looked down at me. "What do you mean?"

"About Ciaran. He kept a book that he wrote all his prophecies and stuff in, like a journal or something. Brassal and Alva were in charge of executing his will, and apparently in it, Ciaran asked that the journal be burned when he died, but no one could ever find it. I bet that's what Taron wanted."

I looked up eagerly awaiting his reaction, but if I'd expected his excitement to match my own, I was sorely mistaken.

"How did you come to find out about this?" he demanded, his eyes critical.

What the hell, he was mad at me?

"I... asked a friend."

"You what? What friend?"

"Steven."

"You spoke to Steven about this?"

Clearly he wasn't happy, but what I couldn't figure out was why. "Yes," I said, feeling slightly defensive, "what's the problem? He's not going to say anything, and I found something out, didn't I? Isn't that what we were supposed to do?"

"That is what Cormac was supposed to do. You were to wait until I spoke to Brassal about getting the books from the archives. Didn't you hear a word I said this morning?"

"No one even talks to the poor kid, who's he going to tell?"

"That's not the point!" he scolded. "If you are going to take part in things like this with us, you can't take matters into your own hands..." He sighed and closed his eyes for a moment. "We'll discuss this later. Right now there is a more pressing mater to be dealt with."

Yeah, the fact that Bastian knows about me and the Iris?

Though given his reaction to finding out I'd talked to Steven, I figured I should hold off on telling him about that until later.

"Cormac was able to find out where Shea is buried," he continued, "but, in doing so, he also discovered that someone else has been asking after Shea lately, specifically where he was laid to rest. Any family or friends Shea may have had would not have needed to ask for his location, which leads me to believe–"

"That someone else is going to try to read him?"

"Or try to tamper with what memories are left," Jocelyn nodded. "I'd hoped to avoid a reading, but if someone else is interested in Shea, we need to get to him before they do. Cormac, Alex, and I are going to the cemetery now. If we are lucky, the other person would not have had the chance to visit the site yet."

"But if they have how will we know?"

"I will be able to tell. We should be leaving within the hour," he said stopping at the hallway leading to his room. "You go back to your room and stay there until we return. If anyone asks, we went for a tour of the countryside, but you were not feeling up to joining us."

"Wait, what?"

"We'll come for you when we get back and–"

"No, I want to come." No way was I getting left out. "Please? I won't get in the way or anything…"

"You should stay here, Becca."

"But why? Cormac and Alex will be there, won't they?"

"Cormac knows where to go, and we may need Alex to cover us."

Was he really going to shut me out after one little mistake? "Is it because I told Steven stuff I shouldn't have? Look, I'm sorry, I didn't mean–"

He cut me off, his expression slightly uneasy. "It's not that, Becca, it's… This isn't something…" He paused, glancing away, then finally said, "You don't need to see this."

I saw a shadow in his features as he looked out the window across the hall and suddenly I felt guilty. Here I was, getting offended and angry for being left out when he was only trying to keep me from a potentially disturbing situation. I wasn't sure what specifically he was worried about, but whatever it was, he needed to know that I could handle it. Yeah it was weird, and yeah, I was more than a little creeped out by the idea, but if I wanted to be a part of the Order, then I needed to show him I could handle whatever situations arose, and didn't need to be sheltered or protected when things got difficult.

I waited quietly for him to turn back to me before asking one last time. "Please," I said again, gently this time and meeting his eyes. "I want to go. I'll be fine, I promise."

He took a long breath before finally nodding. "All right," he said, though he still didn't sound thrilled with the idea. "Go and get your coat and meet us in the lobby in twenty minutes. The car will be waiting."

"How long will it take to get there?" I asked as we pulled out of the manor drive and onto the road.

"Shouldn't be more than a half hour or so, I'd guess," Cormac said. "I just hope we will have the place to ourselves, and not run into any other visitors."

"That's why we brought Alex," Jocelyn said.

"Yes, but it would be easier to not have to worry about hiding. Though I'm actually quite looking forward to seeing the place," he mused aloud as he skimmed over the list of directions in his hand. "I hear it's quite lovely."

"Lovely?" I echoed.

"Well, you know…" he glanced back at me from the passenger seat, "as cemeteries go. It was established by the Bhunaidh more than four centuries ago, and I'm told they have always made sure it was well cared for."

"So only Bhunaidhs are buried there?" Alex asked from next to me in the back seat.

"Oh yes," Cormac nodded.

Well sure, if they can't bear to intermingle with regular people when they are alive, why would they want to in death…?

Keeping my more bitter thoughts to myself, I sat quietly trying to enjoy the drive, when I suddenly realized just how quiet it really was. Maybe it was the gentle hum of the car, or the wide open spaces rushing past us outside the window, but suddenly I felt an overwhelming sense of calm that seemed to grow by the minute. It was almost like my insides were taking a deep breath.

Then it hit me. It wasn't the car that was quiet – it was my mind. For the first time since arriving at the manor, I wasn't surrounded by hordes of Holders, each one with an ability fighting for recognition in my mind. I'd grown used to it after the first few hours, but I'd also forgotten what it felt like to be alone – or relatively alone, anyway.

Relishing in my newfound peace, I sighed almost involuntarily as I rested my head back on the seat of the car and gazed lazily up at the roof.

"You OK over there?" Alex asked, eyeing me with a grin.

"It's so quiet," I told him with a drowsy smile.

His eyebrows pulled together slightly, but eased into a smile as he realized what I meant. "Nice to be away from the masses?" he said, sliding his hand underneath mine and lacing our fingers together.

"Mmmhmm," I hummed, giving his palm a squeeze.

I sat for a while letting my brain enjoy the solace, however the less cluttered my mind became, the more it was able to focus on the question I'd been wondering about ever since Jocelyn had told me what we were on our way to do.

"So…" I said hesitantly, hoping I wasn't about to make things awkward. "Mind if I ask how this works, exactly?"

"How what works, dear?" Cormac asked

"The whole reading Ciaran thing. Doesn't seem like it would even be possible given his… you know… condition."

"It's not exactly a reading," Jocelyn answered. "A true reading is scanning thoughts and memories. When a person dies, obviously they are no longer able to think, so thoughts would be out of the question. However, just because a person's mind ceases to function doesn't mean their memories are lost."

"It doesn't? Kind of seems like it should," I said.

"The mind and saol of a person are very closely knit," Cormac explained. "Experiences become memories, memories can alter feelings, emotions grow from those feelings, which inspire new experiences, on and on throughout the span of our lives. All of those feelings, thoughts, emotions, and memories are each a different facet of your essential being – your saol. They coexist together within you, playing and building on one another and making you who you are. Now your saol is also, of course, your life energy, which is extinguished upon your death, but even when gone, its shadow remains on and in your body like a fingerprint, marking you. That fingerprint is made of everything your saol contained: your memories, your ability, your personality… all of it. The downfall is that this fingerprint is literally on the body itself, so over time when that begins to disappear, any information it may have stored is lost."

This had to be the most interestingly macabre thing I'd ever heard. "So then, if I am understanding this, you could read a dead person too, right? Read him and see what his ability was?"

"In theory, yes," Cormac said, "though I am nowhere near powerful enough to do it myself, few are. In fact other than Jocelyn, I've never heard of anyone able to successfully read people who have passed."

"Yes," Jocelyn sighed, "but I have never attempted it on anyone who was more than a few months gone, and even then there was precious little to work with. After three years I don't hold out much hope."

"Well, the most recent memories should be the strongest," Cormac said, patting his arm supportively. "Let's just hope that whatever we wish to learn happened within the final few months of his life."

After that, no one said anymore, which was fine by me as I'd hit my freaky limit for one afternoon. We rode quietly for a while until Cormac's light snoring broke the silence, and I decided to follow his lead. I laid down against Alex's chest – who also looked as though he was about to nod off – and felt his arm come up around me before sliding off into a peaceful sleep.

Sadly the peace didn't last long, as a short time later I woke up to the subtle but undeniable feel of abilities gently nudging at my own. As I felt the car turn into a parking spot and shut off, I realized that we'd arrived, while the nearby abilities told me that Cormac had been right: we were going to have company.

Alex stretched underneath me and sat up taking me with him, giving the top of my head a kiss as he went. "Looks like we're here," he said, turning to face forward as he stretched out his back again.

I popped the door open and climbed out, taking my first look at the towering wrought iron entry way of the cemetery and being immediately impressed. And OK... a little scared. I mean, the thing was straight out of a gothic novel, and cool as it was, I also wasn't ashamed to admit that I was happy we'd come during the day.

I gazed out over the rows of intricately carved headstones, and while I didn't see anyone else in the cemetery itself – which I'd expected as the abilities I sensed were too muted to be coming from so close – I also didn't see anything or anyone even remotely nearby.

"Is there anything else around here?" I asked Cormac as he stepped out of the car.

"No dear, not for miles."

"That's weird," I mumbled to myself, looking out over the open fields, doing my own perimeter check. I could feel abilities other than Jocelyn, Cormac, and Alex, but if the only other Holders were miles away, I shouldn't have been able to feel them at all, at least not without the Iris. The abilities I was sensing were muted to be sure, but they were still strong enough for me to feel, so where were they coming from? There was no one else around as far as the eye could see. At least no one... alive...

Oh God...

My head snapped back toward the headstones as my mind replayed our conversation from the car.

Saols left fingerprints on the dead.

Prints that faded over time.

Prints made of memories... and personalities...

...and abilities. *Oh God...*

CHAPTER 14

It was them – the dead people. I was sensing the abilities of the dead.

"Oh God," I breathed, stumbling backwards until I hit the car. "Oh God, oh God…"

"What's wrong?" Alex asked, rushing over as I pressed my palms to my forehead.

"Oh my," Cormac said, putting a hand on my back. "You can feel them, can't you, dear?"

I nodded without looking up, worried what might come out of my mouth if I opened it. I wanted to keep it together, but the feel of decaying abilities swirled around me, clinging like spider webs as I tried to swat them away. Their eerie echoes wafted through my mind like ghosts, turning my blood to ice water in my veins.

With my eyes squeezed shut I did my best to maintain control, until I felt a pair of hands gently but firmly take hold of my shoulders. "Becca," I heard Jocelyn call over the chill in my head. "Becca, look at me." I lowered my hands and looked up, hoping he didn't notice how much they were shaking. "Listen to me," he said softly, "I want you to forget about everything else you feel, and focus on the three of us. Concentrate on our abilities and let the rest fall into the background."

I did what he said, directing all my attention to his, Cormac's, and Alex's presences in my mind. They were clear, bright, and strong, but more than anything they were familiar. Next to their vivid glow, the rest of the brushes on my mind were muted and dull, like flashlights glowing under a blanket. Keeping my concentration on the living, I opened my eyes slowly, letting my focus calm me and ease the anxiety crawling across my skin.

"I know it's difficult," he continued, the empathy thick in his voice, "but what you are sensing from the others... you can't think of them as abilities. Their true abilities died with them, just as their thoughts and memories did. You are only feeling the shadows that those things left behind for us to find. Think of them as diaries these people might have kept or letters they may have written – they were made by them and left behind; they are not a part of them."

I let his words resonate, allowing them to relax my heart rate as they sank in. Somehow he'd known exactly what to say, and as I finally regained control of myself and pushed the echoes safely to the background of my thoughts, I don't think I'd ever been more grateful. But then I suppose it shouldn't have come as a surprise. The empathy in his eyes as he spoke had told me that he knew the fear and panic I was feeling all too well, and I couldn't help but wonder why. He'd been alive over two hundred years, God only knows the things he'd been through in all that time. He'd said that he fought in the First World War; had he struggled to ignore the thoughts of the dying on the battlefield? How many cries for help had he been forced to hear without being able to answer? Had there been someone there to help him when it all got to be too much? Again I realized just how little I knew about him, but for the first time I found myself truly wanting to learn more.

But now was obviously not the time, so instead I met his eyes with the barest of smiles. "Thank you," I breathed, happy to have my feet solidly back under me.

He nodded before releasing me and stepping back, but still looked wary. "Stay with her," he said, glancing at Alex who was back at my side a moment later.

"No," I protested, as Jocelyn turned to leave without him. "You need him with you. What if someone comes?"

"I can hide them from here," Alex said.

"Not as easily. I'm fine now, really. We can all go together," I said, straightening my shoulders. "I mean it, I'll be fine."

They all looked hesitant, but I kept my head high and hoped they would buy my confidence, only a portion of which was hyperbole. I'd been the one who insisted on coming out here with them in the first place so I could prove that I was capable and didn't need to be handled with kiddie gloves when things got rough, and that was still what I intended to do. Admittedly it hadn't gone well thus far, but in my defense the whole "sensing the dead" thing was a twist I hadn't seen coming. But minor freak-out aside, the outing wasn't over yet, which meant there was still time for me to buck up and save face.

After a long moment, Jocelyn finally agreed. "All right," he said, looking me over once more then shooting Alex a blatant "keep an eye on her" glance. "Let's go."

We walked through the gates and into the perfectly manicured yard, following Cormac toward the section of plots that Ciaran was supposedly in. As we passed by headstone after headstone, I noticed that they were all very similar to one another, while at the same time very different from anything I'd ever seen before. They were very tall – most looked to be over five feet – with large, amazingly detailed Celtic crosses making up the top portion of the stone. Each cross was ornately carved with knot work and other Celtic and religious symbols, all fashioned in the same ancient style, so that they coordinated perfectly with one another while each one still remaining entirely unique.

However, beyond the intricate gothic stonework, there was something else that stood out about the gravestones, which was the lettering on their faces. The first line of text was the person's name, as would be expected. But beneath that, where you would normally find the years of birth and death and maybe a denotation from surviving loved ones, like "Beloved Husband" or "Honored Father," there was only one single word on each of the stones, written in Gaelic.

"What are those?" I asked Alex as we fell slightly behind Jocelyn and Cormac. "The words under each of their names on the markers?"

"Their abilities."

"Ah." Guess I should have figured. If ability was the most important thing to these people in life, why not in death?

"Reader... Caster... Healer..." Alex began reading, nodding at each of the stones as we passed. "Reader... Kinetic... Discerner... Alchemist... Porter... Another Reader... Mentalist..."

"Wait," I asked, recognizing the word. "What is that? Someone called me that last night."

"Well sure, that is what they all think you are. A Mentalist is someone who can practice Mentalism. You know, like Jocelyn: mindreading, thought control, that sort of thing."

"Really? I've never heard him called that. I didn't even realize it had a name."

"Sure it does. Though," he admitted, "you probably wouldn't have heard Jocelyn called that, or at least not often. Most Mentalists are only able to manipulate one facet of the mind, but since Jocelyn has control over all the mental aspects, it kind of puts him in a league of his own. But Ryland is considered a Mentalist."

"And why aren't the years on the stones?" I asked as we continued up the path.

"To hide their ages. Holders are the only ones buried here, but that doesn't mean that they are the only ones who visit."

"Right," I nodded, having not considered that a cemetery filled with stones all claiming to belong to people hundreds of years old when they died might raise a few eyebrows. "I guess that's smart."

"It should be..." Cormac said, pausing up ahead and scanning the nearby headstones. "Ah, there," he pointed to a large stone at the end of the path.

It was one of the largest I'd seen in the whole cemetery, with a towering stone cross sitting atop the elaborately carved base stone, framed by two life-sized angel statues on either side like beautifully intimidating guardians. Their weatherworn faces held an unsettling expression that hovered between serene and menacing, while their wings were poised just shy of open as though they could spring to life and fly off at any moment. Even the path itself seemed to service only this one monument, turning abruptly at its foot then looping all the way around the plot before meeting back up with itself like a lasso. I leaned in as we approached the island of grass and read the script inlayed on the face of the headstone.

Ciaran Oengus Shea
Fáidh

"Wow," I whispered, admiring the grandeur of the scene. "He must have had a lot of money."

"Unlikely," Cormac said. "Bhunaidh like Ciaran who have no family at the time of death have their departing arrangements handled by the head family. When this sort of thing," he motioned to the monument, "is done, it usually denotes someone with either a high standing in Bhunaidh society, or, as I would wager is the case here, an extremely rare or exalted ability."

We all stood quietly at the edge of the path for a moment before Jocelyn sighed quietly and stepped up onto the grass. He took a knee a few feet from the headstone and bowed his head, staring unseeing at the grass in front of him, while Alex, Cormac, and I hung back on the path and waited.

And waited...

...and waited.

I had never actually seen a mind reading done, but as the minutes began to tick by, I started to wonder just how long something like this normally took. Did it always take a while, or was this one harder because the person he was reading was dead? Was he having trouble? Alex and Cormac didn't seem worried, so should I just relax and wait it out? Probably. Was it OK to lean against one of the nearby headstones when my legs started getting tired? Probably not.

Round about the ten minute mark, and just before I had a chance to really get antsy, the stiff tension in Jocelyn's form broke and his shoulders dropped.

"Anything?" Cormac asked.

Jocelyn shook his head, rubbing his eyes like he was massaging a headache. "No. Or at least nothing I can make out. There are fragments of something toward the end of his life, but there is so little it's like trying to reach out and grab smoke."

Cormac took a step toward him. "Could you see if anyone has been here before us? Was anything tampered with or changed at all?"

"No," Jocelyn answered, "there were no signs of anyone else even so much as having tried to read him. We are the first. Not that it's done us any good," he added with a frustrated scoff.

"Well," Cormac said, attempting to lighten the mood, "at least we tried. And now we can rest assured that no one else will be able to garner anything from Mr Shea, so all in all, not a wasted trip."

But Jocelyn wasn't ready to leave. "I want to give it one more go," he said, rubbing his hands over his face then turning back toward the grave.

Cormac frowned, walking up beside him. "Jocelyn, enough. You've done what you can, there is no need to give your mind a beating over it."

"No," Jocelyn snapped, "there is something there…" He paused sighing heavily, shame suddenly hanging on his brow. "I'm sorry," he said, "I didn't mean to–"

"It's nothing," Cormac cut him off quietly, clapping him gently on the arm with a smile, "it's nothing."

As I watched the simple exchange between the two men, I saw something in Jocelyn that I would never have thought I'd see. It was something I doubted that many others would have

even recognized, but I knew it the moment I saw it in his eyes –
because I had seen it so many times in my own.

It was burden.

It was the weight of being special. The pressure of knowing
that he was the second most powerful Holder on earth, and
the belief that as such he *should* have been able to do this, but
he couldn't. It was the fear of disappointing everyone who was
counting on him, worried that he might let us down.

Yeah, I knew all about that – I felt it every day. Jocelyn might
have been the second most powerful Holder, but if those damned
prophecies were true, then I was the first. I was the one who was
supposed to bring an end to Darragh, and save Holder kind,
and a bunch of other stuff I'd basically blocked out and buried.
But just because I'd gotten really good at ignoring my so-called
destiny, it didn't mean that it wasn't always there, hovering in
the back of my mind, sprinkling every one of my thoughts with
just the tiniest hint of fear and self-doubt. For the time being I
was able to fight it, but deep down I knew a day would come
where I wouldn't be able to beat it back anymore.

"We came all the way out here," Jocelyn continued. "I should
at least give it one more try."

With an encouraging nod, Cormac came back to join Alex and
I on the path while Jocelyn took a deep breath and reassumed his
position over the grave. I wanted to help, but there was nothing
I could do. He was the only one who could even attempt to do
a memory reading like this, and even if we could find someone
else, they wouldn't be as powerful as Jocelyn nor would we have
any idea whether or not we could actually trust them. If only
there was a way to add to Jocelyn's power and maybe... give
him a boost...

But maybe... Could I...?

Without taking the time to think it through, I gently reached
out toward Jocelyn's ability, melding it with my own. This
would normally be the point when I would be able to assume

the ability of the person I was connected to, but due to a block Min had placed on my scaith, I knew I wasn't going to be able to draw his ability into me… but could I push mine out to him?

I focused on the glow of Jocelyn's ability in my mind, but instead of pulling it toward me as I normally would, I began to funnel my own power into it as slowly and carefully as I could, feeling the two energies swirl together and change, like pouring red punch into lemonade. As I watched the globe of power grow, I got excited. Was it working? Had I really–

"*Gah!*" Jocelyn suddenly gasped, his whole body pitching forward as his hands fisted the grass.

Oh God, what had I done?

Immediately I broke all connection with him and stumbled backward, terrified he was hurt. "I'm sorry!"

"Oh my!" Cormac cried out, reaching for Jocelyn.

"I'm fine," Jocelyn assured him, breathless. "I'm fine. It was just all at once… there was so much…"

"What happened?" Alex asked, putting his arm around me as I stood motionless, my hands shaking.

"I'm sorry," I stammered again. "I didn't mean to… I'm… I'm sorry…"

Jocelyn looked up at me, still clutching the ground. "That…" he asked, attempting to catch his breath. "That was you?" I couldn't decide if the look in his eyes was shock, fear, or awe, but in any event I didn't like it.

"I'm sorry," I said, "I didn't mean to hurt you, I just… thought it might help…"

"It did," he said, squinting almost as if he was confused by his own words. He stood slowly, glancing at the grave then back to me. "Do it again."

"But," I motioned down to the patch of ground he occupied a second ago.

"It's all right."

"I don't want to hurt you."

His eyes softened as he shook his head. "It didn't hurt," he assured me, "it simply caught me off guard. I'll be ready this time."

Burrowing myself just a little deeper into Alex's side, I nodded, still unsure, but willing to trust Jocelyn's judgment. If he said he'd be able to handle it then we had to at least try. I should have been happy to finally get a chance to help, and part of me was. But there was a much larger part of me that was still reeling from seeing Jocelyn fall to the ground, not knowing what I might have done to him. No one had ever reacted so violently to anything I'd done with my ability, and the idea that I could actually hurt someone without even realizing it, wasn't one I enjoyed. Making a mental note to never do anything to anyone again without first asking permission, I took a deep breath and looked up. "OK."

Once again Jocelyn turned back toward Ciaran's grave, and once again I joined our abilities and began to slowly feed my strength into his, watching him closely for any signs of pain or distress. The moment our abilities melded, I did see a slight waver in his stance, but instead of sending him to his knees, it seemed to flow through him, easing the tightness in his muscles and relaxing the strain from his face. When he closed his eyes a few seconds later and a slight grin lit his face, it didn't look as though he was working at all.

"There are scattered partial memories," he began, "but only one full enough to read. It is from the last day of his life. It's a prophecy, something regarding his journal…"

The journal again. There had to be something to that thing…

"It looks as though this prophecy was his last one."

"That's probably why it's still so strong," Cormac mused quietly.

"But it is only a portion of it," Jocelyn said, his brow furrowing slightly. "The first line was written earlier in the day, but I can't make it out. This memory only contains the second half." He paused again while we waited anxiously. "*…can pierce the shroud…*" he dictated, finally needing to concentrate a bit,

"*…of my sight.*" I waited for more, but after that, he opened his eyes and stepped away from the grave.

"Wait, that's it?" That couldn't be it.

"That's all," he nodded, and I broke our connection.

"'Can pierce the shroud of my sight'; what does that even mean?" I asked.

"I don't know. We need the first half, but that portion of his memory is gone."

"And there was nothing in the memories that were left saying what it meant?"

"I could only see that he seemed to believe that it was in regard to his journal, but that was all."

"Hmm," Cormac hummed thoughtfully. "Odd for a Seer to know what a vision pertains to."

"What do you mean?" I asked

"Seers only receive messages, not their meanings. Unless it contains a specific reference, prophecies tend to be very vague and their wording cryptic."

"Yeah, I noticed," I grumbled.

Cormac turned to Jocelyn who joined us back on the path. "And there was nothing else? Perhaps earlier in his life?"

"Nothing discernible," he said shaking his head, "only fragments too small to read."

"Wait," I interjected, turning to Jocelyn. "You said that the first part of the prophecy had been written earlier that day? As in written down onto something? Was he writing the part that you saw?"

"Yes," he cocked an eyebrow at me. "There was a side table next to the bed he was in."

"Was the first part of the prophecy on that same page?"

"Possibly, but I'm not positive. He wasn't looking at the page while he was writing, so anything else on it wasn't a part of the memory."

"But he wrote it that day, and if that was the day he died, he probably didn't get out of that bed…" I tapered off, almost laughing at where my train of thought was taking me.

She was going to flip...

"What are you getting at?" Alex asked from my side.

"Don't you see?" I said. "Sounds to me like all we need is the room where he died... and a Time Walker."

CHAPTER 15

It only took about half the drive back to the manor to convince Jocelyn to bring Chloe out to be our Time Walker. He'd agreed that time walking back to Ciaran's last day and reading the prophecy for ourselves would be the best way to proceed, but getting him to see that Chloe was our best choice for our walker took a little convincing. However, with Alex and even Cormac on my side, it wasn't long before he saw that Chloe was truly the only option. There weren't any other walkers at Adare that we were certain we could trust, and although Chloe wasn't a powerful enough walker to be able to get what we needed on her own, if I was able to help her the way I had Jocelyn, she should have no problem getting us the remainder of the prophecy.

When we arrived back at the manor, Jocelyn went to call Mr Anderson and tell him that he would be bringing Chloe with him when he came out. After that, he and Cormac were due to meet with Brassal and a few of the other men for drinks and billiards in one of the lounges where they planned to try and find out where Ciaran might have spent his final days. They took Alex with them so that he could do some invisible poking of his own, while I, on the other hand, was off to nowhere, to do another round of nothing. Awesome.

I made my way back to my room, irritated that my bout of usefulness in the cemetery had been so short lived, and I realizing how tired I was getting of being the only one who never seemed to have a job to do other than take up space. Sure I was supposed to do "research," but until we actually got the books from the archives I couldn't even start that, and pretty much everything else I'd tried to do thus far – talk to Steven, spy on Bastian, and so on – had gotten me into trouble. But at least my room was safe, and actually, I was feeling a little worn out from the ordeal in the cemetery and could use a rest. But sadly, there was no rest to be had.

"Becca!" I heard Alva call just before I could make it into the hallway.

Great. "Hello," I smiled, turning to greet her.

"I'm so glad I caught you, dear," she said, coming up and placing a hand on my shoulder. "I was just on my way to your room."

"Oh?" No way this was headed anywhere good…

"Yes, I was coming to let you know that the reception tonight for all the young Holders has been moved from the terrace to the library."

"Reception?" Guess I should have read that itinerary I got at check in.

"Oh yes, it's a wonderful time. There will be food and music and all the younger members of our company will be there. You know, without all us old folk getting in the way," she winked, making what I assumed was a joke. "We will all be having dinner downstairs, so you will have the place to yourselves."

"We don't all have dinner together?" I asked. How was I going to get out of this if I didn't have Jocelyn or Cormac to use as an excuse?

"No, not tonight. The second night is always our social evening. The first night is the gala, then the social, then we will all be back together tomorrow night for dinner and the theater troupe performance."

"That sounds like fun." God help me.

"Wonderful!" she beamed. "And I will make sure to let Bastian know you will be there tonight so he doesn't miss you."

I tried not to cringe as her eyes twinkled mischievously. She really was trying to get Bastian and I together. I didn't know what pissed me off more: the idea that she was treating me like a broodmare for her prized stud, or the fact that she was actually lending credence to his cover story. Unable to fake the sort of response I knew she wanted, I simply did my best to smile, which seemed to be enough. She patted my arm once more before turning back the way she'd come, leaving me to resume the walk to my room.

When I finally got there, I kicked my shoes off and flopped onto my freshly made bed, trying to fight away the knot of dread already rolling around in my stomach. A room full of teenaged Holders, staring, whispering and judging me, with no Jocelyn to draw any of the attention away. Oh yeah, this was going to be great.

As I kicked back the covers and snuggled down into the mountain of pillows, I did my best to look on the bright side. After all, I would have Alex there with me to keep me company. Actually, it could be nice, the two of us together, no Jocelyn hanging over our shoulder. Of course we would still have to be careful, but at least we could be seen together without raising suspicion. It would simply be me, hanging out with the only other person there that I knew – nothing weird or suspicious about that. Hell, if we played our cards right, it might almost be like a date. And then maybe after the reception…

With a smile I dozed off, just maybe looking forward to the evening after all.

"What do you mean you're not coming?"

"I'm sorry, Leannán," Alex said as he adjusted his tie. "I wasn't invited to the youth reception, my invite is for the adult dinner."

I was beyond miffed. After my nap, I'd gotten all ready for the reception, fully believing that Alex and I would be going together. I'd come down to meet him so that we could walk up together, but instead of being in his own room I had found him in Jocelyn's, dressed and ready to go – just not with me.

"That's crap," I said. "You're not an adult."

Alex cocked his eyebrows. "Pardon?"

"You know what I mean," I rolled my eyes, "not an adult like them." I waved at Jocelyn and Cormac.

"The old men," Cormac chuckled as he checked his tie in the mirror.

"No," Alex said, "but I am twenty-two. They have to draw the line somewhere."

"Yeah, but you're close enough. Couldn't they have at least asked?"

"There was no need to ask," Jocelyn said, taking his sport coat off the hanger and sliding it on. "As far as anyone knows, Alex is here as my associate. They would have had no reason to think that he would have any interest in the reception for the younger members. The fact that they included him in the invitation at all is fortunate, so we are not about to complain."

"Well, there is no way I am going to this thing by myself," I said, fully prepared to spend the rest of the night in my room.

"Oh yes you are," Jocelyn said, straightening his cuffs. "Everyone here will either be up at the reception or at dinner with us, and you will not be the only person missing."

"No one will even notice," I insisted, though I could already tell I was yelling at a wall.

"We both know that is not true," he said, turning off the lamp, "and we also agreed that you would do everything you could not to draw undo attention to yourself, and hiding in your room will do exactly that."

"Fine," I sighed, realizing there was no way I was going to win this. "But I am leaving the second it becomes socially acceptable to do so."

"Which will not be before 9 o'clock," he added for me.

"*Nine?*" I whined, but was interrupted by Alex taking my shoulders and turning me around.

"Come on," he laughed, as he guided me toward the door. "Don't make it worse."

A few minutes later, after bidding the men a bitter farewell, I took to the stairs like a convict to the guillotine, each step slower than the last. Truth be told, I could have gotten out of it, but that would've meant that I would have had to tell Jocelyn the truth; that I was scared. Scared of having to deal with all the staring and whispering on my own. Scared that Shannon would be there talking about me to anyone who would listen. Scared that I would have to admit to myself that I wasn't as tough as I'd always thought I was. And I couldn't do that. I wanted Jocelyn to know that I could be relied on as an active member of the Order, and allowing him to find out that I was worried about idle gossip and catty bullies would not help my case. So off to the reception I went.

As I neared the library and began to see other Holders my age, I decided that if I had to spend the evening socializing, I might as well make the most of it. When I'd met Shannon's father that afternoon, I'd decided that I'd had enough of being intimidated by strangers, and I meant it. I was done hiding and ready to take this auburn haired bull by the horns and show her that I was not about to be daunted by anyone, especially not someone I thought as little of as her.

With my new plan driving me, I set my sights on the library keeping my chin held high, pretending not to notice all the eyes following me as I made my way up to the door. The long room hummed with voices as I made my way in, scanning the dozens of faces for my target. I spotted her about half way down the length of the room to my right. Here we go; this was it. I was going to walk up to her, introduce myself, and end this nonsense once and for all. Shannon Gallagher, prepare to be met.

Although... I did have to pass right by the drink table to get over to her... and I *was* really thirsty... Maybe I should grab a punch on my way...

Thirty minutes and two drinks later, I was standing at the end of the drink table hating myself. Why was this so damn hard? Was it because I missed out on the normal high school experience? Was that where you were supposed to learn all this stuff? I'd kept my eyes on her the whole time I'd stood at the bar, trying to figure out what the hell it was about her that got to me so much. Had it been Chloe, or Ryland, or anyone else in my shoes, I would have told them to rise above it and not to give her another thought. So then why did I constantly let her beat me? I mean, what was there to be afraid of? I hadn't even *met* her!

Finally something in me snapped. No more. I threw back the last of my punch, gathered up more bravado than I wanted to admit I needed, and walked across the room without so much as pausing to take a breath. Before I let myself change my mind, I stepped up to the small group that Shannon was talking with and introduced myself.

"Hello," I said, praying my voice wouldn't shake as they all turned toward me. "I hope I'm not interrupting, I just wanted to come and say hi. I'm Becca."

"Yes, of course," one of the girls to my right said. "It's lovely to finally meet you. I'm Aoife."

"Brennan," the boy next to her said, offering me his hand which I shook.

"I'm Kerra," the girl opposite me said, "and this is Miach," he motioned to the second of the two men who also offered me his hand.

"Pleasure," he said.

"And Shannon," Kerra added with an uncomfortable nod when it became clear that Shannon was not going to introduce herself.

"Yes," I said turning to Shannon, my courage growing. "It is nice to finally meet. I've heard a lot about you."

Shannon looked down at me, her smile somehow only adding to the contempt in her eyes. "Have you? How kind of you to say."

"How are you enjoying your time with us so far, Becca?" Miach asked after a strangely awkward pause.

"It's certainly been interesting," I said, going with the nice version of the truth.

"You grew up in the States, yes?" Kerra asked.

"Yes."

"How long have you been in Ireland?"

"Almost three months now."

"Quite a big change, was it?" Brennan asked.

"Not as big as I thought it would be."

The conversation continued pleasantly as I answered questions, surprised to find that they all seemed genuinely interested in what I had to say. Turned out that Aiofe had done a semester abroad in America studying at Harvard, and Brennan had been accepted for a semester at Columbia the following spring. It was turning out to be a far pleasanter conversation that I would have thought possible. The only problem was the fact that there was one member of our circle who was decidedly not participating.

"That reminds me," Kerra said, after Aiofe made a comment about enjoying some of the current American fashion trends, "your gown was stunning last night, Becca. Who was your designer?"

"Madame Loute."

"Oh, isn't she fabulous? She did the gown for my last birthday, I just loved it!" Kerra raved.

"And isn't her shop amazing?" Aiofe asked.

"Spectacular," Kerra agreed.

"I actually didn't get to see it," I said. "We didn't have much time, so she came out to St Brigid's to make mine."

"Wow," Kerra said. "I didn't know she would even do something like that."

"Becca," Shannon said suddenly, causing all of our eyes to fly in her direction. "I could do with a refill," she said, holding up an empty glass I hadn't even realized she'd been holding, "would you care to join me?"

"Sure," I said, noting how the other four decidedly turned away and began casually talking amongst themselves as though obeying some silent command. Did this chick seriously run the world, or was it all just a coincidence? I wasn't sure why, but somehow it didn't feel like the latter.

We walked silently together, stopping at the drink table so Shannon could fill her glass, then stepped off to the side and looked out over the room.

"This must be wonderful for you," she said after a taking a dainty sip of her punch. "All this attention."

"Actually, I don't really care for it," I said, trying not to let my sudden nerves show.

"Come now Becca," she chided, a snide edge to her tone, "false modesty may be better than none, but it still isn't very attractive. I think we both know that you are quite enjoying the spotlight. So much so that when it doesn't come to you on its own, you have to go and seek it out." She lifted her glass slightly and gestured with it toward her friends.

"I wasn't seeking anything," I said, mortified that I was actually blushing.

"Of course you were," she said taking another sip. "If not, you would have stayed over at the drink table where no one had even bothered to notice you."

"Well, it seems like someone took the time to notice me," I challenged, "or she wouldn't have known where I was standing."

She glared down at me, her face a perfect mask as her hazel eyes frosted over. "Yes, well it's always easy to spot the thing that doesn't belong."

"What is your problem?" I asked, beyond sick of her crap.

"That's simple; I don't tolerate mediocrity. And I certainly don't celebrate it. My friends may have been kind enough to humor you, but don't mistake cordiality for acceptance. Learn where you belong," she handed me her empty glass with the slighted jut of her chin as though I was nothing more than one of the staff, "and we'll get along fine."

With that, she turned on her heel and floated back over toward her friends, leaving me standing with her discarded glass while everyone around us pretended not to be watching out of the corners of their eyes. I set the cup down on the end of the drink table, straining to keep my face relaxed and casual as though nothing at all had happened – even though it was clear they all knew better.

Desperate to leave, but not willing to let them see me cower, I feigned an interest in the hors d'oeuvre table, which just so happened to be on the way to the door.

Don't walk too fast, they're watching. Keep smiling…

I scanned the selections thoughtfully, not actually seeing a single one.

Don't let your hands shake, they'll see. Keep smiling…

Pretending not to find anything that I wanted to try, I glanced over to where Shannon and the others were gathered, to see if any of them were looking at me.

Don't let them see you looking. Don't let your nostrils flare. Keep smiling, keep smiling…

When I was positive that none of them were looking, and that the majority of the people around me had lost interest and moved on to other entertainment, I took my opportunity and slid quickly through the door and out of the room, not stopping until I was down the hall, down the stairs, and around a corner, tucked into a small dark alcove in an unlit hallway, completely out of sight. Backing all the way against the alcove's high window, I stood there for I'm not sure how long, silently venting all the things I couldn't bring myself to say to her face.

Mediocre? I'll show you who's mediocre… And your friends were not humoring me, you cow! What's wrong, mad that they wanted to talk to me more than you? Gee I wonder way that could be… Oh! causeyou're an evil bitch!

I leaned back against the window and crossed my shaking arms, refusing to let the tears I felt stinging my eyes fall. It was bad enough I was hiding for the second time in two days, I was not about to add crying to the list of things I could be ashamed of having done this trip. But much as I hated running and hiding, there was no way I was going back up to that reception, 9 o'clock or no. Now the only thing to do was figure out how I could get back to my room from here without anyone seeing me.

However, just as I went to come out of my hiding nook, I heard the tap of footsteps in the adjacent hall coming my way. Having no desire to get caught hiding in a corner like scared cat, I stepped back against the window and slid behind the long velvet curtain, pulling myself completely into the shadows.

I held my breath as the silhouette of a man appeared, quickly turning the corner from the main hall into the one I occupied, ducking behind a stone pillar just across from where I stood. He hesitated there for a moment with his back pressed to the pillar and his head turned to the side, listening carefully as he remained perfectly still. When only the echo of silence followed him, he glanced around once more before stepping out from behind the pillar and into a ray of light from the window he passed beneath.

It was Bastian.

I'd wondered why I hadn't seen him at the reception – who knew it was because he was busy playing shady secret agent?

Ducking his head, he continued on down the dark hall, quickly and quietly like a sinister breeze. I watched him turn to the left at the far end of the hall before I stepped out into the light myself and followed him, my adrenaline already pumping. Sneaking around again, was he? Well, his luck was about to run out.

I hurried down the hall, peeking around the corner I'd seen Bastian turn before tiptoeing down it as well. I began to worry I'd lost him until I heard low voices carrying from an open door a short way off. Barely allowing myself to breathe, I crept into the hollow of the door next to the occupied room, craning my neck to hear what was being said.

"So he did go?" an older man's voice asked.

"Yes," said another man, "this afternoon."

"Did he get anything?"

"Not sure. The four of them went together, so it was too risky to follow, but they were only gone just over an hour. That would mean he spent less than twenty minutes at the grave."

My chest clenched as I deciphered their words. "Grave'." "Four of them." They were talking about us.

"Doesn't sound like enough time to get anything. Especially if he didn't know what to look for."

"But if he didn't find anything, there is no way Liam will be able to, even with the help."

"Doesn't matter, we still have to try. If the weather holds out, we go immediately after the game. If it doesn't, then we leave at dawn…"

He continued to speak but my ears went numb the moment I realized that his voice was getting louder. They were headed for the door. Panic clawed my back as my eyes darted around me looking for a place to hide. I couldn't let them find me – not after what they would know I heard – but there was nowhere to go. My only option was to bolt back down the hall and pray I made it to the first turn before they looked in my direction.

Without another thought, I backed out of the cover of the doorframe, preparing to run as fast as I could, but instead felt my heart stop as I bumped into the chest of someone who'd been poised directly behind me. I turned to see Bastian, his face like stone as he looked down at me while at the same moment I heard a hand grasp the handle of the open door. Before I could conjure a coherent thought, Bastian grabbed my shoulders and spun me around to face the door. His arm like a steel beam, he locked me against his chest while his free hand came up to cover my mouth and nose. I couldn't move, I couldn't scream, I couldn't even breathe. All I could do was watch as the door swung open, and then…

…everything went black.

CHAPTER 16

It all happened in the timespan of a blink; the world around me went black, there was the sensation of falling, then suddenly the darkness burst to life again, only now I was now looking at a wall in what appeared to be one of the manor's guest suites. As I tried to remember how to breathe, I felt Bastian slowly release me. "Easy," he cautioned quietly, as his arms opened, his hands spread wide as though to keep me calm.

I tried to speak but I couldn't seem to coordinate my brain with my mouth. What the hell just happened? Where were we? Were we alone? Should I run? How did... we...

"Whoa," Bastian said, quickly grabbing me as my legs gave out. "That's why I said easy," he chuckled as he lowered me into an armchair a few feet away. Luckily for him I was still too close to passing out to mind that he found any of this amusing. "Deep breaths," he said before stepping away, returning a moment later with a glass of water. "Here." He handed me the glass then took a seat in the chair next to me, looking oddly relaxed. "Sorry, under normal circumstances I would have warned you, but there wasn't time. Though for future reference, if you close your eyes you won't get dizzy."

I emptied the glass in three gulps, allowing the cold water to ease the hot tingling in the front of my forehead. Once I was sure I could raise my head without getting queasy, I looked up at him, hoping my death grip on the glass would hide the fact that my hands were shaking.

"Better?" he asked.

I stared at him blankly. "That's something of a loaded question."

He huffed a laugh, though oddly enough, there didn't seem to be any arrogance or derision lurking under the sound. He still gave off a cocky sort of air, but now instead of haughty and off-putting, it was almost playful. "I suppose it is, but that's why I brought you here; I think we need to talk."

"I'd say so," I agreed, not nearly as calm as he clearly was. "And we can start with you telling me what the hell you just did to me."

"If memory serves," he smirked, "I believe I saved you from being discovered as probably one of the clumsiest spies in history."

"OK, first off I was doing fine until you showed up, and secondly, you know that's not what I was talking about. Where are we and how did we get here?"

"A," he began counting on his fingers, "you were *not* doing fine. You were seconds away from being seen, and I can assure you that would not have ended well. Cleen and McGary are not the sort of men who would take kindly to being followed and eavesdropped on, particularly by one of the subjects of the conversation. And B, we are in my room. I ported us here after you nearly got us caught."

"Ported..." That's right. I'd forgotten he was a Porter. Well if that was porting, it was pretty cool – if not borderline vomit-inducing. Too bad now was not the time to dwell on it. "What do you mean got 'us' caught? I was following you. What were you doing over there if you weren't with them?"

"The same thing you were, trying to hear what they were saying. I was just doing a better job of it."

"I guess I'm just not as practiced at spying on people as you are," I challenged, crossing my arms and waiting for the denials to begin.

He looked long and hard a me for a moment before letting out a long breath. "Yes," he said, "you're probably right."

I froze for a second, totally thrown. "Right about what?"

He paused again, holding my gaze long and hard before speaking. "All of it," he finally said. "The spying, Pennsylvania… everything."

I stood there motionless, staring at him, trying to figure out what in God's name was going on. I'd expected the moment when he finally broke down and admitted I'd been right about him to feel satisfying and triumphant, but this wasn't right. He'd been fighting me tooth and nail since we'd met, hitting me with nothing but denials and excuses every time the subject came up, yet now, out of nowhere I was supposed to buy that he was ready to come clean? Yeah right.

"You are so full of it," I said, in no mood for whatever game he was playing.

"What?" Obviously not the response he'd expected.

"I don't buy it. And if you think you can play me by telling me what you think I want to hear, you've got another think coming."

"Hold on," he said, his face both amused and annoyed, "you have been harping on at me for two days to come clean, and now that I do, you don't believe me?"

"It's too easy. You're up to something."

"You can't just make this easy, can you?" He rubbed a hand over his face, more annoyed than amused now. "I did just save you when I could have left you to hang, doesn't that at least earn me the benefit of the doubt? Just listen to what I have to say."

"Listen?" I snarled, as the fragile hold I had on my temper snapped like a frozen twig. "No. No, I won't listen. Why the hell should I? So you can spout more lies, or pacify me with whatever you think I want to hear? Well, you can stuff it."

I stood, and turned toward the door, but Bastian caught my arm before I could storm off. "Becca, please–"

"No!" I pulled my arm free. "I'm done with you; I'm done with all of you! You are absolutely the worst kind of people and I am through playing your games. You all think you can hold yourselves above everyone else when the truth is you don't even deserve the abilities that you think make you so great. And now you, who have done nothing but treat me like an idiot from the moment we met, have the audacity to act like *I* owe *you* something – are you out of your mind? But then why would I expect special treatment when you treat even your own brother like trash? But then I guess he deserves it," I laughed once without humor. "After all, the way he is, he's barely worthy to do your laundry, much less share your blood, isn't that right?"

Bastian had stood quietly while I ranted, never once interrupting me with even so much as a sideways glance. However, the moment I mentioned Steven, a fierce and strangely familiar fire lit under his eyes, and I knew I'd struck a chord.

"Steven," he said, taking a slow step toward me, "is the best man that I know, and I am *proud*" – his intensity almost turning the word into a growl – "to call him my brother."

I tried not to shrink back under his glare. "Certainly didn't seem that way this morning."

"That's because you don't understand how things work here. You think that defending someone means confrontation. That crossing your arms and stomping your foot is the only way to stand up against wrong. That may have been how it worked for you back home, but here, yelling and screaming will get you nowhere. They," he pointed angrily out toward the hall, "are in charge here, and if you want any chance of winning in their game then you must play by their rules. It might not make any sense to you, but I do what I do because I am the only thing that stands between them," he pointed again and I was shocked to hear the unveiled loathing slicing though his tone, "and my brother. And I am not going to do *anything* to jeopardize that."

I looked up at him, trying my hardest to see any trace of deceit or manipulation on his face, but deep down I know that I wouldn't find any. If there was one thing I knew, it was the look of someone whose only concern was protecting their brother. I used to see it every day in the mirror, and now it was staring back at me again, but this time through the eyes of another. I might not have understood everything he'd told me, but what I did know was that for the first time since we'd met, he was being honest.

"You know," I sighed, "that's the first thing you've said that I actually believe."

"I'm glad," he said, still serious, but no longer severe. "Does that mean you're willing to hear me out?"

"Yes," I nodded once, my eyes still locked on his. "But it better be good."

With a satisfied breath, he finally broke our stare-off, glancing down as he began slowly pacing around the center of the room. As he gathered his thoughts, I retook my seat in the chair I'd occupied earlier and waited patiently – albeit skeptically – for him to begin.

"Steven and I grew up like all other Bhunaidh children. Private schools, private tutors, private lives. We had no friends outside of other Bhunaidh children until we began attending school, and even then we were instructed to keep to our own kind as much as possible. We were tutored rigorously in the Bhunaidh histories, customs, and ways, always accepting everything that was taught to us without question or complaint, all in anticipation of the day our Awakenings would occur. The Awakening of a Bhunaidh child is more than simply the day his or her ability appears, it also marks their induction into Bhunaidh society. Finally being accepted into the 'proud and ancient majesty'" – he rolled his eyes – "of the Bhunaidh fold was everything we were taught to want, and as children it was all we could think about."

He stopped for a moment, leaning against the enormous four-poster bed, bracing his hands on the footboard as ripples of a deeply harbored anger began to seethe under his skin.

"I was fourteen when my Awakening occurred," he continued, his grip on the bed becoming rigid. "As we were twins, everyone expected Steven to follow closely behind me, and when he didn't, my parents became impatient. They arranged for him to be awakened manually by an Alchemist, which is when we discovered that there would in fact be no Awakening because there was no ability. I was sad for him of course as I knew better than anyone how disappointed he was, but I was sure that both he and my parents would come to accept it, and that eventually everything would be fine." He laughed, though the sound was dark. "And the fact that I actually believed that just shows how blind I truly was. Up until that point, I had spent my life believing that the fundamental lesson in all the Bhunaidh teachings was the importance of family – that that was what we held most sacred. What I didn't realize was that family and lineage are not one and the same, and that it can be very easy to mistake someone loving *who* you are, for simply loving *what* you are."

He stopped, taking several breaths as he stared at the floor while I fought back the sympathy I felt trying to claw its way out of my chest. No, damn it! I would not feel sorry for him. At least not until I could determine if all this was true, or if he just knew that a story about a helpless brother would be the best way to win me over. Though, skeptical as I may have been, I couldn't help but notice that something was different about him – something more than just his lack of obnoxious ego. There was a realness about him that I hadn't seen before. An emotional undercurrent to his words that ran deeper than the shallow surface façade he'd worn throughout our past conversations. Something that was strong as it was vulnerable, and definitely couldn't be faked.

"Suddenly," he began again, the strain in his jaw making his cheeks quiver, "the world didn't look at Steven as my brother anymore. As far as they were concerned, he was just this thing that followed us everywhere, fouling the air with his tainted blood and burdening my parents with his presence. Parents who never once tried to defend him or stand by him, but instead bemoaned their 'great misfortune.' Parents who, instead of accepting their child for who he was, accepted condolences from their friends who couldn't believe that such a horrible fate had befallen them. *Parents*," he spat the word, "who expected me to behave as they did, shunning my best friend – their *son* – for no reason at all."

He stopped again, this time for so long that I wondered if he was done. "I appreciate you telling me this," I said sincerely, not wanting to belittle what he'd shared. "Really I do. And to be honest, I understand far better than you know, but this isn't exactly helping with my overall confusion." In fact, I'd say it had more than doubled since the start of our conversation.

He nodded with what might have been a smile and came back over to sit in the second armchair. "Bear with me," he said, "we're getting there." He paused again quickly before beginning again, his emotions back under control. "Of course I refused to go along with everyone's sudden intolerance of Steven, instead turning my back on my parents and all the rest of the people I could no longer put up with, and putting all my energy into finding a way to help him."

"If things were so bad, why didn't the two of you just leave?"

"We… were going to," he told me, shifting uncomfortably. "That was my first plan. We would do what we had to until we turned sixteen and had full access to our financial accounts, then we would leave and start new elsewhere. However," he hesitated, looking away, "matters changed and we realized that would not work as we'd hoped."

"What happened?"

"There were complications." He said it casually, but there was nothing casual about the way his hands fidgeted in his lap. Before I could question further, he moved on. "After that," he continued quickly, "I floundered a bit, not sure what to do. Actually," he smiled, raising an eyebrow at me, "I became quite a bit like you.

Standing up to the ones who shunned Steven, convinced that if I was strong and didn't back down that eventually I would be able to change their minds. But I was fooling myself. There is no changing the minds of people who refuse to listen, and for all my efforts I only seemed to make the matter worse. Finally, I became so desperate that" – he bowed his head as though he were ashamed – "I decided to seek the help of Darragh."

My eyes popped open. "You what? Please tell me you're kidding…"

He shook his head. "I'm not proud of it, but at the time there didn't seem to be any other way."

"What did you think he could do?"

"Show me the process of taking and assuming abilities from others."

"You wanted to give Steven someone else's ability? You do know that involves killing the Holder you take it from, right?"

"I did know that Darragh killed for his abilities, but that didn't necessarily mean that was the only way it could be done. Maybe there was a way to harmlessly take the ability of a Holder who was about to die of natural causes, or perhaps take small bits of power from several Holders with the same ability and combine them, I don't know. It was totally and utterly stupid, I know that now, and honestly a large part of me knew it then, but again, I was desperate. My brother's life was disintegrating and I refused to do nothing but stand by and watch, but I swear to you, I only ever intended to learn the process so that I could try to adapt it. I would never have killed anyone."

"I'm glad to hear it," I said, "though I think there may have been a better chance of Darragh killing you."

"Probably. But luckily, Ciaran intervened before I was forced to find out."

Immediately my ears perked up. "Wait, Ciaran Shea?"

Bastian nodded. "He'd had a vision of my yet-to-be-arranged meeting and was able to stop me before I did anything foolish."

"So you knew Ciaran?"

"I did. That's why when I found out that you were looking into him, I realized that we might be of use to one another."

"How did you find out about that?" I asked with a squint.

"Steven told me."

"He ratted me out? He promised not to tell anyone!" *Oh, he was so dead...*

"Well, as far as Steven is concerned I'm not 'anyone.' And just so you're aware, he only told me after he came to your gallant defense. He gave me quite an earful for yelling at you the way I did."

"Good," I raised my eye brows, "you deserved it."

"Maybe," he allowed, a smile twisting his cheeks. "But I think we've gotten a bit off topic."

My glare turned wry. "I happen to be enjoying this topic, but if you insist, go on."

"Thank you," he clipped, a smile hiding in his eyes. "So as I said, Ciaran had a vision and came to see me. In exchange for not informing my parents about what I'd been planning to do, Ciaran insisted I tell him what was going on. When I explained what I'd wanted from Darragh and why, he told me that if I was willing to allow him, he could help."

"Help Steven?"

"Help me to help Steven, yes, but not in the way I'd expected. He explained that not only was my attempt to cut a deal with Darragh reckless, it would also have been futile as only Holders can assume abilities taken from others. The new ability actually bonds to the one the person was born with, thus if there is no ability already present, the new ability has no way to be absorbed."

"Ciaran knew how to steal abilities? I thought Darragh was the only one who knew how it was done."

"So did I, but it turned out that Ciaran was the one who first told Darragh it could be done, though he didn't know how, nor did he realize the lengths Darragh would go to in order to make it a reality."

"So Ciaran and Darragh actually knew each other?"

"Quite well from what I understand. Darragh had a talent for seeking out the most powerful Holders and keeping them close, and Ciaran was one of the most gifted Seers to have ever lived. There was a time when the two of them worked closely together, Darragh giving Ciaran a home, protection, and anything else he may have needed, while in return Ciaran kept Darragh appraised of all his visions and prophecies. Their arrangement remained for decades – until the day when Ciaran shared a vision which prompted Darragh to single-handedly kill every member of his own bloodline."

My stomach turned. "Darragh killed his own family? All of them? Just because of something Ciaran said?"

Bastian nodded slowly. "Every last one."

Dear God...

"What was it?" I asked, trying to hide my fear under the far less vulnerable emotions of shock and abhorrence. "What did Ciaran see? What could make a man – even a man like Darragh – do that to their own family?"

"I don't know. Ciaran never told me, but I do know he carried the guilt of it to his grave." He paused a moment looking away, and I had to wonder just how close the two of them had been. I could have asked, but as it wasn't really the time, I sat quietly until he turned back and continued. "That was when he finally left Darragh and came to us – or to my grandparents, I should say, as it was long before I was born. He told them he wished to join with the Bhunaidh, and considering that his bloodline was pure and the fact that they enjoyed the idea of finally having a Seer among their ranks, they welcomed him onto the fold."

"And Darragh never came after him?"

"Honestly, that is the part I have never understood. There was no doubt that Darragh knew where Ciaran was, but anytime I would ask him about it, all he would ever say was, 'Darragh and I have an understanding.' Yet despite the 'understanding,' Ciaran seemed to constantly be on edge, forever looking over his shoulder. Most people attributed it to simple paranoia or assumed he was beginning to lose his mind to his ability as was so common with Seers, but the truth was he knew he was being watched."

"But if he was so paranoid," I asked, my skepticism rearing up again, "why did he trust you enough to tell you all this?"

"Because, as mentioned earlier, he wanted to help me. I'll admit that at first it seemed odd even to me, but then I began to see how similar we really were and wondered if he saw it as well. He'd been watching the situation with Steven and saw how much it had changed me. He knew that I'd come to see the Bhunaidh way of life for the hollow sham that it was, but like him, could not risk leaving the measure of protection it provided. Maybe it was what he saw of his own struggles within me, or perhaps it was to help allay some of his underlying guilt for the deaths he felt he caused, I'm not sure. But whatever the reason, he decided to take it upon himself to show me that if I truly wanted to help Steven have a better life, lashing out and fighting was not the way. The collective mindset of the Bhunaidh was one that had been too long standing and rigidly formed to be broken, but that didn't mean I couldn't twist and manipulate it from within. In other words, he taught me to play the game."

"The game?"

"This," he waved his hand around the room, "them, all if it. It's a game. Say the right things and play by the rules; you win. Say the wrong things or step out of bounds; you lose. Simple as that. Ciaran convinced me that if I acted the part and became who they expected me to be, that I would be able to reassume my standing in Bhunaidh society, and that using that standing to my advantage would be my true power. I was skeptical at first, but as I had nowhere else to turn, I decided it was worth a try. After talking with Steven and making sure he was agreeable to this new approach, I swallowed my disgust and assumed the mantle of a true Bhunaidh. I retook my place at my parents' side, mirrored the pride and contempt that everyone around me seemed to wear like a second skin, and – at least while in public – began treating Steven the way everyone else did. My parents remember it simply as the day I 'returned to my senses,' when little did they know it was actually the day I finally took control. Control I used to convince my parents to allow Steven back into the private academy we'd both attended, because it was 'just so embarrassing to be without him and let all the other students know that he was no longer worthy.'"

"And that worked?"

"I'd begged my parents to let him stay when they pulled him out just after his failed Awakening, and they had barely heard me. But one single mention of being embarrassed for my family name, and lo-and-behold, Steven was immediately reenrolled. That was when I realized that Ciaran had been right and that true power lay not in fighting my position, but using it."

"OK... I get that, but how did all this lead to you sneaking around hallways and eavesdropping through keyholes? Not to mention land you in my math class?"

"It started out as simply a way to try to help Ciaran. He was convinced that there were several members of the Bhunaidh that were secretly informants of Darragh, so I decided to look into it so that I could help put his mind at ease. However, the more I learned, the more it became apparent that not only was Ciaran correct, but that the informants were actually using Bhunaidh resources to help Darragh's operations. They provided him information from the archives when needed, even stealing volumes on occasion, and of course they kept a tight watch on Ciaran for him. There were also times when they acted as middle men, often meeting with other of Darragh's spies and relaying information back and forth."

"Kind of smart, really," I mused to myself. "I mean it's no secret that you all don't exactly like getting your hands dirty when it comes to Darragh. No one would have looked twice for spies here."

"A fact I'm sure they have counted on," he agreed. "Being both outraged that these men were getting away with betraying their entire race to a madman, and excited that I had finally found some way I could truly be of use to someone, I made espionage something of a hobby. Any time that was not spent away at school, I did my best to attend as many gatherings and functions as possible, make as many visits to the individual men's homes, and did anything else I could manage to learn as much as possible. My hope was that if anything serious were to be plotted, I would hear enough about it to remain one or two steps ahead and be able to prevent any sort of disaster. It was slow going at first and there were some very near misses – though none quite as near as the one I just rescued you from," he chuckled.

"You did not *rescue* me, you abducted me," I corrected, not about to be looked at as some damsel in distress.

"But once I got the hang of it," he continued, acknowledging my protest with nothing more than a snarky grin, "and began to incorporate my porting, I actually became quite good. But despite my growing proficiency, oftentimes, there simply wasn't much to be learned. Then finally, I received my big break. It was the thing that I was sure would put me ten steps ahead of everyone including Darragh, and oddly enough, it didn't come from, as you say, sneaking around halls and listening at keyholes, but from Ciaran, and was given quite by accident. He and I were discussing the Black Iris one afternoon, and he happened to mention something about the person destined to awaken it – a person he quite clearly referred to... as *she*."

"Ciaran knew about me..." I whispered, only realizing after the words were out that I probably shouldn't have confirmed it and instead played dumb. "How?"

"A vision, most likely. When I asked about it he denied having said it, but the look on his face was as good as a confession."

"Is that how you found out where I was? Did he know that too?"

He nodded. "At first he wouldn't say, claiming it was for both your safety and mine, but when I learned from one of my many bouts of eavesdropping that one of your father's most trusted associates was yet another of Darragh's informants, Ciaran became worried that you and your brother may be in danger. He couldn't risk sending word to your father when there was a traitor so near him, nor could he go to check on you himself as it would call too much attention to the situation. I, on the other hand, was about to leave for my next semester of school anyway, and with some careful planning, would not be missed. With both Ciaran and Steven's help, things fell quickly into place, and before I knew it I was in the States attending high school."

"You were where?" I asked, making a show of leaning in.

"In school with you."

I put a hand to my ear dramatically. "I'm sorry, one more time..."

"In Moon Area High School, Pittsburgh, Pennsylvania, attending your classes as Brian Connor," he said, eyeing me exasperated. "Satisfied?"

"Marginally," I nodded. "Go on."

"The plan was to assess the situation, then come home and decide how to proceed, but it was about that time that Ciaran began to fall ill." He paused, looking down at his hands. "He died while I was away. When I came home I was on my own. I didn't know what to do or who I could trust, so did the only thing I could – I waited. Waited for a chance to share what I knew with the right people, while in the meantime make sure nothing bad happened that I could prevent. I hadn't expected the opportunity to fall at my door the way it did, but when Steven told me what you said earlier, I knew this was what I had been waiting for."

When he stopped, I knew I should probably speak, but I didn't know what to say. I just looked at him, one last time waiting for a flash of falsehood or some other sign that he was working me over, but yet again, all I found looking back at me was sincerity that was as irritating as it was genuine. "Do you have any idea what you've put me through the last two days?" I asked after a moment.

"I know."

"No, you don't know! Don't tell me you know! I have been going out of my mind! Do you realize I called my mother to have her try to look you up in my yearbook just so I could prove to myself and everyone else that I wasn't crazy?"

"I didn't take a picture–"

"I know!" I growled, taking a few deep breaths as I reined my anger back in. "What exactly do you want?"

"I want to help," he said. "I know things that can get you the answers you need."

"Why? What do you get out of it? And don't say something stupid like, 'it'll be fun' or 'because I'm bored.' This is a serious matter, and I want a serious answer."

He looked me right in the eye and didn't flinch once. "I will be able to do what I can to make sure that Ciaran's work isn't used to cause more destruction or death than he believes it already has. He lived too much of his life in shame for what his visions brought to pass, and I won't allow his work to fall into the hands of the one man he sought to keep it from."

I sat there as the desire to believe and the desire to keep hating him wrestled in me like two bears fighting over one cave. The real problem was that as I looked into his calm yet slightly tentative expression, I knew that one of those bears was right and the other one was just being stubborn and petty. Much as I may not have liked it, this man was serious and more than that, he just might have the answers we needed; in which case, there was only one way this could end. I stood up, looked hard at his still seated form one last time, then offered him my hand. Following me to his feet, he glanced down at my waiting palm and smiled, taking it into his own and shaking it.

"I still don't like you," I grumbled, not willing to surrender totally.

"You don't have to. You just have to be willing to give me

a chance. And who knows," he grinned as that playfully cocky glint came back into his eye, "you may find I'm not so bad once you get to know me."

"Yeah, not likely," I scoffed. "And just so you know, I'm not the only one who matters here. There are some other people we need to go talk to who may or may not kick you to the curb, so just keep that in mind."

"Well, I suppose there is no time like the present to find out. Shall we go and speak to them?" he asked, turning toward the door and offering me his arm.

I eyed his outstretched arm with a cocked brow for a moment before passing it by and walking over to the door. "Let's go."

"See," he chuckled as he followed behind me, reaching around to open the door with a smirk I tried to ignore, "you're warming up to me already."

CHAPTER 17

"How were you able to enroll in school in the States without the help of your parents?" Jocelyn asked Bastian as the three of us plus Alex and Cormac sat in Jocelyn's suite a short while later.

"Ciaran was able to procure paperwork stating that he was my guardian and arranged everything via phone."

"And your parents knew nothing about it?"

"No."

"But your academy in France shows you as enrolled that year, how is that possible?"

"I was technically enrolled," Bastian answered, not bothering to ask how Jocelyn would have known that. "I attended the first week of classes in France, after which I enrolled myself in an intensive study program that required students to live away from school with an academic sponsor. I had participated in the program before: once I lived in Germany with a professor for a semester, then the following year I was sponsored to Italy by an artist."

"And Ciaran registered as a sponsor and chose you for himself?" Jocelyn guessed, putting it together.

"Yes. Both the school and my parents believed I was studying with a historical sociologist out of Greece, leaving me free to attend school in the US."

It had been going on like this for almost a half hour, and honestly, I wasn't sure who I was more impressed with: Jocelyn for giving Bastian such a hard time, or Bastian for holding up like a trooper under the pressure.

When I'd told Jocelyn that Bastian and I had talked and that he wanted to help us with the Ciaran issue, I thought for a minute that he might tear me a new one right there in the hall for once again telling someone outside our circle about what we were up to. However, once I had vouched for him and explained that Bastian had actually been the one to seek me out, he agreed to hear him out. The fact that I'd left out the whole "he saved me when I was spying-slash-taking matters into my own hands again like you told me not to" thing was neither here nor there.

Jocelyn, Cormac, Alex and I had gone straight to Jocelyn's room where Bastian was waiting, and the second the door closed behind us the explanation-turned-interrogation began. Bastian opened by relating his story to the three men while I listened carefully to make sure that what he told them was exactly the same thing he'd told me – which of course it was. The only differences I noticed that he left out were the more personal parts of the tale involving Steven, but as those bits were private and not exactly pertinent to the investigation into Ciaran, I let it go. The fact that he'd felt comfortable enough to tell me the entire story was enough for the time being, and to be honest, almost flattering.

Almost.

When Bastian had finished, Jocelyn's questions began and hadn't stopped for what was closing in on forty-five minutes. He grilled him like a pro, going over every aspect of Bastian's story with a microscope, covering all potential gaps or loopholes, and thoroughly examining all his motivations and reasoning. Had I not been there to see it first hand, I wouldn't have thought the old boy had it in him, but Jocelyn worked Bastian over like a seasoned interrogator, leaving no corner of his story unexamined.

Finally, he seemed to reach the end of his string of questions and stepped back, crossing his arms as he studied Bastian carefully. "You understand," he said, "that this is not a situation what we have found ourselves in before."

"I realize that," Bastian nodded respectfully, "and I also realize that you may find it difficult to trust me given that I have admitted to keeping things from you. But I hope you believe me when I say that I was only withholding information because I had no way to know who could be trusted. Once I realized that one of your own men was disloyal, I thought that no one was above suspicion, which made any effort to contact you too high a risk. If I attempted to send a message and it was intercepted, my involvement could have been exposed, and given that mine is not the only welfare resting on my precarious position amongst the Bhunaidh, it was not a risk I could afford." Jocelyn considered his words carefully, and while it was clear that he still wasn't thrilled, I could also see that he understood. "If," Bastian added, after a pause, "you believe that examining me further would make you all feel more comfortable, I am more than willing to offer you my mind for confirmation of what I have told you. I assure you I have nothing to hide, and am at your disposal if you wish."

Wow. Offering up his mind for a reading? Obviously he was serious about all this, and I hated to admit it, but I was impressed. Of course there was always a chance he was bluffing – misdirection was something of an art form to this guy – but to brazenly manipulate the principles of one of the most powerful Holders in history? No way he had balls that big...

Jocelyn considered him for a long moment before finally shaking his head. "No. If you are going to work with us we have to trust you because we believe you are worthy of our trust, not because we can't prove otherwise. If in fact you were on close terms with Ciaran through the later years of his life, then I do believe that you may have information that could greatly benefit us in our investigation, so provided there are no other concerns..." He paused, glancing to the rest of us who shook our heads – or rather, Cormac and I shook our heads while Alex stood silently, "then we would be grateful for your help."

"I am happy to be of use," he smiled, then looked wary. "My only fear is that the information I have will not be what you wish to hear."

"Anything is more than nothing, lad," Cormac said. "We will work with whatever you can give us, and who's to know, perhaps your knowledge combined with what we have been able to gather for ourselves will lead us toward the answers we need."

"I hope so," Bastian said.

"Let's start from the beginning," Jocelyn said, turning the chair from the desk around and having a seat. "What can you tell us about Taron? How did you find out that he was betraying us?"

"I first realized it several years ago when he attended a meeting with Darragh's other spies within the Bhunaidh."

"And just how many spies are we talking about here?" Ciaran asked.

"Four that I can name; McGary, Barra, Ryan, and Cleen."

"Not Barra!" Cormac said, appearing to know the person fairly well.

"Yes," Bastian said, "I've seen him several times." Cormac sighed, shaking his head, and Bastian continued. "There is one more, but I am not certain who it is, though I suspect it may be some type of Mentalist. Whoever it is, they keep themselves at a distance from the rest, and may even have their ability disguised, I'm not sure."

"The holes…" Jocelyn mumbled to himself.

Bastian paused looking at him, but Jocelyn waved his hand cueing him to go on. "Over the past several months," Bastian continued, shifting back to topic, "Taron was contacting the four of them more often than was usual in an effort to help with their work on Ciaran's notebook."

"So they are after the notebook?" Cormac said.

"Do you have any idea what Darragh wants from it?" Jocelyn asked. "The prophecies naturally, but which specific one?"

"I don't know," Bastian replied, "but it would have to be something Ciaran saw in the years after his and Darragh's separation. Anything before that Darragh would already know."

"So something new?" Alex said.

"Or perhaps a continuation or completion of an older prophecy. Seers do not always receive their visions all at once."

"Whatever it is, over the past few months Darragh has become desperate for it," Bastian said.

"The past few months?" I mused aloud. "So this sudden desperation would coincide with Ry and I coming to St Brigid's..."

"It would seem that way," Jocelyn said.

"What's the connection?" Alex asked.

"There is no way to know until we find the notebook. Bastian, do you have any idea where it might be?"

"I know exactly where it is," he replied. "It is with Darragh."

The room was suddenly so silent it was like a switch had been flipped. "Wait," I said, blinking quickly, "it's what?"

"I'm sorry," Bastian said, his eyes hopping from face to face, worried at our reaction. "I should have been more clear; Darragh and his men are not *looking* for the notebook, they are already in possession of it. As I told Becca, I was in the States when Ciaran passed and was unable to get the journal to safety before Darragh's men took it."

"So that's why your parents could never find it to burn?" I asked, remembering what Steven had told me.

"Yes," Bastian nodded my way, "one of Darragh's men – I'm not sure who – was able to get hold of it before it was destroyed and Darragh has had it ever since, so the problem isn't finding it... the problem is reading it."

"Reading it?" Jocelyn said.

"It appears that Ciaran had the foresight to have a charm placed on his journal before passing that keeps it from being read. That is what Darragh has had all his people working on: a way to read the prophecies the journal contains."

"What did the charm do?" Alex asked, suddenly more interested.

"Did it code the writing, or something to that effect?" Cormac said

"The writing is gone," Bastian said.

"Gone?" several of us said in unison.

Bastian nodded. "The pages are completely blank."

"Maybe the journal was switched out for another one…" I suggested.

"Doesn't seem so," Bastian replied. "From what I understand, an Alchemist has been able to confirm that a cloaking charm was placed on the pages of the journal themselves, and given all that I know they have tried thus far, it appears that the charm was designed to be unbreakable."

"Can't we just find the person who cast the charm?" I asked.

"Darragh's men have searched extensively, but haven't been able to come up with anything," Bastian said. "The person is either someone that Ciaran had no formal ties to or someone who died a long time ago, but if the charm is in fact unbreakable, then it makes little difference."

"Why?" I asked.

"An unbreakable charm," Jocelyn explained, "is just that – unbreakable. Even the Alchemists who cast it are unable to reverse or change its effects. That is why they are so seldom used."

"But why the charm?" Alex asked. "Why not just destroy the journal and be done with it?"

"Exactly," Bastian said. "If Ciaran wanted to make sure his work was entirely unreadable that is what he would have done, which is why I believe that the journal contains something potentially damaging to Darragh. If Ciaran had received a vision or prophecy that somehow revealed say, Darragh's ultimate downfall, or maybe a weakness somewhere in his operation, that would explain the charm."

"It wasn't just anyone he was trying to keep from reading, it was Darragh," Jocelyn completed the thought.

"Hold on, what?" I asked, hoping I wasn't the only one not understanding.

"If Ciaran had seen something damaging to Darragh, he would have wanted to keep it hidden from Darragh, but still make it available to someone who might be able to use it against him. That is likely what the charm was meant to do – prevent the information falling into the wrong hands, and keep it safe for the right hands."

"I get that," I said, "but if there is no way to break the charm, then how is anyone, good or bad, supposed to see what it says?"

"If the charm was created only to keep some people out, then we don't have to break it," Jocelyn said. "We only have to find a way around it."

"And that is what Darragh has been trying to do?"

"Yes," Bastian said.

Suddenly, Jocelyn's words from the reading at the cemetery flashed in my mind. "*...can pierce the shroud of my sight,*" I quoted. "What if that's it?"

"What?' Bastian asked, though I could see the others' eyes light up as they had the same thought I did.

"'*Pierce the shroud*'," I said. "Like, see though the cover, and '*sight*,' you know, like foresight. Maybe his last prophecy was actually telling us how to read the journal!"

"Could be," Cormac said, "but we'll need the rest to be sure."

"I'm sorry," Bastian said, his eyes wide as they jumped from person to person looking for an explanation, finally landing on me. "I'm a bit lost."

"Jocelyn did a reading at Ciaran's grave today," I told him, "but the only thing he could get was a portion of Ciaran's last prophecy: '*...can pierce the shroud of my sight.*'"

"We weren't sure what to make of it," Cormac told him, "but this may well be it. However, we only have the last bit of the full prophecy and we will need it all to be able to make any sense of it."

"Is there any way to find out what the first portion was?" Bastian asked.

Jocelyn crossed his arms. "We have a Time Walker coming to see if we can look back and see the rest of the message, but in order to do that we need to find out where Ciaran was staying when he passed away."

"He was at one of my parents' summer cottages," Bastian said.

All three of our collective heads popped up while Cormac leaned in expectantly. "He was?"

"Yes, the whole of the final two months of his life."

"And you're certain about this?" Jocelyn asked, seeming to be hesitantly hopeful himself.

"Positive." Bastian nodded once. "His doctors ordered him to check into hospital when his heart condition became dire, but he flatly refused, likely because of his ever growing, though not unfounded paranoia. Rather than allow him to stay in his small home all on his own, my parents finally convinced him to move into their large holiday cottage where there was a house keeper and cook always on staff, and where they could arrange for a trusted live-in nurse to look after him as his condition worsened."

"And you know where it is?" Jocelyn asked. "Would you be able to take us there?"

"Of course. It's outside of Durrow, not terribly far from here. My parents often let it out during the spring and summer, but it ought to be vacant now."

Cormac rubbed his hands together happily. "Brilliant."

"When would you like to go?" Bastian asked.

"As we are clearly not the only ones interested in all this, the sooner the better. Our Walker arrives tomorrow morning, so any time after would be fine. Also, if what you said is true and Doyle,

McGary, and the rest of the informants are watching us, we will have to be more cautious. *No one* can know anything about this," he said to the group, though I didn't miss – or appreciate – the pointed glance he shot my way at the end. "I realize that we need to tell Brassal and Alva as it is their property, but if there is–"

"No we don't," Bastian stopped him, his brow lowering slightly the way it always seemed to when the subject of his parents entered the conversation. "Telling them we wished to visit would do nothing but raise questions that we are not prepared to answer. As their son, I am inviting you all to the cottage as my guests. Nothing more is needed."

Jocelyn didn't look thrilled, but he nodded. "All right. Though I take it this also means you do not intend to tell them you are assisting us?"

"No."

"I am willing to respect the fact that you are an adult and capable of making your own decisions, but I must say that I am not entirely comfortable making an arrangement of this nature with you behind the backs of your parents. Particularly when I know they would not approve."

Bastian's brow darkened. "With all due respect, there is little they do approve of. I understand that my joining with you on this project may put you in an uncomfortable situation, but I'm afraid I must insist that my parents, or anyone else for that matter, not find out that I am involved. My security, and more importantly that of my brother, rests on my position within the Bhunaidh which would be damaged beyond repair if I were to be in any way connected to investigations into Darragh."

"Then I suppose it's fortunate," Jocelyn said, "that as a competent and legal adult, your decisions are your own, and I have no business interfering."

Bastian's shoulders visibly relaxed. "Thank you," he said sincerely.

After a few more minutes of logistical discussion including the decision to tell Mr Anderson to meet us at the cottage with Chloe the following day instead of coming all the way to the manor and risk being seen by the wrong people, Bastian commented that we had all been missing from our respective events for far too long and should get back before anyone took notice. He left to make a belated appearance at the youth reception while Jocelyn, Cormac, and Alex were late to play cards and have drinks with the other men in one of the upper lounges. Having no intention of going back to the reception I'd run away from earlier, I made an excuse about being tired and asked if I could just go back to my room and go to bed. Thankfully, Jocelyn agreed without giving me any grief and I turned to go, but stopped as Alex spoke up for what may have been the first time that evening.

"I'll walk her back so she isn't seen skipping the social," he said, with a weird severity to his tone I could tell he was trying to hide.

"Not a bad idea," Cormac said.

Jocelyn nodded his agreement. "We'll be in the north lounge," he told Alex as he followed Cormac up the staircase.

"I'll be there in a minute," Alex said, and we stepped off down the hallway together.

I eyed him suspiciously as we made our way toward the main hallway, trying to figure out what was going on. As soon as we rounded the corner and I saw that there was no one nearby to overhear, I opened my mouth to ask what was up. But as it happened, he beat me to the punch. "OK, what the hell is going on?"

"What?" I asked, taken aback. I had never seen him that irritated before. "What's the matter?"

"What's the matter?" He eyed me like I'd lost it. "Seriously? Bastian, Becca, that's what's the matter! Not eight hours ago we were hiding in a hallway, following him around like a couple of second-rate spies, all because *you* were convinced he was the root of all evil, and now all of a sudden not only do you bring him in to join us, but you are vouching for him to Jocelyn? What happened?"

"Right," I grimaced, starting to walk again. "Sorry, I should have caught you up. You're right, this morning I did think he was evil, and trust me after you left it got a while lot worse before it got better, but it turns out that I might have been wrong... about some stuff, anyway. Though," I raised my chin, "I was right about him being the one who went to school with me, just... you know... for the record." The cock of his eyebrows told me he was not amused so I pressed on. "Anyway, yes, this morning I was convinced he was up to no good, but we talked tonight and it turns out that we actually have a lot in common."

"You were talking? Where, at the reception? Did anyone hear you?"

"No, no we were alone."

He blinked. "Alone?"

"He," I paused with a wince, knowing I was going to get in trouble for this one, "he kind of saved me earlier. See, I left the reception because of this bitchy chick – long story – anyway, I was hiding out in a hall and Bastian came sneaking down it acting all shady and whatnot, so I... kind of... followed him."

"*Becca!*"

"I know, I know, I shouldn't have gone without you, but you weren't there, and he was snooping around, and I was already in a bad mood... Anyway, it turned out that Bastian was actually sneaking around to spy on Doyle and McGary who almost caught me, but Bastian was able to grab me and port us both to his room before they saw us. Then we started talking, and I realized that I may have been wrong about him – not about what he was doing, but why he was doing it."

He eyed me sideways. "Is that supposed to make it OK? The fact that not only did you nearly get caught eavesdropping on two of Darragh's spies, but then you and Bastian had some quality alone time in his bedroom? Oh yeah, I feel much better..."

"Oh, come on," I rolled my eyes, "you know it wasn't that kind of 'alone time.'" As we reached my door I took his arm and turned him to face me, taking both his hands in mine. "Hey, I'm sorry. I shouldn't have gone snooping without you."

"No, you shouldn't have."

"I'm sorry," I said again.

"And?" he prompted lifting an eyebrow.

"And... I love you?" I smiled innocently, not sure what he was after.

"And," he said, sternly though with the slightest trace of a grin, "you won't do it again. And," he added, quickly putting a finger on my lips before I could speak, "you are going to *mean* it when you say it this time."

"*I weant it wast wime!*" I mumbled against his finger.

"Obviously it slipped your mind," he glared with a grin, freeing my lips.

I sighed. "I know. I'm sorry. I won't do it again, I swear."

He nodded, satisfied. "And I love you too," he said, pulling me in and kissing me sweetly.

I mmphed softly as the kiss ended, the fuzzy feeling in my stomach brushing away all the remnants of the thousand and one unpleasant emotions that had come at me over the past few hours and replacing them all with a warm and drowsy calm. I looked up expecting to find Alex back to normal as well, but something about him still seemed a little off.

"What's wrong?" I asked, wrapping my hands around his waist and joining my hands together behind his back.

He hesitated a breath before answering. "So this Bastian, you really believe we can trust him?"

"Much as I hate being wrong," I said, "yeah, I do. He's actually not such a bad guy, and it really does seem like he's going to be able to help us. Even if he is occasionally annoying," I added more to myself. Alex nodded but didn't seem convinced – if anything he may have seemed worse. "It will be fine," I tried again, willing him to believe me, "trust me."

"I do," he said with a bit more gravity than I would have expected.

"You know," I said coyly, trying to lighten the mood, "Jocelyn and Cormac are in the lounge..." I left my thought hanging as

I slid my hands around his sides and up his chest letting them finish my not-so-subtle hint for me.

Alex smiled, pulling me closer. "They are, but they are also expecting me."

"Right." *Damn...* "You couldn't come up with an excuse?"

"If I did, do you really think Jocelyn would buy it after what happened last night?"

"No," I grumbled, deflated. "This isn't working out as well as I thought it would."

"No, definitely not," he agreed, rubbing my upper arms. "But don't worry, we still have plenty of time."

"Yeah." Though it was starting to look as if the likelihood of this actually happening was shrinking by the day...

He took my face in his hands and kissed me once more, stroking my cheek with his thumb. "Goodnight, Leannán," he breathed against my mouth sending a fire ripping though me that made me wish with all my might that everyone else on earth could find a way to just disappear for the next few hours.

But of course they didn't, so of course he had to go, and yet again I was left to crawl under the covers wishing my enormous bed didn't feel so empty.

CHAPTER 18

The fog hadn't even lifted the following morning before Jocelyn, Alex, and I pulled up to the Bloch family cottage in County Offlay. Cormac had stayed behind to keep up appearances, and Bastian had made his own way separately to ward off suspicion, so it had just been the three of us on what had turned out to be a peaceful morning drive. Jocelyn and Alex had ridden up front listening to the radio and talking idly about a few of the men they'd seen at the card games the night before, while I spent the trip stretched out across the backseat, enjoying the loud hum of the engine as it tried to lull me to sleep. But relaxing as the ride might have been, the moment I saw the white St Brigid's van waiting for us in front of the cottage, I knew the peace and quiet was over.

"Becca!" Chloe squealed, running up and throwing her arms around me the moment I stepped out of the car. "I missed you so much!"

"It's been two days, Chloe," I laughed, hugging her back, not wanting to admit out loud how much I'd missed her too.

"I know, I'm just so excited! I can't even tell you how happy I was when Mr Anderson told me!" she beamed, starting to ramble. "It wasn't even difficult to wake up so early this morning, which you know I usually hate, but I was so excited I didn't mind at all, I was even awake before my alarm sounded, which never happens! I only hope I brought the right clothes with me, I was worrying over it the entire drive out, but you can tell me what to wear since you've been here a while and have seen what they've been wearing, I mean I know I won't really get to meet anyone so it really doesn't matter, but still…"

"Take a breath, hon," I laughed, as I wriggled out of the death grip her arms held around my neck.

Alex cleared his throat deliberately from just behind us where he stood leaning against the car. "*Why hello, Alex*," he said with a wry smile, beginning a mock conversation with himself. "Good morning Chloe. *It's nice to see you.* Good to see you too…"

"Hi Alex!" Chloe giggled. "Missed you too!"

"Yeah," he chuckled. "I can see that."

"No, I have! I've missed you all; Lorcan has been so boring these past few days! But you've been having fun, right? Is Adare amazing? Oh my gosh, what are your rooms like? I bet you've met loads of people! How was the gala?"

"We can get to all that on the way back, I promise," I grinned, "but for now, you've got work to do."

Chloe's eyes opened wider as a whole new sort of excitement lit them. "Do you really need me to time walk for you? Is that honestly why I'm here, so I can help?"

"Something like that," Jocelyn cut in, "though you won't be walking so much as lending your ability to us and teaching."

Lending? Teaching? "Whoa," I said, getting a strange feeling I knew where this was headed. "What do you mean?"

"Chloe is here so she can instruct you on how to use her ability," he looked at me calmly, "so that you can get us what we need."

My stomach dropped along with my jaw. "Wait, *I* have to do this? You can't be serious! We can't trust something this important to me; I've never time walked before! I thought I was just going to feed her ability like I did for you."

Jocelyn shook his head. "She won't be able to handle that kind of power. It's no insult to you, dear," he said turning to Chloe, "even I had trouble controlling it. It wouldn't be safe."

"Don't worry, it's easy," Chloe glowed, obviously just happy to be of service. "I can teach you. It will be fun!"

I smiled and nodded, but from the corner of my eye I locked glances with Alex for just a fraction of a second, which was all it took.

"Chloe, while we're waiting, let's get your stuff moved into the car."

"OK," she said happily, leading him over to the van.

"*Thank you*," I mouthed.

He winked quickly before following Chloe, allowing me to slip over to Jocelyn and pull him aside without her noticing.

"What is going on here?" I whispered to him as we stepped off to the side. "I know she isn't exactly the strongest Walker out there, but this wasn't the plan."

"This *was* the plan."

"You never said that!"

"I didn't want you to worry," he said, still annoyingly calm, "or worse, find a Walker within the Bhunaidh and attempt to practice before we got here."

"I wouldn't have done that!" I totally would have done that.

"Well, I apologize, but I wasn't willing to risk it. The fact is, we need a powerful Walker we trust. Chloe is more than trustworthy, but she lacks the strength we need. You have both."

Not sure whether I should be flattered he had so much faith in my abilities, or insulted that he kept the plan from me to begin with, I moved on to the big issue which he was clearly overlooking. "Thanks for the vote of confidence and all, but what exactly do you expect me to do? If I assume the Walking ability from her, then I can only be as strong as she is, and if you don't think she could do it on her own, why would I be... any... different..." I tapered as the answer occurred to me and I looked to find confirmation written on his face. Of course, I should have realized – I *was* different. Sure, what I'd said was true; I was only ever as powerful in any ability as the person I assumed it from. However, there was one substantial exception to that rule that I hadn't considered until right then. "The Iris."

Jocelyn nodded. "I asked Mr Anderson to bring it with him. With that, you will have the power of a full Time Walker and then some."

"That might be true in theory, but you seem to be forgetting that I have no idea how to use the thing!"

"You've used it before."

"Oh yeah, and that turned out great…" Ciaran's secrets or no, I wasn't in the mood for yet another near-death experience.

"The only times it has harmed you were when you were not wearing your scaith, and…" he gestured to the large emerald charm hanging against my chest, "you are. You will need to learn to use the Iris eventually, and there is no reason we can't start today."

"Nothing like a little on the job training…" I mumbled, not at all loving this idea.

"Besides," Jocelyn said, leading us back over toward the others, "a Time Walker is the perfect ability to learn with. It is a subtle power and is entirely enclosed to the user. You are the only one who will be able to see or hear any of the effects from the walking, which means there is no chance of injuring anyone if something goes wrong."

"Even Chloe?"

"Not even Chloe. But if it would make you feel better, I will monitor her while you are walking, to be safe."

I'm not sure that "better" was really the word, but it did make me feel at least a little less like a potential wrecking ball, so I nodded.

"Where's the Bloch lad?" Anderson asked as we joined him by the van. "Didn't he come out with you?"

"He drove separately and had to stop by the housekeeper's home in Durrow for the key, but he should be along shortly."

"He's here," I corrected, turning to look down the road in the direction of the approaching ability I felt.

"You're sure it's him?" Anderson asked.

"Unless there is another Porter who followed us out here, then yes." Though given the interest in Ciaran, I guess nothing was impossible.

But thankfully it was him, and a moment later he was stepping out of a ridiculously cool black sports car, tucking his sunglasses into the inner pocket of his jacket like some slow-motion shot out of an action movie. But that ever, I was not about to let myself be impressed by this guy.

But God damn, that was a cool car...

"Gentlemen," Bastian said, nodding to Jocelyn and Alex as he approached.

"Any trouble?" Jocelyn asked.

"Not at all," he said, pulling a key ring out of his pocket. "I was able to get away this morning without anyone realizing, and I told the housekeeper that my mother was in need of a few books from the office here. All's well."

"Good. Bastian," Jocelyn motioned to Mr Anderson, "this is Christopher Anderson, another of our associates."

Mr Anderson took Bastian's hand and shook it heartily. "Good to meet you, lad."

"Pleasure," Bastian smiled.

"He was kind enough to bring us our Walker," Jocelyn said as he turned to Chloe, "Miss Chloe Quinn. Chloe, this is Mr Bastian Bloch. His family owns this property."

Bastian took Chloe's hand and bowed over it politely, and again, his stuck up air seemed to be gone, replaced by charm that seemed to be working on Chloe, but I for one found annoying. "It is lovely to meet you, Miss Quinn."

"Thank you," Chloe answered with a coy tilt of her head.

Ugh... Come on Chloe, don't get sucked in to his crap...

"Shall we then?" Jocelyn asked stepping off toward the house as the rest of us followed behind, though Chloe took a bit longer to move.

"I like your car," she said to Bastian, still blushing.

"Thank you," he said. "I've had it about a year now."

"It's lovely…"

I grabbed Chloe's shoulders and physically turned her away from Bastian and the car. "Let's go Chloe," I groaned, guiding her toward the house. "Trust me, his ego doesn't need it," I told her, glaring back at Bastian when he chuckled, which only made him laugh harder. Jerk.

We made our way up to the cottage door, though I had to admit, the word "cottage" was a bit misleading. Yeah, the stone walls and ivy gave it a country sort of feel, but when I thought of a "cottage" I pictured something more like what Little Red Riding Hood's grandma would have lived in, not a two story building that could have comfortably housed a family of six or more. Once inside it looked even less like what one would find in the country, with a state of the art kitchen, modern electronics including a huge flat screen TV in the living area, and fireplace with a pushbutton starter. Not going to lie, I'd have been more than happy to spend the last few weeks of my life in a place like this.

As Bastian led us from room to room, Jocelyn looked over everything carefully, until finally we reached a bedroom on the upper level and he stopped. "This is it," Jocelyn said. "This was the room he was in during the memory I saw. It is arranged a bit differently, but I recognize the book case and the window. This is the one."

"OK," I said, glancing around. "Now what?"

"Now," Jocelyn said, looking between Chloe and me, "I think we should do a practice run. Start with something simple just to get a feel for it, and we can go on from there."

"Oh," Chloe said, hearing her cue and stepping up next to me. "OK, well, first thing we need is a date to visit." She stood perfectly still for a moment, her eyes glazing over slightly. "Hmmm…" she said after a long pause. "I'm trying to find a date for you to try, but all the days I keep checking are the same and no one is here. There is nothing for you to see."

"The house is empty most of the time," Bastian said from the corner. "Try a Monday – that is when the housekeeper is supposed to be here."

Chloe's eyes glassed over. "Ah," she said after a moment, "there she is. OK, Becca, what you need to do is... I guess you'd... hmm..."

"Yes?"

"I'm not sure, I suppose you'd start the way you always start." She motioned back and forth between us, trying to make her point.

I reached out with my ability and joined it with hers. "Done."

"Do you feel anything?" she asked.

"Not really, but then I never do."

She pursed her lips, looking a bit unsure. "All right... Well, what I do is think of the date in a certain way, and then that day will appear in place of everything you see now. It will become the only thing you can see."

"What do you mean by 'a certain way'?"

"I... don't really know. I just... it's like..." She bit her lip, thinking.

"Take your time," Jocelyn said as she struggled for the right words.

"Aye, it's not easy, is it?" Anderson said. "I couldn't describe how to impart for the life of me."

That gave me an idea. I'd become good at Imparting and to do that all I had to do was think the words I wanted to say and direct them through the ability I was assuming. Maybe the date thing would work the same way.

"What was the date?" I asked Chloe. "Let me try something."

"The second of October this year."

With a long breath I pictured the date in my mind, forcing the thought through the bright hazy glow of mine and Chloe combined abilities, and suddenly everything around me began to change. It was almost as if the world were made of tiny tiles, each one flipping over in a rippling wave then realigning themselves to reveal a similar but still very different image of the room I was in. Jocelyn, Alex, and everyone else who had been crammed in the space a second ago disappeared, and the door which we had shut behind us now appeared to stand open. There was a broom and dustpan leaning against the right-hand wall that had not been there before, and a portly woman in high-waisted jeans and faded sweatshirt suddenly stood at my shoulder, spraying cleaner on the window that was right behind me, and scared the ever-loving out of me.

"Oh!" I yelped as I stumbled backwards. And then in a flash, it was all gone. The woman, the broom, the open door, all vanished leaving me tripping backwards into the desk, everything in the room back to the way it was when I'd started.

An instant later the room erupted with questions as five pairs of hands shot toward me.

"Becca?"

"Whoa there, lass!"

"What just happened?"

"Are you all right?"

"You saw it, didn't you?"

"Yeah," I said to the last question, as I regained my balance. "I saw it... or I saw something. There was a woman cleaning the window..."

"Yes!" Chloe beamed, clapping her hands excitedly. "That was it! You did it!"

"And on the first try too," Mr Anderson commented. "Well done!"

"It wasn't too hard," I told them. "It was actually a lot like Imparting. But what happened?" I turned to Chloe. "Why did everything just vanish like that? I mean, I was scared when I saw her so close, but it only caught me off guard, I didn't break our connection or anything."

Chloe looked down, her face falling a bit. "Sorry, that's my fault."

"What do you mean?" I asked.

"You moved your foot when you stumbled. I can't move while I time walk, remember?"

"Oh, right."

"Any move at all of your foot will do it. You can move just about anything else – your arms, your head, your waist – just so long as your feet don't move."

"Got it," I smiled, feeling guilty for having brought up her shortcomings in front of so many people. "Let's go again."

For the next few minutes I tested my new ability, picking different dates, then moved on to learning how to choose the time of day, though Chloe's lack of power made that part a bit more difficult. Finally, I came back to the present time, feeling more comfortable and even enjoying myself, but the fun wasn't to last. Much as I was still dreading the task ahead, I knew I couldn't put it off any longer.

"Are you ready?" Jocelyn asked when I glanced his way after a nervous breath.

"I guess." As ready as I was going to get, anyway.

He walked over to the desk against the wall next to me, reaching into his vest pocket as he went and pulling out a worn leather pouch. My throat tightened slightly when I finally saw the Iris as he drew it from the pouch and set it down on the desk with a gentle metallic *thunk*.

"Just take it slow and you'll be fine," he said to me quietly before turning back to the group. "Bastian, do you happen to know the date that Ciaran passed, or perhaps just a general timeframe to give her a starting point?"

"It was when you were in the States, right? So coming up on four years ago?" I asked, hoping we could get at least a little more specific than just the four months he spent in school with me or we might be there all night.

"It was November third," he said confidently, though there was a hint of sadness there too.

I nodded and Jocelyn returned to his spot by the door and waited quietly with the others, while I looked down at the small hunk of metal and stone sitting on the desk waiting for me. Honestly, I hadn't even seen the thing since that afternoon in

Aimirgin Hall back at St Brigid's when it both saved me and almost killed me, and much as I wanted to be able to play the role of tough chick in front of all the eyes I felt on me, I was having a hard time making my hand go near it.

"OK," I sighed, trying to kick my bravado up a notch. "Here goes. If I inadvertently kill anyone, allow me to apologize ahead of time."

"She's kidding, right?" I heard Bastian whisper.

"Sure, sure," Mr Anderson whispered back. Then after a pause added, "Though you may want to step back a bit... just in case."

Great. Thanks Anderson.

Gritting my teeth I lifted my hand with every intention of grabbing hold of the thing and getting this over with, but against my will my fingers stopped shy and came to a rest on the surface of the table while I prayed that it looked to everyone else like I'd meant to do that and hadn't chickened out. I could do this, damn it, I knew I could! Nothing was going to happen, nothing bad anyway, it was all just in my head. But frustratingly enough, knowing that something is only in your head doesn't make it any easier to get past – even though it seems like it should.

My fingers twitched, trying to work up the nerve for their second try, when suddenly a shadow fell over the desk between my hand and the Iris and quickly shaped itself into script.

"Don't worry, Leannán. You've got this."

I smiled with a silent sigh as the words dissolved away as quickly as they came. I did have this. I might have been unsure, but Alex wasn't, and even when I couldn't totally count on myself, I knew I could always count on him. So long as he had my back, everything would be fine.

With Alex's support to push me, I locked my stance, held my breath, reached out, and took the Iris.

CHAPTER 19

The effect was instantaneous. The barest touch of my finger on the Iris made the curtain of fog around my mind fall like a wet blanket, and in a blink, everything was as clear and bright as cut glass. I held my breath for a second as I waited for discomfort, or pain, or chaos, or any of the other things that had occurred at one point or another during my previous Iris encounters, but there was nothing. All I felt was a freeing clarity that felt as natural as breathing.

I scanned out around me with my newly heightened sense and felt the presence of the other abilities in the room, marveling at the change in them. The individual glows from each of them that were fuzzy only a moment ago, were now concentrated and crisp globes of radiating power. The difference in the before and after was like comparing a cotton ball to a marble. Or maybe stars would have been a better comparison, as now I was no longer limited to the five other Holders in the room, but to Holders across the country and beyond, each of their abilities spread out across my mind like stars in a clear night sky.

Charged up as I was, it took almost no effort at all to find Chloe's ability and lock onto it. The Iris made the link between us strong as a steel cable, fusing our abilities together, charging and magnifying the gifts of time walking as they flowed into me, transforming me into a full-fledged Time Walker. I took the date Bastian provided and pushed it through my new ability and watched as the world around me shifted, this time with a smooth and confident transition that no longer felt fragile and shaky, but stable and strong.

As the room around me began to change and the day of Ciaran's death came into view, the first thing I noticed was the considerable change in light. The curtain over the only window in the room was drawn, allowing only thin slivers of light in through the gaps in the fabric, while the only other light came from a small lamp with a dim bulb sitting on top of a chest of drawers. I turned to get a better look at the second half of the room and, after noting with relief that the images didn't disappear the moment I moved my feet, I found that the largest changes in the scene had occurred on and around the desk and bed area. A plethora of pill bottles and other medical paraphernalia now lay strewn across the desktop, and what wouldn't fit there was stacked on the desk chair and on the edges of several of the bookshelves. Around all the makings of the pseudo-pharmacy were piles of books, pens, papers, notebooks and all sorts of other things laying haphazardly in, on, and all over pretty much everything else in the room. In a word, it was a mess.

"Enough, you old shrew!" a voice rasped, making me jump. My head snapped toward the bed where a man was laying down as a woman stood over him, appearing to have just finished administering some sort of medication.

The woman tried to smile despite her obvious irritation. "If you'd be so kind as to hold yourself still, it wouldn't be so difficult, Mr Shea."

Mr Shea. It was him.

"Becca?" I heard Jocelyn's voice call me from what now appeared to be only an empty patch of air. "Is everything all right?"

"Yes," I whispered, then remembering that Ciaran and the woman weren't really there and couldn't hear me, I repeated in a normal speaking voice. "Yes. It worked, Ciaran's here, I see him. There is a woman here too, his nurse I think. He's," I paused with a grin, "calling her names while she's trying to give him a shot."

"That sounds about right," I heard Bastian chuckle quietly from his corner. "Old boy never did like to be tended to or fussed over."

"Can you see anything on the nightstand to the right of the bed?" Jocelyn asked. "That is where he was writing in the memory."

I stepped around the nurse who was gathering up her things from the edge of the bed. "No," I said, scanning the tiny table, "nothing, just a glass of water."

"There now," the nurse said, piling some trash and empty dinnerware onto a tray. "You have a rest, and if the rain holds off, we can have a walk this afternoon."

"I don't want a bloody walk, now be gone woman!" Ciaran yelled from the bed, the effort of raising his voice winding him so much that he slumped back against his pillows as he tried to catch his breath.

"All right, all right," the nurse sighed, shaking her head. "I'm going, don't upset yourself."

As the door clicked shut, I looked around, not sure what I should do. Since there was nothing on the nightstand as of yet, then I had to have arrived at a point in the day before he'd written the first portion of the prophecy, but what exactly did that mean? Was I going to have to just sit here for God knows how long and wait it out? Was there a fast forward feature to this time walking thing? Maybe if I–

"Sorry about that one," Ciaran suddenly said as he stared blankly at the ceiling above his bed, still huffing and puffing a bit. "She has a tendency to prattle on."

Who was he talking to? I looked around to see if there was someone else in the room that I had missed, but it was only him. Was he talking to himself? Praying out loud, maybe? They had said that he'd gone a little crazy toward the end; maybe he'd lost it and actually thought there was someone with him.

"Thirty seven after ten," he continued, looking over to the clock that sat on one of the higher bookshelves. "That's the time that very clock had on its face in the vision where I watched you arrive. That's how I knew you'd come. How I know you're here."

Again I looked around. "Who's here…?"

"What is it?" Jocelyn asked.

"I don't know," I shook my head. "He's talking to someone."

"I didn't want to stay here, in this cottage," Ciaran continued, "but when I saw this room, I knew that this was where I was supposed to be. I knew this was where you would come and I had to be here when you did. I've been waiting for you, Rebecca."

My eyes popped open with a gasp as every hair on my body prickled. It was me – *he was talking to me.*

"What's wrong?" I heard Jocelyn ask, but I shushed him quickly and stepped closer to Ciaran's bed.

"Many months ago," Ciaran went on, "I received a vision of your arrival. You used the Iris to enhance the ability you garnered from your friend in order to come and see me here. That is how I found out about you. About who you are and what you can do."

"Oh my God… this is so creepy…" I breathed, barely believing what I was hearing.

"What's happening?" Jocelyn asked again.

"He's talking to me," I told them all. "He's actually talking to me. He knew we were coming and that I was going to find him."

"Really?" Chloe whispered.

"What did he say?" Bastian asked.

"That's incredible!" Anderson said.

I silenced them all with a quick raise of my hand just as Ciaran spoke again. "Not only do I know that you are here," he continued, "but I also know why." He reached under the blankets and pulled out a black book that was so old it looked as though it might fall apart at any moment. He opened the front cover and took out a small folded piece of paper, holding it out in front of him. "You came for this."

He paused a moment, then reached up behind himself and took hold of the large round topper to the left hand post of his headboard and began to unscrew it until the entire wooden ball came off into his hand. He brought it down to rest in his lap, then rolled the little piece of paper he'd taken from the book and slid it into the hole on the bottom of the post head. "I have never read it," he said, straining to return the post head to the top of the headboard, using all of his quickly waning strength to twist it back into place, "but I know it is what you have come for. It will still be in there waiting for you when you arrive," he said, seeming oddly confident. With a raspy sigh, he sank back onto his pillows, once again winded and breathing heavily. "May it serve you well." His eyelids began to fall. "Good luck Rebecca," he whispered as the last of his energy seemed to give out.

My stomach tightened as I began to panic, only one thought rambling through my mind. *Oh God, don't die, don't die, don't die, I cannot stand here and watch someone die without completely freaking out, please don't die…*

But to my immense relief, instead of stopping, his breathing simply transformed from the shallow puffs of exhaustion, to the long, deep draws of sleep.

With my fear subsided and my adrenaline pumping, I couldn't get back to reality fast enough. My only thought: getting into that bed knob. I plunked the Iris down on the desk, instantly snapping the heightened strength of my ability and shattering the scene around me, hurling me back in to the present day. As I stumbled backward from the force of the transition, Jocelyn caught my arm at the last second, keeping me upright as I got my bearings once again.

"What happened?" came the first of the tumult of questions that were all too jumbled together for me to even put names to the voices.

"What did he tell you?"

"Are you all right?"

"You're not hurt, are you?"

"Did he really know you were there?"

Back in control of my motor skills – though still blinking somewhat spasmodically – and momentarily ignoring the other five people in the room, I hurried over to the bed and began twisting the round post head off of the frame. It was tight at first, but quickly gave way and began to spin, up, up, up, until it teetered and fell off into my hand. Holding my breath, I peered down into the small threaded hole at the base of the knob, praying that the tiny piece of paper would still be in there.

"What in bloody hell is going on?" Anderson asked, everyone else in the room having fallen into a confused silence.

"What's going on," I answered with a smile, as I stuck my finger into the hole and pulled out the folded coil of paper, "is that I am getting us what we need."

"How…" Bastian whispered through the line of stunned faces, "how did you know that was in there?"

"Ciaran told me," I said, tossing the knob onto the bed. "I watched him put it in there for me to find. He told me that he didn't know what it said, but that it was what I wanted."

"He'd known you would be there?" Jocelyn asked, sounding impressed though not entirely surprised.

"Yes," I nodded as I walked over to join the group and began slowly unrolling and unfolding the note. "He said he'd had a vision months before where he'd seen me use the Iris and time walk back to see him, and he said that this," I paused, finally getting the paper open, "was what I had come for."

I passed the note off to Jocelyn who read it aloud. "*Look into the shew and find the origin…*"

"That's all?" Anderson asked.

"That's all," Jocelyn answered. "If this is the first portion of the prophecy I saw him complete in the memory, then the entire thing would read: *Look into the shew and find the origin that will pierce the shroud of my sight.*"

"Great," I grumbled, "can't just be easy, can it?"

"Actually," Bastian shrugged, "it's more straightforward than Seers' prophecies usually are."

"Straightforward? How is that straightforward? And what's a *shew*? Not like... you know," I raised my foot, "a shoe, right?"

"No," Bastian chuckled, to which I glared. "It's a shew stone, or seer stone. Seers use them to help see certain visions more clearly. Think of it like an antenna."

"So," Alex cut in, "if I'm understanding this, it sounds as though all we need to do is find this shew stone, and it will tell us how to read Ciaran's notes?"

"Hang on now," Anderson said, rubbing his head. "How do we even know that this is actually what we were after? I thought you said that he wrote the first part of the prophecy earlier the day he died?"

"That was simply my suspicion," Jocelyn said. "I was never certain. If Ciaran knew Becca would be there to hear him and he went to all that trouble to leave this where he knew she would find it, then he had to know that this is what we need."

"The two parts do make sense as a whole," I allowed, though I still wasn't thrilled with the riddle-esque structure of it.

"But then," Anderson continued, "when did he write that second bit that you saw? And how could he possibly not have known what was written on that scrap of paper if he'd wrote it himself?"

"The portion of the prophecy I saw him write must have come to him later on that day, or perhaps that night. As for why he didn't know what was on this," he lifted the paper, "it's hard to say."

"It could have been a trance," Bastian suggested. "Ciaran went into a trance at least once a week all in the time that I knew him."

"Then that's likely it," Jocelyn agreed.

"Wait, what's a trance?" I asked.

"Seers often put themselves into a trance state to receive more concentrated and powerful visions. That is when they would also make use of their shew stone," Jocelyn explained.

"Ciaran would stare into the thing for hours on end, while one of his hands wrote continuously, almost working separately from the rest of his body. He would often fill whole pages of his journal in just one sitting."

There was a long pause, then finally Jocelyn folded the paper back up and tucked it into his pocket. "I believe Alex is right," he said. "We need to find Ciaran's shew."

"I have it," Bastian said, "or, rather, my parents do. They kept it after he passed, as they considered it to be an artifact of Bhunaidh history. It is locked in the vault at our family estate. I could have it delivered to Adare in a day or two tops, though," he grimaced, "for that I will need my father's permission..." He sighed, brushing off his sudden worry. "But not to worry, I can come up with something to tell him without rousing suspicion."

"Good," Jocelyn nodded slowly.

"But will that do us any good?" Alex asked. "I thought that shew stones only worked for the Seers they were made for. Even another Seer shouldn't be able to see anything in his stone."

"It's true," Bastian agreed, "I've seen Ciaran's stone myself, and I've never seen anything."

"Well, Ciaran seemed to believe that there was something there to be seen, and in any case, it is still the most natural next step for us to take. Perhaps all that is needed is a clear idea of what we are looking for, which," he patted his pocket, "now we do." Did we? I certainly had no idea what he'd meant by "origin," but I let it go. "Or," Jocelyn continued, "maybe there is in fact nothing, and this will all turn out to be no more than a dead end. I don't have the answers, but I do know that the only way to get to them is to have a look at this shew for ourselves and see what there is to see."

He looked as though he was going to say more, but it was at that moment I felt the faintest tickle of two new abilities against my mind. They were abilities that I knew didn't belong to anyone in the room, and they were growing stronger by the second. Sucking in a sharp breath, I snapped my head toward the window, every nerve in my body on edge. "Someone's coming," I said, and immediately every eye in the room flew to me then the window, then back to me.

"This way?"

"Are you sure?"

"Can you tell who they are?"

"I don't see anything."

It was Jocelyn's calm but pointed voice that finally cut through the nervous chatter. "How many are there?"

"There are two of them," I told him.

"And you're sure they are headed this way?" he asked.

"Yes," I answered, "but I'm not sure who they are. One I think might be that McGary guy, but the other I'm not sure." *Damn it, why hadn't I been paying better attention?*

"I'll bet they followed us," Bastian said.

"But they are only arriving now?" Alex countered.

"It can't be a coincidence," Bastian insisted.

"We can't be seen here," Anderson said, "not all of us together like this."

"What do we do?" Chloe whispered, her hands fidgeting nervously as she looked from face to face.

Jocelyn quickly stepped over to the desk and picked up the Iris, stowing it safely in his inner jacket pocket. "Anderson is right, we can't be seen here. We will have to find a way to get out without them seeing."

"They are too close and there is only one road," I said. "They will see us drive away."

"She's right," Alex agreed, "and even if I hid us, I wouldn't be able to mask the sounds of our cars."

"They'd figure it out for sure," I finished, my heart rate picking up as I felt them growing closer.

"There they are," Anderson said, pointing toward the window, "coming round the bend, just down the way. We're running out of time."

"Everyone away from the windows," Jocelyn ordered. "Alex, hide the cars."

Alex glanced out quickly at the three vehicles parked out front. "Done," he nodded a moment later.

"Good," Jocelyn said with a short breath. "If they can't see the cars, then they shouldn't know that we're here. We will let them come, wait for them to leave, then we can follow behind."

"And if they come up here?" Chloe asked, her voice smaller than usual.

"Aye," Anderson said, "if they are here for the same thing we are, then they'll end up in the same place we did."

"I can hide us," Alex tried to assure them.

"No," Bastian said, raising a hand, "there is no way that will work."

"I can handle it," Alex said through his teeth.

"I'm sure you could keep us hidden to the eye," Bastian allowed, talking quickly, "but there is only so much you can do. Even if they don't come up here, what if someone sneezes, or moves even slightly and the floor creaks? Or if, heaven forbid, they do come in here, there is no way we can possibly fit in this room with the addition of two more people without bumping into something or someone."

"Do you have something better in mind?" Alex asked with a burn in his eyes like I'd never seen before.

"I do," Bastian nodded, walking quickly to the door. "Are they in sight of the driveway yet?"

"No," Alex said, squinting out the window, "but nearly."

"Keep all the cars hidden except mine, I'll need it," Bastian said, to which Alex nodded, though I could see his jaw was still locked tight. "I can take care of this," Bastian continued, turning to Jocelyn, "just wait here and keep watch." After only a second of hesitation, Jocelyn gave him a nod, followed a moment later by the crunch of tires on the gravel driveway. "Everyone stay out of sight and as silent as possible," he whispered, then without warning, he looked over at me and took my arm. "Not you," he said, pulling me out of the corner I was prepared to hide in and taking me with him toward the door. "I need you with me."

Chapter 20

Before I could put my confusion into words, Bastian had towed me out of the room, down the hall and to the stairs.

"Hey," I whispered sharply, pulling my arm free before he could drag me down the steps. "Do you maybe want to fill me in on what the hell we are about to do?"

"We," he paused, leaning down the staircase and listening for a moment, "are going to scare them."

"Scare them? Are you kidding?"

"No," he said, then hurried quickly down the steps.

I followed behind him as quietly as I could. "Seriously? That is your big plan? Jump out from behind a wall and say 'boo'?"

"There are many different kinds of fear," he said as we reached the first floor. "We are simply going to exploit the kind that stems from not wishing to be caught doing something you shouldn't be."

"What do you need me for?"

"You are my excuse for being here."

"What does that–"

"As much as I would love to fight with you," he cut me off sternly, but still with the shadow of that smirky grin I hated, "there really isn't time for this at the moment. What do you say we save it for the ride back, and for now you zip it and trust me, hmm?"

I was about to let him have it, but when I heard the sounds of car doors shutting and realized that our visitors had arrived, my rant stuck in my throat. We were out of time, and like it or not, as I had no plan of my own, I knew I was stuck with his. God damn it, why did he always have to be right?

"Ass," I growled under my breath.

"Thank you," he said, recognizing the compliance under my fury. *God, what I wouldn't give to rip that smile right off his face…*

"What are we going to do?" I asked, trying to curb my more violent thoughts.

"We just have to let them know we're here. Ah, good," he added almost to himself as he stretched to look out one of the windows at the end of the hall where the hood of a green car was just barely visible. "They parked along the side. They won't have seen my car."

"OK," I said, not sure what we were waiting for, "so let's go confront them."

I took a step toward the main door, but Bastian stopped me before my foot hit the floor. "No," he grabbed my shoulder, pulling me back, "not yet. We need to wait for them to come in."

"You really think they would just break in?"

"Probably. Though as it stands they won't have to. I didn't lock the door."

"Why not?"

"Why would I?"

Mumbles at the door ended our argument, and I held my breath as I heard the handle wiggle then the door gently click open.

"Look here," a voice said, blowing in through the door with a puff of cool, misty air, "wasn't even locked."

"Here we go," Bastian breathed at my ear. "Act natural and follow my lead." Then, without giving me the chance to complain or protest, he placed a hand on my back and pushed me forward, wrapping his arm around me in a more-than-just-friends kind of way. My first instinct was to push him away, but as we rounded the staircase and came into view, my nerves got the better of me and I tensed up.

"Mr McGary?" Bastian said, feigning surprise as we approached the two men frozen in the doorway, looking at us the same way one might look down the barrel of a shotgun.

"Bastian," McGary said, recovering quickly though still visibly on edge. "Do forgive the intrusion…" he paused, blinking a bit too fast. "I was not aware anyone would be here."

"Yes, well," Bastian said, perfectly assuming the flippant and haughty demeanor I'd not seen on him since our meeting in the hallway the morning before. "I found it simply horrid that Rebecca had yet to see the sunrise over a proper Irish countryside, and thought she might enjoy a morning away from… the crowds," he finished with a strange inflection in his voice.

"Ah," McGary nodded, a reciprocating tone in his own voice. "One does need privacy from time to time."

"Indeed," Bastian agreed.

Privacy? What were they…

Then suddenly my brain started assembling all the pieces: the hand around my waist, the excuse to get me away, the privacy comment – were they implying that Bastian and I had come out here… *romantically?* Oh, was he going to get it for this one…

"Again, so sorry to interrupt," McGary continued. "I simply wished to show Mr Ryan," he motioned to the other man with him, "your lovely cottage. We were out for a drive and he mentioned that he would like to look for a let this spring."

Please. He was so full of it…

"Of course, of course," Bastian said easily. "No trouble at all!"

"We will be on our way," McGary said, stepping backwards preparing to flee, "and again, do forgive our intrusion."

"Not at all," Bastian assured him, "and by all means, do not go on our account."

McGary turned back with a squint. "Pardon?"

Yeah, pardon?

"Becca and I are due back to Adare for lunch and were just leaving ourselves, so by all means feel free to look around."

"That is most generous of you, but we couldn't impose," Mr Ryan said, speaking for the first time.

Impose... right. Because breaking and entering is fine, but imposing is crossing the line.

"It's no imposition," Bastian told them, leading me over to the door. "Just remember to lock up when you leave," he added, shaking McGary's hand.

"Well... that is very kind of you, thank you," McGary answered, obviously shocked.

"It's nothing," Bastian assured them, sounding as though he was barely interested. "Are you ready my dear?" he asked, looking at me.

I nodded with my best try at a smile, so lost and confused that I was afraid to speak for fear I'd say something I shouldn't.

"Good day, Miss Clavish," Mr McGary said as I turned to go.

I nodded again to both Mr McGary and Mr Ryan, then walked out the door and toward Bastian's – apparently – lone car in the front drive, hoping my confusion and irritation was somehow reading as simple embarrassment. Bastian said goodbye once more, then jogged up behind me, still a picture of smooth ease. When we got to the car, he reached around me and opened my door, playing the part of the perfect gentleman.

"What are you doing?" I hissed out from between my teeth.

"Trust me."

He shut the car door behind me, waved one last time at the two men still standing in the doorway of the cottage, then climbed into the driver's seat and drove us off down the road, not looking back once.

"What was that?" I screamed, the second we turned the bend around the small hill in the meadow. "You just left them there! I thought you were going to scare them, not invite them to stay! What about everyone still hiding upstairs!"

"They won't go upstairs, I would stake my life on it. Trust me, the only thing they want to do now is get back to Adare as soon after we do as possible, be seen by as many people as possible, and make sure that no one starts talking."

"You don't know that!"

"Yes, I do," he said, entirely confident. "And second, they *were* scared, so as I see it, both missions were accomplished brilliantly."

"What was the point of scaring them if it wasn't to make them leave?"

"To make them talk."

I stared at him blankly. "What?"

"They were just caught trying to break into a house, and narrowly escaped suspicion – or at least so they think. They are now sitting alone – or, again, so they think – in a house with at least five minutes to burn before they can leave. Do you really think they will have nothing to say about the situation?"

"You were setting them up?"

"Let's just hope it was worth it."

"Wait," I said, looking around and realizing that we were getting further and further away from the cottage. "We aren't actually leaving, are we? Aren't we going to circle back around or something?"

"Why would we do that?"

Was he serious? "Because there are other people back there that might need our help!"

"They will be fine. I told you, they're not going to go upstairs."

"And I told you, you don't know that!" I snapped. "Turn around."

"Pardon me?"

"I said turn around, we are going back. There is no way in hell I am just going to leave my family in danger and just hope everything *works out* the way you *think* it will! Now *take me back!*"

Without warning, he slammed on the brakes and yanked the steering wheel, fishtailing us off of the road and onto the grass field that stretched out to our left. We bumped and bounced violently over the rocky dirt field for several dozen yards, until we reached what looked like an abandoned stone barn which behind and then turned off the car.

"What are you doing?" I asked, trying to keep up my fire and not let on that I was a little freaked out.

"I am forcing you to trust me," he said seriously, his annoying smile gone.

"I told you to take me back."

"This," he ignored me, and pointed out to the road we were just on, "is the only road leading to or away from the cottage. There is no other way to get anywhere unless you are on foot. We are going to sit here for five minutes, and I promise you that within that time, McGary and Ryan will come driving by, headed back to Adare, completely unaware that there was anyone in the house with them."

"And if they don't?"

"Then I will take you back as fast as this car can go."

"No, I'm not staying here, they could be in trouble. What if something happens?"

"I think they are all more than capable of taking care of themselves."

"Well, maybe I'm not willing to risk that!"

"It looks like you don't have a choice."

Was that so? I'd show him. I threw the door open and got out, ready to get back on the road and walk if I had to.

"Becca," he called, coming after me. "Please don't make me spend the next five minutes porting you back to the car."

"You can't keep me here," I ground out, balling my fists.

"I'm fairly certain that I can."

I was a breath away from punching him square in the face, wrestling his keys from him, and flooring it back to the cottage… but then I felt something. There were three abilities brushing my mind when a moment ago there had only been Bastian's.

Two new abilities had appeared and were growing stronger by the second – the same way they had when I'd felt them in the cottage. McGary and Ryan.

It was them.

I slowly turned around to face the road, took a few steps forward and looked around the corner of the decaying barn to the road, careful to stay out of sight. McGary and Ryan's abilities were growing stronger at a rate that told me they were approaching very fast, and before I knew it, the green car I'd caught a glimpse of outside the window of the cottage came barreling down the road, going well above whatever the posted speed limit was. They flew by the barn we were hiding behind without slowing, then raced off into the distance, their abilities growing fainter and fainter as the silhouette of their car faded into the distance until both finally disappeared completely.

I stood staring at the now empty patch of horizon, feeling all my anger and worry drain out of me like water from an unplugged tub. Then, to top off both my relief and my chagrin, I felt several other abilities come into my range – abilities that I knew very well. They approached just as the first two had, though not as quickly, growing stronger and brighter until the white St Brigid's van came into view with Anderson at the wheel, followed closely by the car we'd taken out, carrying Jocelyn, Alex, and Chloe. They approached, passed, and left, safe and sound, completely unharmed, and totally unaware that I was looking on.

He'd been right; Bastian had been one hundred percent right.

As I watched their cars shrink to dots in the distance, I heard the grass rustle as Bastian stepped up behind me.

"I know these people, Becca," he said gently. "I know how they think, what they do, who they are. What I know can help you – I can help you – but you have to let me."

"I am not going to apologize for wanting to be there for them," I said, quietly, my temper gone. "They're my family, and my family always comes first."

"Of course. But had I taken you back and McGary or Ryan had seen you, what then?"

The truth? I probably would have floundered, not come up with a good enough excuse as to why I'd come back, made them suspicious, maybe even have gotten us all caught, and who knows what from there. I didn't answer him out loud, but I couldn't help from bowing my head a little.

"Sometimes," he said, his tone telling me that he knew I understood, "the best way to help someone is to trust that they can handle themselves, and step back."

"I'm not good at that," I admitted, turning toward him but keeping my head down.

"I can see that," he grinned, though for some reason I didn't find it quite so annoying.

But then how could I be anything but grateful? He'd been right and hadn't rubbed my nose in it, he'd had a chance to shame me and hadn't taken it, and had even talked to me gently and with understanding when he could have just as easily scolded or schooled me. I wasn't about to say anything about it, but that didn't mean I didn't appreciate it.

I looked up, matching his cocked eyebrow with one of my own. "Shall we go?" I asked, realizing with a weird sort of relief that the tension which had hovered invisibly between us since the gala had thinned.

"Yes," he replied, one half of his mouth pulling upwards as we walked back over to his car. "And on the way," he added as we both opened our doors and got in, "you can do a little explaining of your own, starting with," he turned the ignition then glanced sideways at me, "what exactly was going on back in Ciaran's room."

The majority of the ride back to Adare was spent explaining my ability to a raptly attentive Bastian. Of course he'd already known that I was the one who could use the Iris, but what he hadn't known was what that meant. I was actually impressed that he'd been able to stand there the whole time we were in

Ciaran's room and watch everything happen without asking even one question – had it been me, I probably wouldn't have been able to stop asking.

As we rounded a large patch of trees and Adare came into view off in the distance Bastian finally spoke. "So," he said with a shake of his head, "you can do... everything?"

"Yep," I nodded. "Anything that anyone around me can do."

"But if you're alone, you can't do anything?"

"That's right."

"And the Iris takes it all into overdrive?"

"Pretty much," I laughed.

"Wow," he said, looking me over quickly with a squint.

"That's right," I smiled, making a show of flipping my hair. "I'm awesome."

He chuckled, rolling his eyes. "Something like that. Must be hard though," he said after a moment.

"What?" I asked, feeling oddly exposed all of a sudden.

"Seems like a lot of pressure, that's all."

I looked out the window at the grass and foliage as it whisked by. "It's... fine." When I saw him glance at me though the reflection on the glass, I pursed my lips and tried to ignore the skepticism on his face. "You wouldn't understand," I mumbled, sinking further into the seat.

"No," he shook his head, resting back casually. "What would I know about the pressure of living up to expectations...?"

I sighed, but didn't say anything. I knew he'd understand but I wasn't in the mood to share. Or maybe it was that I didn't want to actually admit my insecurities out loud, but either way, I decided it was time for a change of subject.

"I think I've done enough explaining for one day, now it's your turn," I said, shifting in my seat to face him. "Let's talk about how you made me look like some floozy, who would sneak off to a private cottage with a guy she'd only just met."

"To McGary and Ryan?" I raised my eyebrows with an affirmative glare. "I did no such thing."

"Oh please," I scoffed, "it was more than clear what you were implying."

"I was merely implying that they were intruding on something intended to be a private encounter. Anything else they may have derived was nothing but speculation. Besides, I really don't see the problem," he shrugged. "I had to tell them something that they would accept without question, and that might be a touch embarrassing."

"A touch? I'd say it's well more than a tou–"

"Not for you," he interrupted, "embarrassing for them."

"Well congratulations, you covered us all."

"It was not my intention to make you uncomfortable – and what, pray tell," he added, with his mouth in a grin as he pretended to be offended, "is so embarrassing about being found with me? You could do a lot worse, if I do say so."

"This is not about you, it's about me! I don't need rumors going around the manor about how you and I snuck off for a..." I waved my hand, looking for a word.

"Shag?" he suggested, his grin turning to a full on smile when I blushed.

"I was going to say *tryst*, thank you," I informed him, raising my chin with a scowl when he chuckled.

"A rumor would require those who saw us tell someone what they saw, and to do that they would have to admit to being there, which is the last thing they will want to do. If I thought you would be in any danger from them, I would not have involved you. Believe it or not, I am not one to sully a lady's good name so carelessly. You can rest assured that your reputation will remain unscathed."

"It'd better," I huffed, though deep down I knew he was right. McGary and Ryan weren't about to open themselves up to questions by spreading gossip, and as for the two of them, I didn't give a rat's tail what they thought.

As we pulled onto the long driveway for the manor, I was looking forward to getting out of the small car and stretching my legs… until I felt an all too familiar ability brush my mind and I looked up to find Shannon and her mother standing at the entrance of the manor, apparently waiting for the valet to bring their car.

"Oh no…" I breathed, closing my eyes for a second.

"What's wrong?" Bastian asked, his brow somewhere between worried and confused.

"Your girlfriend is up there and for some reason she hates me," I said, the truth coming out before I could stop it.

He looked up ahead to the figures standing at the top of the drive, his expression flipping instantly from confusion to an eye roll of annoyance. "Shannon is not my girlfriend."

"Really? Sure sounded like you two had a thing… from what I heard, anyway," I said, remembering the overheard conversation in the bathroom.

"I can assure you there is no 'thing' – much as she and her mother may wish otherwise," he added with a slight grimace.

"Oh," I said, strangely happy to hear it. "Well, good. You could do better." He huffed a laugh. "But if you aren't together, then why does she hate me so much?"

He shook his head with a smile, though there was more distaste in it than humor. "That's easy; you stole her thunder."

"Her what?"

"Shannon is a Healer like her father, however unlike most of the other women in the Bhunaidh, she is a full Holder, and as such she is quite powerful. I'm sure you know how rare it is for a woman to have an ability that is as developed as her male counterparts." I happened to think it was crap, but I was aware of it, so I nodded. "The strength of her ability makes her rare, which makes her a big deal around here. She is always in the spotlight at gatherings like this, not to mention being number one on my mother's personal list of girls to marry me off to… that is, until the daughter of *Bronntanas* blew in."

"Wait, she's jealous? Are you kidding me? *That's* the reason she's been treating me like scum on the floor?"

"Shannon and I have known one another since we were too young to recall, and she has never been one to tolerate anyone getting in her way. And unfortunately for you, she sees you as just that."

"Can you just drive around and let me off somewhere else?" I asked, mortified that I was actually nauseous at the thought of having to walk by her to get inside.

"What are you worried about?" When I didn't answer, his voice grew softer. "Listen to me, don't let her get to you. She is not worth a second of your time. Shannon and her mother represent the worst sort here in this association of hypocrisy and condescension. Brush it off."

"I am," I answered without looking up. "I mean, I want to… I'm just… I'm not used to…" My voice died off and I gave up, not knowing what was worse: wanting to hide from Shannon, or having actually admitted it to someone else.

"No," he said, a sneaky grin in his eyes. "I have a better idea." He pulled up to the entrance of the manor, just as calm as could be, while I tried to keep from looking like a cat about to be thrown in a bathtub.

"What are you doing?" I hissed as he grabbed the handle of his door.

"Don't worry, it will be fun."

"I've done this a few times now, and it has never been fun."

"That was because you didn't have your secret weapon," he said, stepping out of the car, then leaned back in back in with a wink. "Me."

Oh right, because having them see me with you will make things better…

I didn't dare look anywhere other than at the dashboard as he came around the car and opened my door for me, leaving me no choice but to stomp down my cowardice and step out.

"Bastian, please, I don't want to do this," I whispered, not knowing what he had planned, but twitching at the thought of what it might be.

"You don't have to do anything," he said softly. "All you have to do…" He paused, pulling my arm through his as he assumed the usual self-assured mask that he was never in public without, "is smile."

Unable to make myself do anything other than comply, I put on my best happy face and let him lead me away from the car and toward the manor. As Bastian handed the car keys to the valet, I ventured my first glance over to the two women watching us with the same cocktail of emotions you might have while watching footage of a natural disaster: shock, horror, disbelief, fear, with just a tad of vulnerability. As I turned my eyes back toward the entryway, my smile became natural as a wave of rippling triumph washed over me. I knew that taking pleasure in the discomfort of others was kind of evil, but at that moment, I didn't care. Far as I was concerned, they deserved it. As Bastian and I walked past, I was able to lift my head up and walk tall for what felt like the first time since we'd arrived at Adare, and it felt amazing. After all the things she called me, and despite all the reasons she thought I was beneath her, I'd gotten the thing that she wanted most. Or at least she thought that I had, and that was all that mattered. I wasn't going to be her doormat any more, and I was done taking her crap. I was back in control – I was free.

Take that, bitch…

CHAPTER 21

"Oh my gosh, oh my gosh, oh my gosh…" Chloe breathed in wonder as she stepped into my room at Adare for the first time.

"Pretty cool, right?" I asked, enjoying the "kid on Christmas morning" look on her face.

"*Cool*?" she repeated, looking at me like I'd lost it. "It's the most amazing thing I've ever seen!"

"Here you go," Alex said, setting her small suitcase on the ground next to the bed. "Enjoy your stay, miss," he smiled, tipping his imaginary bellman's cap.

"Thank you Alex," Chloe said dreamily, not even looking at him as she continued her wide-eyed appraisal of the room.

"If you are waiting to be tipped, you might be here awhile," I snickered, as Alex took a spot by my side. With a grin, he bent his knee, bringing his foot up from behind and kicking me in the butt. I swatted his hand away with a playful shove, only giving in because Jocelyn stepped into the room behind us.

"All right," he said, closing the door. "Is everything brought in?"

"That's all of it," Chloe said, skipping over. "I only had the one bag."

"Good," Jocelyn nodded. He looked Chloe over for a moment as she did her best to appear calm and attentive. He took a slow stride toward her, lowering his head and looking out gently but sternly from beneath his brow. "Now: rules. You are not to leave this room."

"Yes, I know," Chloe said obediently.

"The only way you are allowed outside these walls is if Alex is with you and hiding you."

"Of course," she nodded.

"It is imperative that you are not seen. No one can know you are here."

"I understand."

"And the same goes for the rest of you," he looked over at Alex and I as he pointed to Chloe. "She is not here."

"Got it," I said as Alex nodded.

With a deep breath Jocelyn stepped back, looking satisfied. Honestly I was surprised he'd even allowed Chloe to stay with us, and hadn't sent her back to St Brigid's with Mr Anderson. He'd said it was because we might need her time walking again, and I guess that was true, though I was pretty sure it wasn't the real reason. More likely he realized that it was downright cruel to bring the poor girl all the way out here and get her hopes up only to send her straight back home again. There was no harm in letting her stay as long as she kept her head down, and I was happy to have her with us. Sure my room would be a bit more crowded and we'd have to share a bed, but the room and bed were more than big enough for the both of us. There was also the minor issue of the lack of privacy should Alex finally be able to spend the night, but that also wasn't a big deal, considering that he still had a room to himself that we could... make use of.

"As for the rest of us," Jocelyn went on, "we will await word from Bastian regarding the shew. He is trying to determine if and when he can get it here, and believes he will know by tomorrow morning at the latest, so until then, go about your day as usual. Speaking of which," he glanced at his watch, "we are due at lunch any minute." He looked over to me as he opened the door. "We will see you there, don't be late."

"I won't," I assured him, concealing an eye roll. As he walked out into the hall, Alex followed behind him, but not before brushing his hand against mine with a heart tickling goodbye smile. A moment later, they were both gone.

"This is so amazing!" Chloe squealed under her breath the second the door closed. "It's like I've gone to heaven!" She floated over to the bed and fell backwards onto it with her arms stretched wide.

"I'm glad it didn't disappoint," I smiled, going to the mirror to look myself over. "I'll come back after lunch and we can hang out. Will you be OK until then?"

"I'll be perfect," she sighed, rolling over on her stomach, letting her feet dangle behind her like a child. "Don't hurry back on my account, I'll have plenty to do!"

"There's really not much to do here, is there?" Chloe asked the next morning as we sat on my bed, picking at the last of our room service breakfasts.

Lunch the previous day had taken a lot longer than I had anticipated, flowing right into a guided tour of the gardens that I couldn't weasel out of, then straight into dinner, which left Chloe on her own in the room for the better part of seven hours. When I'd finally gotten back after dinner, we were both wiped out and had decided to go right to bed. By the time we woke up the next morning, I could tell the charm and allure of the castle setting had worn thin for poor Chloe, and boredom was starting to take over.

"Sorry, hon," I said, popping the last of my toast in my mouth.

"Oh, no," she said quickly, as though determined to stick to her "this is the best thing ever" mindset, "don't be sorry, it's fine, really. I simply should have packed better, you know… brought… more to do…"

"Don't worry," I told her, pushing my tray away and folding my legs up under me. "So far, there is nothing planned for today, so we can hang out all morning. And later, Alex can swing by and maybe get you out and about for a little while."

"That'd be nice," she admitted, sliding off the bed and going over to the window. "Looks like it might be a clear day, maybe we could go outside. What is the garden like this time of year?"

She looked to me for an answer, but I wasn't paying attention. I was distracted by the rustling I heard at the door. When she saw me listening, Chloe also went still, tuning her ear and quickly drawing the same conclusion I had – there was someone out there. My pulse began to pound, but I stayed still, not sure what to do. Who was it? Not a friend or they would have knocked. Was someone listening to us? Were they trying to get in? Should I call for help?

We stared at the door until something began to force its way through the gap between it and the floor, which is when we both caught our breath. Jumping off the bed, I waved toward Chloe who took the signal and ran for the bathroom, shutting herself in. Determined to catch the intruder in the act, I ran silently over to the door, took a shaky breath, and flung it open to find... Steven. He was crouched down, attempting to slide a note under the door, looking up at me like someone had just popped a balloon right behind his head.

"Steven!" I sighed, rubbing my face. "What are you doing down there? You scared me."

He stood timidly, still holding the note in his hand. "S-sorry, I didn't w-want to dis-sturb you."

"Don't be silly," I smiled. "What's going on? Is everything OK?"

"I h-have a me-essage from B-Bastian."

"Oh," I took the folded piece of paper from his hand, "great. Here," I said, poking my head out and checking the hall quickly, "you should come in before someone sees you."

He nodded and stepped in, scanning the hall once more himself before shutting the door. "Th-thank you."

"It's OK, Chloe," I called toward the bathroom as I opened the note. She peeked out, but hesitated when she was someone with me. "It's fine," I motioned for her to come out.

"I thought no one was supposed to know I'm here," she whispered, still hanging back.

"It's all right, Steven's a friend. Steven, this is Chloe Quinn, she came up to lend us her time walking ability. Chloe, this is Steven Bloch, he is Bastian's brother."

"Nice to meet you," Chloe said, finally coming to join us.

"It's a p-pl-leasure," Steven said, taking her hand and bending over it politely.

I grinned to myself when I heard Chloe gasp and saw her cheeks flush at his show of chivalry. She might have to be stuck in one room for the duration of the trip, but at least she was able to get a little of the old world regality I knew she'd hoped to find at this place. That was nice at least.

"Becca," I began to read Bastian's note aloud. "I'm sorry to say the gift I promised you won't arrive until tomorrow, but the books for your project arrived today, and I would be most happy to go over them with you this evening, if you are free. Best Regards, Bastian." I lowered the letter, feeling my face wrinkle in confusion. "Gift? Project? I mean, I get that he was trying to be discreet, but if I can't even understand it…"

"Your father req-quested books fr-rom the a-archives," Steven said. "They have ar-rived and y-you and Bastian are su-upposed to go th-through them."

"Right," I sighed, "I forgot that was my job. So I guess that makes my 'gift' Ciaran's shew stone. Well," I refolded the letter and tossed it onto my dresser, "I guess that's better than nothing. Thanks, Steven."

"You're we-elcome," he smiled, turning to leave.

"Do you want to stay? We were just going to hang out here and maybe watch a movie?"

"I wo-ould, but ha-ave to get b-back before they s-see I'm gone."

"Yeah sure, more important things to do, I get it," I squinted jokingly. "Well, if you get bored, we'll be here."

"Th-thank you."

I opened the door and leaned into the hall to make sure it was clear before Steven gave us a farewell smile and slipped out of the room like a shadow, hugging the wall as he hurried out of sight.

As I locked the door behind him, I couldn't help but smile. "It's nice to see him helping out," I said, "the poor kid's had it rou–" but my throat seized up when I turned back around and saw the stricken look of horror on Chloe's face. She hadn't moved since coming to stand by us from the bathroom, and the terrified look in her teary eyes made her seem fragile as glass.

"I…" she rasped, her voice thin as a reed, "I…"

"Chloe?" I took her trembling hands in mine. "Chloe, honey, what's wrong?"

She didn't move, continuing to stare blankly at the door. "I… I don't… I…"

I started to panic. "Chloe," I begged, fear making my voice harsh. "Tell me what's wrong. What happened?" My own hands started to shake as I led her over to the bed to sit down. I'd never seen anyone like this before, what in God's name had happened? She was fine a minute ago. I quickly decided that she had one last chance to talk to me, or I was calling for help. "Chloe, please…"

Finally looking away from the door and over to me, she blinked rapidly, the tears that had been sitting on her lids spilling down. "I… He…" she stammered again, this time picking up her hand and showing it to me. It was the hand that Steven had taken.

Wait a minute.

She'd been fine… Steven had come in… touched her hand… She'd gasped… blushed… hadn't spoken since… fell apart the second he left…

No… freaking… way…

"Chloe, look at me," I said gently, taking her shoulders and turning her to face me. "Did you just…" I paused as her eyes met mine, "…Is he your…"

Instead of answering, she began to hyperventilate, but having been there myself, that was all the answer I needed. No doubt about it – she had bonded. Steven was Chloe's Anam.

"OK," I sighed, trying not to smile. "OK, take it easy, sweetie." I began rubbing my hands up and down her arms trying to sooth her. "Everything's fine, just breathe."

She looked up at me with a face both crazed and confused and started to ramble. "It's not fine! How can you say it's fine? It's not fine! It's horrible, and it won't stop, and this isn't right! Wait!" Her head snapped up suddenly. "He's a Holder, this can't be right! You and Alex are supposed to be the only ones like that, not me. I'm supposed to have a normal person, so this is a mistake, right?" she asked, almost hopeful as though she'd found some loophole.

"Sweetie, Steven's not a Holder."

"But you said he's Bastian's brother?"

"He is, but for some reason he was born without an ability," I told her, clearly bursting her bubble. "He's just a regular guy."

"But... but..." she stuttered, her panic setting back in.

I lifted her chin, hoping to get her to focus on the positive. "Chloe, I knew it's sudden, but this is a good thing! You've found your Anam, it's what you've always wanted! What you've been waiting for!"

"No!" she jumped up off the bed and started pacing back and forth in front of me, "no, this isn't right, it wasn't supposed to feel like this! It was supposed to be wonderful and romantic and amazing, not terrifying and nerve-racking and... are you *smiling*?"

Damn it, I was. "N-no..."

"How is this funny? This isn't funny!"

"I know that, I'm sorry," I assured her, standing and leading her back to the bed, biting back my grin. I hated myself for letting her think I would laugh at her state, but something about it was just so oddly cute – not to mention amusingly ironic.

"What do I do? Tell me what to do," she pleaded. "I changed my mind, I don't like this, how do I make it go away?"

"It doesn't go away," I said, sitting her down again next to me, desperately searching for the right thing to say, "or I mean, it changes. Well, not changes, really, but gets better…" God I sucked at this! I'd been through this, I should know what to tell her, but for some reason I couldn't put what I was thinking into words. Then it hit me. "You know what?" I said, perking up as suddenly I knew exactly what to do. "Why don't we call Alex?" If there was anyone who always knew the right thing to say, it was him.

I hurried over to the phone and dialed the number to his room, crossing all my fingers that he would be there.

"Hello?" he answered.

"Hey, it's me, you need to come to my room."

"Is everything OK?"

"Not really. I mean it's nothing bad, exactly, I just… need help."

"Be right there."

"He's on his way," I said, hanging up and turning back to Chloe – or at least where she had been a second ago. "Chloe? Chloe!" I yelped when I saw her at the door with her hand on the knob. "Where are you going?"

"I don't know," she admitted with a whine as I took her hand off the handle. "I feel like I should be out there, he's out there. I don't know how I know, I just do. I can feel it. It's like this thing," she fisted her hand over her chest.

"Yeah," I said, leading her away from the door and into a chair across the room. "That happens when he's nearby, you'll get used to it."

"Oh…" she whimpered, hugging herself tightly as she began to whisper hysterically, "this isn't right, this can't be right. Are you sure I can't go out for just a moment?" She looked up at me, then quickly shook her head. "No! No I don't want to. I can't see him, what would I say? Oh, this is horrible, why did I ever want this? I didn't want this, this wasn't what was supposed to happen…"

Knock, knock, knock!

I ran over to the door, letting out a breath of relief when I saw a nervous Alex standing behind it. "You're just in time," I told him quietly as he stepped in.

"What's going on?" he asked, scanning the room quickly and seeing the trembling form in the far chair. "Chloe?" he said, hurrying over and taking a knee in front of her chair. "What happened?"

"It's horrible…" she squeaked. When she didn't continue, he put a consoling hand on her knee and looked over to me.

"Well," I said walking over. "Steven came to bring me a message a little while ago. He and Chloe met."

"OK," he said, his brow furrowing as he tried to understand. "And?"

"And… they shook hands…" I said, raising my eyebrows to stress the point.

The confusion on his face remained for a fraction of a second before it fell to a blank stare. He looked at me, then to Chloe, then back to me. "You don't mean…" he trailed off, finishing the thought with his eyes. I nodded, once again biting my lips to keep from grinning. At my confirmation, a spark lit behind his eyes as well, and he bent his head down to try and hide his smile.

But it wasn't hidden well enough. "You're laughing too?" Chloe yelled as she shot up out of her chair. "Why is everyone laughing? This is not funny!"

"Of course it's not," Alex assured her, quickly getting himself back under control. He took her hands and brought her back down to the chair, pulling the nearby ottoman over and sitting in front of her. "I know it's not funny. It's scary, and it's intimidating, and it's overwhelming." She nodded with a sniff. "I know. But I promise it won't stay that way forever. It's difficult now because it's new, but soon you'll adjust, and when you do, you'll realize that it truly is everything that you'd dreamed it would be. That and so much more. You'll have a connection with someone like you've never imagined possible, and all you'll wonder is how you'd gone so long without it." Chloe's shoulders relaxed as she absorbed his words, her red eyes watching him calmly while I tried to blink away the mist I felt filling my own. "He will become your entire life," Alex went on, "not replacing, but enhancing everything you already love, making your world richer just by being there. You can't go without them, and it's scary. I'm not going to lie to you, that part never fully goes away. But in the end, you wouldn't trade it for anything."

When he finished, Chloe took a deep breath as though letting his words resonate, while I did my best to fight the choking knot in my throat. I'd known he would know what to say to Chloe to calm her, but I hadn't expected him to turn me inside out in the process.

"Thanks," Chloe finally said with a weak smile.

"No problem," he tapped her under the chin. "Just give it time. Now," he said standing and pulling her up with him, "why don't you go freshen up a little bit…" He wiped one of the tear tracks off of her chin with the back of his hand, "and we can all go out for a walk and get some air."

With a nod and another sniff, Chloe left for the bathroom, while Alex turned and walked slowly my way.

I crossed my arms, avoiding his eyes with a shy stubbornness. "You suck," I mumbled, my voice thick with the tears I was still trying to subtly blink away.

Smiling, he took my face into his hand and pulled me to him, wiping away the lone tear I'd let escape with his thumb. He brought his lips down to meet mine in a kiss so warm and soft I wanted to wrap myself in it like a blanket and never leave. After a lingering moment he broke the kiss and pulled back ever so slightly, his lips grazing mine as he spoke, "I love you, too."

With the sound of the faucet in the bathroom turning off as our cue, we separated, him kissing my head quickly before he went while I wiped away what was left of the moisture in my eyes.

"So," I said, clearing my throat, "what do we do now?"

"I guess someone should go and tell Jocelyn."

"Yeah," I agreed, "maybe he can figure out a way to get Steven to come back to St Brigid's with us."

"You think Jocelyn would try to bring him over?"

"Apparently he's tried before, but Steven has always said no."

"Why?"

"Jocelyn thinks it's because of his parents. That's why he never pressed the matter. But those times it had only been for Steven's sake, to try and save him from his life here, but now," I motioned to the bathroom, "there is obviously an entirely new reason."

"I know the Bhunaidh don't look fondly on bonding, but even still, Steven would have to know about it. Maybe if Jocelyn spoke to him, and tried to explain?"

"That's it," I whispered, my eyes glazing over as the answer suddenly occurred to me. I hurried over to my shoes and slid them on. "Stay with Chloe, I'll be back."

"But Jocelyn's at the—"

"Not Jocelyn," I interrupted, "I need to go see Bastian."

"What? Why?" he asked, suddenly looking wary.

"To tell him, so he can help us," I said, running a brush through my hair. "If anyone can explain what's happened and talk Steven into coming to stay with us, he can."

But Alex still looked unsure. "And you are sure he will?"

"If there is one thing I am sure of, it's that he loves his brother and wants him to be happy," I told him, going back over to him and pecking him on the cheek. "He'll help, I know it. Keep an eye on Chloe for me, will you? Take her for a walk, get her a snack, whatever you have to do, just keep her away from Steven."

"No problem," he said, smiling stiffly then looking away.

"I'll be back soon," I called over my shoulder as I pulled the door open and hurried out. I wasn't sure where Bastian was, but I didn't care if I had to search the entire castle from top to bottom, I would find him and get him to help. Chloe deserved her happy ending; I was going to make sure she got it.

CHAPTER 22

"Bastian?" I called when I arrived at his room and saw that the door was ajar. I knocked gently before poking my head in to find Bastian standing by his bed, rolling up the sleeves of his collared shirt. When he looked up and saw me something flashed across his face that was too quick for me to read. But before I could ask, the question answered itself.

"Becca!" came Alva's surprised voice from the side of the room I'd not seen. "What a surprise!"

"Oh, I'm sorry," I stammered, my brain scrambling for the right thing to say, "I didn't mean to interrupt…"

"Not at all," Bastian said, stepping forward to pick up the proverbial dropped ball. "It was wretched of me to keep you waiting, I am terribly sorry."

"Waiting?" Alva asked, an excited flicker in her eyes.

"Yes," Bastian lied casually. "I promised Becca a walk this morning, but today's workout delayed me."

"Now Bastian," Alva scolded, coming over and taking my hand, bringing me out of the doorway and into the room. "Is that any way to treat a lady?"

"It's not a problem," I said, doing my best to play along. "I understand."

"You know boys," Alva sighed, putting her arm around me and leaning in, "always with their games and toys. But don't worry, it isn't you dear," she assured me with a wink, "nothing can keep Bastian from his daily fencing practice."

"Oh?" I raised my eyebrows feigning interest. *"Fencing" again, huh? Yeah right...*

"Heavens, yes. He's studied rigorously for years, isn't that right dear?" she beamed at Bastian.

"It's just a hobby," he shrugged passively, though the tension in his shoulders didn't match his tone.

"He's too modest, why I don't think I've ever seen someone as dedicated–"

"All right, Mother," he sighed, coming over with his shoes dangling from his front two fingers. "That is quite enough boasting for one morning."

"It's not boasting, it's pride," she corrected in that very motherly way, "but if you insist."

"I do," he said flatly, slipping on his first shoe.

"Very well then," she said, then added with a look that was intended to look stern when it was clear that deep down she was thrilled, "but don't you treat this gorgeous woman so carelessly again."

"I wouldn't dream of it."

"Well, I certainly don't want to be in your way," she said, backing toward the door with a look on her face that was almost embarrassing it was so transparent. "You two have a lovely time."

"We will," Bastian said with his usual smirk.

"Thank you," I added, not sure what else to say.

With one more awkwardly suggestive smile, Alva floated out of the room, being sure to guarantee us privacy by shutting the door as she left. Bastian stayed perfectly still, listening for a full five seconds before finally looking back over to me, one eyebrow raised. "You seem to have made something of a habit out of testing my ability to improvise."

"Sorry, but I needed to talk to you."

"It couldn't have waited until tonight," he asked, sitting as he tied his second shoe, "or didn't you get my note?"

"Yes, I got it, that's sort of why I'm here, and no, it couldn't wait."

He must have heard the urgency in my voice because it reflected in his own. "What's wrong? Has something happened?"

"Yes, but it's kind of random. It's got nothing to do with Ciaran and all that, it actually has to do with Steven."

He stood, utterly serious now. "What about him?"

"It's not bad," I told him, hoping to quell the worry I saw in his eyes, "it's actually kind of great. Turns out Steven is Chloe's Anam."

All expression fell from his face. "What?"

"I know, right," I smiled. "Who knew? She bonded to him when he stopped by to deliver your note."

"And you're sure?" he asked, face still blank.

"Oh yeah. I was there, it definitely happened."

"Does Steven know?"

"No, she didn't react until after he was gone. That's why I came," I explained, his lack of response beginning to make me uneasy. "I was hoping you could talk to him. Let him know what happened, and maybe try to convince him... to..." But my thought died when he turned and wandered off as though he was in a trance, his face still entirely unreadable. "Bastian?"

"This can't happen," he whispered, pacing slowly back and forth in front of his bed. "It can't."

"Well, it did," I said, growing annoyed, "so now we have to deal with it."

"No, *we* don't" he pointed out toward the hall, "*she* does. Steven cannot find out about this – *no one* can find out."

"Excuse me?" I demanded, my temperature rising. "Do you even realize what you're saying?"

"Do you?" he growled. "Do you have any idea what will happen to him if anyone finds out that someone has bonded to him? Do you know how the Bhunaidh regard the Anam bond?

What it represents to them? Steven has more than enough failings in their eyes, the last thing he needs is this to top it all off."

I couldn't believe what I was hearing. "So what are you saying?"

"I'm saying that Steven is never finding out about this. He will continue on with his life as though he and Chloe had never met, and she…" He hesitated slightly, "she will…" He paused again.

"What?" I snapped, my teeth grinding together, "*'get over it'*? Are you out of your mind? She didn't choose this, no one does, it just happens! Hell, she's spent the last hour trying to wish it away. How dare you tell her to get over it, you have *no* idea what she is going through."

"What she is going though is regrettable, but is also not my primary concern, Steven is."

"So what, that gives you the right to run his life? To deny him what would be the most amazing relationship he'll ever experience just because you 'say so'? You don't have that right any more than you have the right to keep Chloe away from the person she's bonded to."

"I have *every right* to do whatever I can to keep my brother safe."

"Not if it means dictating his life."

"At least he'll have a life!" he yelled.

"He could have a better one as Chloe's Anam!"

"You don't know that!"

"*You* don't know that, because you don't get it! You don't even realize what you'd be keeping him from!"

"*Yes I do!*" he roared, shocking me silent. The very air around us held its breath as we stared at one another, my eyes wide in skeptical surprise, while his wavered in indecision for a long moment before finally breaking like an angry wave. "It's everything!" he yelled, "It's devotion! It's love! It's a link that you can't break no matter how far you go!" He let out a shuddering breath from between his teeth, as the tension in his muscles started to relax as he lost steam. "It's having someone with you always, even when they are not actually there because a part of them is in you. It's knowing that there is someone thinking about you every moment they're not with you, wondering what you're doing and worrying over whether or not you're OK." Hanging his head, he rubbed a hand through his hair and sank down onto the edge of the bed, his elbows resting heavily on his knees as his shoulders sagged forward wearily. "It's everything."

I'm not sure how long I stood there staring at him, but I couldn't help it. I was totally at a loss. Never in a million years would I have guessed it, but now, looking at his defeated form hunched at the edge of the bed, it was blatantly obvious.

Bastian was bonded.

I'd known that Bastian was a good actor when it came to fooling everyone, and playing "the game," as he called it, but it wasn't until that moment that I realized just how good he was.

With a quiet sigh, I walked over to the bed and sat down next to him, following his example and staring down at the floor. "How long?" I asked after a moment.

There was a long pause before he answered, "Five years."

Wow. "And no one knows?"

"Steven," he said, sitting up, "but no one else."

Another quiet moment passed before I shook my head, unable to suppress a smile. "You are quite a piece of work, you know that?"

He glanced sideways at me, grinning in spite of himself. "You're one to talk."

"Yeah, well, I'm worth it," I said, batting my eyelashes, while he huffed a laugh and sighed. "So," I said with a cheeky grin, bumping his shoulder with mine, "what's her name?"

He laughed strangely and reached into his pocket. Pulling out a silver pocket watch, he flipped open the cover and handed it to me. At first there was nothing to see other than the time, but a second button next to the watch face opened a hidden compartment that held a picture. I looked down at that photo and saw blonde hair, pretty blue eyes, an attractive smile... and I couldn't have been more shocked.

"Oh," I said, embarrassed at how surprised I was. "I'm sorry, what's *his* name?"

Bastian chuckled at my reaction. "Justyn Niprùt."

"French?" I guessed from the accent.

He nodded, something helpless in the way he watched his hands as they lay in his lap. "He was born not far from Nice. He and his sister attend school with Steven and I. I bonded to him during my first semester back after my Awakening."

"Does he know?"

"About me? No. We've been," he paused as though he couldn't find the word, "together, for a while now, but the only time we have is at school. During breaks we'll meet up every morning to talk online or maybe video chat, that sort of thing."

I closed my eyes with a smile as I remembered the sounds of a computer coming from behind the door that morning Alex and I had followed him. "Fencing?" I asked, shaking my head. So that's what he'd been up to. No wonder he'd panicked at the thought of getting caught.

He nodded with a chuckle. "My parents believe me to be an expert with the amount of hours I've put in to practicing. Truth is, if anyone ever did come at me with a foil, I would be in quite a lot of trouble. But no," he said, sobering again, "Justyn knows only that Steven and I have a complicated home life, as that's all I've been able to bring myself to tell him. He has no idea what I am, what I can do, or why he'll never meet the rest of my family."

"Because they wouldn't approve?" I knew it was a stupid question, but I couldn't stop it.

"Approve?" He laughed without humor. "In the eyes of the Bhunaidh, the Anam bond is a curse; a terrible weakness that we are expected to rise above The idea that we could be tied forever to a person of no ability or standing is unacceptable, and to succumb to such a thing is a disgrace."

"But it has to happen sometimes, doesn't it? I mean, it's not like it's something that anyone can control."

"It can't be controlled, but it can be avoided. In order for the bond to be formed, you must make physical contact, and most Bhunaidh don't even enjoy sharing a room with average people, much less allow themselves to be touched by them. But of course, every now and then one of our number will suddenly disappear from society for reasons unknown, or perhaps begin to take frequent extended holidays," he emphasized the words suggestively. "Occurrences like those are never openly spoken of, but of course the rumors circulate and scandal ensues."

"That's so stupid…" I mumbled, rolling my eyes.

"Yes, it is," he frowned. "So no, to answer your question, my parents would most certainly not approve. Though even if they could somehow bring themselves to overlook the fact that I had 'allowed myself to succumb to the great weakness of our kind'," he quoted with derision, "they would never forgive me the fact that Justyn is male, and as such, guarantees them no traditionally begotten grandchildren, thus bringing an end to their long and prestigious line."

"Steven could still have kids," I suggested.

"If Steven himself is no longer welcome in the family, what makes you think any children of his would be?"

"Oh yeah…"

"Unfortunately for them, I am the one on whom all their futile hopes for the future lie. Though it's my own fault, leading them on the way I do and allowing them to believe whatever they wish. I suppose no plan is perfect."

"Is this why you couldn't leave?" I asked, motioning to the watch as I closed the cover and handed it back to him. "You told me that initially you and Steven had planned to leave as soon as you could but that things changed and you couldn't. Was it him?"

He didn't answer at first, but the guilt on his face told the tale. "I would have gone," he finally said, almost defensively before calming again, "or at least I like to believe I would have. But Steven said no. He knew – we both did – that if we left…"

"That you'd never see Justyn again," I finished for him.

He bowed his head. "We would have had to leave school. At that point I didn't know Justyn well enough to justify visiting him outside of school…" He tapered off again, but this time I didn't interrupt. "Steven knew that I had bonded, and he refused to follow through with our plan to leave when he knew that I would suffer – so we didn't go." He paused, collecting himself with a deep breath before going on. "That was when I became desperate to find a way to help him, even going so far as to consider working with Darragh. I had ruined our only chance of getting away, and Steven's only chance at a better life… I had to find a way to make it up to him."

I could see this was difficult for him, so when he didn't continue, I gave him some time, choosing my words very carefully before I spoke again. "I know what it's like to live only to protect and care for a little brother who can't always defend himself. And I know that you want to be able to give him the life he should have had. But you can do that now," I said gently. "He could be happy with us. Actually, I think maybe you both could." He glanced up like he might argue, but instead looked at me with what might have been the slightest hint of hope in his eyes. "Steven could finally be himself," I continued. "He wouldn't have to worry about hiding or being ashamed. He'd have Chloe to love and support him, and he would finally be able to branch out and have a life that is all his own. And by the way, Steven isn't the only one not living the life he deserves. Without Steven here to protect, you could you could stop spending every moment of your time pretending to be someone you're not, and start living the life you want. You could come with us, or go be with Justyn, maybe something in-between, or who knows, maybe something you haven't even thought of. I understand why you didn't want to go before, but things are different now. You and Steven are both adults, you and Justyn have a stronger relationship and no longer need school as an excuse to see one another, Steven has a real chance at happiness, and most of all, you have somewhere to go, with people who can help you both. You don't have to be on your own anymore."

He sat quietly for a long time while I waited, toes tapping nervously in my shoes. Eventually he rubbed his hands over his face and up through his hair. "I'm sorry," he said, looking up to meet my eyes. "I shouldn't have reacted the way I did. Of course Chloe bonding to Steven is a good thing for them both. The news simply caught me unawares, and I overreacted."

I snorted a laugh. "Yeah well, lucky for you, you're talking to the queen of overprotective freak-outs," I smiled, "so don't worry about it."

"I'll talk to Steven. I'll let him know what happened, and tell him what the options are, but as to what he wants to do from there, that part will be up to him. As much as I like to believe that I know what's best for him, in the end it should be his decision."

"What about you?"

"Depends on what he chooses. There is nothing I'd like more than to leave all this behind me forever," he admitted, looking idly around the room, "but if he decides to stay, I won't leave him here alone."

"I don't blame you."

Our eyes locked for just a second as he finished and something passed between us – something new, but still very familiar. He was a man doing everything he could to look after his brother. He didn't always know what to do, or the best way to do it, but he did the best he could. He may have overreacted and lost his temper from time to time, but that goes with the territory when you are fighting for someone you love. I'd found him annoying, frustrating, and exasperating, but truth be told, deep down… he was just like me.

He let out a long breath with a stretch, breaking the serious tone we'd been in for far too long with one of his trademark smiles. "Now then," he said, turning toward me and leaning back casually against the bedpost, his eyes filled with a humorous sort of skepticism, "we've covered my Anam, let's hear about yours."

"Sorry?" I said, trying to play it off, fully aware that I wasn't at all convincing.

"'*You* don't know what it's like,' that's that you said," he reminded me, cocking his brow, "not, '*we* don't know,' or '*no one* knows,' but '*you* don't know.'"

"I think you're reading way too much into my word choice."

"I don't think so. You fought far too vehemently and are far too knowledgeable to have only heard accounts of bonding from others." He crossed his arms. "Come now, out with it. I'll not be the only one giving up secrets today, now let's have it."

I wanted to deny it again, but the look on his face told me there was no use. He knew he was right and wasn't going to let it go until I admitted it. "OK fine," I huffed. "Yes, I've bonded with someone."

"There, see? You can't fool me." He folded his hands behind his head triumphantly. "So, what is his name? Where is he from? What monastery does he reside in?"

"Monastery?"

"Of course. For surely only a monk would have the patience for you… *Oof!*" he huffed, laughing as I smacked him with one of the enormous pillows from the head of the bed.

"You're hilarious," I sneered through a grin. "For your information, it's Alex."

He blinked, his eyebrows furrowing. "The Alex that you brought with you? The Caster?"

"That's the one."

"But he's a Holder, how on earth did that happen?"

I shrugged. "Who knows? I'm weird, remember?"

"Does he know?"

"More than that, he's bonded to me too."

"You're joking," he gawked with a surprised laugh.

"Nope."

"I'll be damned," he chuckled. Then a strange flicker sparked in his eye. "Well, I suppose that explains a few things…"

"What?"

"It's nothing," he said, but his snicker said otherwise.

"Don't give me that, what are you talking about?"

"It's no big thing," he insisted, "it's just, well, I've gotten something of an evil eye from Mr Bray on more than one occasion over the past few days," he told me, biting back a smile. "Now I know why."

Immediately I rolled my eyes. "Oh please," I scoffed. "If anything, he's eyeing you because I spent the first two days we were here convincing him that you were a jerk and he's having trouble giving up on the idea."

"Sure," he said, clearly pacifying me. "That's probably it."

I could see he wasn't convinced, but I let it go, as the whole notion wasn't worth arguing about. Alex was my whole world, he knew that. Sure, he hadn't been a fan of watching Bastian and I dance together, but that was nothing. He knew better than to actually be jealous.

"Anyway," I said, happy to change the subject, "if we are through discussing secrets and hidden lovers, I need to go see Jocelyn."

"I suppose we are," he nodded, standing and adjusting his shirt. "As it happens," he said as we made our way toward the door, "I was headed to see him myself before you arrived. I didn't think it wise to send him a note as I did you, so he still needs to be caught up on... certain deliveries," he winked. His hand paused on the door handle as he glanced over and offered me his free arm, his expression settling into the casual superiority of his public mantle, though he didn't quite hide the grin behind his cocked eyebrow. "As I happen to be going your way," he said in his too-cool-to-care way, "would you do me the honor of allowing me to escort you, Miss Clavish?"

"If you insist," I said dramatically, adopting a lofty manner of my own, raising my chin as I took his offered arm, "the privilege is all yours."

"Not bad," he chuckled under his breath as he pulled the door open for us. "You don't have my knack for delivery, of course, but not a bad start."

Luckily, there was no one to see the two of us come out of his room – as I couldn't even imagine the sort of rumors that would start – nor was there anyone in the main hallway or any of the lounges and seating areas we passed.

"Where is everyone?" I asked, actually enjoying the quiet.

"If I had to guess, I'd say the back lawn, either watching or partaking in the games."

"Games?"

"This morning is the field games tournament. Rings, skittles, lawn darts, that sort of thing."

"I'm going to assume those are all games?" I asked with a laugh, finding "skittles" particularly amusing.

"Of course," he said with a dramatic gasp as we turned down the hallway that Jocelyn's room was in. "How long have you been in country, now? I should think that at least you would…" But I silenced him with a slow raise of my hand as I concentrated on the two abilities I suddenly felt in one of the approaching rooms. They stood out to me because all the other rooms in that hallway were currently empty, making them the only abilities other than Bastian's that were anywhere nearby. However, it wasn't until I realized that I recognized them that my heart rate began to pick up. One was clearly Mr McGary, and the other I couldn't put a face to, but I knew I'd felt him somewhere before.

"What's wrong?" Bastian whispered, instinctively glancing around for trouble.

"Two people, one McGary and one I'm not sure of," I told him, the tension building in my stomach with every step.

"What are they doing?"

"I can't tell."

"Do you know where they are?"

"Yes," I nodded, my jaw tight, "they're in Jocelyn's room."

CHAPTER 23

"What could they possibly have been after?" Cormac wondered aloud as he, Jocelyn, Alex, and I sat around in the window-lined sunroom after lunch that afternoon. Most of the others guests had returned to the lawn for the second round of games, leaving us free to talk, so long as we kept an eye out and our voices down.

"We couldn't tell," I said. "I was worried it was the Iris, but theoretically they shouldn't even know it's here. Though, it was probably a good thing you had it on you, all the same."

"Indeed!" Cormac agreed. "Can you imagine?"

"Luckily, whatever they wanted, it didn't look like they found anything."

"And you are sure they didn't see you?" Jocelyn asked, looking pointedly at me.

"I'm sure," I nodded confidently. "We listened at the door until we heard them coming, then hid around the corner until they were gone."

"What were they saying?" Cormac asked.

"Not much," I frowned. "There was a lot of shuffling, then McGary called down to the front desk and requested a cleaning for the room."

"Clever," Cormac mused. "Come in for a search, ruffle things up, then call the housekeeper to tidy up after you. Even had something been out of place, you would likely have just assumed it was done during the cleaning."

That was smart. Sneaky bastards…

"After the call," I went on, "the other man – Cleen, according to Bastian – said that they weren't having any luck and should go." As it happened, Bastian had also told me that Cleen was one of the two men I had been spying on the night he had to port me to his room, which was probably why his ability felt familiar. However, as Jocelyn was still unaware of that little near-miss encounter, I left that bit out. "They both made a point in noting the time as they left the room, and then they were gone."

"The time?" Alex repeated. "Like they were late for something?"

"No, like seeing what the time was," I clarified. "Real specific too, down to the minute. In fact, Cleen even checked his watch again when they reached the end of the hall before they went their separate ways."

"What are you thinking, Jocelyn?" Cormac asked, having noticed the change in Jocelyn's face as I was talking.

Jocelyn leaned forward, resting his folded hands against his mouth. "There is only one reason I can think of as to why they would have needed to know the exact time. But I can't be sure unless…"

We all sat pensively, waiting for him to go on, but the rest of his thought never made it into words. After a long pause, he finally closed his eyes and let out a sigh, as though having made some silent decision that he was unhappy about but resigned to.

"Unless what?" I prompted, itching to know what he was thinking.

"Did you hear the time they said?" he asked me, though whether he was ignoring me or answering me, I couldn't tell. "What was it?"

"11.37," I said.

"Who said it, McGary, or Cleen?"

"McGary."

He nodded, but instead of explaining the question, he grew very still, his eyes clouding over the way they had at the cemetery. It was almost like he was doing a reading, but there was no way...

Right?

I mean come on, a reading on McGary? *From here?* Not a chance. McGary wasn't even in the room! He was probably at the games, which were on the other side of the manor, not to mention surrounded by dozens of other people. No way Jocelyn could pick his lone mind out of a crowd that big from this far awa–

"He's on the lawn watching the cricket match," Jocelyn said suddenly.

Holy... crap...

Much as I tried, I couldn't keep my jaw from dropping just a bit. I looked over at Alex who must have been enjoying my face as he was covering a smile.

"Seriously?" I mouthed silently, glancing between him and Jocelyn.

"*That's nothing,*" Alex casted onto the table in front of me, "*he could read Min right now if he wanted to.*"

I shook my head, trying to keep my awe under wraps. I knew I really shouldn't have been surprised, as I was more than aware that Jocelyn was incredibly powerful, having heard it time and time again. However, just like reading the dead, hearing about something and seeing it firsthand are two very different things. Though for some reason, the display of power was getting to me in a strange way that I didn't understand.

"*You're scared,*" the shadow in the back of my mind whispered, "*because you know that, powerful as he is, you are even more so...*"

A cold shiver of fear rippled through me as I kicked the unwelcome thought away, stuffing it back in the dark where it belonged.

"Damn it," Jocelyn mumbled suddenly, rubbing his eyes and breaking his haze.

"What happened?" Cormac asked.

I leaned forward, consciously keeping the tremor out of my voice. "Did you find out what they were doing?"

"I did not find what they were doing," he said with a frustrated sigh, "because the only thing there to find was exactly what I expected – a hole."

"A memory hole?" I whispered.

"Like the ones you found in Taron?" Alex asked.

"Exactly like the ones I found in Taron," Jocelyn nodded. "So much so, that I can all but guarantee that they were made by the same person."

Cormac looked puzzled. "How did you know that McGary's memory of this morning would be gone?"

"The time," Jocelyn answered. "I've been thinking a great deal about the memory holes ever since Bastian mentioned that he believed there was a fifth informant who was a Mentalist. I've come to believe that whoever it is, is an Observant, not a Compulsionary."

"Wait," I cut in, "a what?"

"All Mentalists can read minds to one extent or another," Cormac explained, "but Observant Mentalists are the ones who can erase thoughts and memories, and Compulsionary Mentalists are the ones who can alter or change them. Neither can do both – present party excluded, of course," he added glancing at Jocelyn.

"The only reason," Jocelyn continued, "that McGary and Cleen would have needed the time, was if they were working with an Observant who would need it to know what portion of their memories to cut."

"Couldn't the Mentalist just read the memory then cut out the parts they wanted out?" I asked.

"They could, but depending on the strength of the Mentalist's abilities, it could take a great deal of time. Cutting a clear chunk, from one predetermined point in time to another, would be far quicker, not to mention cleaner if he or she wasn't overly familiar with the process."

"So what now?" I asked, leaning back in my chair.

"The plan stays as it was," Jocelyn said. "Tonight, you and Bastian will see if there is anything of use to us in the books from the archives, and tomorrow we will see what we can garner from Ciaran's shew."

"Do we really still have to go through those old books?" I groaned. "I mean, I got it when we were looking for stuff on Ciaran, but now we don't need that anymore, right?"

"No, we don't," Jocelyn said, "but we do need anything we can find about the seeing ability as a whole, particularly with regards to shews and seer stones. We don't know exactly what we are looking for tomorrow, but the more information we have, the better off we will be."

"What about our mystery Mentalist?" Cormac asked, drawing the attention away from my grumbles. "If he is removing crucial memories from all of Darragh's informants, then it sounds like he may be the one chap who would have all the information we need to know."

"I agree, but if he is as careful as Bastian believes him to be, then drawing him out won't be easy."

"But at least now we know he's here," Alex pointed out. "He would have to be in the manor if something from this morning is already gone from McGary's memory."

"True," Jocelyn agreed, "and that is a place to start. In the meantime," he said, "I am going to return to my room and double check that nothing is missing, then rest for a while before dinner."

"I say," Cormac stood with a stretch, "a rest does sound lovely."

Jocelyn and Cormac began talking casually as the four of us left the sunroom, while Alex hung back to walk with me a few steps behind them.

"How did your talk with Bastian go?"

"It was interesting," I grinned, "that's for sure."

"What do you mean?"

Oh nothing, just that he's secretly bonded to a guy from school that no one knows about but Steven and I...

"I'll tell you when we're alone," I whispered. "But he is going to talk to Steven about coming back with us, so we'll see."

"That's great."

We arrived at the hallway with Cormac's room, and he turned off with a wave, and I realized that while Jocelyn and Cormac had announced their plans, no one had asked Alex and I what we were going to do. No orders, no plans, nothing. Maybe it was by design, or maybe it was an oversight, but either way, I got excited.

"Don't look now," Alex said with a smile, apparently having the same realization I was, "but we it appears we might have some free time."

"I was thinking that too," I grinned, "but I didn't want to jinx it."

"You feel like taking a walk?" he asked, sharing my tentative excitement.

"Sure," I said, fighting the urge to slide my hand into his, "that sounds great. But shouldn't we check on Chloe?"

"Looked in on her right before lunch, she was out cold."

Alex hadn't had much luck in getting Chloe out for walk while I was talking to Bastian, so instead he'd taken her to Cormac who had been able to procure a sleeping draught from one of his Alchemist friends. Good thing too, because I have no idea what we would have done with her the rest of the day. Now she could sleep off the emotional rollercoaster that was the first several hours of a new Anam bond – which, take it from me, was the way to do it – and the rest of us could have the afternoon off.

"Good," I said, "she needs it."

"So, then you're free?" he asked, his eyes lighting up.

"Always," I smiled.

I wasn't sure if he truly wanted to take a walk, or if he was just being discreet and really had something a bit more... *private* in mind, but to be honest, I didn't care. It felt like I hadn't seen him in ages, and as long as we got to be together, it didn't matter what we did. Finally it would just be me and–

"Bastian?" Jocelyn said suddenly.

I looked over to the adjacent hallway where Bastian was indeed walking toward us.

"Good afternoon," Bastian said with a polite nod, ever conscious that someone might be watching. "I wonder if you would mind sparing me a moment of your time? If you are not presently engaged, of course."

"No, not at all," Jocelyn said, "In fact I was just on my way to my room, if you would care to join me."

"Thank you," Bastian nodded again, joining our group as we continued down the hall.

A few steps later and we reached the corridor that held Jocelyn's room and turned down it – all of us, that is, except Alex who hesitated.

"What's wrong?" I asked, turning back while Jocelyn and Bastian continued on, having not noticed.

"I don't think they really need us," he shrugged, "why don't we just go?"

"But it sounds like something might be up," I said as I kept going, waving for him to follow. "Besides, even if he did want us, it's not like he could have said so."

"Yeah..." he mumbled with a weird grimace, glancing away for a second.

"Don't worry," I smiled, "it'll only take a second."

I caught up to Jocelyn and Bastian just as they were stepping into the room, with Alex bringing up the rear.

"Is something wrong?" Jocelyn asked as soon as the door closed.

"No," Bastian said, "but I wanted to let you know that I misjudged the amount of time it would take for the delivery from the vault. I appears the shew will be arriving tonight."

"Tonight?" I reiterated, all but overjoyed.

"Yes," Bastian confirmed, "should be about 6 this evening."

Woohoo! That means no dusty book duty!

"I know it's a bit earlier than expected," Bastian said, leaning his forearms against the back of the nearest armchair, "but this may work out better. It would have been difficult for us to all have a coordinating time tomorrow to disappear without being missed, but with the council dinner tonight—"

"—everyone who would have cause to miss us will be occupied," Jocelyn finished his thought.

"Exactly."

"You aren't supposed to be at the dinner?" Alex asked, though I couldn't tell who he was talking to.

Jocelyn shook his head. "I am not a council member, and Bastian, if I'm not mistaken, is still too young. Yes," he said, actually looking pleased, "this should work out well."

"Good," Bastian said. "The box will come to my room, so if that is acceptable to everyone, we can have a look at it there. Though," he added, "Becca and I won't have had time to look through the volumes from the archives."

Damn it, Bastian, shut up!

"True," Jocelyn said, while I silently cursed Bastian into oblivion. "Why don't you have a look at them now?"

"I am available if you are," Bastian said looking over to me.

"It would seem as though I am," I said gritting my teeth.

Damn it, damn it, damn it!

"This is so boring…" I droned, pushing yet another utterly unhelpful book to the side and reaching for the next. "How long do we really have to keep this up?"

Bastian and I had been locked in the parlor next to the library for over two hours, flipping through musty book after musty book, looking for anything at all about Seers, and coming up empty handed. I was tired, I was irritated, the dry rotted dust from the old leather was starting to make my eyes itch, and worst of all I had a sickening strain in my chest that would not go away. Normally, that sort of strain meant that I was near Alex, but this time it only served as a physical manifestation of my guilt for leaving him and our plans to walk to play research assistant. I had asked him to come and help, but he'd only made some thin joke about not being in the mood to do homework and said he'd rather just go lie-down. I could tell he was disappointed; so was I, but then I guess we should have known better than to get our hopes up.

"Until we find what we need, or get through them all," Bastian said from across the table. "And what are you complaining about? I should be the one desperate to be done. Your work partner has been nothing but a delight," he rested back in his chair with a grin, "it's mine that's been whining and moaning since we arrived."

"I'm not whining, I'm voicing my displeasure."

"Consider it voiced," he chuckled.

"And I have every right to moan, since it's your fault we're here."

"What are you talking about?"

"'*Becca and I won't have had time to look through the volumes from the archives,*'" I quoted with an exaggerated impersonation of his voice.

His eyebrow cocked while he continued to flip pages. "Did you have something better to do this afternoon?"

"As it happens, yes, I did."

"Then why didn't you say that when I asked if you were available?"

"Because it wouldn't have mattered, Jocelyn would have made me come anyway."

"Then shouldn't you be mad at him instead of me?" he asked coolly, not lifting his eyes from the book in his lap.

"Yeah, well, he's not here."

"Lucky him," he chuckled, clearly amused by my griping – which of course only made me angrier.

"For the record," I glared. "I'm not like the other girls you know; I will throw a book at you."

"And I am not like the other guys you know," he smiled, glancing up. "I'll throw it back."

Luckily, before I could actually consider making good on my threat, I realized how childish I was being and gave up. Bastian didn't deserve this from me, and I knew it. With a heavy sigh, I crossed my arms on the table and let my head fall against them. "Sorry," I mumbled into the table. "I'm just frustrated."

"It's fine. Actually, I'm rather enjoying our quality time together."

Hmm... Quality time...

Suddenly an idea hit me and I looked up at Bastian with a bright-eyed grin. "I think we need a break."

"I'd agree," he said skeptically, "but I can already tell that nothing good is going to come of that face..."

"Teach me to port."

"I'm sorry, what?"

"Teach me to be a Porter," I said, standing and walking over to his side of the table.

"Now?"

"Sure, why not?" I took the book from him and set it aside. "Like I said, we need a break, and we may as well do at least one constructive thing this afternoon."

"What do you call this?" he motioned to the books stacked on the table.

"A waste of time."

"I'll have you know that time spent in my company is never a waste," he said looking down his nose dramatically, "and as for this, we are assisting with the investigation into Ciaran's notebook."

"Oh, come on, do you really think we are going to find anything in these things?" I lifted a book and let it *thunk* back onto the table. He didn't answer, but his expression gave a definite no. "Exactly, so why not take a few minutes to actually do something productive?"

"OK, I'll make you a deal; you finish going through this one…" He handed me the book I'd taken from him and stood, "and I will teach you to port."

"Deal," I agreed excitedly. "But hang on, where are you going?"

"If I am going to teach you, I need to go get something. Now sit," he ordered, taking my shoulders, turning me around, and pushing me down into his empty chair, "and read."

"Fine, but you better come ba–" But I choked on the last syllable when, without warning, Bastian vanished. Like a bubble popped in midair; there, then gone.

Wow, that was cool…

I opened the book and began to skim through, once again finding nothing at all of value. By the time I got the rest of the way through the book, more than ten minutes had passed, and I started to wonder exactly where Bastian had gone. However, the exact moment that I shut the book and set it aside, he came walking back in through the parlor door – the timing of which seemed like an awfully large coincidence.

I glared at him. "You were standing out there waiting for me to finish, weren't you?"

"Would I do that?" he asked innocently.

"What is that?" I asked, ignoring his denial in favor of the silver charm I saw hanging from a cord in his hand. As he got closer, I could see it was a thick round circle about an inch and a half or so in diameter, with a hole in the middle. It looked a little like a small flattened doughnut.

"This," he handed me the charm, "is my *ancaire*, or anchor. Every Porter has one – only one – and it is how we get around. We are tied to it, the way other Holders are their Sciath."

"You don't have a Sciath?" I asked, as I examined the cool metal ring in my hand.

"No, only my anchor. It is both a Porter's ability and weakness all in one."

"What do you mean?"

"The term 'anchor' is quite literal," he said, taking the ring back. "I am anchored to this charm – tethered to it." He set the anchor down on the table next to him, and began to slowly walk to the other side of the room. "I can travel by traditional methods anywhere I choose to go, be it across the room, or across the country. But when I port," he paused, having reached the far corner of the room, then disappeared as he'd done before, only this time he reappeared an instant later, right next to where his anchor sat on the table, "I can only port to where my anchor is."

"Hold on," I said, my heart racing at what I'd just seen. "You mean you can't port anywhere you want to go?"

He shook his head. "As I said," he picked up the anchor and held it up, "strength *and* weakness. I can only go to where my anchor is, be it two inches or two countries away."

"So that's why we ended up in your room that night? Because that's where your anchor was?"

"I usually keep it there during events like this, as obviously it does no good to keep it with me."

"I didn't see it."

"It was on the bureau behind us. I'm never sure what direction I will be facing when I arrive, but I am always within arm's reach of it. Or as close as physically possible if it is, say, inside a drawer, or in a trunk, or something like that."

"Wow," I said, crossing my arms and leaning back against the table. "So how far can you go? Is there a limit?"

"That depends on the strength of the Holder. The weaker ones can go only a few feet from their anchors, while the strongest can be on the other side of the world. I have not tested it that far, but I can tell you that I am able to go from Pennsylvania to France with no trouble." He grinned. "I ported back and forth several times during my stay in the States."

"But how could you go back and forth, I thought it was a one way trip?"

"It is, which meant I could travel back and forth as quickly as the postal service could deliver."

"Postal… oh," I nodded, seeing what he meant. "You would port to France, then mail your anchor back to Pennsylvania, and vice-versa."

"That's it."

"Cheaper than flying, I guess. And what about taking people with you? Can everyone do that?"

"Again, it depends on strength. Some can take nothing, others can take anything. Personally, I am on the stronger side, and can take with me anything that has a mass smaller than my own. Clothing and anything else attached to you will port with you on their own, of course."

"Wow." I couldn't remember if that was the second or third time I'd said that, but I couldn't seem to come up with anything else.

"Well?" he asked, almost seeming excited himself. "What do you say? Ready to give it a try?"

"Yeah, but," I hesitated, "I mean, I want to, but I don't have an anchor. How will I be able to go anywhere?"

"Normally, that would be a problem, yes. Each Porter's anchor is made for them and honed to their specific ability, which means you can only go to your own. But you are not a Porter, you are simply going to be using my ability which is tied to my anchor. I would take that to mean that you would have to use mine. But don't worry, you'll feel it. And as far as what to do…"

"Yeah, yeah, I know," I cut him off, "you can't explain it. It's fine, trust me, no one ever can."

"They can't?"

"No, but I get it, it's inherent, you can't explain it, so on and so forth."

"I can explain it."

I blinked. "You can?"

"Sure, it's quite simple, really. All you have to do is let go."

"Let go?"

"Give it a try and I think you'll understand. Oh," he added, a smile in his eye, "don't forget to close your eyes."

"Right," I said, happy that he'd reminded me, as that dizzy feeling from the first port wasn't something I wanted to relive.

Taking a breath and squeezing my eyes shut, I reached out and merged our abilities, and from the moment our two energies melded together, I understood every word of what he'd said. Not only could I feel his anchor, which was undoubtedly working for me, but I could feel it pulling, attempting to draw me toward it. I couldn't tell its distance by only the feel of it, and had I not known where I was, I wouldn't have been able to tell if it was in the room with me or hundreds of miles away. All I knew was that it was calling me, like a helium balloon being called toward the clouds, and all I had to do to cut the string that held it down was let go.

So I did.

Just like the first time, there was the sensation of falling, and then suddenly I was grounded again. I had done it. With a satisfied smile, I opened my eyes… to find that I was standing not four feet from Jocelyn.

"*Gah!*" he yelled, stumbling backward.

"*Agh!*" I screeched, my hands flying to my mouth.

He stumbled backward at the shock, grabbing both the bedpost to steady himself and his chest as it heaved under his gasping breaths. "*Becca?*" he choked out. "How in God's name…?"

I was in his room. Somehow I'd ported myself all the way from the library parlor to Jocelyn's guestroom. Apparently, I wasn't as good at this as I'd thought.

"I-I don't know," I stammered, still shaken and desperately trying to ignore the fact that he had nothing on but pajama pants and an undershirt, "I was… We were trying…" I frantically looked around myself to try and figure out what had happened, which is when I saw it. Sitting on the nightstand right beside me, no more than an arm's reach away, was the square leather pouch that I'd seen Jocelyn take the Iris out of back at the cottage. "Oh…" I said, as confusion cleared and embarrassment set in.

The Iris. Looked like I had an anchor after all.

I turned sheepishly back toward Jocelyn who was still catching his breath. "Well," I said, an awkward grimace, "that's good to know…"

CHAPTER 24

"The Iris? Hmm..." Bastian mused, as he and I sat in his room later that evening, waiting on everyone else to arrive for the shew experiment. "We probably should have considered that."

"Probably, yeah," I agreed.

"I'm just glad you're still here," he said with remnants of shocked fear in his voice. "You scared the life out of me!"

"Scared *you*? What about me?"

"You may have been surprised, but at least you ended up somewhere you were familiar with. For all I knew," he threw his hand up, "you'd ported yourself to China! I damn near panicked!"

"Aww, that's so sweet," I fluttered my eyelashes. "You'd miss me."

"Yes," he laughed, "that's it. I'd thought it was because I didn't want to be the one who *lost* the daughter of *Bronntanas*, but sure, I'd miss you, we'll go with that."

"Yeah, well," I said, acknowledging his joke with a sneer. "I'm just glad Jocelyn didn't decide to lock me in my room for the remainder of the trip."

"What did he say?"

"Not much actually. Once he caught his breath, I just explained generally what we'd done, and left."

"That's good, yes."

"Sure." If not a bit unsettling. "Though the image of him in pajamas is one I could have done without."

He chuckled, the sound somewhat evil. "You should be grateful," he glanced sideways at me, "after all, it could have been worse…"

"*Agh!*" I squeezed my eyes closed, as he laughed, "*Seriously? What is wrong with you? Not cool. Not. Cool!*"

Before Bastian could disturb me further, there was a knock at the door, and I ran to answer it.

"Thank God," I said, knowing it was Alex before the door was even fully open. "You're just in time."

Alex looked confused as I pulled him the room. "Did I miss something?"

"Welcome, Mr Bray," Bastian said, still laughing quietly. "We were just discussing Becca's luck."

"Not cool," I repeated, glaring at him.

"OK," Alex said, as I wondered why there was a sudden odd tension in the room. "Anyway, Jocelyn wanted me to tell you that we are to start without him and Cormac. Jocelyn thinks he found a lead on our mystery Mentalist, and he and Cormac went to check it out, but he said that one or both of them should be here shortly."

"What did they find?" I asked.

"He didn't say, just that time was of the essence."

"That's interesting," Bastian said, standing and walking over to a box I hadn't noticed before, sitting on the floor beside the couch. "Well, if they are delayed, we might as well have a look then." As he reached inside the box, Alex and I took a seat on the couch and watched as he carefully withdrew what looked to be a heavy object that was wrapped in a wrinkled black satin cloth. Shifting it in his hands until it was right-side up, he set it down on the coffee table in front of us and pulled off the satin cover to reveal what looked to be a large glass ball, sitting on a silver three-legged stand that had intricate patterns of Celtic knots and design work carved into the metal.

"This is it?" I asked, more than a little surprised. "It looks like something a fortune teller at a carnival would use."

"And who do you think the first fortune tellers were?" Bastian asked, tossing the satin aside and sitting next to me on the empty side of the couch.

"Oh," I said, leaning in for a close look, "right." I admired the carvings and tiny details for a moment, waiting for someone to make a suggestion, but no one seemed to know what to do next. The craftsmanship on this thing was amazing; too bad it didn't come with instructions. Unable to wait anymore, I broke the silence. "So, what exactly are we supposed to do here?"

"I suppose we start by doing as the prophecy says, and see what happens," Bastian suggested.

"Look into the shew and find the origin that will pierce the shroud of my sight," Alex recited.

"OK," I sighed, "then we'll look. But what are we looking for?" I wondered aloud.

"The origin," Bastian said, though I could tell he was being smart.

"Gee thanks," I squinted at him. "I meant, what does that mean? What's an origin?"

"Could be any number of things," Alex said. "I guess we'll know when we find it."

"Should we take turns?" I asked with a shrug.

"We should," Bastian said, "though in the interest of time, I think you should go first."

"Why me?"

"Because, I think we all know that if anyone is liable to see something in that thing, it is going to be you."

"But no pressure or anything, right?" I added sarcastically.

"Of course not," he said, though the sound was oddly sincere. I looked over at him to see him looking back with nothing but casual confidence. "If you see something you see something. If you don't you don't. Either way, we will deal with it."

As unexpected as his words were, they brought me a welcome rush of calm and I turned back to the shew with a reassured breath, ready to give it my all.

"What do I do?" I asked, shifting forward in my seat a bit. "I mean, I know I look at it, but I'm looking at it now, and I've got nothing. Did you ever see Ciaran use it?" I asked Bastian. "Did he do anything special?"

Bastian blew out a long breath as he thought back. "The only times I actually saw him use it, he was in a trance, but I'm pretty sure he could use it out of trance as well."

"OK... that doesn't really help..."

"Can you sense it at all?" Alex asked, speaking up for the first time in a while. "The way you sense abilities?"

"The stone? No. It's just a thing, like any other thing as far as I can tell."

"Just take your time and concentrate," Alex said.

"Exactly," Bastian nodded, "draw from..." he gestured vaguely to my head, "whatever you have going on up there, and see what you come up with."

I still had a ton of questions, but as I knew that no one had any answers, I also knew that any further questioning was really just me trying to stall. Realizing it was now or never, I took a deep breath and leaned forward, focusing all my energy and attention onto the melon sized globe in front of me.

I looked at it for a moment, then adjusted my eyes, relaxing them so that I was almost looking through it, focusing deep down on the center of the orb. As I stared, I got the feeling that maybe there was something to what Alex had said about sensing it. My ability still wasn't picking anything up, but maybe I could get something if I treated the stone itself as an ability. I honed my power, directing it at the ball in my sights, channeling everything I had toward it, hoping to see a flicker, or a flash, or anything else that would let me know I was on the right track. I continued to push my ability outward, pouring it into the stone, feeding it, surrounding us both in power and energy until the air around me hummed. I pushed my eyes further into the stone, diving down into the heart of the rock itself, watching the way the curve of the crystal bent the light and warped the reflections and images of the room around us. With one final push, I fixed my gaze on the pinpoint in the center of the form that was untouched by the waves and curves of bent light surrounding it. I forced the last of my strength into the perfectly circular, perfectly clear spot and saw...

Nothing.

With an exhausted huff, I closed my eyes, retraced my ability, and collapsed backwards on the couch, out of breath and discouraged. But a glance around showed that drained as I felt, it was possible I hadn't gotten the worst of it. Both Alex and Bastian were bent forward in their seats, their shoulders hunched as they gasped for air. Alex was rubbing his temples while Bastian had one hand on his forehead and the other braced against the coffee table like he'd been about to fall.

"Holy Mother of God..." Bastian mumbled as he sat up slowly, his eyes far too wide.

Alex looked over at him, and the two exchanged a glance. "You too?" Alex asked between breaths.

"What happened?" I stuttered, my head flying back and forth between them. "Are you all right?"

"We're fine," Alex assured me, though his hand was still shaking slightly.

"Yes," Bastian agreed quickly, "fine."

"Clearly you're not fine, now what happened?" I asked again, panic that I'd hurt them bubbling up in my throat.

"We're OK, Becca, really," Alex said, "it was just a bit... intense for a second there."

Suddenly, I realized what I had done and my heart clenched like a cramp. Why hadn't I thought about what I was doing? I'd been so concerned about doing everything I could to see something in the stone, that I hadn't considered that there were two other Holders in the room who could be affected by me filling the air around us with the full force of my ability.

"You're too powerful, you're going to hurt people..." the shadow in my mind whispered, rearing up yet again.

"I'm so sorry," I gasped, my chest heaving now not for air, but from fear. "I didn't realize... I didn't think... I'm so sorry!"

"Hey, hey," Bastian said, smiling down at me, "calm down, no harm done."

"Everything's fine," Alex said, placing a hand on my back.

I let the fear slowly subside as I looked up at the reassuring smiles on their faces, both of which seemed to be back to normal.

"You're sure?" I double checked, knowing that no matter what they said I was never going to do that again.

"Absolutely," Bastian winked.

"What about you," Alex asked. "Are you OK?"

"I'm fine," I told him. "It took a lot out of me, but I'm better now."

"Good," Alex breathed, the concern lifting from his eyes.

"Yeah," I huffed with a frown. "Too bad it didn't get us anywhere. I did everything I could think of, and still there was nothing to see."

"All right, well at least we gave it a shot," Bastian said, taking it far better than me.

"A blind shot in the dark, maybe," I mumbled, reaching forward and picking up the stone and holding it in my lap.

"You said the Iris gives you more control, do you think having it would help?" Bastian asked.

"I doubt it," I answered, slowly turning the stone around in my hands and looking at the pattern on the stand. "If the stone had something to focus my ability on, then maybe, but there is nothing. Like I said, it is just a thing."

"All Holder artifacts are just things to anyone other than the person they are intended for," Alex mused.

"True," Bastian said, "but maybe that's the answer. Maybe we could find a way to trick the stone into thinking you're Ciaran."

"The only way to even try to do that would be to have me assume his ability, and even if I were willing to go and rob what little energy is left from his grave – which I am not – there is no way there would be enough for me to work with. And even then, I would still have no idea what to do."

The boys continued to spitball, while I kept looking over the shew, seeing if there was anything we might have missed. But there was nothing. The only marks it had on it at all was a three digit number etched into the center of the underside of the stone. It was in the dead center of the circle made by the open middle of the stand, and was only visible when the entire thing was turned upside down, almost like a serial number or limited edition notation.

"Hey," I said, interrupting a conversation I'd not heard as an idea came to me. "We are supposed to find an origin, right? What if that means the origin of the shew itself?"

"What do you mean?" Bastian asked.

"It looks like there is a serial number on here: 812. Maybe if we can find out where this came from, the answer will be there?"

"That's a bit short for a serial number," Alex pointed out.

"Not to mention impossible," Bastian said, leaning over to see for himself. "That stone was custom made for Ciaran hundreds of years ago, long before the creation of the serial number." He took the stone from me and held it up for a closer look, confusion wrinkling his forehead when he saw what was there.

"I know," I said, annoyed at how literally they were taking me. "I don't mean like a serial number from a factory, I'm just saying that the number might be able to tell us where it came from, or maybe who made it, I don't know."

"The number," Bastian said, looking hard at me as though for confirmation.

"Yes," I nodded.

"812?"

"Yes," I stressed, getting annoyed.

He looked over at Alex, tipping the bottom of the stone toward him so that he could see. Alex stared at it for a moment, then he and Bastian exchanged yet another private glance, this one far more serious.

"Where is the number again?" Alex asked as they both turned to me.

"Right there," I pointed to each digit, "8, 1, 2" but I stopped when I realized they were looking at me strangely. "You…" I glanced between them, "you don't see it?"

The chilling silence was all the answer I needed. I looked back down at the stone and the three numerals etched onto its surface – numerals that I could see plain as day – and knew this had to be it.

"Well," Bastian sighed, apparently drawing the same conclusion I had, "it seems as though we've found our 'origin in the shew.'"

"But, how is that an origin?" I asked, trying to wrap my head around the idea. "It's just a number, how are we supposed to figure out what it means?"

Bastian folded his arms and leaned back in his seat. "A number that's an origin? Sound to me like it would be a date."

"A date! Yes," I said, growing excited, "812… 8-12! August twelfth! What happened on August twelfth? Something with Ciaran maybe?" But I stopped speculating when I saw Bastian shake his head.

"812 would only be August twelfth in the US. Here, the day comes before the month."

Everything in me ground to a halt as his words rang through me. "Day first…" I whispered as my stomach rolled.

"Right, so it wouldn't be August twelfth, it would be – "

"December eighth," I finished, staring down at the tell-tale etching in the stone. "My birthday."

"It is a cloaking charm," Min's voice called through the speaker phone in Jocelyn's room. "I would wager anything on it. And if the prophecy is as you have read it to me, then it is more than likely that the charm on the shew that is keeping the date hidden, is the same charm that is on Ciaran's notebook keeping the writing hidden."

As soon as Alex, Bastian and I had realized what the number on the shew meant, we went straight down to Jocelyn's room, where he and Cormac had just returned from their investigation. Once we told them what had happened and what we'd found, he'd called Min for an explanation.

"But hang on," I said, not loving where this was going, "if I can see the number on the shew and it's the same charm, wouldn't that mean that I would also be able to read Ciaran's notebook?"

"That is exactly what it would mean," Min said. "You are clearly the person Ciaran intended to leave his prophecies and visions to."

I wanted to ask "why me?", but as I knew the answer, I didn't bother. Though, after everything that had happened so far that week, I was seriously considering getting the question printed on a T-shirt.

"Thank you, Min," Jocelyn said, walking over to the phone. "I'll call you later with any updates, and to discuss the other matter."

Other matter? What else could possibly be going on?

"Very well," Min answered. "Good evening everyone."

After a collective goodbye, Jocelyn hung up the phone and turned back to us, leaning back against the desk with his arms crossed. The room was quiet for a second, but no way was I going to let that last.

"So the way I see it, we're done," I said, trying to hide the mild hysteria in my voice. "I mean think about it, if I am the only one who can read that notebook, all I have to do is never read it. Darragh will never get whatever he wants from it, all his minions," I gestured toward the hall, "will keep searching aimlessly, and we can all go home."

"I understand how you feel, dear," Cormac said gently, "but I do not believe that it is quite that simple."

"He's right," Alex said, his tone not nearly so calm. "What if they find out that you can read it? They will come after you."

"They don't know it's me," I said. "They don't even have a way to figure it out. We only did it a few minutes ago. All we have to do is destroy the shew, and we're good."

"That may not be enough," Bastian said. "After all, we have no idea what they already know. Cleen and Barra knew that you all had gone out to the cemetery, we heard them discussing it," he glanced at me, while I prayed Jocelyn wouldn't question the revelation. "McGary and Ryan followed us out to the cottage, Cleen and McGary searched this very room." He paused, shaking his head. "Clearly they know something, and just because we don't know what that is, doesn't mean we can make the assumption that they won't eventually find a way to put the pieces together."

"Bastian's right," Jocelyn agreed, corking my next argument. "It's true, they may never have the means to figure any of this out, but we can't take the risk. We need to find out exactly what they know, and how much of it they have relayed back to Darragh. Only then will we know for certain how safe we are."

"You mean by finding the Mentalist?" Alex presumed.

"I do," Jocelyn said, "and I suspect I may know who it is: a man named Niall Molony."

"Is it?" Bastian asked, sounding both annoyed and vindicated. "He was one of the ones I suspected, but it's so hard to get hold of him, I was never able to be sure."

"It is very hard to get a hold of him, you're right. From what I understand, he is rarely seen, and even when he attends functions like these, he stays away from the crowds and only makes the occasional appearance."

"He's also incredibly paranoid, and suspicious to a fault. Keeps everyone at a distance, no matter their standing or position."

"Sounds like a man with something to hide," Cormac said.

"Is that what you were doing just now, while we were with the shew?" I asked. "Were you trying to read him?"

"No, I only wanted to see him for myself. I wouldn't dare chance reading him."

"Why not?" Alex and I asked together.

"Because he would know. A Mentalist can almost always feel when their mind is being accessed or tampered with, and if he were to realize I'd attempted to read him, he would likely panic and leave, not only taking anything he may know with him, but also alerting the other informants that I was on to him."

"I agree," Bastian said. "When it comes to Molony, spooking him is the last thing we want."

"But if you can't read him, how are we going to find out if he's the Mentalist we are looking for? And even if he is, how will we learn what he knows?"

"Once we can verify that he is in fact the one we want, there are… *measures* I can take to garner information from him, but first I have to know for certain that he is the one extracting memories." His tone made me want to know what sort of "measures" he was talking about, but at the same time it made me too afraid to ask.

"I'd hoped to be able to read him myself this evening," Cormac said, "but, as you know, I need to make contact in order to determine his ability, and I was never able to get near enough to even consider it."

Bastian drummed his fingers looking thoughtful. "No, that won't work either. He has to know you are a Reader; were you to touch him, he would realize immediately what you'd done. It has to be something more subtle," he mused, pacing slowly, "something he wouldn't think to expect. Not to mention quick, as in past years he has left immediately after the Founders' Banquet." He stopped and looked up at Jocelyn. "You didn't by chance receive an invitation for it, did you?"

"The banquet, no," Jocelyn told him, "but I didn't expect to, as I was given to understand it is only for direct descendants of founding members."

"It is," he sighed. "Molony will be there I'm sure, he always is, but even if I could get you invited, that wouldn't do a lot of good."

"Besides that, it would be highly suspicious," Cormac pointed out, "particularly if Molony and his counterparts already believe we are up to something."

"Also true," Bastian frowned.

But then something sparked in him, causing his eyes to open a little wider and his pacing stop. I watched as the spark grew, quickly building into a full-fledged idea, and a slow grin began to play at his mouth.

"How would you feel," Bastian said with sly edge to his tone, "about partaking in a ruse involving my parents?"

"I suppose," Jocelyn said tentatively, "if it's necessary."

"How about you?" Bastian asked.

"Who, me?" I asked when I realized he was looking at me. He nodded. "I guess, what did you have in mind?"

"We get engaged."

"What?" I asked, not sure if I should laugh or not.

"Hear me out," Bastian said, raising his hands. "If we become engaged, or at least allow everyone to believe we have, you would automatically be expected to attend the Banquet with me. Unlike Cormac, you only need to be in his general proximity to be able to determine his ability, and best of all, no one will suspect a thing. Everyone expects us to become engaged as it is, we'll simply be playing into their hands."

Much as I hated to admit it, it wasn't a bad plan. We could get what we needed without turning any heads, and I rather liked the cloak and dagger feel of it all. "What happens when it's over?" I asked.

"Engagements end all the time, even around here. I'll tell my parents that we decided against marriage, for some reason or another. My mother will of course be disappointed, but she'll get over it, no harm done."

"What do you think, Jocelyn?" Cormac asked, as he had yet to offer his opinion.

"It does make sense," Jocelyn admitted, then looked at me, "so long as you are sure you can handle it. A matter like this is more than simply telling everyone and being done with it, you will have to be able to play the part of someone who intends to join Bhunaidh society."

"I think I can handle it," I told him confidently. "Besides," I glanced at Bastian, "I know a pretty good coach."

Jocelyn stood quietly for a while I waited to hear his decision, hoping he would see that he could trust me with this. Eventually he looked over to Cormac who was waiting patiently with the rest of us. "What do you think?"

"I think it is our best bet," Cormac said.

"Alex?" Jocelyn said, moving his gaze to him.

Alex hesitated a second before answering. "It makes sense."

"Very well then," Jocelyn nodded, coming back to look at me. "If you are sure you are up for it, then that is what we will do."

CHAPTER 25

"Morning lovebird," I sang to a still sleeping Chloe the next morning, "time to get up."

"No," she groaned, rolling over and burrowing into the comforter.

"Yes," I laughed, sitting next to her on the edge of the bed. "You have been asleep for almost twenty hours," I told her, pulling the blanket down so I could see her face. "You're not a bear, you need to eat."

"Twenty hours?" she asked, her voice cracking.

"Yep, but a sleeping draft will do that."

"What did I miss?" she asked.

"Oh, not much," I told her with a nonchalant wave. "I learned to port, found a hidden number in the shew, realized that I am the only one who can read Ciaran's journal, and Bastian and I got engaged."

Her eyes were like golf balls. "*Engaged?* Wait, how long was I out again?"

"It's not real," I laughed, "we're just pretending to be engaged to get me into a party. But never mind that, I can explain later. What about you? How do you feel?"

She propped up onto her elbow and pursed her lips. "I don't know," she said, her eyes darting around as though she was doing an internal inventory. "OK, I think."

"Do you remember what happened yesterday?" I asked cautiously, hoping I didn't incite a second wave of hysterics.

"I bonded," she said in awe as though she was both remembering it and learning about it for the first time. "I bonded to Steven."

"You did," I smiled.

"I remember, but it feels different now."

"The first day is the worst. From here on out, you should be OK."

"Where are you going so early?" she asked, looking down to see that I was dressed.

"It's not early," I told her, "and I am going to grab some breakfast for both of us before it ends. Want anything special?"

Before she could answer, there was a knock at the door. Chloe threw the fluffy comforter over her head, and as soon as I saw she was hidden I opened the door.

"Bastian?" I stepped to the side so he could come in. "What are you doing here?"

"I am here to escort you to breakfast. After all, we're engaged now; we can't very well show up on our own. Good morning Chloe," he added as she came out of hiding.

"Morning," she said, trying desperately to tame her wild hair with her fingers as she slid on her pink robe and matching fuzzy slippers.

"We've been engaged for less than a day, it's not like anyone knows yet," I objected.

"Please tell me you're joking?" I stared blankly at him. "Becca, I can all but assure you that there is barely a soul left on this entire estate that has not heard about the two of us by now. Gossip is sustenance around here, and when my mother is at the lead, it spreads faster than a spill on a rug."

"Oh," I said, not expecting the sudden rush of nerves. "Sure. Yeah, OK, that's fine. No problem."

"All right then, are you ready?" he asked, reaching for the door.

"Sure," I nodded, fighting the butterflies that were chasing away my appetite. "Chloe, we're going to go, will you be OK for a little while?"

"I'll be fine. And don't worry about bringing me food, I can just call down."

"Actually," Bastian said to me quietly, "I don't believe Steven has had anything to eat yet this morning."

The mischievous light in his eye caught fire in mine, and I gave him a quick nod. "Do it."

Taking the cue, Bastian walked over to the phone and dialed. "Yes, hello," he said very officially when the line was picked up. "I need to order the breakfast tray for two, please. Yes, this room. Thank you."

"Thank you, but I'm not that hungry," Chloe said as he hung up. It wasn't until he picked up the phone and dialed again that she began to look worried. "Wait, what are you doing?" she asked, her eyes bouncing from Bastian to me and back again, "What is he doing? What are you doing?"

"Steven, it's me…"

"*No!*" Chloe screamed under her breath, slapping both her hands over her mouth.

"…listen," Bastian continued, fighting a smile, "I'm taking Becca over to breakfast, would you mind coming to her room and eating with her friend Chloe? She could use some company."

"*No,no,no,no,no!*" Chloe continued to whimper.

"Great, thanks," Bastian said, throwing me a grin. "Bye."

He replaced the receiver in the console with a satisfied smile, while Chloe could only look on in horror. "I can't believe you did that!" she said, or rather tried to say but her voice was so high it was barely audible. "And you," she turned on me, "you let him do it! You knew what he was doing and you let him!"

"Sweetie, this is good," I said, forbidding myself from laughing at her predicament… again. "You need someone to hang out with, and you are going to have to get to know him sooner or later."

Her head shook in what looked like a nod, though it may have been more comprehension than actually acceptance. "Oh my gosh… oh my gosh… he's coming here… right now… to see me…"

"He did say he needed to get ready, so you probably have a few minutes," Bastian told her.

"Get ready?" her eyes widened. "I need to get ready!" Then without another word, sprinted into the bathroom and closed the door.

"We'll leave you to it, then," Bastian called after her.

"Yeah, good luck hon, have fun!"

"I'm still mad at you!" she yelled from behind the door, mumbling over what sounded like a toothbrush.

"Come on," Bastian said, taking my arm and pulling me with him out the door. "She needs to do this on her own."

"I know," I said begrudgingly, knowing he was right, but still wanting to be there for her.

"They will be fine. And just to make sure, we can compare notes later after we talk to them," he grinned.

"Speaking of talking to them," I said, taking his arm as we walked down the hall toward the smells of warm bread and sausage. "I take it from your call that you haven't yet told him about what happened?"

"Haven't had the chance, but that is probably for the best. Better that they meet once or twice before he finds out. No need for them to both be nervous, the situation is stressful enough as it is."

"You're probably right."

"And while we are on the subject of nerves and stress," he segued casually, "are you sure you are all right?"

"I'm fine."

"I can feel your hand shaking on my arm."

Damn.

"It's nothing," I said, as each step we took toward the breakfast room made me more and more of a liar. "Just a little anxious. I mean I knew this would happen, obviously. I just… I don't know… thought I'd have more time to ease into it. But I can handle it," I added quickly, not wanting to lend any credence to Jocelyn's hesitations the night before.

"You can handle it."

"That's what I said."

"I know, but when I said it, I believed it. You only want to believe it."

I scowled at the floor. "You really suck sometimes, you know that?"

"You are overthinking this," he said, laughing off my jab. "It's simple, give them what they expect. Do what they would do in your place. You have been watching them for almost a week now, you know what to expect from them, now reflect it back. Oh," he stopped suddenly, reaching into his pocket, "almost forgot. You'll need this," he said pulling out an unmistakable velvet box and handing it to me.

I opened the lid and found a ring with the biggest diamond I had ever seen outside of a cartoon. "Please tell me that's not real," I said, already fairly certain it was.

"Not only is it real, it is a rose cut diamond that has been in my family since the middle of the sixteenth century."

"Are you out of your mind, I'm not wearing this!" I shut the box and shoved it back at him.

"You have to; everyone knows this ring, they'll expect to see it on you."

"I don't care, I'm not wearing something you could buy a small country with! What if I break it?"

"Break a diamond?" he cocked an eyebrow. "That would be impressive."

"You know what I mean!"

Taking the box, he pulled my hand through his arm and continued leading me down the hall, removing the ring from its velvet compartment along the way. "This ring belongs to me now. It was given to me years ago by my mother so that I could bestow it on whatever lady was deemed fit to be my wife. Of course we both know that will never happen, but that's not the reason you shouldn't worry about it. As far as I am concerned, all this thing represents is the expectation of my family and ideals of a life I have fought for years to separate myself from. The fact that having you wear it helps in a ruse actually gives it a purpose I can support. Don't think of it as a priceless keepsake that you have to protect, think of it as a mask designed to help you fill the role they expect you to play."

I still wasn't happy about it, but given that I didn't really have a choice, I nodded, and he slid the ring on my finger just as we stepped out into the open corridor that led directly into the breakfast room.

As the sounds of talking voices and clinking plates reached me, the butterflies that had been with me since Bastian arrived in my room turned to stones, sinking to my feet and making them drag. When the curious eyes of the dozen or so people talking outside the room began to turn and watch our approach, I had to tighten my grip on Bastian's arm to keep from running.

He put his hand over mine reassuringly. "Easy," he whispered in a tone only I could hear, "you can do this."

"I don't know," I said, my voice shaking.

"I do. Keep your head up," he instructed gently without looking at me or even moving his mouth, coaching me secretly as we walked. "Don't shy away when they look at you; point your chin; pull your shoulders back; smile." I let his words echo in my mind like a mantra, following each piece of advice to the letter. After a few minutes I started to feel the change in myself, slowly growing more comfortable under the cold judgmental eyes of those we passed. By the time we reached the entrance of the breakfast room, a few of those eyes even began to look at me with approval, and I realized that Bastian had been right; I could do this.

When we paused at the door, Bastian glanced down at me for the first time, his aloof public mask in place. "Shall we eat, my dear?" he asked, his eyes searching me carefully.

I lowered my eyelids slightly and raised my nose. "Of course," I said, smiling up at him with a cool and haughty confidence that could rival his own.

A flash of laughter passed behind his eyes as he looked back out over the room. "Thattagirl," he breathed with the glimpse of a smile, placing a hand on my back and leading me into the room.

The next two days of my life became about one thing: playing the part of Bastian's fiancée. I'd been offended before, when Jocelyn had suggested that I might not be able to handle the role, but now I totally understand why he'd been worried.

It. Was. A. Lot.

Bastian and I were together almost constantly and spent most of our time in the public eye. There were meals, socials, casual gatherings, formal gatherings, outings, open events, and private events. Not to mention hordes of people to meet, dozens of names and titles to remember, and all the while keeping up the polished façade of a genuine Bhunaidh-in-training. I was exhausted.

But at least all my hard work wasn't going unnoticed. Everyone was buying my act, from Bastian's family, to the other Bhunaidh guests, to even the staff – though admittedly I was always nicer to them than I was supposed to be. Bastian was constantly complimenting my progress, assuring me that he himself hadn't taken to "playing the game" as quickly as I had. Even Jocelyn seemed to approve of my performance.

The icing on the cake would have been the chance at an early meeting with the mysterious Mr Molony, though of course that would have been too easy for my luck to allow it. Had it been anyone else we were trying to see, we undoubtedly would have run into them during all our mixing and mingling, but not Molony. Apparently, he was known for making himself scarce, usually not even staying on the estate. Bastian didn't expect him to make another appearance until the banquet, and after two days without so much as a sighting, it was starting to look like he was right.

And so, we waited.

Though if there was one person not at all unhappy about the prospect of passing the days at Adare, it was Chloe. She and Steven had become inseparable over the past few days, and I had never seen her happier. They spent nearly every waking hour together, which really wasn't hard considering neither of them had anything else to do, and the change in them both was astonishing. In a matter of days, Chloe had gone from an over the top perky girl, into a joyous and refined woman. The change was subtle, but those of us who knew what it was like to have a bonded Anam, knew that it was just the gentle shift that came from having a greater purpose. And as for Steven, he was talking, smiling, and laughing so much that even his brother could hardly recognize him. Bastian was beside himself, constantly telling us that he hadn't seen Steven that happy and carefree since they were kids. He finally had someone to love him exactly the way he was, and to a person who had never known the feeling, it was like opening your eyes for the first time. It was magic.

On the afternoon of the third day, I finally found myself with some alone time – having graciously opted out of a car tour of the countryside, citing my inclination to motion sickness – and was looking forward to spending some time with Alex and Chloe who I'd not been able to say more than a few words to in days.

I stopped by Alex's room, but he wasn't there. When I didn't find Chloe in our room either, I realized that Alex was probably with her as she would need to be hidden if she was out for a walk. I wandered around some of the more private areas that I thought they might have gone to, finally ending up in the back hallway not far from my room where I'd met Steven on that first day. When I approached the window seat I saw both Chloe and Steven sitting together smiling and talking as though they'd known each other for years, with Alex sitting on the top step of a downward stairwell further up the hall. I waved as I passed by the happy pair in the window seat, not wanting to interrupt, and walked up behind Alex who smiled when he saw me coming.

"Hi," I said, sitting down next to him.

"Hi."

"Giving them privacy?" I asked, looking back toward the window seat.

"As much as I can while still being able to hide them."

"How are they doing?"

"Great. They are together almost constantly," he said, breaking my heart with the longing in his voice.

"I guess it's good that neither of them really have anything to do," I said, realizing only after I said it that it sounded like a justification of my own absence.

"Yeah," he said simply, looking down at his hands. We sat quietly for a few minutes, until I saw that his gaze had wandered over to my hand and, more specifically, the enormous rock it held. He reached over and took hold of my fingers, lifting them up for a better look. "That's... something."

"I know," I said as he released my hand. "Hard to believe something that is worth so much money could be so ugly." I chuckled, but his smile was forced. "Hey," I nudged him with my shoulder, "you're still OK with all this, right?"

He laughed once without humor. "*Still* OK with it? What makes you think I was ever OK with it?"

"Because you said you were! Jocelyn asked you what you thought, and you said, and I quote, 'It makes sense.'"

"Of course I said that, what was I supposed to say? It *does* make sense, that doesn't mean I like it."

"Alex, you know I'm only doing this because it's what we all decided. It's not like I'm having fun pretending to be Princess Pompous all day." He nodded but it took too long. Checking the hall quickly, I took his chin and kissed him gently hoping to ease his frustration. "Don't worry," I said with a smile. "Tomorrow night is the banquet, then after that, this will all be over and things will go back to the way they were." Again he nodded, but again he didn't seem convinced.

"Want to take a walk?" I asked, hoping it would take his mind of things.

He smiled slightly, but shook his head. "I shouldn't leave them, someone could come along."

"Oh, right," I glanced up the hall. "Forgot about them. That's OK, I should probably start getting ready for tonight anyway." I stood up.

"Plans?" he asked, not looking up.

"Yeah, there is a youth social tonight I have to go to. But it shouldn't be too late, and I was thinking that, if you wanted, we could watch a movie in your room after."

He looked up with his first real smile. "I'd like that."

"Great," I smiled back, happy both to have plans with him and to see that he seemed better. "I'll see you then."

I turned to go, but before I could step away, he reached up from his seat on the step and grabbed my hand. With a look on his face that I'd never seen before, he got up, took me into his arms, and kissed me like he might never see me again. The surprise of it nearly threw me off balance, but his arms held me tightly, clinging to me like they'd never let go. It was deep, fiercely strong, and knee-shakingly passionate, but there was something else about it. Something that I couldn't quite discern but that struck me as almost... desperate?

"I love you," he breathed against my mouth, not even giving me a chance to respond before capturing my lips again. After a long moment he released me and stepped back, his face once again unreadable. "See you tonight," he said with the shadow of a grin.

I nodded with one last smile and left, a quiver of worry in my chest. Something was going on with him, but I couldn't tell what it was. He was usually so open about things, but this time it was almost like he was afraid to share. But what could possibly be that bad? I knew he missed me, because I missed him, but that wouldn't bother him this much. I also knew that he wasn't loving the fact that I was running all over town pretending to be engaged to another guy, and while he should have spoken up before it happened, I can see why he didn't. But even that wasn't all that big a deal considering he knew I was only doing it because I had to. No, it was something beyond all that, and I was determined to make sure that before we did anything else later that evening, I found out what it was.

CHAPTER 26

"Wow, look at you," Chloe said as I stepped out of the bathroom that evening.

"You've seen this outfit before," I reminded her, grabbing my earrings from the dresser and putting them on.

"I know, but not with your hair done and make-up on. Have you ever worn make-up this many days in a row?"

"Very funny. What do you have planned tonight?"

"Don't know yet. Steven said he wanted to talk to me about something, so we are meeting up later, and from there, who knows. What about you? Ready to party?" she asked, doing a little dance.

"I guess. Though to be honest, I'm really nervous."

"Why? You've been mingling with the bigwigs for days now, this is only the younger ones. It should be a piece of cake."

"And it probably would be if Shannon wasn't going to be there. I've barely seen her or her mother since this whole engagement thing, and I have no idea what to expect from her."

"Why are you still letting that spoiled little harpy get to you?" Chloe asked, having been all too caught up on my Shannon drama. "She's horrid, not worth a moment of your time, you know this, and yet you still let her frighten you into a state? Why?"

"I don't know," I moaned, plopping down into the edge of the bed. "I can't help it. I'm not used to dealing with people like her, at least not when they are coming after me. I defend other people, that's my thing. I'm no good at fighting when it's just me out there."

"But that's just it, love, you don't have to fight," she grinned, coming to sit next to me. "You've already won. You got her man."

"Yeah," I snorted, "except he wasn't ever her man, and I don't really have him."

"But she doesn't know that, now does she?" I shrugged. "Of course not. Listen to me, it's all attitude. I know you know that, now you just have to use it. You are too strong to let someone make you feel the way she has. Time to man up... or lady up, if you will."

"I know, I know," I groaned.

"Good," she said, "now get up and put your shoes on, Bastian will be here for you any minute."

With a huff, I pulled myself onto my feet, and as if on cue, there was a knock at the door.

"Evening Bastian," Chloe greeted him as she opened the door.

"Good evening Chloe. Is my date ready?"

"She's shoeless, but otherwise…"

"I'm ready, I'm ready. Come on," I hooked him by the arm and towed him out the door. "Let's get this over with."

"And a good evening to you too," he snarked, freeing his arm with a chuckle and following behind me.

The social that night was not in the manor itself, but in a large tent that was set up outside. On approach it looked like your typical white, wedding reception style tent, but the moment we stepped inside, it was like being in a high end club. The walls were draped with dark fabric, there were clusters of leather furniture dotting the perimeter, a huge under-lit fiberglass dance floor stretched the entire center of the floor, and all that was just the décor. A DJ booth took up one of the shorter walls, while a wet bar flanked by dessert tables spanned the opposite. There were servers passing drinks and hors d'oeuvres, lighting that set the mood without giving you a headache, and even a waterfall of fog with tiny flecks of glitter that cascaded over you as you entered, almost as though you were stepping into another world.

"Would you like to sit?" Bastian asked over the music.

"Sure," I called back.

We found a crescent-shaped white leather couch that was thankfully closer to the bar than the DJ, and took a seat. As we looked out over the dancers on the floor, I began to carefully scan the room for Shannon, not willing to let her catch me off guard.

"She's over there," Bastian said, leaning into me and nodding toward a group of people on the opposite side of the room.

"Got it," I said, embarrassed to have been caught. But Bastian either didn't notice or was kind enough not to rub my face in it.

The evening crawled by uneventfully as we sat on our couch. Occasionally someone would come over to say hello to Bastian or congratulate us, and we would converse, but thanks to the volume of the music, conversations were generally short.

About an hour into the night, Bastian slid closer to me and leaned toward my ear. "You don't seem to be enjoying yourself."

"Sorry," I said. "This isn't really my thing."

"So I see. Would you like to leave?"

"No, I'm fine, really," I smiled. There was nothing I wanted more than to take him up on his offer, but I told Jocelyn and everyone else that I could do this, and sitting through uncomfortable parties without running away at the first opportunity was part of the job.

"You're not fine," he said, standing then taking my hand and pulling me up with him. "But lucky for you, I know exactly what you need."

"Is that so?"

"It is," he said with a wry smirk. "You need to dance."

He tried to lead me out on to the floor, but I was able to stop him before anyone took notice. "OK, no, this is not what I need," I said, my eyes silently begging.

"Why not? We've danced before."

"Yes, but this isn't the kind of dancing that I'm any good at," I told him, cringing at the thought of trying to dance to the modern club anthem currently thumping in the air.

"Well, that's where having a marvelous partner such as myself is a blessing. For where most people hear only a generic dance beat, I hear only a salsa."

"No... this?" I pointed up with an expression like he'd lost his mind.

"Why not? Can't you hear it?"

I began to count the steps in my head to the beat and though I never would have come up with it on my own, turned out he was right.

The look on my face must have given me away, because he grinned and held out his hand. "May I have this dance?"

I looked at his waiting palm and grinned in spite of myself. "Why not?"

For someone who had been dead set against dancing, it turned out to be the most fun I'd had since coming to Adare, and just what I needed to get me out of my funk. We danced the salsa, rumba, a two-step waltz, and even a tango, all to modern pop and dance-mix songs that I never would have even thought to attempt a traditional style of dance to. It was a blast. Even the fact that we had to remain serious while on the dance floor didn't dampen my enjoyment, as it became almost like a game: who could make the best dance-face without laughing. Bastian had been right, dancing was exactly what I'd needed to get me feeling relaxed, happy, and back in the groove. Unfortunately, after dancing seven consecutive songs, the same could not be said for my feet.

"I'm going to sit the next couple out," I told him when he tried to take my hand for the upcoming number.

"You sure?"

"My feet are," I smiled.

"Lightweight," he teased with a *tsk*. "Come on, we'll get something to drink."

But no sooner had he finished speaking than a different voice pierced the air behind us. "Good evening, Becca."

It was her.

I turned toward the sound and saw Shannon standing not four feet away from us, looking stunning in a black cocktail dress, and offering me something she never had before – a smile.

"Hello," I nodded, not entirely sure what was going on.

"Shannon," Bastian greeted her, with a kiss to her hand. "You look lovely as always."

"Thank you, Bastian," though somehow the tone she used was more of an "of course I do." "Becca," she turned to me, "would you mind terribly if I borrowed your escort for the next dance? That is, unless you planned on dancing yourself," she smiled politely.

Please, bitch, you knew I wasn't, you saw me leaving the floor...

"Of course I don't mind," I said, placing my hand on Bastian's arm. "He's all yours."

When I looked up at Bastian, I could see something was wrong, but I couldn't tell what. Then again, I had just given Shannon permission to fawn over him for at least the next two minutes, so maybe a slight panic was justified.

"I'll just be sitting," I told him, nodding to our still-vacant couch.

He looked down at me pointedly for a fraction of a second. "Tell her no," he whispered quickly from between his teeth.

"Bastian," Shannon called him, something like triumph lighting her face. "May I have the honor?"

He hesitated a long breath before answering, looking at me expectantly. Did he really want me to tell her no? Why? He couldn't be that desperate not to dance with her, could he? Was I missing something? His face told me I was, but all I could do was furrow my eyebrows the tiniest bit and let him know I didn't understand.

"I... suppose," he finally agreed, "if Becca doesn't mind." He glanced at me once more.

"Not at all," I said, determined to be the bigger person, "have fun."

With a cordial smile, I turned and walked back over to the couch, proud of the way I'd handled myself. Clearly she'd thought she could get a reaction out of me by trying to dance with my fiancée, but the joke was on her. No more petty games for me, I was rising above it all.

Or so I thought.

However, the moment I sat down and looked back over the room, I saw that something was very wrong. Almost every eye in the tent was suddenly on me, their owners whispering, and pointing, some even covering up laughter. They would watch me, look over to Shannon and Bastian on the dance floor, then come back to me, all while I pretended not to see them. Clearly Bastian had been trying to warn me, but what had I done? I'd been the bigger person; I'd done the right thing.

Hadn't I...?

But the question hadn't even fully formed in my mind before I began to pick up traces of the ever-growing current of whispers flowing around the room. "Can you believe her? For heaven's sake, they are supposed to be engaged... Doesn't know how things are done... Look at her, she has no idea... I expected more from her... Well, she is American... Completely clueless..."

Focusing my gaze on the natural center of the room, I called up every lesson I'd learned over the past few days and fought to keep it together.

Don't shrink away from their stares...

Don't let them see you sweat...

Make them believe you don't care...

That you can't see them laughing...

...or hear what they're saying...

But what had I done?

Helpless and confused, I looked out to the floor, hoping to catch Bastian's eye, but instead all I found waiting for me was Shannon's – and it told me everything I needed to know in two silent words: *I win.*

In that instant, everything came together and I realized my mistake. I'd unwittingly let her beat me by allowing her to exploit my ignorance. Clearly I should not have stepped aside and let Shannon dance with Bastian. Maybe it was because we were engaged, or maybe it was a general territory thing, I had no idea. But for whatever the reason, it was obviously not the way things were done here unless you were the sort of person willing to be stepped on. I'd just let Shannon prove to herself and the rest of the world that she was still top banana, and the worst part was that she'd known I would. She knew that Bastian would never be so rude as to refuse her a dance in a public setting, and she also knew that I wouldn't know enough to refuse her for him. She'd played me and won, fair and square.

But of course that wasn't enough. Now that I knew it, she had to rub my face in it.

Fully aware that I was watching, she took her victory to the next level. She began dancing around the floor like a professional, adding spins and flourishes every chance she got, whether the move called for it or not. Bastian may have been leading, but Shannon was obviously running the show, forcing him to match her style and intensity with every step she took.

Her message was clear; she was better than me, more refined than me, a better match for Bastian, and above all else, she had beaten me.

And now, everyone knew it.

But as I watched them dance though tear-stung eyes, I realized something. Something I'd already known, but now was magnified by his stoic and formal movements compared to her flowing and natural ones. He couldn't stand her. And that show was my secret weapon.

Smiling more naturally now, I watched them finish their dance, no longer minding the stares and whispers from the rest of the room. When they finished, I stood with a confident smile and applauded, prompting everyone else to follow my lead. When Shannon looked up and saw me, her triumphant glow began to fade.

"That was incredible," I beamed, walking out toward them as the applause died down and the next song started up. "I wish I could move like that."

"You're too kind," Shannon said, her smile forced now as she tried to play off her complete and utter confusion.

"Would you care for another dance, my dear?" Bastian asked me.

"I would, but are you sure you wouldn't like a rest?"

"No," he took my hand. "I am quite all right."

"In that case, I would love one," I said, letting him lead me past a dazed Shannon and onto the floor.

"I'm so sorry," he whispered as soon as we were out of earshot. "I tried to tell you–"

"It's fine," I smiled as I turned to face him. "Don't worry. I've got it under control."

"It looks that way," he grinned, glancing quickly over my shoulder to Shannon. "What's the plan?"

"The plan," I raised my eyebrows, "is to smile."

I grinned up at him as I took his hands and started moving my shoulders to the beat. The fun upbeat pop song that was playing had been exactly the sort of music I'd hoped for when devising my little scheme, and it only took a second for Bastian to pick up on my groove and start moving with me. What we were doing wasn't a swing, or a mambo, or a cha-cha, but rather a hybrid, taking moves from all those dances and more, combining them and weaving together an improvisation that was all our own. It was bouncy, it was quirky, and it was *fun*.

"Come on," I said, when I saw that Bastian was pressing his lips together, trying his hardest to remain casual and aloof. "I know you want to smile, let it out." His cheeks quivered, but he still fought it. "Come on..." I said, making a face as I dusted off my shoulders to the music. He huffed a chuckle through his nose, but that wasn't good enough – I wanted teeth. A few beats later he led me in a turn, and when I came back around with my eyes crossed, I finally broke through his shell. He let out a laugh that had the whole room looking at us, and it was at that moment that I knew I'd done what I had set out to do. We were having fun. Together.

It no longer mattered that Shannon had danced with Bastian, because now she was the one who looked like a fool. I was the one he wanted to dance with. I was the one who truly knew him. I was the one who had a real relationship with him, even if it wasn't quite what they all thought it was. Bastian was currently wearing a smile – a real smile – which was something that I knew the vast majority of the people there had never seen on him before. And that was because of me. Shannon could do what she wanted. I was the one with the real power.

And now, everyone knew it.

By the time the song was coming to an end, we had the attention of the entire room, and almost every face watching us had at the very least an amused grin or smile playing on it. Every face but Shannon's, that is, which glared at the floor in front of her as her cheeks flushed from cream to pink to red.

Bastian finished our dance by twirling me into a playful dip, igniting a round of enthusiastic applause, intermixed with the occasional hoot, whistle, and finally, a tinkling shower of metal clinking on glass. I glanced around and realized that many of the onlookers were tapping their drinking glasses with a spoon or whatever other bit of metal they had at their disposal, and anyone who has ever attended a wedding knew exactly what that meant.

"I'm not sure if it was part of your plan," Bastian said as he brought me up slowly, "but I think we may have to–"

Before he even had a chance to finish I took the side of his face in my hand... and I kissed him. He reciprocated immediately of course, pulling me against him, and inciting a fresh wave of applause and reaction from the crowd. We held there for an extended moment, and let me just say, as far as kisses went...

...God, was it weird.

Not that anyone else could tell as we were both acting the part brilliantly, but if it came down to it, I think I would have been more comfortable kissing Ryland.

Awkwardness aside, there was something else grating at me as we released one another and walked back to our seats on the couch. It was the same feeling I had a few days before in the library when I'd felt bad about having to bail on Alex to leaf though books. The pull in my chest, the lead in my stomach... it was guilt.

"Are you all right?" Bastian asked from my side.

"I'm good," I replied, taking a few deep breaths which helped the discomfort in my chest to ease. "Sorry about..." I gestured to the dance floor, "you know, that," I finished, sheepishly.

"Nothing to apologize for," he said. "In fact, you might be something of a genius. Though I will say," he lowered his voice, "between the smiling and the kissing, I do feel a bit used." He winked with a grin. "But if Shannon sulking in the corner over there is any testament, I'd say it worked."

And she was. She was sitting in a chair, arms crossed, and eyes burning a hole into the chair across from her. I'd really done it, and evil as I knew it was, I loved it! As the last of my discomfort relaxed from my chest, I suddenly had the need to walk, be free, and celebrate.

"I'm going to go get some air for a few minutes," I told Bastian. "Do you mind?"

"Not at all. In fact, I think I'll have a drink. Care for anything?"

"No, I'm all right. Be back in a few minutes."

With a smile and – yeah, I'll say it – a strut, I walked through the tent, back through the sparkly fog, and into the chilly night, taking a deep breath of the damp fragrant air.

I did it. I really did it. It was over. No more having to deal with Shannon and her crap. No more dreading every gathering, every meal time, and every hallway for fear that she would be there. I was free.

I wandered up the pathway to the manor, enjoying the feel of exoneration, but it wasn't long before I discovered that my newfound freedom did not include a freedom from nature, and realized that before I went back into the tent, I should probably visit a ladies' room. Being closer now to the manor than to the tent, I decided just to go back to my room to freshen up in privacy instead of fighting the lines and tight quarters that the tent's small private facilities would likely have. I made my way inside, finding myself hoping that Chloe would still be there so that I could tell her that I'd taken her advice and won the day. However, when I approached my room I could tell something was wrong.

"I know I said I would take you," I heard Alex's voice echo out from the half open door, "but I can't tonight, I'm sorry."

"It's not a problem dear," Chloe replied, her voice heavy with concern, "but I wish you'd tell me what's the matter."

"Nothing, I just need to lie…" but he stopped the moment I pushed the door open, his shoulders tensing tightly.

Chloe saw the reaction as well and suddenly looked very uncomfortable. "Tell you what," she said, glancing between us after a long pause, "I think Steven is still in the back hallway, I can go and meet him on my own. Don't worry, I'll be careful," she said, then slipped out the door and closed it behind her.

"What…" I looked around, trying to figure out what I'd missed. "What's going on?" Alex still hadn't turned to face me, so I came around him and immediately saw that Chloe was right, something was very wrong. His face was tight and his jaw locked, and no matter where I stood, he wouldn't make eye contact with me. "Hey," I said, reaching out and holding his upper arm, cringing when he didn't yield at all under my touch. "What's wrong?"

He pursed his lips for a second but then glanced away. "I'm tired," he said, his voice low and sharp. "I need to go to bed."

He turned to go, but I stepped in his way. "Alex, stop doing this," I insisted, "tell me what is wrong." Again he didn't answer, but when he turned his head I saw the shine of tears on his cheek. Oh my God, *he was crying?* But then I looked closer and saw it wasn't tears sparkling in his skin... and in his hair... and on his shirt... it was...

Glitter.

The same glitter that was falling from the fog fountain over the only door into and out of the tent.

"Why is there glitter in your hair?" I asked.

Once again he didn't answer, but he didn't need to. In a blink it all made sense. The way he was acting, the glitter, the pulling in my chest that I had attributed to guilt...

"You were *there?*" I breathed, my eyes narrowing in furious disbelief. "You were *following me?*"

"You're mad at me?" he countered, looking squarely at me now.

"Yes, I'm mad, you were spying on me!"

"*You kissed him, Becca!*" he yelled.

"So what?"

"*So what?* Are you serious?"

"It was an act, Alex! We were doing what they expected us to do, it didn't mean anything, how could you possibly not know that?"

"It didn't look much like an act," he said. "None of it did. It looked like you were having a pretty good time."

"I was having a good time, what's wrong with that? I'm not allowed to have fun unless it's with you?"

"You know that's not what I'm saying, having fun isn't the issue."

"The issue is that you don't trust me!"

"Maybe it's that I do trust you and I shouldn't!" he gestured sharply out toward the lawn.

·"Were you even going to tell me? Did you think I wasn't going to...?" My face fell and my blood pressure rose as I remembered that tonight hadn't been the first time I had the "guilty" feeling. "The library," I growled under my breath. "Tell me that wasn't you." He glanced down for a split second, but that was enough. "How many times?" I demanded through clenched teeth. "How many times have you followed me?"

He hesitated, which told me I wasn't going to like the answer. "A few."

I was done. I pressed my lips together, locking in the tirade that wanted to spill from them and stormed to my dresser. I looked myself over and when I was happy with what I saw – besides the bright red cheeks – I grabbed my lip gloss, reapplied it, and stuffed it in my pocket.

"What are you doing?" Alex asked.

"I," I said turning back to him with a glare, "am going back to the party, because it's where I am supposed to be."

"Fine!" he said, reaching for the door, his eyes shining brighter than they had a moment ago. "Have fun!"

"I will!" I shot back as he flung the door open. "And don't you dare follow me!"

But my only reply was the slam of the door.

Chapter 27

Madder than I'd been in weeks, I stomped all the way back out to the tent, huffing like a wild stallion.

How dare he not trust me! What had I ever done to give him reason to spy on me like that? OK, yeah, I just kissed a guy, but even if it hadn't all been an act, that would still only give him reason to spy on me from tonight on, not days before it happened!

Collecting myself only just enough to be seen in public, I made my way back into the tent and over to where Bastian sat waiting for me.

"There you are," he said, setting down a near empty plate of mini desserts. "I was getting worried." Then he saw my face. "Or maybe I still should be."

"It's nothing," I grumbled. "Sorry I took so long."

"Did something happen?"

I sighed, and he slid closer so I wouldn't have to yell. "I went in to use the bathroom in my room, and Alex was there. We got into a fight."

"Why?"

"Because he's been spying on me."

"What do you mean?"

"I mean, following me around and watching me. Like tonight," I gestured to the dance floor, "he was here, and saw me kiss you."

His eyes popped open. "So you're telling me there's a black eye in my future." He nodded. "Great."

"Not likely," I grinned. "And anyway, he has no right to be mad!"

"Well, I don't know about that," he raised his hands when I threw him a look. "Just saying, I wouldn't care for it either. But even still, it's strange that he would get *that* upset about it, knowing about my..." he paused, "situation."

"Actually, he doesn't know about it."

"You didn't tell him?" He sounded surprised. "Don't misunderstand, I appreciate the discretion, but you probably should have told him."

"I was going to, but we really haven't had a chance to talk the past few days," I admitted. "Not privately, anyway. But that's not the point, your situation shouldn't matter. He should trust me no matter who I'm with. Trusting a person only when there is no possibility that something could happen isn't trusting them."

"I suppose that's true," he considered.

"And it's not just tonight," I told him. "He's been following me for days. He was even there the day you and I were in the library parlor skimming books for two hours."

"Really? OK, yeah, that is a bit strange."

"Right? I mean, if he can't trust me, then who can he trust?"

He pondered for a second before downing the last of whatever was in his glass. "I hate to take sides," he said, leaning and putting the empty glass on the table at the end of the couch, "but it does seem like he might be overreacting."

"Thank you!" *At least someone had my back tonight...*

"Either that," he chuckled, "or your boy has some deep seated abandonment issues."

He chuckled again at what he thought was a joke, taking the last tiny pastry off his plate and popping it in his mouth. I didn't hear the next thing he said, nor did I look up when the server walked by and took the empty plate and glass away. I simply sat, starring at nothing as the world around me fell off into the background, replaced by the stabbing echo of two words: abandonment issues.

How could I have been so blind?

Alex had been abandoned by his parents when he was still a little boy. The two people that he inherently believed would always be there left him for dead in an asylum. I knew all this of course, but as ashamed as I was to admit it, it was easy to forget. He was just so well adjusted and happy that it seemed almost impossible for him to have suffered so much as child. But he had suffered, and no matter how content and happy he appeared, I knew that deep down, he had scars.

I should have been the one who understood. The one who was there by his side to offer comfort and reassurance whenever past wounds came back to threaten him. But instead, I got so wrapped up in intrigue, games, and petty pride, that I hadn't been paying attention. I'd misinterpreted all the signs I'd seen and who knows how many I'd missed altogether. This wasn't about trust; it was about fear. He was scared...

...and I was an ass.

"Becca?" Bastian called, looking at me as though I might fall over. "Becca, I'm sorry, I didn't mean to upset you. I was only kidding."

"I know," I assured him. "It's not you, I promise. But I need to go."

"Of course," he nodded.

Without another word, I stood and left the tent, not bothering to don my air or mask my features. I didn't care who saw me or what they said. All I cared about was finding Alex and doing whatever it took to fix what I'd done.

I went straight to his room, and when I didn't sense him in there, I tried both Jocelyn's and Cormac's with no luck. I stopped by my own room thinking Chloe might have some idea as to where he might be, but she was gone too, most likely still with Steven. I quickly changed from my party clothes into a long sweatshirt, jeans and comfortable shoes, prepared to search every inch of the manor until I found him, no matter how long it took.

Using every faculty at my disposal, I looked, listened, and sensed my way through the hallways and common areas, praying for anything that would lead me to where he'd gone. He wasn't in the back hallway, or the any of the upstairs lounges. I couldn't feel him in the foyer, the library, or the reception room. And there was no trace of anyone in the large empty gallery or the dark and cold sunroom. It wasn't until I took the hall along the west wall that I felt the brush of his familiar ability calling to mine. I followed its glow until I reached a large double door leading to the west lawn. I looked out through the glass and saw that he was outside, sitting on the wide steps leading down to the grass, almost completely hidden from view behind one of two large pillars that were holding up the balcony above.

I stepped out into the night air and walked up to the pillar, wanting to speak, but with no idea what to say. He had to know I was there but he didn't look up, so I went over to the single step between the one he was seated on and the stone pillar, and gently slid myself down behind him, one leg on each side. I wrapped my arms around his shoulders and leaned into him, resting my cheek against his back.

"I'm so sorry," I whispered.

I felt him swallow, then tip his head down as his hands slowly came up and held my arms tightly to his chest with a shuddering sigh. I leaned back, taking him with me until my back rested against the stone pillar, and his rested against my stomach. He turned his head, nestling into my upper arm, while he continued to clutch my hands and forearms, clinging to them like a scared child would a stuffed bear. We sat that way for a long while before he finally spoke.

"I trust you," he said, the hoarseness of his voice tearing at my heart.

"I know you do."

"You were right, I shouldn't have followed you. I'm sorry."

"It's OK."

"I knew it was wrong, and I didn't do it because I didn't trust you. You were just…"

"Tell me," I urged, when he didn't continue.

He sighed. "You were starting to have so much fun getting to know Bastian, and working on everything with him. And then the engagement and how well you did fitting in with everyone. I know you were doing it because you had to, but you really seemed to be enjoying it too, and…" he paused again, "I started to worry."

"Why didn't you just talk to me?"

"Because," he shrugged against me, "I was embarrassed. I knew I was being insecure. It was my problem, not yours."

"Except there's no such thing."

"I know," he said, giving my arms a squeeze.

After a minute or two of silence, I felt him open his mouth to say something but then close it again. A moment later he did it again… and then again. I could tell he wanted to say something, but as much as I didn't want him to hold back, I also didn't want to seem like I was forcing him.

Fortunately, on the fourth try, the words finally came. "I think about things sometimes. I don't want to but I can't help it." He paused while I waited quietly. "I've always known how lucky I am. The kids I grew up with, most of them don't have what I do. My life at St Brigid's, all the people there who care about me, the education I've gotten and the work I get to do… it's amazing. And for a long time it was enough – more than enough. More than I ever thought I'd have." He paused again, swallowing twice before continuing. "But then I met you. And feeling the way I do about you… having what we have… if you were to…" He tried again. "If…" He took a deep breath. "All that other stuff, it isn't enough anymore. I couldn't go back."

"Alex," I said, blinking away tears as I rested my cheek on the side of his head and aligned my lips with the top of his ear. "I am never, *ever* going to leave you. And if you need me to, I will tell you that every single day for the rest of our lives." I waited a moment, allowing my words to sink in before I went on. "But, that being said, there is something you need to realize." He looked back at me over his shoulder, then sat up and pivoted slightly so our shoulders were perpendicular. "I want you to understand," I said, able to meet his eyes for the first time, "that things are different now."

"What do you mean?"

"I mean in you. There is a quote that says, 'Fate decides who walks into your life, but you decide who you let walk out, who you let stay, and who you refuse to let go.' I know when your parents left, you didn't have a choice. You were just a kid, and at the mercy of those bigger than you. But you are in charge now, and you don't have to let anyone leave you if you don't want them to."

"You can't stop people from leaving."

"No, probably not," I admitted, "but you can follow them." I paused as I watched a thin veil of calm begin to settle over him as he considered what I'd said. "Now, as already stated, there is nothing that will ever make me leave you. But," I grinned, "let's just say, for sake of argument, that some aliens show up one day and take over my body."

"Aliens?" he grinned.

"Why not? If you asked me, I should be the one they look for first. After all, I have access to some pretty mad skills, remember?"

"Right," he chuckled. "OK, so," he motioned for me to continue, "aliens take over your body…"

"Yes. If they take over my body, and realize that you are a clever guy and might figure them out, they could force me to leave. And if that were to happen, I need to know that you wouldn't just let me go."

"I guess I see your point," he smiled.

"Nope, not good enough, I want you to say it." He cocked his brow at me. "I'm not going to be able to sleep at night knowing if aliens show up I'm screwed." We shared a laugh, but whether he knew it or not, I was serious. Sobering, I took his face in my hand and held his eyes with mine. "Really though. I want to hear you say it. 'I will always follow you.'"

He studied me for a moment, his grin slipping away. Taking a breath, he slowly repeated the words, the weight on his shoulders visibly lifting with each syllable. "I will always follow you." When he finished, a smile lit his eyes that made my own misty, and a blink later he had my face between his hands and was kissing me so happily and lovingly that I think I may have actually sighed out loud. "I love you so much," he whispered, resting his forehead against mine.

"I love you too."

We held there for a joyously languid moment, until I felt his shoulders shake as he huffed a laugh. "Now if only you could burn away the image of you and Bastian, we'd be good," he said with a grin.

"Well," I said with a wry glance. "I do know a guy…"

"Oh sure, that'd be a great conversation."

"No," I agreed, "it'd be terrible. But no worries, I think I can take care of it."

"Oh?"

"I might know a little something about Bastian that may help you out."

"Which is?"

"The fact that he is bonded as well. To a guy from his school named Justyn."

His jaw dropped. "You're kidding."

"Nope. Told me about it the morning I went to talk to him about Chloe and Steven."

"That's incredi–" He stopped, his eyes narrowing. "Wait, you've known for how long, and you're only telling me *now*?"

"I know, I'm sorry. I was going to tell you but I didn't get the chance, and then our plans got messed up, and then I didn't see you…" I sighed with an apologetic grimace. "Let's just say I suck all around on this one."

"Or," he suggested, "what do you say we go with we both suck, and agree to talk next time."

"I can go with that."

"So," he said, pulling himself up to his feet, and taking my hand and bringing me up alongside him. "Are you still up for that movie?"

"Hmm," I hummed suggestively, taking far too long a time fixing the collar of his shirt. "I'm not sure I feel like a movie."

"Well," he ran his fingers lightly down my arm, "I suppose we could always find something else to do."

Sliding his hand around mine, he led me back inside and down the hallway toward the wing with his room. I wasn't sure I'd ever had such a rollercoaster of a day, but now that it was all over, I had to say that I was proud of us. We'd fought – really fought – for the first time, and odd as it may sound, I was glad. Too many people think that when a couple doesn't fight that they are strong, but I have never bought that. The question should never be "do you fight," but "can you fight," because fights happen, that's just the way it is. What's important is how you handle it. The strongest couples aren't the ones who avoid fighting, but the ones who do fight and are able to grow from it, and come out on the other side with something better than they had before.

I'd always known that nothing would come between Alex and I, but that was just the "what." Now that I saw that we could handle what problems we did have in a way that only made us stronger, I finally knew the "how."

We were almost to Alex's room when we passed by the hallway with Jocelyn's room, and I noticed Chloe walking along the wall. "Chloe?"

"Hi guys," she waved, coming to meet us.

"What are you doing out here, someone could see you," I scolded her.

"I know, but don't worry, there hasn't been anyone by and I've been very careful."

"What are you doing down here?" Alex asked.

"Waiting for Steven," she said, excitement glowing on her face. "He went to ask Jocelyn if he could come to St Brigid's!"

"Really?" I gave her a hug. "That's fantastic!"

"I know, I didn't even ask him. That's what he wanted to talk to me about tonight; he wanted to make sure I wouldn't mind!"

"That is great Chloe," Alex said, "but you still shouldn't be out here on your own. We'll stay and hide you until he comes out."

"Oh it's OK, it should be any minute. I actually thought they'd be done by now, but Steven talks slow when he's nervous."

"That's strange..." I said, my attention having slid from the conversation to Jocelyn's room. "Chloe, have you been here the whole time?"

"No, I've been walking up and down the back hallway too."

"What's the matter?" Alex asked me.

"I don't feel him in there."

"Jocelyn?" he asked.

I nodded, walking over to the door and knocking. "Jocelyn?" No answer. "Jocelyn? Steven?" I called, pounding the door harder. And that's when I felt it – a cold draft blew across my ankle from under the door.

My head snapped to Alex, fear tight in my voice. "We have to get this door open."

He looked around quickly and ran for a small rough iron decorative table just down the hall while I turned back to the door and gave a hard kick to the wood next to the handle.

"What's wrong?" Chloe asked, her hands beginning to shake. "What's happening?"

"Watch out," Alex said suddenly, having returned with the table in his hands. With a heave, he swung the table at the door and sent a crack splintering down from the handle to the floor. Two more hits and it burst open, sending wood shards and dust flying in every direction. I ran into the room at full speed, only to stop short when I saw the scene that lay beyond the ruined door, my heart stabbing into my throat. The window was broken, the room was destroyed...

...and Jocelyn and Steven were gone.

CHAPTER 28

I couldn't move.

I couldn't think.

All I could do was stare at the empty shambles of the room in front of me, as fear burned like acid in my stomach. Why? How? Who?

The sound of Chloe's hyperventilating finally shoved me out of my shocked haze. "Oh God," she croaked, "oh God... oh God..."

I snapped my head over to Alex. "Go find Cormac." With a nod he was gone, doing his best to shut the destroyed door as he left. I darted over to the floor next to the desk and picked up the overturned phone and hit the button for the front desk.

"*How may we be of service this evening, Mr Clavish?*" a woman's voice answered making an assumption due to the call's room number.

"This is his daughter," I told her, trying to make sure my voice sounded as collected as possible. "Please listen very carefully; I need someone to go out to the youth mixer that is happening right now on the lawn, and tell Mr Bloch that his fiancée needs him come to Mr Clavish's room immediately. This is an emergency, and it is imperative that this message reach him as soon as possible, and confidentiality is of the upmost importance. Do you understand?"

"Yes, of course, Miss Clavish" the woman replied, her tone reflecting the urgency in my own, "right away."

I hung up and turned back to Chloe who was still standing by the door, her face a pale bloodless gray. Swallowing my own dread, I walked over to her and took her shaking hands. "Chloe," I said firmly but as gently as I could, "take a deep breath for me, OK?"

She looked at me but the panic remained. "Where are they?" she asked, her voice squeaking and breaking, "Who would take them? Why? What do they want? We need to tell someone, maybe someone knows, maybe they can–"

"No," I stopped her, grabbing her arms tightly as she went for the door. "Chloe, listen to me…"

"We can't just stand here" she yelled, tears tracing down her cheeks, "we have to do something!"

"And we will," I said firmly, forcing her eyes up to mine, "but first you need to listen to me. I know you're scared, but the last thing that is going to help Steven and Jocelyn right now is us panicking. Alex has gone for Cormac and Bastian is on his way. When they get here, we will come up with a plan and I swear that we will get them both back," I promised, wondering silently how sure I really was, "but until then, we can't just run out and start telling anyone who will listen."

"But what if someone can help?"

"And what if the first person we tell is secretly working with the ones who took them?" She stopped, her eyes widening. "Exactly," I nodded, "that would only make things worse. I know you want to help them, but to do that we need to keep our heads and think."

She didn't respond for a moment but I could see the rationale settling in. "OK," she finally whispered, nodding her head spastically, clearly still panicking but at least somewhat in control of herself again.

"Good," I said giving her arm a squeeze. "Now, I want you to think back. Did you hear anything while you were out there? Anything at all?"

"No," she shook her head, "but I wasn't out there the whole time. I didn't want anyone to see me, so I tried to stay by the back hallway and only come up to the door every once in a while." Guilt shredded her face as she brought her hands up to her mouth. "Oh God, I should have stayed!"

"It's not your fault," I tried to assure her just as Alex and Cormac arrived.

"Heavens above…" Cormac whispered as he took in the scene. "Do we have any idea when it happened?

"Sometime in the last hour or so," I told him as Alex stepped up and put an arm around Chloe, leaving me free to step away.

"Oh!" Cormac gasped suddenly. "The Iris! Tell me he didn't have the Iris on him!"

I spun around, my eyes darting around the room, desperately searching for the square pouch of stiff leather.

"He must have," Alex said. "He said it was always on him."

"Not always," I said, running to the small table it had been on the afternoon I'd ported to it. "He kept it on him whenever he left the room, but while he was in here…" I left my sentence hanging as I searched the table, its one drawer, and the surrounding area. Just as I was about to span out my search, I looked toward the bed and saw something poking out from under the portion of skewed bed sheet that lay on the floor. I reached under and felt a cool blast of relief as my fingers immediately recognized the feel of the worn leather and firm rounded disk beneath.

Cormac sighed loudly, wiping his brow as I pulled the pouch out from hiding and glanced inside to make certain that the Iris was in fact there. "Well, I suppose that's something," he said.

As I got to my feet the door opened again, this time for Bastian who eyed the splintered wood of the door in disbelief. "What the hell happened to the do–" but he choked on the word as the room itself came into view. "What happened in here?" But before anyone answered, his eyes darkened as he looked around at the faces in the room and realized that one which should have been present was missing. "Where is Jocelyn?"

"We don't know," Cormac told him.

"Someone broke in," I motioned to the window, "and took him, and then we broke in," I motioned to the door, "when we realized he was gone."

"And?" he asked, seeing the trepidation on my face and correctly assuming there was more.

"Bastian…" I said, not wanting to tell him, but knowing I had to, "When Jocelyn was taken, Steven was in here with him." I winced as his already concerned face froze over. "They took him too."

I could see the terror singeing his eyes, but his years of practice burying emotion and playing whatever roll needed playing came to his aid, allowing him to keep it together – even if just barely. "What do we do?" he asked after a couple of hard breaths.

"We get them back," I said, my voice as deadly as I'd ever heard it. "And to do that," I paused, opening the pouch in my hand, "we need to see what happened."

Without so much as a blink of hesitation, I slid the Iris out into my hand, welcoming the rush of power I'd feared only days before. Letting my worry for Jocelyn and Steven drive me, it took less than a second to link up with Chloe's ability, and a second more to find the spot in time less than an hour before, when Steven arrived in Jocelyn's room. Entering into that place in time, I let the scene play out in front of me, watching as Steven and Jocelyn began their conversation about St Brigid's and the future. Eager to get to the break-in, I instinctively guided my ability, pushing it forward and watched as the passage of time within the scene sped up before my eyes, like fast-forwarding a movie. I hurried past the several minutes that Steven and Jocelyn talked uninterrupted, allowing everything to return to real-time when I saw a dark shadow loom in from the window.

"Someone is outside," I dictated to the others in the room who had fallen silent when they realized what I was doing. "At the window."

"How did they get all the way up to the second story?" Cormac asked.

"Can't tell," I said. "Looks like he might be on a ladder."

I continued to watch, holding my breath as suddenly the window burst open, shattering the bottom panes of glass and wrenching one of the hinges clean out of the frame. Jocelyn and Steven both spun toward the noise just as the intruder jumped down into the room.

"It's Ryan," I said, finally seeing his face.

He came forward and was about to make a move on Jocelyn but stopped, cursing when he spotted Steven bolting for the door. Quickly using his ability to pull Jocelyn's feet out from under him and stop any immediately threat of him escaping or calling for help, Ryan then turned to Steven who was mere inches from the door, taking hold of him kinetically at the last possible moment, and locking him in place. Jocelyn scrambled to his feet, but with Steven frozen and apparently unable to speak, Ryan was now free to focus his attention on making sure Jocelyn stayed just shy of the upper hand.

"What do you want, Ryan?" Jocelyn asked, standing poised like a snake ready to strike.

"You," Ryan answered. "Your presence is requested."

"Then take me and let him go," Jocelyn gestured toward Steven, never taking his eyes from his attacker.

"He wasn't supposed to be here. Now he comes too."

"I'll stop you," Jocelyn threatened, his slow nod making it clear that the interference he planned to use would be of the mental variety.

"Awful risky with me holding the boy, don't you think? Why, say you were to make me lose focus and I was to smother his lungs or crush his skull?"

Either one of them may have been bluffing, but I knew Jocelyn would never gamble like that, not with someone else's safety. But even had he wanted to try something there wouldn't have been time, as a moment later a second head appeared in the window.

It was Barra. "What in bloody hell?"

"Just get the boy," Ryan barked, releasing Steven who fell to the floor with a gasp, "I can't hold them both."

Taking advantage of what may have been his only opportunity, Jocelyn lunged toward the phone, knocking almost everything off the desk in the process, but had only barely touched the receiver when he too went perfectly still just as Steven had done.

"A good attempt," Ryan snickered, "but you're not as young as you used to be."

"Barra was there too," I said, having almost forgotten about updating the others anxiously waiting in the room. "Ryan told him to restrain Steven so he could hold off Jocelyn. Steven's free of Ryan now, but Barra has him…"

I clenched my teeth as Ryan approached Jocelyn, worried that he might throw a punch at him or take some other cheap shot now that Jocelyn was completely vulnerable, but he didn't. All he did was reach out quickly to the hand hovering over the phone, I guessed to move it and everything else out of reach – though that seemed odd now that Jocelyn could move. It wasn't until I heard the sharp intake of air from Jocelyn's rigid form that I realized Ryan had taken a cheap shot – the cheapest shot of all.

"His ring," I gasped out loud, "Ryan took Jocelyn's ring."

"Oh no!" I heard Cormac breathe. "He'd be completely incapacitated!"

Sure enough, Ryan released his hold on Jocelyn a moment later, only to laugh as Jocelyn fell to the floor with a thud. His eyes were squeezed shut, while his rock-hard fists ground into his forehead, all to the sound of an unending stream of painfully labored breaths hissing in and out from between his clenched teeth.

"Not so tough now, aye?" Ryan laughed again, giving him a swift kick in the ribs.

It wasn't until I felt Alex's hand gently rub my back that I realized I was shaking. "Easy," his soothing whisper came from behind me.

I nodded, drawing strength from the warmth of his hand, and regaining control with a deep breath. "Ryan and Barra are discussing what to do," I said, dictating the scene to the others matter-of-factly, trying to detach myself from the image of Jocelyn crumpled on the floor seemingly only a few feet away. "They don't want to risk leaving Steven behind now that he has seen them. Barra is wrestling him over to the bed while Ryan is taking something out of his coat... a small bottle. He is dumping whatever is in it onto a corner of the bed sheet... now he's holding it to Steven's mouth." I paused, watching poor Steven give one last lunge to try and free himself before losing consciousness. "Whatever it was, it knocked him out."

I heard Chloe choke back a whimper from behind me and I instantly felt guilty. In my attempt to be blunt and unattached, I'd forgotten about how the others might react. Deciding it was best to hold my tongue all together, I stopped my narration and watched quietly as Barra put an unconscious Steven down on the bed and went to the window.

"I'll climb down, you lower the boy to me, then follow with him."

"Right," Ryan said nervously, "go on then, we've already been here too long."

Barra hopped up on the window ledge but turned back before taking the jump down. "Where's the ring?"

"Here," Ryan said, pulling it from his pocket.

"Better leave it, they might have a call on it."

"Hadn't thought of that." Ryan quickly surveyed the room, then walked to one of the armchairs and stuffed the ring down behind the seat cushion.

Satisfied, Barra jumped from the window, while Ryan kinetically lifted Steven, sending him out the window a few moments later. Once Barra had Steven, Ryan turned to Jocelyn who was still hunched over on the floor, grinding his hands into his head. He pulled the debilitated man to his feet, and with a good deal of kinetic assistance, led him across the room and out the window, disappearing into the frosty air.

"They're gone," I said, sliding the Iris back into its pouch, wincing inwardly at the uncomfortably helpless feeling that crept over me at the separation.

"How?" Bastian asked as I walked over to the armchair and started digging under the cushion. "How could they have gotten both of them out of here without being seen?"

"Once Steven and Jocelyn were both incapacitated, Ryan used his ability to take them out the window," I explained, pulling the ring out from the folds of the chair leather.

"They left it?" Alex asked seeing the ring. "Why?"

"They said that we might have a 'call' on it. What's a call?"

"A call charm," Cormac said. "It is a charm designed to be put on an object so that it can never be lost. All you need is a small piece of whatever the charmed item is and you can locate it instantly."

"And they thought we could use it to find him?"

"Yes," Cormac nodded, "and they would have been right. All of our Sciaths are charmed with calls, Min has seen to it. She has a small bit of the metal from each of our settings in her office in case of emergencies."

"But how do they expect to get anything from him without it?" Alex asked.

"And why was he like that?" I added, not completely sure I wanted to know.

"Without his Sciath, Jocelyn has no control of his power," Cormac told me gently. "He hears every thought within the radius of his ability which, as you know, is all but limitless. His mind is now flooded with noise and confusion, but worst of all, there is no barrier between his mind and everyone else's around him. Every ounce of his strength will have to be focused on containing his power and keeping it away from the thoughts and memories of others, or risk damaging or even destroying the minds of anyone within his reach in the blink of an eye. As for how Darragh will make any use of him, I am not sure, but it wouldn't be difficult for Darragh, or anyone else with the ability of alchemy to create a temporary Sciath for him. It would not be even remotely as strong as his true one, nor would it be tailored to his needs, but it would suffice for the purposes of allowing him to speak and giving him a moment of relative peace."

"What do we do now?" Chloe's voice trembled, understandably uninterested in Sciath talk.

"We go talk to the one man who knows everything there is to know," I said. "Molony."

There was a collective nod of agreement, but Alex's brow furrowed. "But how? We don't know where he is. The banquet is the only place we know for sure he'll be."

"No," I shook my head, "we can't wait until tomorrow, that's too long."

"But we don't know where to find him..." Alex pressed, while I looked over to Bastian, relieved when I saw that he had followed my train of thought.

"We don't," he said grim determination set in his eyes, "but my parents do."

I nodded, but still eyed him hesitantly. "Are you sure you are up for this?" I asked, knowing that there was no way we could approach Alva and Brassal without them learning everything that Bastian had fought for so long to keep secret.

"He's my brother."

It was all he said, but it was enough. His love for Steven was the only reason he maintained the pretense he did; why wouldn't he be willing to give it up to save him?

I turned to Cormac. "Call Min and the others and let them know what's happened."

"Of course," he nodded.

As he went for the phone, I turned to Alex, but he beat me to the punch. "I'll stay here with Chloe," he said, echoing my thoughts exactly, "and try to get the door back up. Go with Bastian and see if you can help." I was going to ask if he was sure, but one look in his eyes and I saw there was no need. When it came to Bastian he understood now, and even if he hadn't, this wasn't about us. It was about getting Jocelyn and Steven back safely, and I knew that we were all willing to do whatever it took to make sure that happened. "Everything will be fine," Alex whispered, wrapping his hands firmly around mine.

I knew what he meant, and I tried my best to smile. We both knew that he didn't know how things would turn out, but he wanted me to know that he knew how scared I was even if I couldn't bring myself to say it. As always, he was able to see through me to everything I thought I was keeping hidden, and vulnerable as it usually made me feel, right then it gave me a comfort that I could be nothing but grateful for.

"OK," I said louder as I gave Alex's hand a squeeze and stepped back with a deep breath, "are we ready?" I looked over at Bastian who gave me a nod, and let the adrenaline of action distract my mind from the nauseating worry. "Then let's go."

"What is all this about, Bastian?" Alva asked, as she, Brassal, Bastian, and I arrived at the Blochs' guestroom and quickly ducked inside. As Bastian ushered his parents into the parlor area of the suite, I made sure to scan the hall and surrounding areas once more with my ability, making sure we weren't being followed before shutting and locking the door behind us.

"It better damned well be important enough to warrant interrupting a formal dinner." Brassal clipped, rounding on Bastian the moment they reached the parlor. "Do you have any idea what the other guests at dinner must be thinking of us?"

Seriously? What they were thinking of them – was he kidding? Couldn't he tell that this was serious, or at least give us the benefit of the doubt before assuming we were just wasting his time? Sure, Bastian and I had cut their dinner short when we'd urgently insisted on speaking to them privately, but we had been more than discreet. Granted our caution was more to do with the fact that we didn't know who in the room full of diners may have been listening in, than it was to help the host and hostess of the evening save face, but either way, Brassal had no reason to be complaining.

"With all due respect, Father," Bastian ground out, apparently unwilling to tolerate his father's narcissism, "I don't give a devil's ass to what they are saying about any of us, and neither should you. There are far more serious matters to worry about right now." It looked like Brassal might have been a second away from erupting, but Bastian continued before he could begin, "Jocelyn and Steven have been abducted."

The expressions on Brassal and Alva's faces instantly fell black, then morphed into something between anger and shock. "What in God's name are you talking about?" Brassal asked.

"Jocelyn and Steven have been taken," Bastian repeated, his posture as rigid as his gaze.

"When?" Alva gasped.

"By whom?" Brassal added on top of her.

"About an hour ago," Bastian said. He paused for only a moment as a silent debate flashed behind his eyes. As I waited for him to decide what to say, I wondered just how much he was going to reveal, but as it turned out, I didn't have to wait long. "They were taken by Mr Ryan and Mr Barra whom, along with Mr Doyle and Mr McGary, have been working as informants to Darragh, and assisting him in many of his various operations."

The room fell silent as death, and I found myself afraid to breathe. Though awkward as the moment was, I had to hand it to Bastian; he hadn't wasted any time. He'd laid it all out, and was ready to deal with the consequences, come what may. But impressed as I was, the shift on both Brassal and Alva's faces had me growing concerned. It was obvious that they were shocked, but I wasn't so sure that the news about the four men was the only thing sparking their surprise, and while I could understand Bastian's direct approach, I began to wonder if it was really for the best.

"Have you lost your senses?" Brassal scoffed after a moment, "Those men could not possib–"

But Bastian stopped him. "I assure you I am very serious," he replied, his flat tone reinforcing the words. "We have been watching the four of them for some time, and–"

"*We?*" Brassal interrupted this time, "who is *we?*"

"Jocelyn, Becca, and the rest of their party." He paused with a tense huff before going on. "But only since meeting with them here at Adare. Prior to our arrival, I worked on my own, and have been observing them secretly for years. Because of this, I know for a fact that not only are they conspiring with Darragh, but have on multiple occasions assisted him in his various operations."

A deep red hue began to flood Brassal's face. "You've been *spying* on them?!" he hissed, his nostrils flared.

"Bastian," Alva breathed, her hand flying to her chest as she made a show of being appalled, "what were you thinking?!"

Bastian's hands began to shake. "*What was I thinking?*" he hissed "*That* is what you want to discuss! Did you not hear me? Steven is gone! Jocelyn is gone!"

"What was Steven doing in Jocelyn's room?" Alva asked, sounding far more irritated than worried.

"It doesn't matter right now," Bastian yelled though his clenched jaw, then ran his hands through his hair with a shuddering breath, in a last ditch effort to keep it together. "All that matters," he continued, his temper just barely under wraps, "is that we speak to Niall Molony, and you are the only ones who know where he is."

"Molony?" Alva's eyebrows furrowed.

"Don't tell me you believe Molony is involved in your

ludicrous conspiracy theories as well?" Brassal asked with what was almost a sneer.

I could see Bastian was about to snap, and know that wasn't going to get us the information we needed, I quickly put a hand on his arm before he could speak. "We are not sure of his involvement," I said, while Bastian ground his teeth next to me, "but we do believe he may know what has happened."

"That's preposterous," Alva insisted, waiving her hand dismissively.

As Bastian's eyes followed the flip of her wrist, he lost the battle against his rage. "Is it?" he challenged, sarcastic malice dripping from each syllable. "And why is that, pray? Because you *know him* so well? Because of all the years you've spent as his *closest friends?*"

"You will mind your tongue, young man," Brassal warned, but Bastian ignored him.

"Or," Bastian went on, "could it be that you refuse to believe that any of the mindless, self-absorbed, wastes of matter that you so proudly associate with, could be anything but loyal to your worthless kind?"

Brassal stepped toward his son with a terrible fire in his eyes, and for a second I thought he might hit him. In the end he didn't but action or no, the threat of violence continued to waft from him as he spoke, like the billowing scent of too much cologne. "I will not tolerate such disrespect from you, boy. I don't know what has gotten into you, but you will find a way to control yourself this minute." Bastian didn't respond, but stood rigidly, shaking with frustration. "I realize," Brassal went on, backing down slightly, "that this is a troubling situation. Clearly you are not yourself, and as I understand your being upset, I am willing to forgive you on this occasion. But do not mistake my forgiveness of your outburst for clemency of your professed past actions. These claims of spying and so forth will be addressed at a later time, is that clear?" Bastian nodded, the hope in his features growing. "However, for now, all our energy needs to be put into the situation at hand."

"Oh goodness, yes," Alva said, seeming truly worried for the first time since we'd arrived at the room, "there is no time to lose."

Bastian let out a shuddering breath, his shoulders sagging in relief. "Thank you," he said, glancing down at me as I smiled back, hopeful for the first time since finding Jocelyn's empty room.

"Of course, dear," Alva said, "after all this affects us as much as it does the two of you."

"Indeed," Brassal agreed, then turned to Bastian. "Who else is aware that this has happened? Have you spoken to anyone about it?"

"No," Bastian answered. "Only Becca, Cormac, Alex and myself, as we were there just after it happened."

"And there was no one else nearby? No one who could have overheard?"

"No, I don't believe so," said Bastian, his tone echoing my own growing confusion.

Why would it matter who knew?

"Good," Brassal said seeming somewhat satisfied, "in that case, we may not be too late. Alva," he looked to his pensive wife, "go back to the dinner and make sure nothing has reached them there. I will go to the front desk to see if anything has been reported, and go to Jocelyn's room and see what needs to be done there. The key will be staying in control of the situation, and if we are lucky and work quickly, none of the other guests will have cause to find out that any of this has happened."

"Oh my, can you imagine? Everyone finding out that the *Bronntanas* was attacked at our own event? We would be ruined!"

"Pardon me," I said, unsure if I was misunderstanding, or worse, understanding perfectly, "you do realize that my father has been taken by Darragh, right? And what that could mean?" I added, suppressing a tremor.

"Of course," Alva said, stepping over to me and taking my hand, "and it is just awful to be sure. However, I think there is something you need to understand, my dear. Your father and his associates have been involving themselves in Darragh and his affairs for many years. This sort of thing was bound to happen eventually, I'm afraid."

Brassal huffed in agreement. "Precisely why one should keep to their own affairs. Meddling brings nothing but trouble."

The horror on my face must have shown through, because Alva placed what I'm sure she thought was a comforting hand on my shoulder. "But you needn't worry. You are practically family now, and we will do everything we can to make sure that you are undamaged by all this."

"Undamaged in the Bhunaidh society, you mean," I clarified, not sure what my expression looked like from the outside, but whatever it was, it didn't seem to faze her.

"Exactly," she smiled, eliciting the same feeling in me as would scratching on a chalkboard. "And you'll never have to worry about Darragh, or any of that awful business at the school again."

I wanted to reply, but I was beyond words. Not only were they not interested in helping the man they claimed to worship, but they'd not made a single reference to the fact that their own son was also gone. Jocelyn had "brought it on himself," and all that mattered now was covering it up so that everyone could save face. They would leave Jocelyn and Steven – and probably anyone else for that matter – to rot while they carried on as the center of their own universe.

I should have been mad. I should have been screaming, fighting, and yelling, with a red face and clenched fists. But now was not the time for my temper. Now was the time to get the information I needed, and yelling and screaming wasn't going to get me there. Bastian had taught me that when dealing with people like this, there was another way. He may have forgotten, but I hadn't. He took a breath and was about to fume again, but I stopped him with a clam hand on his chest. He'd tried yelling, and it hadn't worked. Now, it was my turn.

"Forgive me," I said, addressing both Brassal and Alva with a direct and stern tone that had them both turning to look at me, "but I'm afraid you have misunderstood my intentions in coming to you. My father and your son have been taken against their will, and I intend to do everything in my power to bring them home. In order to do that, I need to speak to Niall Molony. You can either tell me where to find him so that our meeting can be done quietly, or you can refuse and force me to question every person on this property until I find someone who can help me. And should I have to go that route, I promise you on everything I hold dear that by tomorrow morning, there will not be a soul in or around this manor who does not know exactly what happened tonight, not only in Jocelyn's room, but in this one as well, and I'm willing to bet that if your guests would be upset at the idea of an attack, that they wouldn't take much kinder to the notion of cover-up. As I said, how I get the information I need is up to you, but I will get it. No one stops me from protecting my family. *No one*." My voice had grown more severe with each word, and by the end, great and powerful Brassal and Alva Bloch were watching me like stubborn mice under the eyes of a hawk.

"So what's it going to be?"

CHAPTER 29

Not thirty minutes later, Alex, Bastian, and I stood in one of the restricted upper level hallways, invisibly waiting on the room service staff member to make his or her appearance. They'd said it would take twenty minutes when Bastian had ordered the dessert, and nearly seventeen minutes had passed since then. Wouldn't be long now.

It's always both a relief and incredibly annoying to learn that something you've been looking for has been right under your nose the whole time, and Mr Molony was no exception. As it turned out, he'd been staying at Adare with the rest of us all along. He'd contacted Brassal and Alva and told them that he wished to reside on the estate this year, but that he required a room that was away from the rest of the guest suites and common areas, as well as total secrecy in regards to where he was. Alva had managed to arrange a room for him within the restricted wing of the upper floor, and had personally made sure that all the other guests believed that he once again was staying elsewhere. The only people who knew the truth were a select few members of the Adare staff, and of course Brassal and Alva, who had not been at all happy about sharing the information.

"Just curious, but do we have a plan B?" Alex whispered as we waited, all eyes glued on the top of the stairs at the other end of the hall. "What if he doesn't take the tray?"

"We'll come up with plan B if we need it," I answered, more than a little nervous myself, "but for now we just have to hope he does."

"Seems we are about to find out," Bastian said, gesturing to the stairwell where the silhouette of a head was rising up into view. "Ready?" he asked Alex, as he pulled his anchor out of his pocket and removed the thick metal ring from its chord. Alex nodded and Bastian dropped the anchor into his outstretched hand.

"Be careful," I mouthed, which he answered with a quick "don't worry" grin, before slipping off down the hall toward the oncoming room service waiter.

Bastian and I both held our breath as we watched Alex silently approach the unsuspecting waiter, deliberately eyeing the tray the waiter held as he went. Pausing when he reached the halfway point in the hall, Alex allowed the waiter to walk by him, then turned and fell into step just behind his elbow as he passed. With his face in the very image of concentration, Alex ever so carefully reached around the oblivious waiter, and placed the anchor on the corner of the tray next to the empty coffee cup. He had only enough time to push the charm under the rim of the cup's saucer and leap silently to the side, before the waiter arrived at Molony's door and shifted the tray away, allowing him to knock. Out of danger, Alex stepped over to join us again where he received a proud grin from me as well as a "well done" eyebrow raise from Bastian.

"*Are you ready?*" Alex cast into the air in front of me as the waiter's knuckles thumped on the door.

All I did was glance up at him, but I knew he could see the answer in my eyes; I was more than ready – I was anxious. Molony knew where they'd taken Jocelyn and Steven, I knew he did, and for all the newfound restraint I'd been able to use with Alva and Brassal, I'd already decided that Molony would get none. I knew what I had to do, and I was prepared to do it, no matter what it took, and for the first time since finding out about my power, I was glad to have as much as I did. The knowledge that I had so much at my disposal was not only comforting, but emboldening, and though I may not have actually been able to use most of it, the bits that I could use were about to rain down on Molony like cinders from a firework.

"Room service," the waiter called when no one responded to his knock.

"I didn't call for room service!" a harsh voice barked from behind the door.

"Y-yes," the waiter stammered, shaken, "forgive my interruption sir, but I bring the evening's desert course at the request of Master and Mistress Bloch. They send it with their regrets that you were unable to make it to the formal dinner tonight, but look forward to seeing you at the banquet tomorrow."

Bastian made a small sweeping gesture toward the conversation, eyeing me sideways. When he'd called down to order the dessert, I'd given him a hard time for using too much detail, though it would appear that he'd known what he was doing – and wanted to make sure I knew it.

"Yeah, yeah," I mouthed with an eye roll, inwardly happy that he was keeping his sense of humor about him, at least to a small degree.

The waiter began to fidget as the silence drug on until finally Molony snipped, "Just leave it!"

The waiter did as he was ordered and set the tray down in front of the door, then took off toward the staircase as fast as a walk would allow. He barely had time to make it down to the first landing before I heard the shuffle of a lock, squeak of a doorknob, and groan of underused hinges echoing through the hall. Molony's door was open, but only a few inches at most, and I could see him peering out into the hall like he expected there to be an angry mob with torches waiting for him – which I suppose he did, though we didn't have torches... damn it.

After checking both sides of the hall a half dozen or so times, he must have decided the coast was clear and took to examining the tray at his feet. He looked at it, nudged it with his foot, bent down for a closer look, looked under the upside-down coffee cup, checked under the cloche, and even lifted the lid to the coffee urn and gave it a skeptical smell before he was even willing to lift the tray off the floor. Jocelyn had been right; this guy was as paranoid as they came. Good thing Alex was able to keep Bastian's anchor hidden or there was no way he wouldn't have found it.

Once another thorough inspection of the tray was done, this time at eye level, he finally looked satisfied that it was safe, and took it with him back into the room, securing what sounded like three separate sets of locks the moment the door closed.

"All right," Bastian said, wrapping one of his hands around my arm and the other around Alex's, "here we go. Whenever you're ready," he added, looking at me.

Concentrating my ability on Bastian's, I channeled my power into his just as I'd done for Jocelyn in the graveyard. This boost allowed him to port both Alex and I simultaneously, and a moment later the three of us were in the center of Molony's darkened guestroom. Luckily for us, Molony's back was turned as we arrived, giving Alex the time to hide Bastian and himself before Molony saw them, leaving what would appear to be only me standing there in the shadows.

I took a deep breath, but I wasn't nervous. I was decidedly calm, turning the steady pulse of thumping anger I felt into a driven focus. Reaching into my pocket, I let my hand rest against the Iris and did a quick scan of the abilities currently in the manor, finding the ones I was confident in using so they would be ready when the time came.

And I *was* ready. This guy was mine.

"Good evening Mr Molony."

At the sound of my voice, he spun around with a gasp, dropping the tray he still held at his feet. "Who?..." he gasped again, raising a shaking finger at me. "How did you get in here?! What do you think you're doing, barging into my private room?"

I could tell he was angry, but I could also see that his harsh tone and scowl were attempting to cover up how rattled and even scared he was. "I'm here," I said, "because you and I need to have a conversation. My father, Jocelyn Clavish, was abducted a short while ago. I know you are working with the men who took him, and I know you know where they have gone."

His expression didn't falter even for an instant as I spoke, and had I not been standing five feet away from him, I'd have wondered if he heard me. Just when I thought he wouldn't respond at all, his eyes flashed and suddenly he lunged toward me with his hand out in front of him like a claw, ready to latch onto the first bit of skin it touched. Unfortunately for him, I was ready. Cormac had told us that he needed physical contact in order to read and remove memories, so I'd assumed he try something like this as soon as he realized that I had information he didn't want me having. I found the nearest kinetic, assumed his ability, and had Molony's hand frozen in midair before it had made it even halfway to my arm.

"That," I said, forcing his entire body backwards until he was a safe distance away, "is not how this is going to go."

"Do you have any idea who I am?" he growled, not as phased by my kinetic demonstration as I'd hoped he'd be.

Time to up my game.

I forced him down into a chair and pinned his arms and legs to the upholstered frame. As he struggled pointlessly against my hold, I kinetically raised all the items that had fallen from the room service tray along with several other objects from around the room and began to make them fly them around the room, circling Molony's chair. As the objects started to pick up speed, I lifted the chair Molony was trapped in off the ground, letting him hover in the air as the flatware and knick-knacks orbited him like out of control comets.

"I know exactly who you are," I said, as in the midst of the controlled chaos I found the nearest Imparter and made a second connection with my ability. "*The question is,*" I imparted, "*do you know who I am?*"

The shock I'd been waiting to see finally widened his eyes. "You...? How...?"

He was clearly at a loss, but I wasn't done. For the first time I was embracing what was within me, and I knew if we were going to get what we needed, I had to show this guy exactly who he was dealing with. I wasn't scared of my power anymore and I wasn't going to let anything limit me; not when there were people I cared about in danger.

As Molony hung in the air in front of us, I reached out again, this time melding with Alex. He had not yet had a chance to properly teach me how to cast, but that didn't worry me. It wasn't that I thought I could master the ability without instruction, as that would be far too reckless, but with the Iris to help me, I was confident I could use his Casting ability well enough to make the point. Careful to limit my cast to only the eyes of those in the room, I began to almost effortlessly morph the image of the space around us, twisting and deforming it slowly at first and then faster until finally, Molony found himself no longer floating near the familiar comforts of his guestroom, but the charred branches and haunting smoke of a fire-ravaged forest.

As our disillusioned Mentalist tried to keep his composure, I stepped forward, imparting to him once more over the cast crackle of the flames and howl of the wind. "*And... do you know what I can do? In a word: everything.*"

He didn't reply, but sank further back into his chair when the items whirling around him moved faster and faster, blowing my hair back with the stream of wind they created. The images of billowing smoke began to thicken, closing in around him while I sent a bolt of lightning ripping though the sky. Faster, brighter, louder, building, building, building, until finally I saw the first flash of real terror streak across his face and I knew I had him where I needed him. I instantly severed all bonds with my assumed abilities, and as abruptly as turning off a light, the scene ended. The cast images of the fiery forest disappeared, and Molony's chair came crashing down to the floor of his guestroom with a thud while the plates, flatware, and other items came raining down around him.

Relaxing my stance, I walked toward him as he sat slumped over in the chair trying to catch his breath. "So," I said, hooking my thumbs onto the pockets of my jeans, "here's how this is going to go: I need information that you have. I could go into your mind and find what I need for myself, but I really don't think you want me to have to do that. So instead, you can tell me what I need to know voluntarily, and when I am satisfied that I have what I need, you and I will part ways like this never happened. What do you say?"

He stared up at me, the shock on his face quickly turning to contempt. "Even if I do know what happened to Clavish, what makes you think I'd be willing to tell you?"

"Because something tells me you want to stay on good terms with your boss."

"You're out of your league, princess." I knew his words were meant to shame me, but I could see that what I'd said had struck a nerve. For as much as he tried to hide it, there was a twinge of fear hidden behind his bravado – a twinge I intended to use.

"He must trust you quite a bit," I said, ignoring his comment. "After all, if I'm understanding things right, you are the only person other than Darragh himself who knows pretty much everything there is to know. Anytime someone does something that could be at all traced back to him, you swoop in and remove the memory of whatever they did, leaving you the only person who knows what happened. I have to give Darragh credit, it's actually pretty ingenious. He can have dozens of people working for him, yet only one who knows enough damaging information to ever really be a threat. That's a lot of power – but power always comes at a price."

"Is that meant to be a threat?"

"No, this is a warning. What I said before is true; when it comes to abilities, I can do anything, which includes Mentalism. If I wanted, I could take the information I need right from your mind, but here's the thing… I'm not very good at it. I haven't had enough practice, I guess," I shrugged. "Don't get me wrong, I'm sure if I were to give it a go, I'd be able to find what I need, but odds are I'd make quite a mess in the process – a mess that a practiced mind reader like Darragh would be bound to notice." It took a moment for my words to sink in, but when they did, Molony's face paled. "Tell me," I went on, "how do you think Darragh would react if he found out that your mind – the mind that contains more damaging information than any other – had been compromised? Would he move you into another line of work? Maybe retire you and pay out your pension?" Again he didn't speak, but his face answered for him. "No… I don't think so either."

"You're bluffing," he scowled, but his voice was thin.

Yes I was.

"You're right, I could be," I said, "but that's not a risk I'd be willing to take if I were you. But no matter what you decide to do, I *will* learn everything you know about where my father has been taken and why. So what will it be; will you tell me what you know willingly, or do I have to rummage my way through your mind like a bronco though a glass house?"

After a long pause he finally spoke. "I suppose I have little choice," he said begrudgingly, unwilling to admit that the choice had been an easy one.

"Thank you," I nodded, still serious.

"You want to know where Clavish was nicked off to? He's at Cuniff, one of Darragh's many family estates."

Cuniff. We had a name.

The sudden relief was so strong it surprised me, but I couldn't let it throw off my focus. There was still more to learn. I crossed my arms and pushed on. "Why?"

"There is a book of notes that we have been trying to decipher for some time now."

"Ciaran's journal," I said, "yes, I already know about that. What does that have to do with Jocelyn?"

For the first time since meeting him a slight grin pulled at his face. "He figured out how to read it."

"What?" I tried to make sure my surprise came across as skepticism, but I'll admit I was thrown, and I suddenly realized why Alex had hidden Bastian and himself from me as well as Molony. No way I wouldn't have slipped and glanced at one of them had I been able to see them. "Why would you think that?"

"We came to learn that Clavish and the old man were interested in Shea, so we were told to keep an eye on them."

"Fine, but that doesn't answer my question. Why do you think Jocelyn can read the journal?"

"Darragh has... *ways* of learning these things."

He may have thought that was an answer, but I wasn't playing games. My eyes narrowed as I stepped forward. "I'm only going to ask you one more time."

"The fháil," he said, finally as his upper lip quivered angrily. "He had a fháil planted in Jocelyn's room."

I had no idea what that was, but I wasn't about to let him know that so I moved on. "And the journal? Is Cuniff where he's keeping that too?"

Molony shook his head. "He will not have the book at Cuniff, only a page of it to use for testing."

"So where is the rest of it?"

"I don't know. No one does – not even Darragh."

"That makes no sense."

"That is the only way it can remain completely protected. When he first came into possession of the journal and realized it could not be read, Darragh placed a call charm on it then sent it off with one of his lieutenants, instructing him to hide it – but not before Darragh removed one of its pages."

"He could use the page to locate the book when he figured out how to read it," I mused aloud.

Molony nodded. "And use it as a way to test different methods of deciphering the writing. It is likely that Darragh will have Clavish read the page before he attempts to locate the entire journal."

"What about the lieutenant? He could always go back and get the journal for himself, couldn't he? Or did Darragh have you remove the memory of where he hid it so now you are the only one who knows? Because if that's the case, of course you know you'll be telling me that too."

"Much as I hate to disappoint," he said, clearly enjoying it, "it's a no to both. Darragh didn't want anyone to know where it was, so my services were not required. And as for the lieutenant, when he returned and verified that he had indeed hidden the journal where no one would be able to find it, Darragh saw to it that he was silenced – permanently. Darragh is now the only one who has the means to locate Shea's journal, so if finding it was one of your goals, I would highly suggest you reconsider."

Normally this new development would have upset me, but as it was, the journal no longer mattered. All that mattered was getting Jocelyn and Steven back unharmed, and if that meant we had to give up on finding out what Ciaran had seen, then so be it.

"How do I find Cuniff?"

"You don't. Or, that is to say, you can't."

"Would you care to elaborate?" I prompted when it didn't seem like he would go on.

"It's located roughly twenty miles north of here, but *where* it is doesn't matter. Like all of Darragh's properties, it has fortress charm over it. So I'm afraid you are out of luck."

Before I could reply, a cast message from Alex appeared in my line of sight. "*If it has a fortress charm then he probably has a pass-stone. Ask him for it.*"

"OK, so then it looks like I'll need your pass-stone," I said smoothly, hoping he wouldn't realize that I didn't actually know what I was asking for.

He hesitated glancing away, practically announcing his coming lie. "I don't have one."

"Come on," I rolled my eyes, "we both know that's not true."

He grit his teeth as his anger flared back up. "You told me that if I helped you, Darragh would not find out."

"Yes, and I meant it."

"Bollocks!" he spat. "You claim to want to keep your word, yet you plan to use my pass-stone to rescue Clavish?"

"I don't understand why that's a problem."

"Each stone is unique. All Darragh has to do is see and he will know it's mine"

"Then I will make sure he doesn't see it."

"And how do you plan to do that? Do you honestly believe that Darragh will not wonder how you were able to pass through his charm unnoticed? He will find it and I will be done for!"

"It doesn't matter what I plan to do," I told him. "All that matters is that I promise you, no matter what happens, Darragh will not see your stone."

He looked up with a sneer. "If you honestly believe that I would trust you, you are a fool."

"That may well be, but as you stated so eloquently earlier, you don't really have a choice."

His hateful sting in his eyes lashed at me like a live wire, but I held my ground without so much as a flinch, waiting for him to cave. At first I was confident, but as the seconds ticked by, I started to worry that he'd reached his limit and that I'd have to actually make good on my threat to read his mind. Much as we needed his pass-stone – whatever it was – I didn't know if I could bring myself to do it. Or, for that matter, if I'd be able to figure out how it was done should I try. What if I accidentally erased the very memory I was looking for? Then where would we be?

I was about to give him one last chance to tell me, when I saw his eyes slide over to the floor by the dresser. There were a few different things scattered there thanks to my earlier demonstration, but the one his gaze pointed to was a gold pocket watch that I'd taken from the dressing table and added into my little kinetic tornado. When I stooped down to grab it, I realized that it was quite a bit heavier than it ought to have been, and when I opened the cover I saw why. Inside where the clock face and working mechanisms should have been, there was a fat round rock about the size of a silver dollar and at least three times as thick, that had etching on the surface of it. I turned it out into my hand and looked to Molony for confirmation.

"There," he said from between his teeth. "take it... and get out."

CHAPTER 30

"Yes, that is a pass-stone all right," Min confirmed, turning it in her hand. She and Anderson had left Lorcan for Adare shortly after receiving the call from Cormac, and were now sitting with the rest of us in Cormac's room as we finalized our plan.

"And what does it do, exactly?" I asked.

"It is the only way to breach a fortress charm," she said.

"Yeah, I don't know what that is either."

"A fortress charm is a variation on a protection charm that allows the Alchemist who casts it to have control over who enters their premises and how they are allowed to leave. It is cast on a building or some other confined space, and prevents anyone from seeing the charmed area, entering it, or using any transporting abilities while within it."

"Transporting abilities?" I said.

"Any ability that can physically move a person: porting, kinetics, and so on."

"But the pass-stone will get us around all that, right?" Bastian asked.

"Yes," Min nodded, "so long as you have the stone, you will be able to port out. But take care, for if you were to lose it, you and everyone you want to port would have to be outside the fortressed area."

"We won't lose it," I assured her, "we won't be there long

enough for that. Like I said, we get in, get Jocelyn and Steven, and get out."

"Are you sure you can find this place with only Jocelyn's ability to guide you? Anderson asked me.

"I'm sure. Besides, that's not all we have, we also have a general direction. Molony said it was about twenty miles north, and with that and the Iris to help me, we'll find it." The glow of Jocelyn's ability was brighter than any I'd ever come across, not to mention I was very familiar with it. I may not have been sure what would happen when we got there, but I could get us at least that far, I was sure.

"What about the fháil?" Cormac asked Min. "It's bound to be tied to Darragh, could that help us at all?"

She shook her head. "Most are designed to transmit one time only, it is worthless now."

"What is a fháil?" Chloe asked quietly from the corner, saving me from having to ask myself.

"It is another charmed artifact. The word 'fháil' literally means 'get' or 'acquire,' and that is what it does: acquires information. When casting the charm, you input what you want to learn into the spell, and then place the fháil in the area where what you want is most likely to be found. In this case, they knew Jocelyn was after Shea's book, so Darragh probably set the fháil to alert him when Jocelyn found a way to read it. But it would only have alerted Darragh to the fact that Jocelyn had found the answer, not what the answer was, thus he would not have realized that the one he really wanted was you."

"Aye, probably intends to force Jocelyn to tell him that bit," Anderson growled under his breath.

"That must have been what McGary and Cleen were doing in Jocelyn's room that day; planting the fháil," Alex said, going over to sit by Chloe.

"It's past 3.30," Anderson said as he stood from him his chair. "Not long before sunup now, you three had better be off."

There was a murmur of agreement, and a few minutes later, Min, Cormac, and Chloe left for Lorcan Hall, while Anderson stayed behind with Alex, Bastian, and I. At first light he would drive the three of us as close as he could to where Darragh was holding Jocelyn and Steven, and then leave for Lorcan himself. Alex, Bastian, and I would then find Jocelyn and Steven, I'd feed Bastian's ability with mine allowing him to port all five of us back to Lorcan – where Min was taking his anchor now – and God willing, we could do it all without Darragh even knowing we'd been there.

Sure. No problem...

We were on the bumpy road toward Cuniff by 5 o'clock that morning, and I'd officially been awake for over 21 hours. I should have been exhausted but I wasn't. I also wasn't wired, or jittery, or hysterical – I just... was. Maybe it was the gravity of the situation setting in, or maybe the five to ten minute catnaps I'd had with Alex while we waited to leave that morning had actually done something for me, but in either instance I doubted it. The far more likely reason was that deep down I was forcing myself to rally my strength and keep my thoughts on the job we had to do, because if I didn't, my mind would wander. It would start thumbing through all the things that could have already happened to Jocelyn, and what might be happening even that moment while we were on our way to get him. Had he been given a way to help control his ability now that he was without his ring, or had he been made to suffer all this time with nothing? I was the one they needed to read Ciaran's notes, but I knew – we all knew – that he would never give me up. The only question was what were they putting him through because of it.

I rubbed my hand over the lump in my jeans pocket that was Jocelyn's Sciath ring and let out an involuntarily shudder causing Alex to tighten the arm he had around me. I leaned deeper into his side as he kissed my temple reassuringly. "Everything is going to be fine," he whispered, his lips just above my ear.

I nodded and leaned my head against his chest, thinking that it might be smart to try to squeeze a catnap in before we get there, and praying that no nightmares would decide to creep in along with it.

"Looks like this is the end of the road," Anderson said a moment later.

So much for a nap.

I sat up and looked out to find that Anderson was right, it was the end of the road – literally. Much further and we would dead-end into a large farmhouse not a quarter mile off.

"Was this the right way?" Bastian asked, looking back from the front seat.

I reached into my jacket pocket for the Iris and once again found Jocelyn's ability glowing out in front of us. This time however, it was very strong, which told me it wasn't far off, and its direction was no longer just generally northward, but distinctively to the northeast.

"Yes, we're close." I pointed toward the glow of Jocelyn's ability. "It's that way, through the trees. We're not far."

Anderson pulled the car up to the tree line I'd pointed to and let us out. "Now listen here," he said, stepping out himself but leaving the car running, "you three be careful. There's no telling what you may run into, but at the very least there'll be defense charms and drones to deal with, so stay sharp and above all, stay together."

He continued to speak, but I zoned out the moment I heard the word "drone," feeling my insides recoil. Drones: innocent people whose minds and memories had been totally and irrevocably erased, leaving them empty shells capable of nothing more than taking direct orders. I could remember with stomach churning clarity the look on the face of the drone who had aided Taron in abducting me not long ago. It was a hollow, lifeless expression I'd never forget and, though I'd never admit it, one that had a habit of turning up in my darker dreams.

"And," I heard Anderson continue as I forced myself to listen, "if anything goes wrong, and I mean anything at all, you port back to Lorcan with or without Jocelyn and Steven, do you understand? We can always come up with another plan, but we don't need to add any of you to the list of people needing saved. Got it?"

"We'll be fine," I said, hoping he wouldn't realize that I hadn't exactly agreed.

He nodded, stepping over and giving me a hug, then offering each of the boys a handshake. "All right then," he said with a sigh, "be safe, and good luck."

As he drove away we ducked into the cover of the trees and began situating ourselves for the walk, Bastian relacing one of his boots, me braiding my ponytail into a long plait, and Alex... refastening his belt? It took me a minute to figure out why, but when I did, my jaw almost dropped.

"Whoa," I said, eyeing what was quite clearly a knife hanging from his belt. It was impressive to say the least. It was in a pouch that he had strapped to his belt and I could see that the blade itself was folded down into the handle like a Swiss army knife, but it was much larger and far fiercer than anything your average boy scout would carry. "Where in the world did you get that?"

"Mr Anderson brought it for me," he told me as he pulled it from its case and flipped it open.

"Do you even know how to use it?"

"Sure I do," he said with a wry grin as he began listing its features from handle to tip. "Holding part... sharp part... pointy part."

I rolled my eyes. "Ha, ha."

"Mr Anderson has given me lessons in the past," he smiled, putting his new weapon away. "I'm by no means an expert, but I do OK."

"Anderson knows knives?"

"He served with the SAS for over six years."

"SAS?"

"British army's Special Forces. He became quite proficient actually."

"Are we ready?" Bastian asked, stepping up beside us.

After a nod from Alex I gave one of my own. "Let's go," I said, and turned to lead the way.

As we walked through the wooded area I kept my hands in my pockets, one holding the Iris and the other gripping Molony's pass-stone. I could tell that we were coming close to the area where Jocelyn was being held, but I still couldn't see anything but trees and the occasional patch of brush, so I wanted to make sure I was ready.

"How many others can you feel in the area with Jocelyn?" Bastian asked me as we walked. "Can you tell what we're up against?"

Luckily we were near enough now that I could tell that the area Jocleyn was in was relatively isolated, making the other Holders near him easier to pick out. "There are a few," I said, concentrating on the batch of abilities hovering around Jocelyn's, "more than I would have thought – maybe thirty?"

"*Thirty?*" Alex repeated. "Like, three-zero?"

"What sort of abilities?" Bastian asked.

"Looks like a mix of just about everything, but it's hard to tell this far off."

"Fantastic…"

"Yeah," I nodded, "that's the bad news, but the good news is that most of them are concentrated in one area and it isn't the same area that Jocelyn is in, so we might be able to totally avoid them if we're careful."

We continued to walk for another several minutes until we came to a stream, across from which was a break in the trees. I looked out through the break and saw a large clearing, at the center of which was a large manor house. The house was very large, maybe half the size of Adare, though not nearly as updated or well kept. The gray stone walls were crumbing in areas, and the stone and wrought iron fence that surrounded the house was dotted with gaping holes, some large enough to drive a car through.

"Hide us," I whispered quickly to Alex and grabbed the sleeve of Bastian's coat just as he was about to cross the stream.

"I have been," Alex said keeping his voice down. "Why, what's wrong?"

I gestured out toward the clearing. "We're here."

"Cuniff? Where?" the boys asked over one another.

I pulled the pass-stone out of my pocket and held it out so that they could each put a finger on it.

"That's incredible," Alex breathed, as the manor appeared before his eyes.

Bastian began to shift on his feet anxiously. "OK, now what? Where do we go?"

"Jocelyn is up there somewhere," I told them, pointing to the upper right hand area of the building, "and most of the other abilities I can feel are down there," I gestured to the lower left wing. "If Alex can keep us hidden, I say we go up to Jocelyn since he is the one we can pinpoint exactly, and maybe we'll find Steven along the way. If not, once we give Jocelyn his ring back, he will be able to find Steven's mind and tell us where to go. As soon as we have them both, we get the hell out."

"Sounds good," Alex said.

"OK," I said with a deep breath, "the front door there is the only one I see, so we'll head that way, and since there doesn't seem to be a way to tell where the fortress charm actually starts, until we get inside, we're all going to have to keep hold of the pass-stone."

"Got it," Bastian said. "Let's do it."

I looked to Alex who gave me a nod, and off we went. It was difficult to move at first considering we all had to keep a hold of the tiny pass-stone, but once we were clear of the stream and tree line we were able to find a walking formation that worked and began to make our way quickly over the short dead grass of the clearing.

It wasn't until we were only a few dozen steps from the entrance that we noticed the two men standing guard at the door. We all paused while and Bastian and Alex took a closer look, but I didn't need one. Even from this far off I could see their flat dead eyes and I knew they were drones.

"How are we going to get past them?" Bastian asked, his tone the barest of whispers.

"They won't see us," I said.

"No, but they will hear the door open," he countered.

"Drones are only able to follow one order at a time," Alex said.

"Yes, and these ones are clearly to guard the door," Bastian added.

"Yes," Alex agreed, "but not from everyone. Just follow my lead and stay as quiet as you can."

Unable to question him, we continued to walk toward the door, passing through a gap in the twisted rust wrought iron fence and onto the small front lawn area of the house. As soon as we were through the fence, Alex stopped and tentatively took his hand from the pass-stone, glancing around. After a moment he smiled and nodded, letting us know we had safely made it through the fortress charm and could let go of the stone. I was about to return it to my pocket when Alex held out his hand as though he wanted it. I gave it to him with a squint of confusion, but he smiled, his eyes saying, "trust me."

Stone in hand, he stepped off ahead of us motioning for us to follow behind as he approached the guard drones at the door. That was when I noticed the man walking quickly our way from the wooded area we'd just come from. He was walking directly toward the door as though he'd been here several times before, and as he grew closer I realized that there was something very familiar about his hair... and his clothes...

Molony?

What the hell was he doing here? Had he come to turn us in? To tell Darragh what we'd done in the hopes of saving his own skin? I was about to suggest we make a run for it when suddenly Alex began to walk straight at him not appearing to be concerned at all. Closer and closer they came until it was obvious they were going to collide, blowing our cover and likely getting us all killed. My heart pounding, I opened my mouth to shout out, but Bastian was able to throw a hand over my mouth and silence me just in time to see Alex step into the image of Molony as he approached the door, disappearing completely.

My throat relaxed as I realized that Molony wasn't there with us at all – it had been a cast. Alex knew we'd only get in the door if the drones saw someone they recognized, but he couldn't risk just allowing an image of Molony to just appear out of thin air, so he'd cast an image of him arriving as he normally would before disguising himself. Smart.

Making a mental note to give Alex hell later for scaring me like that, Bastian and I jogged quietly up behind him as he approached the drones, stopping briefly as though to get their approval. I tried not to shudder as their cold eyes slowly came down, looking through him for the count of two seconds then lifted back up, once again fixing themselves out over the clearing. With a cool confidence I'm sure he didn't feel, the still disguised Alex walked past the drones and up to the large weathered door and pulled it open allowing it to stay cracked just enough behind him for Bastian and I to slip through before it closed with a deep thud.

As soon as we were sure the coast was clear inside, Alex returned to normal, hiding himself with Bastian and I once again, and the three of us ducked behind one of the large pillars that lined the entryway. We took a minute to catch our breath and lower our collective heart rates, while I looked around the large foyer and noted with some amusement that overall, it was not unlike the entrance of Adare. There were high ceilings, pillars, a large fireplace, and decorative carvings and hanging on the walls. The only real difference was that Adare was pristine and well cared for, while this place looked like it hadn't seen a dusting rag or mop in decades. The stone walls and floors had moss growing from their cracks, cobwebs hung from nearly every rail and beam, and the dust not only clung to every surface, but hung in the musty air like fog. If we could all manage to get in and out of here without one of us blowing our cover with a cough or a sneeze, it would be a miracle.

Once we were collected and ready, we made our way to the back of the foyer where there was a large staircase that ended up about half a floor then split, leading to both the east and west wings. Knowing that Jocelyn was in the upper eastern wing, I pointed up to the right side staircase and we began to climb, carefully testing each step we mounted to make sure that none of the withered planks would creek or rattle under our weight.

Once we reached the top of the stairs, things became more difficult. There were several hallways to choose from, and now that the glow of Jocelyn's ability was so near, it was becoming difficult to isolate. I could still tell that he was on this level and that he was down toward the end of the building, but now that there were multiple ways to get to the general area we needed to be, it was impossible to know which one was best.

I pointed to the different hallways then motioned to Alex and Bastian. "*Don't go, just look,*" I mouthed silently, adding several hand gestures to make it clear.

We each took a hall, glancing down it to see if there was anything of note, but each one seemed to be exactly like the others; long, dark and empty. That is until Bastian went to look down the last hall that ran along the back wall of the building and motioned for Alex and I to join him. When we got there, we found that this hallway was like the other three except that it was not empty. There was a man who looked to be another drone just leaving one of the rooms about a third of the way down the hall. It may not have been much, but at least it was something.

We waited – my eyes deliberately downturned so as not to have to see his face – for the drone to pass us before we hurried down the hall to the door he'd exited. I could tell that this was not the room that Jocelyn was being held in, but as it was the first room we'd encountered with a person in it, and was at least worth a look. Maybe, if we were lucky, it would be where they were holding Steven and we would be one step closer to getting out of here.

Being the first one to arrive at the door, I took hold of the knob and began to turn it as slowly and quietly as I could, wary that there may be someone else inside who didn't want company. Actually, I was fully expecting it to be locked; however, the further the knob went the easier it became to turn, never once hitting a lock or even so much as a squeaky spring before opening completely. Pushing the door just enough to peek in, I found that indeed there was someone else in the room, and when I realized who it was I had to push a hand to my mouth to keep from laughing with relief.

It was Steven.

I slipped inside and saw that the poor thing was sitting hunched over on the floor in the corner of the room, and had fallen asleep against the hard stone wall. But uncomfortable as he surely was, he was alive, and that was all that mattered. As I hurried over to him I started to wonder if this would end up being far easier than we had expected. I mean, here we were with one of the two people we'd come in after and so far we hadn't had any trouble at all. We hadn't hit a snag bigger than a few drones, and the door to Steven's holding cell hadn't even been locked! At this rate, Jocelyn may just decide to wander out of his holding room and meet up with us on our way out the door. Not that I wanted to take our luck for granted, but if I'd have known it was going to be this easy, I might have even gotten some sleep last night.

"Steven," I breathed, lightly rubbing his leg and praying I wouldn't startle him. Last thing we needed was him yelling out and getting us caught. "Sweetie, it's Becca. Come on, we've got to get you out of here."

I rubbed his leg a bit harder almost impressed by how deeply he was out. Had they given him something? A sleeping draft maybe? It was possible, but why? It wasn't like he...

But my thought imploded as I looked up and realized that though he looked to be asleep, his eyes were actually open.

...and unblinking...

...and empty.

Suddenly I knew exactly why they hadn't bothered to lock the door to his room, and my stomach heaved into my chest. They hadn't needed to lock him up because they knew he wasn't going anywhere – not without a command.

Steven had been droned.

Chapter 31

"Steven?" Bastian croaked, falling to his knees next to his unresponsive brother. He reached out and took Steven's face between his hands, tears beginning to streak his own as he gave Steven's head a shake. "*Steven...?*"

Fighting tears of my own, I ran over to the door and closed it silently, hoping that the thick wood would block at least some of the muted noises the next few minutes were bound to entail. When I got back Bastian had released his hold on Steven and was instead holding his own face as he sat hunched over, trying desperately to keep his overwhelming tumult of emotions from taking over. I knelt down next to him and put my arm around his shoulders wishing there was something I could do, all the while knowing there wasn't anything anyone could do. Steven was gone; his body remained, but his mind – the part of him that made him Bastian's brother – was gone forever. I couldn't even begin to imagine what he was going through, what it felt like.

And what about... oh God... *Chloe*.

After a few minutes, he finally looked up at me, his eyes puffy, wet, and completely lost. "What...?" he stammered, his voice hoarse and thin, "How can...? How can we...?"

He couldn't get it out, but I knew what he was asking and I knew that there was only one answer. I reached back into my pocket and grabbed the Iris, searching through the grouping of abilities that were still at the other end of the building. It took a moment but I finally found what I was looking for: a Porter. He was about as strong a one as Bastian, maybe a bit stronger, and best of all, I could still pick out his ability even after I let go of the Iris and only had my own natural power levels to rely on.

"Where is the pass-stone?" I asked Alex as quietly as I could.

He handed it to me and I passed it directly to Bastian. "Here," I said placing the stone in his hand, "take this and go."

"What?" he asked, looking at me like I'd gone mad.

"I'm serious, take the stone and get Steven out of here. And," I pulled the Iris out and handed it to him, "take this with you."

"I can't leave you two, you'll be stuck here."

"Not if you take the Iris with you. There is another Porter here whose ability I can draw from. Porting is instantaneous, so all I have to do is feed his strength with everything I have and it won't matter that he's not coming with us, it should still be enough to get us home, right?"

Bastian hesitated. "Technically… yes, but what if it's not?"

"It will be," I said. "Besides, we don't have a choice now. There is no way we are going to be able to move Steven without getting caught. You leaving with him now is the only way to get him out of here."

"But even if you can feed the other Porter, all three of you will still have to get outside the borders of the fortress charm in order to port."

"We already know the charm ends somewhere around the fence," Alex gently chimed in. "We can handle it. You need to get Steven back to Lorcan."

The battle going on inside him was apparent in his face, but in the end he knew we were right. "You're sure?" he asked one last time to which both Alex and I nodded definitively. Finally convinced, Bastian slid forward and took Steven's hand firmly with his own, then placed the pass-stone in-between their two palms. Holding the Iris tightly in his other hand he looked over at Steven's blank face.

"Close your…" but he stopped with a wince as two more tears slid down his cheeks. "*Gar do chuid shúile,*" he ordered in Gaelic, and Steven's eyes immediately fell closed. He glanced over to us once more with a sad nod and then… they were gone.

Alex and I stared at the empty patch of floor for a few seconds trying to wrap our minds around everything that had just happened – or at least that's what I was doing.

"So," Alex whispered after a moment, shifting to face me, "can you really get us out of here?"

"Yeah," I said confused. "I said that I could, didn't I?"

"Sure, I just wanted to check… you know, in case we needed to come up with a plan."

A plan? Wait… "Did you think I was bluffing?"

"I wasn't sure."

"But you backed me up?"

"I said we could handle it, and we would have."

I wished I could put a name to the feeling that rolled through me right then, but sadly there wasn't time to dwell on it. "Thank you," I said, hoping he could see how much I meant it.

"I promised to always follow you," he smiled, "and I will."

I leaned forward and kissed him sweetly. "I love you." I whispered against his mouth as I pulled back.

"I love you too," he replied and then sighed, a new determination in his eyes. "Now, let's go get Jocelyn."

Cautious and silent, Alex and I snuck back out into the hall, carefully closing the door behind us, hoping that no one would come by to check on Steven before we were able to make it back to Lorcan. We hurried further up the hall and began searching the maze of corridors for one that held Jocelyn. I still knew what direction he was in, but now that I didn't have the Iris, pinpointing his location was almost impossible. The best I could do now was determine if we were moving closer or further away from him, turning our once strategic search and rescue operation into a glorified and dangerous game of Marco Polo.

For more than twenty minutes we wound our way through the halls and corridors looking for a guarded door or waiting for me to sense something new. But our luck had seemed to run dry, as minute after minute passed and we continued to see and sense nothing.

But then suddenly I did sense something – a whole lot of somethings. The group of people I'd sensed earlier in the lower west wing of the manor were on the move and headed in our direction. The hall we were in was smaller and on the far side of the building, and if they came this way they would have no other choice but to walk right past us. Normally this would be fine, but with the size of the hall and the sheer number of people I felt, there was no way Alex and I would be able to keep out of their way. Invisible or no, one of them was sure to bump into one of us and we'd be caught.

"We've got to get out of here," I whispered, grabbing Alex's arm and pulling him behind me and I jogged up the hall. I knew it was risky to be running in the direction of the oncoming mob, but if we could just get to the alcove we'd passed a short while back, we may be able to stay out of the way when everyone passed by.

Alex followed me without question, and just as I felt the group enter the adjacent hallway, we dove into the shallow alcove and out of the main corridor. Now that we had a modicum of safety, I poked my head out and watched as the first of the bunch – a Reader, apparently, as that was the strongest of the oncoming abilities – rounded the corner and stepped into our hallway. He was an average looking middle aged man, with light blonde hair and rather striking green eyes, but the most unusual thing about him was the silver ring he wore on his right hand that was set with an enormous black gemstone.

As he came closer I felt the other abilities nearing too and looked behind him to see if the other people had rounded the bend yet, but none had. It was still only the one man. Where were the others? I stepped back a bit and held my breath as the man walked smoothly by, thankfully not so much as hesitating as he passed us, and continued on down the hall. I was about to look back out and see if the others had come yet, when I realized that all the other abilities were now coming from the opposite side of the hall. They had walked past at the same time as the Reader. But how? Were they hiding themselves the same way Alex and I were? Were they all...

My thought drifted off as all of a sudden something in me clicked, and my head whipped around to the man whose silhouette was fading into the dim light of the hallway. I was such an idiot – how could I not have realized? More than a dozen abilities... all tied to one man...

It was him...

Darragh had been within five feet of me and I'd not even realized it. With barely a thought I took off after him, crossing my fingers that we hadn't lost him. I knew it was stupid, and reckless, may very well get us caught, but none of that mattered now. All that mattered was that Darragh was headed to a room that was obviously in this portion of the manor, and I had a hunch it was exactly the room we were looking for.

Once again Alex followed behind me, but this time he had questions. "*What's going on?*" he cast as we ran. "*Was that who I think it was?*"

I glanced back with a nod.

"*And you think he's on his way to see Jocelyn?*"

Another glance and a nod.

"*Just checking.*"

A glance and a smile.

We came to the end of the hallway just in time to see Darragh open the door to a stairwell not far down the connecting corridor. Alex and I had seen that door earlier in our search, but the stairs had only gone down and I knew that Jocelyn's ability had been coming from above the ground floor. Thanks to a quick sprint, Alex was able to catch the door before it shut allowing us to slide through before allowing the door to click closed only a second or two after it otherwise would have.

I looked down the curving flight of stairs, but didn't see Darragh anywhere. He wouldn't have had enough time to get so far down that we could no longer see him, so where was he? It was then that I felt a tap on my arm and saw that Alex was pointing up toward what appeared to be Darragh floating in midair above us. And not just floating; he was climbing up higher and higher until he stopped, reached out apparently opening an invisible door and step through it and out of sight.

What the hell...?

Alex crouched down and reached out toward what looked like only empty space next to the top of the downward staircase, but as his arm moved I heard a faint brushing sound. Reaching up with his free hand he took my arm and guided me down next to him, bringing my hand to rest next to his which was not simply floating in empty air as it seemed to be, but resting on the cold hard stone of a step.

"He must have used another charm to hide the steps. If we still had the pass-stone we would probably be able to see it, but without it we will have to walk blind."

I wasn't crazy about the idea, but I also wasn't willing to risk losing track of Darragh, so I nodded.

"One more thing, we should probably take off our shoes. The echo is pretty bad in here."

Again I agreed, slipping off my shoes and setting them next to Alex's in the shadowed corner at the top of the downward staircase, and up we went.

The first few steps weren't so bad, but the higher we got the more the fact that there didn't appear to be anything under my feet than several stories and rock-hard floor began to mess with my mind.

"Don't look down," Alex suggested. "Or better yet, give me your hand and close your eyes."

I did as he said and instantly felt better. Now it was no different than climbing any other staircase in the dark which I'd done plenty of times.

A few more steps and I felt Alex tap my hand signaling that we had reached the top. I waited for him to open the door and lead me through, but it didn't happen. I opened one eye a tiny bit to see what was going on to find Alex slowly feeling the wall in front of us and realized the problem; he couldn't find the doorknob. Terrified as I was to open my eyes, I knew that every moment we spent stuck in the stairwell, Darragh was getting further and further away. Choking back my fear, I opened my eyes and stooped down, wiping my hand on the invisible floor. Once I was sure that it was good and dirty, I lifted it up to my mouth and blew, sending a small cloud of dust and grime billowing at the wall, and as the tiny particles swirled in the air, the faintest outline of a door handle just barely became visible. Wasting no time, Alex made a grab for it and pulled the door open to reveal a small – and thankfully very visible – hallway.

Just like the halls below, this one also had other halls splitting from it, but in this instance there were only two, and there was no need to wonder which to take as only one of them had a doorway that was open, had two drones standing guard over it, and best of all, voices carrying from it.

"I take no pleasure in this sort of thing, my friend," a voice said as we quietly made our way toward the open door, "but you are leaving me with very few options. I have searched for too long to simply overlook that you have found what I need."

Having reached the door at this point, Alex and I crept up to the frame, carefully avoiding the two drone guards who stood only a few feet away, and peered into the room. The first thing I noticed was that it was significantly lighter than Steven's room had been on account of the window that stood open on the wall opposite the door. But other than that it was much the same, with the only other glaring difference being the fact that its inhabitant wasn't a hunched-over Steven, but tense and trembling Jocelyn who sat beneath the window, his fists purple from clenching as they pressed into the sides of his head. He was shaking with the effort to keep his mind and abilities in check, and dripping with sweat. The sight alone made my thoughts turn violent, but I pushed them aside, forcing myself to stay in control.

"We are going to give this another try," Darragh continued as Alex and I snuck around the doorframe and into the small room, keeping ourselves up against the wall so as not to risk being bumped or ending up in the way, "and I'd thank you not to attack me this time, but I think you learned your lesson."

Taking a few steps over to where Jocelyn was seated, Darragh took some sort of necklace out of his vest pocket and placed it over Jocelyn's head. The moment the cord encircled his head he looked up and slowly lowered his hands from his temples, seeming to have been granted some mild form of relief – though, if the trembling of his limbs and the tightness of his jaw were anything to go by, it didn't seem to be nearly enough.

Alex must have seen the look on my face as there was suddenly a message floating in front of me. "*It's probably the temporary Sciath. It wouldn't be nearly as strong as his ring, but that wouldn't matter to Darragh. He doesn't care how much pain he is still in, so long as he is able to talk.*"

"Now then," Darragh said, reaching into a second pocket and pulling out a folded piece of paper, "I want you to either read this, or tell me how I can."

Jocelyn watched him with more malice and hate than I would have ever thought him capable of. However it didn't seem to work, and when it became clear that the stare would do nothing to deter Darragh, Jocelyn moved his eyes to the paper hovering in front of his face. After a long moment, a look of disgusted resignation fell over him and he raised a shaking hand to accept the offered page. I held my breath as he lifted and began to study it, having no idea where he was going with this. I knew he couldn't actually read it, was he bluffing? Trying to throw him off?

But before I could speculate any further, he raised his other hand and quickly ripped the page in half, then again and again, having it in more than eight crumpled pieces before Darragh was able to lunge forward and stop him. The two men struggled as Darragh tried to wrestle the paper from him while Jocelyn did his best to shove the scraps out the open window. Finally, Darragh gave up fighting and reached out again, not for the papers but for the cord and pendant around Jocelyn's neck, snapping it free and sending Jocelyn falling to the floor with a sharp hiss, fists once again smashed into his temples. Once Jocelyn as down, Darragh easily lifted all the bits of paper from the floor kinetically.

"Not wise, my friend," he said as he turned to go. "Enjoy your morning. I will see you again in a few hours." With that, he left the room, shutting the door behind him with a bang. "*Garda an doras*," he ordered the two drones outside, and then he was gone.

Trying to remember to stay quiet, I ran over to Jocelyn and knelt down in front of his rigidly crumpled form. Pulling his ring out of my pocket, I put my other hand over one of his fists, hoping it would loosen enough for me to slip the ring onto one of his fingers, but he seemed completely unaware that I was touching him at all. But then I remembered he didn't need to wear it; all he needed was to touch the stone. Putting the ring on my own hand, I turned the stone toward my palm, then slid the sleeve of his shirt back and took hold of his bare forearm, pressing the ruby of the ring into his skin firmly.

The effect was instantaneous. His eyes shot open as he gasped, slumping forward with a huffed sigh. I leaned forward into him, using my own body to keep him upright so that he wouldn't collapse under the weight of his own shoulders as his mind quieted for the first time in almost twelve hours.

"Becca…?" he croaked quietly looking up. I shushed him quickly with a finger to my lips, but he ignored me, "You shouldn't be here…"

"Yeah," I whispered, "well neither should you. Let's get out of here."

Alex came over and helped me get Jocelyn to his feet then leaned in. "I can't cast anything to them from in here," he said. "We are going to have to get them to open the door for us. I'll go over there and wait while you make a noise. When they open the door to check it out, I will cast an image of Jocelyn as he was before and slip out. Once I am in the hall, give me a second or two then follow me. From out there I will be able to keep them from seeing you open the door and come out. Good?"

I nodded and he took his place beside the door. There wasn't anything in the room I could use to make noise, but Jocelyn took care of it for me, stomping his foot loudly on the stone floor. A moment later the door opened and one of the drones walked in and surveyed the room while Alex hurried out the door behind him. Seeing nothing out of place the drone left, leaving Jocelyn and I alone as we waited the few seconds Alex asked for.

Just as I was about to lead us out Jocelyn grabbed my arm. "Steven, we have to get Steven."

"We have him," I said, "he's back at Lorcan with Bastian."

"Is he all right?"

"He…" I hesitated looking away. "He was droned."

Jocelyn didn't respond but the look on his face was enough. "Ready?" I asked.

"Yes, but how are we getting out of here?"

"I am going to port us back to Lorcan, but we have to get outside and on the other side of that fence first," I told him pointing to the iron fence from the window. "That's the border of the fortress charm, if we can make it to there, we are as good as home."

He didn't ask me if I was sure I could do it, or if it would work – even though he was more than likely thinking it – which

I appreciated, and a few moments later I was working the handle of the door like a safecracker, making sure that the worn old knob didn't make a single sound as I manipulated it, opened the door for us, then closed it again. With Jocelyn finally free, the three of us made our way down the hall toward the door to the invisible staircase, which is when I noticed that Darragh was not as far away as I'd thought he was. When he left Jocelyn's room I had assumed he would go back down stairs, but it seemed he hadn't, instead having gone over to a room on the second hallway of the level we were on now. Good news was he was currently stationary, so there was no immediate need to panic.

When we reached the door to the stairwell, Alex opened it and stepped through, demonstrating for Jocelyn who seemed hesitant at first – not that I blamed him. Knowing I would have to close my eyes for the first part, I let the men go first while I followed, dragging my hand along the wall for support. We arrived at the first landing where we hesitated a moment as Alex and I looked at one another.

"Down further or back the way we came?"

"Let's go down one more and maybe we'll find a door with no drones somewhere out the back."

He nodded in agreement and continued on with Jocelyn next to him and me following behind. Though not following closely enough it seemed, for I hadn't even taken my second step down when my toe caught on the rim of my own discarded shoe, sending me sprawling to the floor with a short but piercing scream.

The cry seemed to echo endlessly from every surface of the manor and for a second, I was literally frozen with fear. The distant sound of feet and yelling brought me back to my senses, and as soon as Alex and Jocelyn managed to drag me to my feet, we were running down the stairs and out onto the ground floor. No longer bothering with caution, we bolted for the nearest door we could find which of course wasn't nearly as close as we would have liked. As we ran, the sounds of shouting grew louder and were joined by the approach of abilities – not Darragh, but individual ones from several different directions which meant it wasn't only drones who were chasing us down.

We reached the door we'd been aiming for and burst through, barely noticing the two drones who were standing guard outside just as the two at the front had been.

Jocelyn however, did seem to notice them, turning back and yelling as we ran, "*Lig aon duine amach!*"

I had no idea what he'd said, but whatever it was, it made the two drones turn back toward the door and shut it, then begin to slide a lock over the two handles as though securing it.

But relieved as I was at the "help" the drones were ironically giving us, something else had caught my eye when I turned back. It was small and white, and lay in the dirt up against the wall of the manor just a short way off from where I stood.

It was one of the small ripped bits of the page from Ciaran's notebook.

Without stopping to think, I turned back and ran for the paper, knowing it may be our only chance to ever find the notebook and learn what Ciaran wanted us to know so badly. Slowing only when I slammed into the wall, I dove down for the scrap of paper then took off again just as I heard the sound of men banging from the inside of the now locked door, clamoring to get out.

"Becca!" Alex screamed from just inside the fence while Jocelyn looked on having already passed though.

"I'm coming! Go!" I yelled, already sprinting toward him.

My feet flew over the cold ground faster than they'd ever gone before, but suddenly as I rounded a large block of stone and displaced fence it all came to a jarring halt as my head snapped to a standstill causing my legs to fly out from under me. I tried to get up but I couldn't; something was holding me back... holding my *head* back.

My hair.

Twisting around as far as I could, I saw that my braid had gotten caught on one of the protruding wrought iron spearheads that was sticking out from the rock I come around. With a desperate cry I tried to yank myself free but it wouldn't come loose. The knot it had caused was too tight and the wings of the spearhead were preventing the hair from sliding off. I continued to struggle and tear at my hair, all the while thinking that this wasn't happening; it couldn't be real. We couldn't have come so far only to fail now. I had to get free – I had to. Alex and Jocelyn couldn't get home without me. They needed me.

The thought make me look up and there was Alex, barreling toward me with a panicked fire in his eyes. A split second later he slid up next to me and grabbed my braid with both hands and tried to wrestle it free from the stake, but it was too late. The loud snap of cracking wood rang out and I knew the men chasing us had broken through the door. Abandoning my braid, Alex reached to his belt and pulled out the knife from Mr Anderson and flipped it open. Three slices later and I was free and being jerked up to my feet.

We ran toward Jocelyn like we were being chased like hell itself, reaching him just as the men from the manor were pouring out of the breached door. Grabbing both Alex and Jocelyn's hands I reached out and melded with the Porter I had felt earlier and funneled as much of my power into it as I could, willing to wait until the last second to leave if it meant making sure we would all make it back. As I continued to pump energy into the Porter's ability something drew my eye up to one of the windows on the top floor of the manor where I saw a shadowy silhouette come into view. His features were shrouded, but his bright green eyes gave him away and I found myself meeting them steadily as I realized that he was in fact the one I was taking the porting ability from. His eyes seemed to want to say something but as the men came running down the lawn I knew our time was up and I shut my eyes and let go, sending us hurtling across the country in the blink of an eye. Yet, as the three of us landed safely in the Inner Chamber at Lorcan and were met by relieved greetings of the residents there, the lingering sound of Darragh's imparted voice echoed through my mind.

"*Nice to finally meet you, Rebecca...*"

Chapter 32

I wasn't sure how much time had passed, but what seemed to be both an instant and an eternity later, I found myself sitting on the side of my bed in my own room, totally alone for the first time in longer than I cared to remember.

Even though it had only happened a short while ago, our return to Lorcan was little more than a blur. The moment that Alex, Jocelyn, and I had appeared on the floor of the Inner Chamber, the questions began as everyone we knew seemed to want something from us.

"What happened?"

"Are you all right?"

"What do you remember?"

"Drink this."

"What happened to your hair?"

"Are you hurt?"

"Were you seen?"

"You look awful!"

"Are you hungry?"

On and on they went until I didn't even hear them anymore, simply nodding when it seemed appropriate and existing in a haze. Eventually I somehow came to be in my room, having vaguely remembered hearing something along the lines of "*she needs rest*" just before the flurry of inquires stopped, finally leaving me in peace.

Peace and quiet anyway, which I quickly found was not the same as peace of mind.

If anything, the sudden silence only seemed the make the tension that was straining in my chest worse, allowing the memories of the morning's events to drift in my mind like ghosts, haunting me from the inside out. I'd not had this problem that morning, on the contrary, I had been calm, collected, and focused. There had been a job to do and I had done it. I'd remained focused and sure, and because of that – and fair helping of luck – we had come out of the ordeal not only with the people we'd set out to rescue, but with the key to finding Ciaran's notebook.

However, sitting alone in my room was not the same as being ushered off to battle, and I was finding that my calm confidence was gone, and all I had in its place was the memories. Unsettling and even frightening memories that I'd collected that day but had been too preoccupied to fully process at the time. Things such as the sight of Jocelyn laying in unbearable pain on the floor as Darragh looked on completely unconcerned. Or the sound of my scream as it echoed through the stairwell, and the feeling that stabbed in my gut when I realized what I'd done. Or the panic I'd felt the moment I realized that my hair had gotten stuck and that couldn't free myself. And of course the worst of them all, the chilling look of nothingness in Steven's eyes when we found him, and the replying one of devastation in Bastian's when he realized that he brother's mind had been lost. I leaned forward on my knees with something between a sigh and a sob.

Oh God... poor Steven...

At some point during the chaos of our return, I managed to hear that Steven had been taken to a secluded room on the far side of Lorcan to be tended to and examined, and that Bastian and a horridly distraught Chloe had gone with him. I wanted to go see him. I wanted to be there for my friends and do whatever I could to help, but for some reason I also couldn't bear the thought of leaving my room.

Feeling utterly defeated and wretchedly alone, I hung my head and ran my hands up over my face and through my...

Oh... that's right. I'd almost forgotten.

Hugging my arms around my chest, I stood and walked over to the mirror above my dresser, not sure what I would find, but knowing I would have to do it sooner or later. It took a few seconds longer than it should have, but when I finally looked up at my refection it was pretty much what I'd expected, and at the same time a whole lot worse. There were scrapes and bruises that I had no idea I'd gotten, and a tear in my shirt that I also couldn't recall the origin of. But bumps and cuts aside, the biggest change was of course my hair – or rather, the lack thereof. The long brown waves that had hung down to the middle of my back were gone, replaced by chunky uneven spikes, ranging from about an inch and a half to two inches long, and were sticking up all across the back of my head. The sides were a bit longer but not by much, and dotted all around my face were a few sparse long pieces that were each still their original lengths, having been pulled free of the braid by my frantic clawing before Alex took his knife to it.

In a word, it was a mess.

I knew it was just hair and that it would grow back, but something about it seemed to be mocking me, as though it were trying to put a visual image to what I felt like inside, and before I could stop it, I felt my nostrils start to flare and a hard lump build in my throat. But I couldn't cry; I had no right. With everything that could have happened that day, and even amongst the things that had happened, I was truly no worse for wear. I was alive, relatively unscathed, my brother and my Anam were both safe, and my mind was still whole and completely my own. Out of all the people in our little group, I was one of the lucky ones. I should have been grateful and been doing what I could to help the ones who truly needed it, not giving myself a pity-party. I should have felt relieved and fortunate, not empty and broken. But as much as I knew all of that was true, for some reason all I could bring myself to feel was scared and alone.

But suddenly, as though I'd spoken the words aloud, a warm pulling sensation began to fill my chest and seep into every corner of my body. I heard the door to my room open, but I didn't turn because I knew who it was. When the door shut again I heard the quiet click of the lock and a moment later Alex stood behind me, slowly wrapping his arms around me, securing my whole upper body gently but firmly to his chest. As we both looked at our reflections in the glass, I lolled my head back to rest in the curve between his neck and shoulder, and knew that we were not the same people who had woken up the morning before. We were different, and it was more than my cut hair or the deep bruise that had formed on Alex's cheek. It was something deeper; something permanent. And though I wasn't sure how, I knew that though the change had been hard, it was also for the better.

Bringing a hand up to the frayed bits of my hair, Alex rubbed his palm softly over the tattered strands, tilting his head down until his cheek rested on my temple and his lips brushed against my ear. "*Tá tú thar a bheith álainn, cuisle mo chroí.*"

I closed my eyes with a sigh as I felt new tears threaten to build under my lashes. A lot of the words were unfamiliar, but I didn't need to know their meaning to know that they were exactly what I needed to hear. I turned in his arms and reached up, pulling his mouth down to meet mine in a kiss that filled the empty cavern in my chest and flushed away my fear like it had never been.

As our embrace began to grow more passionate, I knew that the unconditional love I had for Alex was all I really needed. Despite everything we'd gone through that morning, and the sorrow and suffering that I knew were going on in other parts of Lorcan, the moment we were in was what I let in and surrounded myself with. It was a moment of all-encompassing love, unyielding support, and total devotion, and best of all, it belonged entirely to us.

It wasn't long before our kisses grew deeper and began to hold new and promising undercurrent and I knew – we both knew – that we were ready. But what I hadn't expected was the realization that

I hadn't been ready until that moment. We'd been talking about it and trying for weeks to make it happen, but only now did I see how unimportant all the concerns we'd previously had were. It wasn't about the place, or the time, or what had happened that day. It didn't matter if the bed had a huge four-postered canopy, or only a bare frame without even a headboard, nor was an enormous, luxury suite any better than my small, two room apartment in Lorcan. None of those things mattered, and strange as it seemed, it was almost as though some small part of us had known that all along. Know it, and whether we realized it or not, had been telling us to wait for this very moment to finally give in.

Everything we did, from the interplay of our mouths to the heaviness of our breathing, began to build as each act fed and grew from the last. However it wasn't a frenzied or desperate build, but slow and deliberate, allowing for every touch, every move, and every sound to be savored and explored to its fullest extent. There was no rush. We had all the time we wanted, and we both seemed more than happy to take advantage of the fact.

As our explorations furthered and clothing began to come off, Alex's Sciath eventually joined the pile of discarded items, and when it did, the entire experience was lifted to a whole new level. With all of his emotions exposed and swirling around us like mist over water, I was able to truly let go of all the little self-conscious worries and fears I'd been harboring about what we were doing – and about to do – when I saw that he had them all as well. The shy reluctance, the coy embarrassment, the anxious nerves, all of them mirrored perfectly in his own web of feeling, and yet instead of compounding on each other and worsening my inhibitions, the simple knowledge that I was not alone seemed instead to free me of them almost entirely.

Of course I'd thought about Alex and I together many times in the past, and so obviously I'd had some ideas as to what our first time might be like, but what I hadn't realized was that there was just no preparing for something like this. It didn't even seem possible for the range of emotions and sensations that coursed through me to exist all at once, and yet there they all were. There were some that melded together and complemented each other seamlessly, and others that were completely contradictory, having nothing at all to do with one another. It was beyond understanding and at the same time made more sense than anything I'd ever experienced.

There were times when all I did was think, and times when I couldn't think at all. There were moments when it felt so amazing I wasn't sure I could handle anymore, and moments when I felt like I was only a second or two from getting a cramp. It was amazing, tender, breathtaking, and beautiful, while also being awkward, clumsy, uncomfortable, and strange. And even though it wasn't always easy or graceful, and there was no five star suite or majestic castle, there was the two of us sharing with one another something we'd never shared with anyone before. And as it turned out, that was all we needed for it to be perfect.

Knock, knock, knock!

"Come in," Jocelyn called from behind his office door that evening.

I entered the office to find him sitting in his desk chair, though he didn't appear to be doing any work. "Shouldn't you be... I don't know... sleeping or something?" I asked with a grin as I approached the desk.

"Now? It's almost 7 o'clock. If I sleep I'll be up all night." I cocked an unamused eyebrow at him, but I could tell he was joking. "I'm fine," he said with a small smile after a moment, "I took a nap earlier."

That was good to hear, but I was still concerned. "And you're... OK?"

I didn't elaborate, but the slight softening of his eyes told me he knew what I meant. "Yes," he nodded, glancing down, "I'm fine. Mild headache, but that will pass."

"Good," I said, sliding my hands into my pockets. A short silence followed, but happily it wasn't awkward – perhaps the very mildest version of "almost" uncomfortable, but that was still a vast improvement for us – and I took a seat on the arm of one of the large wingback chairs across from his desk.

"And while we are on the subject of my predicament," he said, looking up, "thank you for coming for me."

What had he thought I was going to do?

"No problem," I smiled.

"You shouldn't have done it," he added, trying to sound more severe though it didn't stick, "but, thank you."

"I pursed my lips with a wry squint. "I'm sorry, am I being thanked or reprimanded? I can't quite tell."

"Both," he grinned, then paused, a shadow falling over his eyes. "I just wish there had been something I could have done for Steven. If only I could have…" but he stopped, letting his thought hang.

"You were a little preoccupied at the time. It's not your fault."

"I know that," he admitted, "but I can't help but feel bad. Not only was I unable to aid him when he needed it, but even now there is nothing I can do to help."

"Actually, that was what I came to ask you about. Is there really nothing at all we can do for him?"

"I'm afraid not," he answered as though he hated the feel of the words on his tongue. "Memories once lost, are lost forever. I do plan to look into the matter as extensively as we can, but in all honesty, I don't hold out much hope."

"So what do we do until then?"

"We care for him here until we can either find help for him or find definitive proof that is there no help, in which case we will go from there. Unless of course his parents would rather he be returned home, but from what I can see, I don't think Bastian is going to present them with the option."

"Good," I mumbled to the floor.

"Though on the subject of Steven, there is one new development you should know; Chloe will be joining with the Order."

"Wait what? Since when?"

"Earlier this afternoon, actually. She came to ask me about it, and I couldn't turn her down, not now."

"I thought she wasn't powerful enough?"

"She's not, but with you able to use and strengthen abilities the way you can, she could turn out to be a worthwhile help. In truth, she already has been; just look at what you were able to accomplish at Adare with her help. Besides, with Steven the way he is now, she just wants to do something, to feel like she's of use to him in some way, and I couldn't deny her that."

I nodded, happy that Chloe would at least have something to put her mind on other than Steven's condition. That was bound to do her good.

"And Bastian?" I asked. "I assume he'll be staying too."

"Yes, and he is welcome to join us for as long as he's here, or even longer if he chooses. He is a powerful asset, and has more than proven himself as far as I'm concerned."

We lapsed into silence again, but then I remembered something. "Here," I said reaching into my pocket and pulling out the small scrap of Ciaran's journal that I'd run back for at Cuniff. "It's from the journal."

"Yes," he said, taking it from my outstretched hand, "I'd meant to ask about that. Going back for it like that may have been the most foolish thing you have ever done."

"Yeah, I know." I shrugged. "Though in my defense, I wasn't really thinking clearly at the time, and it did work out in the end, so…"

"It didn't work out so well for your hair," he said, nodding toward the headband I was wearing in a lame attempt to flatten it enough to be seen in public. "But," he added begrudgingly, "we did make it out, and you're right, having this will help us a great deal. All we need is for Min to make up a call charm with it and Ciaran's journal will be at our fingertips. Let's just hope we can get to it before Darragh realizes we can."

I meant to let it go, but the words slipped out before I could stop them. "Even if he did, I'm not so sure he would stop us."

"What do you mean?"

I hesitated, thinking back to the moments before we ported away and the odd feeling I'd gotten that I realized only now hadn't fully gone away. "He saw us, you know. Darragh saw us as we were about to get away and he didn't do anything. Why didn't he stop us? It would have been easy enough to do with all the abilities he has, so why didn't he?"

Jocelyn pondered for a moment, appearing to taking the question seriously. "I don't know," said finally. "Perhaps it had something to do with the fortress charm, or maybe there was truly nothing he could do. But whatever the reason, we are all home, and I am willing to be happy enough with that for the time being if you are."

I thought for a moment before nodding with a sigh. "Yeah, I guess." I agreed. *For now...*

"And who knows," Jocelyn added, looking down at the scrap of paper, "maybe Ciaran's journal will have something we can use to help Steven."

"We can only hope."

A short while later, I was on my way up to the room where Jocelyn had said Steven was being housed. The location was a bit out of the way, but that was undoubtedly by design so that it would be far enough away from students who wondered the more open parts of Lorcan for classes during the day, thus sparing everyone the worry of a random chance encounter with someone who wouldn't understand.

As I turned down the hall leading to the room, I ran into Bastian who looked as pale and haggard as I'd ever seen him.

"Bastian," I greeted him, trying to smile.

"Becca, oh good, I've been meaning to come see you. How are you? I heard you had some trouble, are you all right?"

"I'm fine. Still a little tired," I added for honesty's sake, "but otherwise good."

"Dear God, your hair," he said stepping to the side to get a better look.

I ran my hand over it a bit self-consciously. "Yeah… Got it caught on a pole. No biggie though. I'll get it cleaned up at a salon and it'll be fine." I said it as casually as I could, unwilling to let the man who'd just lost his brother waste pity on what was little more than a bad haircut.

"Well I'm glad to see you are all right – the parts of you that wouldn't grow back anyway," he said with a ghost of a smile. "And who knows, short hair can be fun. You may even end up liking it."

"Maybe," I said, but quickly moved on to another subject. "So, how are you doing?"

His eyes glazed over as he did his best to answer. "I… I don't know. Honestly, I'm not even sure if I've fully realized yet… I just wish there was… but I know there is nothing…"

"I know," I said, hating the hopelessness in his eyes. "But that doesn't mean we are going to give up. In fact, Jocelyn's wondering if there may be something in Ciaran's journal that could help him." The minute the words were out of my mouth I realized that I probably shouldn't have said them. Much as I wanted to help Bastian's pain, the idea of giving him false hope was even worse than seeing him suffer.

Though luckily, he didn't seem overly excited at my news, instead giving me a small smile. "Hopefully. And thanks to you, we will be able to find out."

I wasn't crazy about the credit, but I didn't argue. "Have you told your parents yet?"

Something flared in his eyes and I almost regretted asking. "No," he shook his head, "and I don't plan to. I have no idea what they would do with the information if they got it, but the prospects make me too angry to even consider. From now on, Steven is done with them – we both are."

Odd how one statement could make you sad and proud all at the same time. But as it was obvious the subject needed changing once again, I didn't belabor it, instead turning to an observation. "You look like you need some sleep. Why don't you go back to your room for a while and let me sit with Steven?" I offered, assuming he would rather Steven not be alone just yet.

"I do need a rest, and was on my way to bed now as it happened, though Chloe is back with Steven, so you don't have to worry about him. I don't think she is going anywhere soon," he said, but his tone had become more sympathetic than sad. "Thank you for the offer though. It really does mean a lot. Actually, I'm not really used to this, but it's... really nice."

"What is?" I asked, not following.

He hesitated but didn't look away, his eyes very sincere. "Having a friend."

I smiled as he walked off, glad that he'd come back with us and was finally going to be able to have the life he deserved – though admittedly the circumstances could have been infinitely better. And speaking of friends, there was one I hadn't yet seen who I was very much worried about.

I continued down the hall, taking the turn where Jocelyn had said to, and the moment I rounded the corner I was met by the heartbreaking sight of poor Chloe. She was sitting on the floor against the wall a short ways down the hall, with her legs hugged to her chest and her chin resting on her knees, eyes fixed on the open door across the hall from her. My stomach felt as though it sunk a bit lower with every step I took in her direction. What would I say? I wasn't sure. What *could* I say? That was easy: nothing. But even so, I was still determined to try.

She didn't look up as I arrived next to her and slid down the wall at her side. Scooting as close to her as I could, I wrapped my arm around her shoulders, and at least felt a bit of relief as she leaned toward me, resting her head against me with a small sniffle. We sat quietly for a long while, looking to the room opposite us where I could see Steven seated on the bed and staring unblinking and unseeing at the wall.

"Don't you want to go in?" I asked her gently, not sure why she was sitting on the floor in the hall when there were open chairs in the room that would have been closer to him and far more comfortable.

"They don't want us to go in until they've finished checking him," she rasped, her voice almost nonexistent. "Said it might not be safe."

I wasn't sure who "they" were or who it might not be safe for, but I didn't question. "You know we're going to do everything we can for him, right?" I asked as I tilted my head toward her, leaning my cheek against her hair.

She nodded again with another sniffle.

The need to find words that would somehow help her or ease her pain was like a virus eating at my heart. But I knew those words didn't exist, so I gave up, and resigned myself to simply sitting with her as long as she needed me, holding her in a comforting arm as she stared in at the man she loved but couldn't save.

I would do it though. I would find a way to help Steven, no matter what I had to do. I would make sure he got to have the life with Chloe that he was so pointlessly robbed of, and no matter how many times they told me there was no way, I wasn't going to give up. I was the most powerful Holder there'd ever been, damn it, and I was going to find a way. These people were my friends, my family. And no one hurts my family.

It seemed almost impossible, but I had everything I needed: I had Alex. I had Jocelyn and Ryland. I had the Order. And no matter what was coming our way, what battles may be looming in the future, or how long it took me, I was going to make sure that, come hell or high water, we all made it through.

Together.

Acknowledgments

If you want to know what writing a book is really like, I'll give you a tip: don't ask a writer. Sure, one could give you an idea of the process, and tell you more than you ever wanted to know about publishing, but that isn't the real story. For the real story, you need behind the scenes footage, and you can only get that, not from the writers, but from the people who surround them. For instance, the writer's friends who have learned never to ask "*How's the book coming?*" when there is a deadline looming. Or maybe their spouse, who could tell you when it is and isn't okay to ask the writer a question without automatically adding a preemptive, "*I know you're writing, but...*"

Family, friends; these are the people that have the information you really want. They are the ones on the front lines, supporting us as writers on an often daily basis, making it possible for us to do what we do. They are the people we couldn't make it without, and I for one want to make sure that each and every member of my own front line knows how much I love them and appreciate all that they have done for me. This one is for you guys because I am the luckiest writer in the world. (And because if any of you decide to publish *How to Write a Book: Behind the Scenes*, I am so totally screwed.)

It always seems that the quietest people have the loudest roar, and I don't think that could be any truer of my amazing agent, Carly Watters of PS Literary. She is as adorable and sweet as can be, but when it comes to her clients she is a tiger, which makes her exactly the sort of person you want fighting in your corner. I am beyond lucky to have her, and can't thank her enough for her endless support of me and my writing.

I'm not sure what I can say about the team at Strange Chemistry other than they are the best people an author could ever hope to work with, and undoubtedly some of the hardest working folks in the industry. They have always had my back, and the understanding and support they have given me this past year means the world to me. And to my fabulous editor, Amanda Rutter, thank you so much for everything you have done for and tolerated from me this year. It continues to be an honor and a privilege to count myself as one of your authors.

This might just be me, but I have found over the years that my fingers have a mind of their own. They edit, tweak, and often completely change the words I am trying to get out, usually without even bothering to run it by me first. Yet, for some reason there are still people out there who agree to read through my work before it has been edited and remains in all its typo-ridden and auto(*un*)corrected glory. These folks deserve far more than I could ever give them, and I can only hope they know how much I appreciate their help. To Cathy Pleskovich and Mary Smith, you keep the world from knowing just how horrible my spelling really is. To Elizabeth Shaw, whether reading my stuff or not, you are always one of my biggest supporters. To Sean Lusk, your notes are nothing short of amazing, and you are nothing short of inspiring. To Liz, Shannon, Vera, Beth, Patti, Julie, and Yelena, you guys give me the encouragement, laughs, and nights out that I need. Love you all! And to Trisha Wolfe and Angela Cook, no one reads like a writer. Thank you so much for your thoughts, your support, and your time.

Finally, to my incredible husband, you make everything I do possible just by giving me a reason to do it. I couldn't ask for a better man or a better friend. All my love.

EXPERIMENTING WITH YOUR IMAGINATION

"(*The Holders* is) an engaging, well-paced story. Julianna Scott is a fresh new voice in the paranormal romance genre."
Juliet Marillier, author of the Sevenwaters *fantasy series*

EXPERIMENTING WITH YOUR IMAGINATION

A tale of phantom wings, a clockwork hand, and the delicate unfurling of new love.

LAURA LAM

SHADOWPLAY

"Pantomime took me into a detailed and exotic world, peopled by characters that I'd love to be friends with . . . and some I'd never want to cross paths with."
Robin Hobb, author of the Farseer Trilogy

STRANGE CHEMISTRY